dare from DEEP WITHIN

dare from DEEP WITHIN

D. L. Sleiman

WhiteFire
Publishing

This is a work of fiction. All characters and events portrayed in this novel are either fictitious or used fictitiously.

DARE FROM DEEP WITHIN

Copyright © 2017, Dina Sleiman
All rights reserved. Reproduction in part or in whole is strictly forbidden without the express written consent of the publisher.

WhiteFire Publishing
13607 Bedford Rd NE
Cumberland, MD 21502

ISBN: 978-1-939023-80-3 (print)
         978-1-939023-82-7 (digital)

ONE

This is killing me!

Curling deep into a corner of the worn couch, Layla Al-Rai blinked away tears and reread the text message from the man she had hoped to marry: *This is killing me!* Then she hit delete. She needed to put Mo far from her mind, forget about what she couldn't have and focus on what she could.

Somehow forget that this was killing her too. Valentine's Day without him had provided a special kind of torture. Things could only improve from here. Right?

Swiping her newly cut black layers from her eyes, Layla surveyed the cozy living room of her little bungalow. She searched out her friends gathered in the well-lit kitchen and honed in on their smiling faces. Allie and Rain had been her strength and comfort throughout the tumultuous first semester of college. These returning students, both independent women in their mid-twenties, showed her what life could be like beyond the veil.

Surely miracles did exist. Despite the fact that Layla was an adult of twenty-two, if anyone had told her six months earlier that her Muslim parents would allow her to share a house with a group of Christian college girls, she would have cracked up laughing. Yet here she was, not only sharing a home but a new Christian believer herself.

"Coffee, Layla?" her roommate Allie called from the kitchen.

"Sure. Plenty of cream and sugar." Coffee, another thing to be thankful for. Nice light American coffee wafting through the air, not her auntie's syrupy Lebanese version. Layla took a deep breath and attempted to ignore the stab of longing in her chest, as if a caffeinated beverage could replace the love of her life.

Layla's good friend Rain plunked down on the arm of the rust-colored couch, pregnant belly and all. Rain didn't live with Layla, but she folded her legs Indian style and wiggled an indentation for her burgeoning rear as if she did. Hugging an oversized coffee mug to her chest, she took a hard look at Layla's face in the dim lamplight. "Hey, we're happy tonight, remember. No more tears."

"I'm not crying." Layla grimaced.

"Then what's that wet thing on your eyelash? You should know better than to try and fool me. The wise, all-knowing Rain sees everything." She took a sip of coffee before hollering into the next room. "Allie, we might have to break out the big guns. Any ice cream in that fridge?"

As if Rain needed ice cream. Layla's lips quivered into a grin. The all-knowing, New-Age hippie guru evidently didn't *see* that she was about to break the couch. Although Rain looked prettier than ever with her café-au-lait skin, corkscrew light brown curls, and peasant blouse that matched her golden-green eyes, she needed to slow down on the weight gain if she wanted to continue perching herself in such precarious positions.

"Never mind, Allie. I'm fine, really. Rain has no idea what she's talking about."

Allie and her little sister Sarah came to join them. Sarah, wearing a long beige skirt and turtleneck sweater against the winter chill, settled herself primly on the edge of an overstuffed chair. Meanwhile, Allie handed Layla a steaming mug of amaretto-scented coffee and plopped onto the couch, stretching her bare ballerina legs onto the glass-topped table.

Could the sisters possibly be more different? Despite their matching blond coloring, Sarah represented everything Allie had left behind from her ultra-conservative past. At least they were getting along these days. Hopefully Allie could help Sarah unwind a bit before she snapped.

"I'm all for ice cream." Sarah brushed her twill skirt down flat. "I don't need an occasion."

Allie took a long sip and sighed. "You'll all have to be content with amaretto creamer tonight. The teenyboppers wiped out the fridge. I swear those girls swarm like locusts."

Layla nodded. "A real-life biblical plague." Allie's nickname for their roommates certainly fit. Those four freshman girls bopped in and out all hours of the day and night. "At least we have some peace and quiet for the moment."

"I don't know how you guys do it." Rain shook her head. "They give me a migraine."

"They aren't so bad once you get used to them." Allie laughed. "Besides, I only have to put up with them until summer. Save your pity for Layla."

Layla didn't need pity. Truly, she was still overwhelmed by the wonder of it all. "The girls are kind of fun. You can't imagine how amazing it is for me just to be on my own, with no auntie watching over my every move." Not to mention having the pleasure of attending a real, live church or the joy of praying when and where she pleased and feeling like someone actually listened.

After twenty-two years in a restrictive culture, Layla was finally free—the constant, nagging fear of Allah's judgement gone from her life—and of course she had her amazing new relationship with Christ, which she was still discovering. Surely giving up Mo was a small price to pay.

"Yeah, I guess surviving a murder attempt puts everything in perspective." Rain placed a warm hand on Layla's.

"Oh my goodness." Sarah's blue eyes grew big and round, all the more obvious beneath her tight chignon. "I forgot about that. You must have been terrified."

The last thing Layla wanted to talk about tonight was her uncle's botched honor killing. "It's over and I'm safe now. That's what matters. I doubt he would have gone through with it, but I'm sure you can understand the teenyboppers look pretty good to me after all that."

"And things are okay with your parents? They didn't disown you?" Sarah sat up a bit taller and leaned in.

Layla couldn't help but feel sorry for the girl. Unlike Allie and Layla's friends at her new church, Sarah looked quite bound by religion herself.

"No, thank goodness," answered Layla. "They didn't disown me. I still can hardly believe it. My mom wouldn't speak to me for a while, but my dad's moderate in his beliefs. He's all for religious reform. I mean, they aren't happy with me, but for now they're paying the bills. So my dream of an engineering degree is still alive. And they've dropped the subject of an arranged marriage, which is way more than I expected."

"Yeah, but she's not supposed to tell anyone. And they made her give up her boyfriend in exchange for tuition, which totally sucks." Rain slammed her cup down on the end table, causing the lamp to shake. "I swear, Layla, you're a grown woman. You should find a job and be done with them."

Rain wouldn't understand. She'd been living with her significant other, James, since she was eighteen. Her parents were off on perpetual safari somewhere in Africa, but Layla needed her family. She loved them, and she longed to honor them in whatever way she still could. Not to mention that boyfriends really didn't even exist in her culture.

Sarah tilted her head and tightened her lips. "We're supposed to honor our parents, Rain. The Bible says so. Layla's doing the best she can in a hard situation. Besides, this is not the right time in her life for a boyfriend. She should focus on God."

Somehow hearing her thoughts filtered through Sarah's judgmental mind made Layla question her own reasoning. "Mo was a huge part of why I came to Christ. So it's not that simple. Without Allie and Mo, I might never have found him. That has to count for something."

Sarah gazed at her sister skeptically. Layla knew the women well enough to decipher the look. *How could a heavy-metal loving, short-shorts wearing, so-called Christian lead anyone to Christ?* Layla stifled a giggle.

Not so successful at restraining herself, Rain snorted. "How about you, Sarah? Any hot guys in your life?"

Red crept up from the edge of Sarah's turtleneck to tinge her face. "No guys at all, hot or otherwise." She patted her fastidious hairdo. "I have no need for men right now. *'Awake not love before it pleases'* and all that. Really, Layla, your parents are doing you a favor. I have no intention of dating. After college I'll consider courtship."

Despite Layla's new appreciation for the Bible, Sarah's habit of spouting scripture left a bad taste in her mouth. She took another sip of amaretto coffee to wash it away.

"Courtship!" Rain laughed out loud this time.

Heat emanated from Sarah's face, but she had no way to stop it. They probably figured she was embarrassed by all this talk about guys. Better they imagine her a pious fool than suspect the truth. Jesse's sexy smile flashed through her mind along with his searing eyes that turned her to melted butter. Sarah gulped and attempted to steady her breathing as guilt washed over her in torrents.

Allie cleared her throat and looked to be choking back a giggle. "So have you decided on a school yet, Sarah?"

Thank God, a change of subject. Although, on second thought,

Sarah doubted God deserved any credit for her relief at the moment. Surely he was standing on alert to zap her with a lightning bolt. She smiled her appreciation to Allie. "I've been accepted here at Old Dominion University and also at a Christian college near Roanoke. But I'm leaning toward ODU. I plan to study languages, and they have Arabic classes, which are hard to find."

Allie twisted to recline her long legs over the back of the couch behind Layla's head. How did Allie do it? Looking relaxed and happy as she lounged in her little hot-pink dancer's shorts, somehow at peace with God and suddenly engaged to the assistant pastor of Sarah's own conservative church in Virginia Beach. Surely Allie was delusional—kind-hearted but nuts. Things just didn't work that way with God.

"Wait a minute." Layla seemed to shake off the funk she'd been in all evening. "Did you say Arabic? *Hal tatakalame Alarabiya?*"

"*Naam ya habibti. Ftakartic betaerfi,*" Sarah answered.

Rain threw up her hands. "Translation please."

Layla sat forward. "I asked if she spoke Arabic. She said yes. She thought I knew, but I had no idea. How'd this happen?"

"I go to a high school for international studies. I hope to be a missionary someday."

Rain sucked in a sharp breath. Layla glanced from Allie to Rain and back again. Allie just shrugged her shoulders.

The heat returned to Sarah's face. Did they suspect she was nothing but a sham? A failure of a Christian? She had planned to be a missionary for years. She wasn't ready to give up her dreams over one little stumble.

"You know, Sarah..." Layla smiled encouragingly. "You could learn a lot from Allie in that department. The way she was just herself and open about both her faith and her struggles meant a lot to me when I was searching for the truth."

"Yeah." Rain contentedly rubbed her protruding belly with her ringless left hand. The woman had no shame. Sarah should be glad

Rain chose life, but still. She twisted her purity ring around her own left finger. Thank God she would never have to deal with the shame of an unplanned pregnancy.

"I'm not as into all the Christian stuff as Layla," Rain continued, "but Allie definitely gave me a better perspective on it. She really changed my ideas about God."

Oh, so they didn't think she'd be a good witness, not as good as Allie. No matter how hard she tried, she'd never be as good as Allie. A heavy lump filled Sarah's stomach.

After eight years gallivanting the globe, living life on her own terms, Allie had returned home to the proverbial fatted calf. Okay, so she was on a dancing "mission" trip and not quite the prodigal child. But after Sarah killed herself to be the perfect daughter and meet every last one of her parents' high standards, it stung to see her free-spirited sister accepted so easily back into the fold. They even bought Allie that flashy red Mini Cooper, while Sarah had no car of her own.

"Hey, Sarah," Rain said with an evil grin, "if you end up going to school here, you could take Allie's bed after the wedding. I'm sure she'll be occupied in a much warmer mattress."

"That would be fun." Layla nudged Rain, otherwise ignoring the inappropriate innuendo, and perked up even more. "I'd love to share a room with you. I could help you with your Arabic."

"Oh, my gosh." Sarah blinked vapidly a few times and squealed in imitation of Allie's eighteen-year-old roommates, wiggling her fingers beside her head. "Like, I so totally get more of Britney and company than I can stand at church every week. Like, I might just die or something."

"That is so her." Rain clapped in delight.

Although only eighteen herself, Sarah had no need for a bunch of immature, boy crazy roommates. This recent incident was just a blip on the radar. She'd get things under control soon enough and had no desire to surround herself by such worldly influences.

"Look, there she is now!" Allie teased.

Sarah turned to the dark window. A shadowed figure stood on the sagging front porch, barely discernible against the soft glow of the streetlights. Her heart sped, but surely it wasn't Britney. The person was alone, and Britney always had a posse in tow.

A soft knock rapped against the door.

Allie stood and shot a questioning glance to Layla. "Too quiet for the teenybopper crew. You expecting anyone?"

Layla just shrugged.

Allie called, "Who is it?"

"Help me, please." A pleading, accented voice filtered through the crack. Its broken timber tugged at something deep in Sarah's being.

Allie shot a questioning glance around the room. Rain hurried to stand behind her, cupping her shoulders.

"Let her in," Sarah whispered.

Allie opened the door. Through it stumbled a slight figure shrouded in black.

TWO

"Layla? Is Layla Al-Rai here?" emanated the familiar voice from the black fabric.

Layla jumped from the couch in response. "Fatima? Is that you?"

A sob broke through the slit of the *niqab*.

The poignant sound rang all too familiar in Layla's ear, a cry she had heard far too often. She ran to her dearest childhood friend, picked up the heavy hem of the full-body veil, and threw it over the woman's head—revealing a golden-haired beauty, stunning despite a split lip and the purple smudge rimming one of her hazel green eyes.

"Oh, Fatima. What have they done to you now?" A wave of nausea rolled over Layla. She gathered the shaking bundle carefully into her arms.

"I am just glad I find you. I was so scared. I could not stay one more minute." Fatima's English sounded rusty. But then, she'd barely spoken it since high school.

"Shh, shh. You're safe now." Layla shot a frenzied glance around the room. How on earth they could protect a battered Saudi Arabian woman from her fanatic father and brothers, she had no idea.

Cold fear crept through Layla as images of her uncle holding a knife over her head flashed through her mind in sharp detail. She shook the memory away. Risking her own life had been hard enough. Layla couldn't bear the thought of Fatima going through that. Somehow Layla had survived, but what if Fatima's story didn't end as well?

Nonetheless, she gathered her courage for Fatima's sake. "These are my friends." Layla gestured around the room and introduced the girls by name, but Fatima didn't seem to register a word. A glazed expression covered her face.

The other women stared on with muted curiosity.

"Remember, Fatima? You've exchanged emails with Rain and Allie. They'll help take care of you. Don't worry. And Sarah is Allie's sister. Sarah, this is my dearest friend from childhood, Fatima Maalouf." Layla stroked Fatima's shoulder, hoping to infuse life back into her.

Fatima blinked and her eyes focused this time. "Rain, Allie, yes. *Allah be praised.* It is so good to finally meet you."

Rain and Allie had been writing to Fatima for months. The girl was desperate for any sort of interaction since she became a prisoner in her own home.

"We're here for you." Rain approached and gave Fatima the standard three Middle Eastern kisses. "Just like I said we'd be."

Layla winced. So this was Rain's idea. Didn't she understand the repercussions? Surely Fatima's family would trace her here. The girl had traveled in full veil for crying out loud, and where else could she possibly have gone? Fatima's family only permitted her to associate with the strictest of Muslims. Layla had been accepted as a neighboring child, but they hadn't even let her visit this winter when she was home for Christmas break.

Allie lightly kissed Fatima's cheeks as well. "How did you get here?"

"Bus," Fatima said through chattering teeth.

They transported the hobbling Fatima to the couch, and Rain tucked in her shivering form with a throw blanket from a basket on the floor. Beneath the *niqab* that had shrouded Fatima in black from head to toe, leaving only a small slit at the eyes for her to see, she had worn a simple pair of jeans and a long sleeved T-shirt, but they did little to keep her warm on this wet, blustery winter night. Sometimes Layla missed the honest snow of Detroit. At least it didn't soak through your clothes like the cold drizzle in Norfolk, Virginia. She could hardly believe Fatima had traveled all this way on her own.

Rain chafed Fatima's fingers with her hands. "You poor thing. You don't even have a coat. Tell us the whole story."

"I'll get you some coffee," Allie offered. "That will warm you up."

"Thank you." Tears streamed down Fatima's face, but the chattering had subsided. "Thanks to all of you." She sighed deeply. "I thought I would not make it."

"So you traveled by bus," Layla prompted, not wanting to overwhelm the young woman.

"Yes." Fatima relaxed into Rain's side embrace and rested her head against Rain's shoulder.

Layla laid her hand on Fatima's knee. "How? Where did you get the money?"

Fatima bit her swollen lower lip. "I stole it."

"It's okay. You can tell us." Rain gave her a squeeze.

"*Eiy!*" Fatima shrieked, grimacing in pain.

Gently pulling the cotton of Fatima's purple T-shirt aside, Layla revealed a bruised shoulder. Her stomach clenched. "Where else are you hurt?"

"My ankle is sprained, I think. And my ribs. Something is wrong with my ribs."

"Dear God." Rain pressed a hand to her mouth.

But it came as no surprise to Layla. She'd seen Fatima roughed up before. Just never this bad or all at once.

Allie brought the coffee. The heat and sweet amaretto creamer delivered the desired effect.

On her own, Fatima began to tell the story. "He's been threatening for months. Father insisted I go to Saudi Arabia and marry some middle-aged stranger who would lock me up for good. He could never risk dishonoring the family by marrying me to a kind American man who might let me run wild, and yet he will not even tell me what number wife I will be to this man. He insists my 'wicked' beauty must be guarded. But he knew he could not force me through an American airport, so he has been punishing me, not letting me leave the house, threatening me, hitting me." She sniffled and took another drink of coffee.

"I'm so sorry." Allie snuggled with Sarah in the armchair.

Sarah shook her head, her mouth gaping.

"Then yesterday I hear him speaking with my brothers and asking them to find something to drug me, to make me calm and sleepy. Roofies, he said. I panicked. Mother was back in the kitchen. My brother's wallet was on the bureau by the front door. I grabbed it, my shoes, my purse, and my *niqab,* and I ran out of there before it was too late. I cannot go to Saudi Arabia and be a man's slave. I simply cannot." Fatima dissolved into sobs.

Sarah spoke up. "We won't let that happen. We can fight this in court if we need to."

"No!" Fatima shrieked even louder than when Rain squeezed her injured arm.

"Let's get you to a hospital and document your injuries. We'll take out a restraining order." Sarah crossed the room and knelt in front of Fatima, beside Layla. "I know how these things work. It will be all right. We have laws."

"You think they care about your laws?" Fatima pressed herself deeper into the couch like a cornered animal. "They will kill me without a second thought. I would disappear and that would be the end. My family can never find me, never know where I am."

Layla agreed. Fatima's family could never know where she was. "Oh, Fatima. I just wish you hadn't worn your veil. You could have blended in so easily without it. No one would know where you went."

"I was...I was scared. I did not think. I just ran. I was feeling safer with it."

This was hardly the time to give Fatima a lesson on Western

Sister Amani - former Muslim → head of Xian TV
prog. fr Muslim women
• Layla Al-Rai, 22 - college - engineering → Xlim. hof. coll.
grew up - Islamic sect in - Detroit
• allie (8 yr. old) Virginia Sister Sarah
• Rain bi-racial "spiritual paren" Rel. - no culture
New Age

" Sister - Briggs - Iraqi (4 yr.) James Allen - heritage
death Native Am.

Layla - living w/ aunt/uncle in Calif.
allie - Andry Norma + sch. boyfriend
dance studies - guest lecture (took classes to j. ach.)
+ daughter Taylor
L - Mo Jhoth So. Lebanon - then Detroit in Kbg.

Brayn - Allie - I feel so lost - God → be lost in Me

culture. Logically, after almost two decades in this country, she must understand that American men were used to seeing female faces and that there was nothing sexual in a woman's facial features to them. She would have been safe enough on a public bus, but a lifetime of cultural training kept her from accepting those facts, especially at a frightening time like this.

"I suppose it doesn't matter. They're going to guess you've come here. Eventually they'll show up. We need to find you somewhere safe to stay." Although Layla doubted such a place existed when it came to radical Middle Eastern men whose honor was at stake.

"You can stay with me, Fatima." Rain laid a gentle hand on Fatima's wrist. "No one in your family knows me. I'm a couple of miles from here, and my boyfriend James has dealt with a few thugs in his time."

Fatima's eyes grew big.

Layla studied the protective way Rain sheltered Fatima in her arms. Staying with Rain and her boyfriend—albeit her committed boyfriend of many years—would be a shock to Fatima, but the plan had merits.

"Or she could stay with my family," Sarah offered, sitting on the floor at Fatima's feet.

"I think Rain's place would be best." Layla nodded. "It's closer in case of an emergency, and the fewer people who know, the better. Besides, James's thug training could come in handy."

"Are you sure you won't go to the police?" Sarah pleaded. "I've studied these cases in school. There really are laws to protect you. You're over eighteen, right? If you weren't it could be tricky, like that poor girl Rifqa Bary, but the courts still figured out a way to help her."

"No, no, please. I just want a place to hide and feel safe. Maybe later I will have no choices, but not now."

Tears welled in Layla's eyes, and as she glanced around the room the malady looked contagious.

"Are you hungry?" Allie stood. "Can I get you some pizza?"

"No. I could not eat." Fatima buried her face in her palms.

"When was your last meal, young lady?" Rain attempted a smile.

"You need food to keep up your strength." Sarah reached toward Fatima but let her hand fall.

"I think we should get her settled at Rain's place first." Layla's mind spun at the potential disaster of the situation. These girls had never met Fatima's family. They couldn't begin to understand. Middle Easterners had their own sort of mafia, and although she didn't know for certain, Layla wouldn't be surprised if Fatima's family was involved in terrorism. They were certainly quick enough to terrorize their own women. "I don't mean to be alarmist, but they could get here much faster by car, even if she had a decent head start."

"Oh, sorry." Allie sat back down. "I didn't realize."

"It's okay. It's a lot to wrap your mind around." Layla gathered up the moist *niqab*.

"Can I use the restroom first?" Fatima whispered.

"Of course. It's right this way." Allie ushered her down the hall.

The rest of them sat in silence for a moment, digesting the enormity of the situation.

Sarah pressed a hand to her mouth. "She's so beautiful and so tragic."

"And her hair—it's almost blond," Rain added. "I thought she'd look like you, Layla."

"I think she has a Syrian grandmother. Middle Easterners come in all sorts of packages, but who would ever know it when they keep half the population hidden behind...what did you call them, Rain?"

"Mobile prisons?"

"Exactly." Layla loved aspects of the Middle Eastern culture, but she never could stomach the subjugation of women, no matter the excuses.

"Any special instructions?" Rain stood to gather her purse and coat.

"Just be a mother to her. You're good at that. Lord knows her own hasn't done a decent job since she hit puberty." Layla pinched her nose. The whole issue gave her a headache on top of her upset stomach. Which came first? The religion or the culture? It was the chicken and the egg all over again. She was thankful to be done with it.

"Is there any way I can help." Sarah's tears spilled down her face. "I want to help."

"Maybe you can bring her some clothes. You're both tiny, and she'll like the modest cut. We'll need to get her some basic supplies tomorrow." Layla put on her coat and pulled out her keys. "I'll drive her and get her settled."

"Okay, I'll head over." Rain waved and walked out the door.

Allie escorted Fatima back to them, wrapped in a warm winter jacket.

"I am ready," Fatima said.

Were they all ready to deal with the consequences of this evening? Layla didn't know, but there was no turning back. If only she could talk to Mo—he'd know what to do.

THREE

Rain resisted the temptation to punch the thin plaster wall of her apartment. No doubt she would leave a hole and frighten poor Fatima in the process. This was precisely why her boyfriend James wanted nothing to do with religion—this shell of a woman huddling near her side—but the God Rain had met last semester could never be responsible for such tragedy. "Everything's going to be all right now, Fatima. Just relax. You're home. Let me show you around."

"Thanks, Rain." Layla smiled her reassurance as they walked deeper into the apartment.

Waving her hand, Rain gestured to the patchwork living area with the comfy, if dilapidated, green couch surrounded by colorful splashes of homemade decorations and items they had picked up during their years of travel. "We have a TV our neighbors gave us. Computer's in the corner on the desk. It's a bit of a dinosaur, but it works. The place isn't very big. Thank God we upgraded last month from a studio to a two bedroom, though, and we won't need the space for the baby for the better part of a year. It will give you some privacy. We'll just need to get you a bed."

She glanced around in search of inspiration. "For tonight let's make do with the couch cushions and a sleeping bag. One good thing about living on the road—you learn to make a cozy bed out of anything."

Fatima huddled farther into the hollow of Rain's shoulder.

"Isn't it nice, sweetie?" Layla leaned against the vintage dining room table that Rain and James had found on the side of the road.

Rain let go of Fatima to light the ginger candle on the counter of the kitchenette, hoping the warm glow and spicy scent would soothe her guest. "Fridge, stove, and microwave are in here, all functional. Do you think you could eat a little something?"

"No. I am so tired. Could I perhaps only sleep?"

"Of course." Rain smiled as she knew she should, but her heart was splintering in her chest. All those years she and James spent helping in homeless shelters, feeding the needy and patching up battered women, she should be prepared for this, but somehow Fatima hit too close to home. After emailing back and forth for months, Rain had become attached to her, enjoying her intelligence, her questions, and her subtle wit. "Come on. Let's get the room set up. Layla, can you grab the couch pillows?"

Fatima hadn't chosen to let herself be abused out of some warped sense of co-dependence. She wasn't homeless because of alcohol, drugs, or mental illness. This woman was a victim in the truest sense of the word.

Rain switched on the light to the spare bedroom. An unopened crib box rested against one wall, and a small stack of baby items sat in the corner. She could clear those out tomorrow.

A protective instinct rose up in Rain like a fierce mother lioness. Just let those jerks show up at her door. They'd be sorry they ever met Rain Butler-Briggs. With her bi-racial heritage, both her father and her boyfriend had schooled her well in the evils of oppression, but this topped everything! This scrap of a girl stripped of all dignity and personhood.

Rain wished she could beat someone up, but for now she'd pour all those nurturing instincts into making Fatima whole and well again. She and Layla arranged the cushions into a bed. Rain dashed down the hall to her room to grab a pair of pajamas, a sleeping bag, and a pillow.

Before long, they had created a safe little nest for their broken bird. Fatima had brought only a large purse with a hairbrush, a bit of makeup, and her Kindle—her gateway to the world for the past six months since Fatima's father refused to let her out of the house anymore.

"Hmm... What else can I get you, honey?" Rain stroked Fatima's burnished golden hair strewn over the pillow, a gorgeous color that no doubt counted as blond in her home country. To think this beautiful woman with her heart-shaped face and delicate bone-structure had been hidden away since puberty, that her brothers and fathers had dared lay their hands on this diminutive creature—it nearly made Rain lose her appetite as well, although that was pretty hard to accomplish these days. "Doesn't seem quite like home yet, does it?"

"I am fine. Truly. I just... I just..."

"What is it, sister?" Layla's chosen endearment appeared to bolster Fatima's courage. "You can ask for anything."

"It is just...this boyfriend. This James. He will see me?" Fatima gulped.

"Oh, sweetie. Don't worry about James." Layla patted her hand. "He's one of the kindest, dearest men I know. And trust me, he only has eyes for Rain."

Fatima cracked a grin.

"The guy wouldn't hurt a fly." Rain tucked Fatima's thick hair behind her golden, shell-shaped ear. "Literally. The crazy man catches them and frees them out the window."

Fatima chuckled at that.

James's handsome mocha face, with his goatee, dreadlocks, and kind eyes, flitted through Rain's mind, sending a pleasant shiver through her. To think she had almost lost him last semester. She rubbed her hand over the child in her womb. The surprise pregnancy had triggered his own childhood trauma, but she had him back safe and secure now. She'd never let anything come between them again.

"He's spent his whole life helping people like you, Fatima." Depositing a motherly kiss on Fatima's head, Rain said, "You're going to love him. We traveled all over America like gypsies to experience the plight of the less fortunate and help those in need. I'm writing a book about it. Maybe you can help me. I know you love to read." That was something Rain had picked up on the road—give victims a sense of purpose, a way to contribute.

"Oh, I would love to!" Fatima leaned up to hug Rain around her waist, sending showers of warmth and hope through her. "My spoken English, it is not so good as it used to be, but I am fine on paper." She sighed and lay back against the pillow.

"Your written English is perfect." Layla tucked the sleeping bag around Fatima's chin.

"It is sad, though, is it not, that I am the less fortunate one Rain must help? I never think of myself like this. So much money. Such a large and luxurious home. But what good...?" Fatima's voice trailed off as her eyes fluttered, golden-brown lashes waving against her cheek like a butterfly. Watching her cocooned in the sleeping bag, Rain thought perhaps Fatima wasn't a broken bird after all. Perhaps she was a wounded butterfly.

With one last kiss, Rain nodded to the door. She and Layla both stood to exit.

"Please be leaving the door open," Fatima mumbled.

"Of course," Rain whispered. "I'm right nearby if you need me."

"My praying man," Fatima said as she drifted toward sleep. "He will wonder about me."

"Don't worry," Layla said. The words seemed to make sense to her, although Rain had no idea who Fatima's *praying man* could be. "You let us take care of you."

Fatima didn't answer, and the women slipped out the door.

"Who is the praying man?" Rain whispered.

"Best I can figure, he must be an American Christian who does regular prayer walks through her neighborhood. They seem to have forged some strange sort of bond. But Rain, really, will James be all right with this?" Layla asked as she slid onto a stool by the kitchen counter.

Rain rested against the counter from the other side. "Oh, sure. You know James. He lives for this stuff. It's been hard for him to focus on work and school with a big hurting world out there. He'll be in his glory."

"So you guys are doing well? He's still excited about the baby?"

"She's all he talks about. He can't decide on a name good enough for her though." Rain chuckled. "Once he felt sure he wouldn't become an abuser like his father, everything changed. He's so thankful that I stood strong and refused to get rid of her. He plans to be the best father in the history of the universe."

Layla smiled. "No doubt he will then. So…the counseling must have worked for him. I'm thinking Fatima might need something like that."

"In time. Don't rush things."

"I'm sure you're right. I'm just anxious to see her get better. Her whole life has been rough, but I've never seen her quite like this." She sat staring into the flame of the candle for a moment, then shook off her trance. "I probably should head home. I'll come visit her tomorrow after my morning classes."

"Sounds good. See you then."

As Layla put on her coat and grabbed her purse, Rain gathered up celery, peanut butter, and a box of organic cookies. Evidently she hadn't lost her appetite after all.

Layla turned to her. "Whoa! Go easy, girlfriend. You're not carrying twins, you know."

"No, but I feel like I am." Rain took the food to the cushionless couch and sat on it anyway.

"All right. I give up. See you tomorrow." The door clicked behind Layla.

Rain bit into the crunchy celery and reveled in its contrast to the smooth, creamy peanut butter. James seemed charmed by her new round figure. His opinion was the only one that counted. Now that this thing with the baby was settled, nothing would come between them ever again.

Not even me? The whisper welled up from someplace deep in Rain's being.

"Don't be silly," she said to herself. God wouldn't begrudge her James. Why should he? Or she, as the case might well be? God would want her to be with the father of her child. She hadn't spoken with God in a while and had simply grown rusty at hearing his voice. Besides, at her new interfaith church, they speculated God was merely a construct of one's own psyche, or that God was an embodiment of their own inherent divinity. Although, Rain had to admit she sometimes missed God, the actual being with a face.

Either way, James was all hers, and nothing would change that. She didn't need a marriage certificate to prove it...although, truth be told, it would be nice.

FOUR

James wiggled his key in the old lock until it gave way and the door let him in. Entering the apartment, his instincts sharpened to alert—a long black cape draped over the dining table, the light shining from the baby's room, an unfamiliar gardenia perfume lingering in the air. His night watchman job at a nearby storage facility had taught him to remain alert to all clues. Since it was located deep in "the wrong side of town," he had already dealt with his share of thieves and vandals.

But even without his newly acquired skills, Rain's guilty expression as she sat watching the morning news on the couch with no cushions would have told him something was up. "Lucy, you got some splainin' to do," he said with his best Ricky Ricardo accent.

"Morning, baby. How was work?"

"Uneventful." He bent over to give her a kiss. "Which is always a good thing."

"Did you get some rest?"

"Yeah, and I managed to study for that anatomy test." Getting back into the swing of school after seven years off had been a challenge, but he was determined to earn his pre-med degree. From there he planned to become a physician's assistant and work for Doctors without Borders, with Rain at his side, penning her next literary marvel no doubt.

"I have a little surprise for you." She smiled up at him with a glimmer in her greenish-gold eyes.

"I suspected as much. What are you up to now, my little troublemaker?"

"Did I ever mention Fatima? Layla's Saudi Arabian friend I've been e-mailing?"

"I think so." He didn't remember specifically, but Rain was always picking up strays.

"Well, she ran away from home, and she's here." Rain bit her lip and wrinkled her nose, waiting expectantly.

"Here...in Norfolk?"

"Here...in our spare bedroom?" Her voice rose at the end like a question.

He laughed. "You're something else. You realize that?"

"Don't act like you mind. You've been itching for a project. She needs us. She's been battered. Her father was planning to drug her, drag her to Saudi Arabia, and marry her off to some stranger. She'd probably be like his fifth wife or something. Now that she's run away, she's dishonored them on top of everything. They might look at Layla's place. It's too dangerous there, so I brought her here."

James emitted a low whistle. He hadn't expected to start the day on such a heavy note, but Rain was right—he did need a project.

"She's in big trouble. If they find her, there's no telling what they might do."

"Don't worry. We'll take care of her."

Rain attempted to jump to her feet but faltered under the weight of the baby.

James hauled her off the couch and into his arms.

Her soft lips pressed warm against his cheek. "Thanks. I knew I could count on you."

He took a deep whiff of her spice and vanilla scent. "So when do I meet this..."

"Fatima."

"Fatima. When do I meet her?"

Rain untangled herself from his arms. "I need to hop in the shower. Why don't you make us some breakfast, then I'll wake her up. The poor thing was exhausted."

"Sure."

Rain hummed her way toward the bathroom as James pulled the oatmeal from the pantry shelf. Comfort food. He hoped it translated across cultures. Smiling to himself, he shook his head. Helping someone in need put a new swagger in his step. Although these days his own woman and daughter were his first priority, that buzz from changing the world never grew old. In this often cruel and random universe, carving out a safe space for himself and a few others, making a small but meaningful contribution, that was the best he could hope for.

After he set the pot to boil, he situated himself at the table with the newspaper. Storms, wars, famine, destruction, not to mention everyday rapists and serial killers, then toss in a few abusers and terrorists like Fatima dealt with—he threw the paper down in disgust. The news was never good. He should stop torturing himself.

A rustle in the hallway caught his attention. He heard a tiny yelp but didn't see anything. Then a dark golden head followed by a hazel eye circled with a purple bruise peeked around the corner.

"Hello," James said tentatively.

"Hello," came the answering whisper. "Where is..."

"Rain is in the shower." James used his softest voice and raised his pitch a few notches. He shrank in his chair, making himself as small as possible—tricks he had learned while working with battered women and children in the homeless shelters.

The girl stretched farther around the corner, her face bruised and swollen but somehow still picture pretty. He hadn't expected that. The tiny creature pulled at his heartstrings, vibrating them into a symphony of compassion.

"You are James?"

"Yes, and you must be Fatima. It's nice to meet you. Rain planned to wake you for breakfast in a few minutes and introduce us."

Fatima sniffed the air with an adorable button nose. "Oatmeal?"

"I hope you like it."

"Yes, very much. Maybe today I will be eating again." With a bracing breath, she took a step around the corner, revealing a slim but feminine physique in jeans and a long sleeved purple T-shirt. He would have never guessed she was from the Middle East if Rain hadn't told him.

"Would you care to join me?" Instinct told James to wave toward the empty chair, but he resisted and wound his arms around his middle instead, intent on appearing as nonthreatening as he could.

She limped her way to the chair on her own and sank into it. Running her hand along the side of her face, she looked down. "I am not used to men seeing me, but I suppose I must adjust."

"We might be living together for a while. I want you to feel safe with me. Would it help if you thought of me as a brother?"

Fatima flinched at the word brother, and James realized his mistake. "Sorry. Not brother. Is there a man that you trust? Feel safe with?"

She thought for a moment. "My uncle, my mother's brother in Canada. He is so kind."

James smiled. "Then just think of me as Uncle James. A very young, very handsome uncle, mind you."

Fatima giggled like a little girl. "Of course, or maybe a brother, but my mother's, not mine."

"Yes, that sounds perfect. I'm here to help you. Rain told me a little about your situation. You need to know things are different now. In America we love and cherish our women. We protect them, and not just physically. We care about their hearts too. I'm making you my sister, Fatima. I never had a little sister, but I'll protect you like my own. The world isn't meant to be such an awful place." He wasn't sure that was true, but after living through his own abusive childhood nightmare, he would make sure it never happened to this woman again.

Tears filled her eyes, and she covered her face with both hands.

"I'm sorry. Did I say something wrong?" James resisted the urge to reach for her. If she wasn't used to being seen by men, surely she wasn't used to being touched by them.

"No, no," she said through her whimpers. As she lifted her head, a wobbly grin spread across her face. "No one has ever said these words to me. Oh, James, I would love to be your sister. I have dreamed of such a brother all my life."

Why not run his heart through a paper shredder? Sheesh! James pinched his tear ducts with thumb and forefinger.

Rain came down the hallway in a bathrobe, rubbing her hair dry with a towel. "Hey guys, you getting introduced without me? Fatima, are you doing all right this morning?"

"More than all right. Thank you so much for bringing me here, Rain. I might even eat some lovely oatmeal James is preparing."

James took in Rain in all her glistening glory. He still couldn't figure out what he'd done to deserve such a treasure. After almost nine years together, Rain still entranced him, even in her oldest terrycloth robe. Karma must finally be on his side. She had the kindest soul of anyone he'd ever met, and she was all his.

His eyes drifted to the belly protruding from under the knotted belt. Soon he'd have a daughter, child of this woman, raised by her hand. He could barely comprehend his good fortune, and to think he had tried to end it all—he swallowed down a lump in his throat. But Rain would never let that happen.

Now he had this precious young woman, Fatima, to take care of and to help find her place in the world as well. "You did good, honey," he said to Rain. "Very good."

He turned his attention back to Fatima and pondered what sort of men could have beaten her. Cowards for sure, conscienceless, stony-hearted men, the kind that thrived on hate, violence, power, and pride. A shiver shot through him. What would it take to protect this girl?

If he were a praying man, now would be a good time. No wonder so many people clung to the superstitions of religion.

Layla dashed out of her engineering class and down the linoleum hallway, longing to get back to Rain's place as quickly as possible to check on Fatima. Last night the poor girl had been exhausted, but Layla had so many questions, and they still had much to figure out.

They would need help for sure. Money, supplies, maybe even some medical care and counseling for Fatima. How could she find the assistance they would require without jeopardizing Fatima's safety?

Pastor Mike at The Gathering, her small church near campus, might be a good person to ask for help, even if she couldn't share with the congregation yet. More than anything right now, she and Fatima needed prayer.

When Layla first began praying for Fatima and reaching out to her, she never imagined it would come to this. Yet God's fingerprint was all over the situation. No sooner had she cried out to him for a new direction in her life than her email had chimed with a heartrending letter from a desperate Fatima. Still, Layla couldn't stop the shiver of fear that shot through her.

Bypassing the crowded main stairway and elevator for the quickest route to the exit, she turned into a dark, old stairwell and started clicking down the five flights to the bottom.

Now she understood how Mo must have felt before she came to Jesus, so badly wanting Layla to find freedom yet terrified of the consequences and danger. She hoped Fatima would find God through this as well...but what would it cost her?

Fatima hadn't said a word about God, although Layla had prayed Jesus would reveal himself to her friend in a dream as he had done for Layla last semester. She paused for a moment on the empty stairway, recalling the wonder and joy of that dream—the honey-thick warmth of the light emanating from his presence and surrounding her, the feel of his divine love wrapping around her. All fear had melted away.

No, she would never deny Fatima that peace. It would be worth any sacrifice.

She continued on her way and turned a corner only to run into some of her old friends from the Muslim Student Union. Layla sucked in a quick breath and pasted on a false smile. To her knowledge, they weren't aware of her conversion yet, and she wanted to keep it that way, especially considering the new complications with Fatima.

"Salaam! Ahmed!" She forced a cheery tone. "Hey, guys. Long time no see."

"Don't blame us. You're the one who seems to have fallen off the planet." Salaam stood right in front of her and drew himself to his full six feet.

Layla did not recall him being so broad shouldered.

"We've been at prayers and meetings as always. The question is, where have you been?" Ahmed rose to the stair beside Salaam, blocking her path.

"Just busy with school. You know how it is." Her smile wobbled.

"No, I don't know how it is to move away from your family for no apparent reason and in with a bunch of infidels." Ahmed stared at her, eye to eye on his perch just one step beneath her, clearly menacing. "Nice hair by the way." He glared at her free-flowing hair, which had been hidden away beneath a headscarf for most of the first semester. Still, she shouldn't panic. Several of the girls in the MSU didn't veil.

Unable to share the reason for the changes in her life, Layla just mumbled, "I'm sorry, guys, but I really need to get going." She attempted to wedge herself through the few inches between them.

Ahmed shoved closer into Salaam, cutting her off. He crossed his arms over his chest. His expression tightened into a glare.

She returned to her step with her heart racing, but she resolved not to let them see her fear. Bullies loved fear. She had to be strong for Fatima. Standing as tall as she could and asserting authority into her voice, she stared back at them with ice in her eyes. "Is there a problem here?"

Salaam, always a decent sort to her remembrance, ran fingers through his hair and looked away. "Don't be like that, Layla. You seem like a cool girl. It's just that a cousin of one of our buddies ran away from Detroit, and rumor has it she's a friend of yours. I don't want to see you get hurt. Make sure you don't get involved in this, okay?"

Layla feigned confusion even as her stomach tied in knots. She gripped her books to keep her hands from shaking. "A friend? From Detroit." She forced a laugh. "Almost all of my friends are from Detroit. You'll have to be more specific."

Ahmed didn't look amused. "Some Saudi Arabian chick."

Her mind spun, desperately seeking the best plan. She knew the Middle Eastern gossip chain traveled at lightning speed yet still somehow had not expected this so soon. Tossing up a quick prayer for guidance, she felt led to try the sympathy route. Salaam and Ahmed weren't truly bad guys. Both were raised in the States and seemed moderate in their religious views.

"*Haram!*" Hopefully the Arabic expression of sympathy would put her on their side. "Could it be Fatima? The poor girl. You don't understand. Her father's used her as a punching bag for years. If she does come here we have to do something. She's a dear, sweet thing and always so frightened. Can I count on you guys to help?"

Even Ahmed softened at that. "It's best to stay out of this stuff.

You should know that. Besides, you don't want to mess with these guys."

Fear darted through Salaam's dark eyes. "He's right. These are some mean dudes."

Layla gulped. She wanted to scream it was because they were so mean that she would die protecting Fatima. Instead, she controlled her voice. "Wow. This sounds serious. What should I do if she shows up?"

She hated holding back the truth, but right now Fatima's safety mattered most.

"Call me. Let me take care of this. You have my cell, right?" Ahmed shoved his hands in his pockets.

"Yeah, I have it."

"We'll get her back to her family where she belongs. This cousin won't hurt her." Salaam fidgeted as if he hoped to convince himself. "He'll diffuse things with her parents. It's for the best. We have to keep these sorts of things in house. Right, Layla?"

Was this guy crazy? Anything to keep the authorities out of it, to keep the Americans from thinking Middle Eastern men were abusers. What if some of them were? Shouldn't they be punished like anyone else? These guys were no better if they would return a woman to that awful home.

Layla shoved all those thoughts aside. For now she needed to appear calm and innocent. "Of course. Thanks, guys. I'm glad you warned me. I'll let you know if I hear anything."

Ahmed snarled one last intimidating, "You better," and then let her pass.

Jerk.

The Middle Eastern mafia struck again. Oh, these guys were probably harmless enough, but plenty of others weren't. She'd heard whispers of terrorist cells in town. Everyone acted like they would never be involved, but someone must.

If she had pulled it off and they believed she knew nothing, she might have bought some time. *Dear Lord, let it be enough. Confuse the enemy and protect Fatima. Help us figure out what to do.*

Layla hoped Fatima's praying man would continue crying out to God on their behalf. The poor guy must be beside himself with worry, but there was nothing they could do about that.

Maybe she should talk to Mo. He seemed to have a pulse on all this, knowing whom to trust and whom to avoid. He'd been in town for years longer than her and walking with the Lord much longer too.

If things continued heating up, she might not have a choice, despite her promise to her parents.

FIVE

Noah Dixon crunched soot encrusted snow as he trekked through the streets of Detroit. Little Arabia, as he thought of this side of town. The call for prayer rang out from loud speakers overhead. "*Allahu Akbar, Allahu Akbar, Allahu Akbar, Allahu Akbar, Ash hadu an la ilaha illal lah....*"

After years studying Arabic to minister among these people, Noah understood every word. *Allah is the greatest. I testify there is no God except for Allah. I testify that Muhammad is a Messenger of Allah. I testify that Ali is an appointed deputy of Allah. Come to prayer. Come to success. The time for the best of deeds has come. Allah is greater than any description. There is no deity except for Allah.*

As the chant met his ears, he cringed. Most people found it lovely, calming even. Although no inherent villainy filled the words, the fact that it greeted his ears in Middle America never failed to alarm him.

Beautiful words? A religion of peace and love? True and yet not true at the same time. Yes the Qur'an contained messages of peace. What no one in the West seemed to understand was that they were later overturned by messages of violence and jihad. He had seen firsthand the violence and devastation this culture could wreak, no more so than in the eyes of the shattered girl on the balcony.

Did she miss him? Did she even notice he'd been sick in bed for days with the flu? He prayed for her anyway and for every one of the lost souls along his route. Love stirred in his heart for the Muslim people, so dear but so bound, longing for peace yet forever trapped in strife. If only he could shout from the rooftops, "Jesus paid the price. He loves you. He can give you the peace you seek."

But they would never listen. Their eyes were blind, their ears deaf, their hearts hardened. For now he would pray and wait for God to open the next door.

He smiled at two veiled teenage girls with their backpacks in tow, heading to school. They shyly giggled and ducked their heads. Precious souls, and at least they looked happy and safe, unlike the girl who most tugged at his heart on this cold morning.

With Bible college finished, Noah had put in applications to a number of mission agencies. Although he spoke Arabic fluently and had studied Islam from several converted sheiks, all the organizations seemed to say the same thing. He needed a job skill. Engineering, they suggested, or a certificate qualifying him to teach English as a second language.

The last thing he wanted was to wait another four years to work at his life's passion. For now he could minister here—through prayers. When God led, perhaps he could outreach in more direct ways. He'd started hanging out at the local hookah bar, and he'd made a few friends over the water pipe. Although he had never even considered smoking a cigarette, if partaking in their culture by sharing a few puffs of apple-scented tobacco opened opportunities to minister, he would not let religiosity hold him back.

He had found his ministry field for now and was praying for future direction, but Noah was in no rush. Could he leave his battered, golden-haired angel anyway? Her haunting eyes drew him, screamed out to him, day after day from her balcony. He still could hardly believe she had removed the facial scarf of her long, black *niqab* to reveal her features to him. All he could figure was that she had wanted someone... anyone...to see her and know her.

Turning the corner to her street, he gazed at the dingy, white stone front of her apartment. From what he could tell, her family occupied half of the large building. They must be wealthy, although paint peeled from the barred windows and litter lined the curb. He had seen a young man with designer clothes and pricey sunglasses walk through the thick metal door on several occasions, his eyes darting about suspiciously before he headed down the street.

What horrors did she face in that house? Did he even want to know? Didn't her tear-streaked face say it all? Each morning she would secretively lift her veil, displaying the day's cuts and bruises on her China doll face surrounded by hair the color of dark honey. He would mouth up the words, *"I'm praying for you."*

And she would mouth back, *"Thank you."* Her kneeling posture told him she prayed as well.

Would her prayers be heard if they were directed to the wrong name? Surely his gracious heavenly Father must see her heart. Noah prayed day in and day out that God would hear her cries and answer her, that he would reveal himself to her, and that he would lead her to safety.

Noah took a bracing breath as he reached her balcony. He looked upward, steeling himself against the pain...but his golden-haired girl was nowhere to be found. Fear knotted his stomach.

Where could she be? Too wounded to crawl to their daily meeting? Locked in her room? Sent back to her own country where she could never escape? Dear God, no!

Had he romanticized the girl? Like Juliette on her balcony, she was the sun he strove toward each morning, but would they similarly be held apart by culture and hate? He hoped not. All he knew was that no other female had ever called to him like this. Somehow he had to protect her. He had to save her.

His chest clutched. He closed his eyes. *Father God, protect her. Save her. Bless her. Heal her. And please God, if you are at all willing, let me find her here tomorrow.*

Layla took a long look at Fatima across the small dining table in Rain and James's apartment, torn between joy that her friend was here and safe and fear for the future. Much of Fatima's color had returned, and the black eye seemed less pronounced.

"You ladies help yourself to tea and Rain's ridiculous organic whole grain cookies if you like." James put the supplies on the island of the kitchenette. "And there's stuff for sandwiches in the fridge. I need to take a nap before my class."

"Dear James," Fatima said, turning to him, "you need not leave. Stay, please, and join us if you like."

James stooped down beside her and put a hand on her shoulder.

Layla waited for her friend to flinch or back away completely as custom demanded, but instead she leaned into James.

He smiled at Fatima. "You two should talk, and I should sleep, really. But I'm right nearby if you need me."

"Okay, thank you, James." Fatima nodded and appeared to be reassured by his promise.

Layla blinked at the odd sight of James's brown hand on Fatima's frail shoulder. Evidently his charm far surpassed her expectations. She had never seen Fatima do anything but cower in the presence of men, yet here she was, bonding with James in one short morning.

James walked down the small hallway, and the bedroom door clicked behind him.

"Did you sleep well?" Layla stood and took two mugs from a wooden hanging rack on the island. "Allie will be bringing a portable bed for you tonight along with those clothes from Sarah."

"I did sleep well. It is the first night in a long time I have no dreams. Thank you so much for helping me, Layla."

"Dreams? What kind of dreams do you have?" Layla bit her lip, hoping Fatima had dreamed of Jesus as Layla prayed she would—as

Layla herself had on a night that changed her life forever. She stood still, staring at Fatima for any clue.

Tears welled in Fatima's poignant hazel eyes. "I do not wish to tell."

"Please, Fatima. It's hard for me to help you if I don't know what's going on."

Fatima wrung her hands in her lap. "They...they are horrible dreams. I hate to speak of such things. Monsters chase me. Monsters with huge teeth that would eat me. They laugh at me. Toss me against walls in a tiny room I can never escape."

"Oh." Layla's stomach roiled. Of course she would have such dreams when her waking nightmares were nearly as bad.

"Please make me say no more."

"Of course...of course, sister. I should not have asked. Only... sometimes my own dreams bring me great comfort and direction." Layla moved to the sink to fill the mugs with water and popped them in the microwave.

"Yes, I remember your dream of Jesus, but I would not want such a dream. This Jesus, I know you love him, but he frightens me as well. Many have died for following him." Fatima closed her eyes as if willing away unbidden images.

A prayer shot heavenward from Layla without conscious effort. *How can she find you when she's so afraid? Oh God, have mercy on this broken soul.*

How could Layla explain? Yes, sometimes Christians gave their lives for Christ, but only because of the evil in this world. She decided the time was not right. "Do you feel better today? Did you eat anything?"

"Yes, James made me oatmeal for breakfast. This is so funny, do you not think, that the man should cook?" Fatima giggled.

Layla giggled along with her, overjoyed to hear the sound. "You've lived here most of your life. Didn't you know that American men cook?"

"Know, yes. See with my eyes, this is different, but he wore no ruffled apron like my mother, thanks God." Fatima raised her hands heavenward.

When was the last time Fatima had made a joke? Layla had almost forgotten her friend's dry wit. She blinked away tears. Turning to the beeping microwave, she asked, "Was it good?"

"The oatmeal? It was very good. I eat the whole bowl, and I have not eaten so much in a long while. Who knew such a big, strong man could handle food?"

Layla's tears turned to a smile. She put the orange-ginger teabags into the mugs and placed them on the dining table along with the whole grain cookies. This apartment always smelled like spices. Layla sat close to Fatima. "You like him, don't you?"

"James? Yes, very much." Fatima whispered the words, causing Layla to raise an eyebrow at her.

Fatima blushed prettily and waved her hands. "Oh, no. Not like that. I only feel so safe with him. He said he will be a brother to me." She giggled again. "Although with his brown skin, I don't know who will be believing. My mother, she would faint at this."

Despite her frustration with Fatima's mother, Layla snorted a laugh. "I would pay good money to see that. So, how are your injuries? Do you think I should take you to a doctor?"

"No, no. I am used to these bumps and bruises. I do not think they will last long. And James, he says he has medical school friends who can come to the house and check if needed." She took a sip of the tea. "Mmm, heaven."

"Sounds like James and Rain are taking excellent care of you. I'm glad we brought you here."

"They are very kind and funny. Not what I would think of a couple who...well, you understand." Fatima blushed again.

"I know it's difficult for you. We're so used to everyone believing the same thing, sharing the same values, but Rain and James are good people, and they're very committed to each other and their baby." Layla sipped her tea as well. Fatima was right—orange-ginger heaven.

"It is a strange family to me. To see this man we call an infidel and this woman we call a...well, you know what we would call her...but to see the peace and joy in their home. To see how they love me and care for me and accept me, although I am so different. They treat me better than my own family. It is hard to believe."

Layla took in the cozy setting of Rain's colorful, Bohemian apartment that did indeed exude an open, loving spirit. "Once you get more involved in the American culture, you'll be very surprised. There are good people and bad people in all sorts of packages. Before long you'll learn to look beneath the surface and spot the difference."

Fatima glanced about and dropped her voice to a whisper again. "They want me to help at a homeless shelter. But I say, no, not for very long time. Right now, I want only to be safe in their lovely little home."

Yes, that's what Fatima needed, a safe haven to heal and grow strong. "Have you thought anymore about the police? Or even the FBI? Maybe we could get you some protection."

Fatima's eyes grew wide as she shrank in her chair. "Or maybe their presence will alert my family where I am."

Layla set down her tea and reached to stroke Fatima's arm. "They're professionals. They know how to be discreet."

"No, I don't think so. I will be fine now." Fatima's breathing sounded labored.

"Please consider it."

Fatima's eyes grew hard and cold, strength coming from someplace within her that Layla had not suspected still existed. She jerked her arm away from Layla's soothing caress and gripped her mug against her slim stomach.

"Fatima, what is it? What aren't you telling me?"

She turned to look out the window. "I will not say it, but surely you must know."

"Know what? Just tell me." Layla stretched her open-palmed hand, as if begging for the answer.

"You've seen my brothers. I can never talk to the police about them, never have the FBI notice they are alive. Do you not understand?" Fatima kept her eyes locked to the overcast sky.

Terrorism! Of course Layla had suspected. The shady, underhanded way they behaved, always checking every alleyway, every parking lot. Anyone fanatical enough to imprison a female in her home would be fanatical enough to fall into terrorism. "And you don't want to...?"

Fatima stared down at her tea, allowing her golden hair to fall forward and hide her face. "I know nothing. I work hard to know nothing. More than that, family is family, no matter what. I have brought enough dishonor upon them." She clenched her jaw to match the hard glint in her eye.

The argument sounded like Salaam's and Ahmed's from earlier that morning. Keep the Americans out of their business. How would things ever change with thinking like that? But now was not the time to give Fatima a lecture. Of all people, Layla understood the pain of dishonoring family in a culture where family and honor meant everything.

"Okay. We'll do it your way for now, but we both know your family will suspect you've come here." No need to bring up the encounter in the hallway and frighten the girl further. "If things get too dangerous, we might have to do something. You wouldn't want to put Rain and James in jeopardy."

Fatima's head shot up, and her eyes lit with compassion. "I am so sorry. I did not consider them. I only thought of me. Please, please, forgive me."

"Don't feel guilty. You're in survival mode right now. We all understand."

"If the danger increases, I will try to find the courage to do something, for Rain and James and their dear baby. I simply don't know what."

Again Layla longed to confide in Mo, the man she still hoped to marry someday. His expertise in this area would help so much. "Let's take it one step at a time. For now, just rest and heal."

"Rest and heal." Fatima repeated the words as if they were the most wondrous in the world.

"And eat." Layla stood and gathered Fatima into her arms.

"Only if James will be making the food." Fatima giggled. "No health food cookies, please."

Layla took a deep breath. Let her friend giggle while she could. If Fatima's brothers showed up, there'd be nothing left to laugh about.

SIX

Sarah frowned as she battled the cold, damp wind on her way to the bus stop. Darkness still reigned, although a hint of orange dawn fought its way through the cloudy sky from the east where the Atlantic Ocean sprawled beyond a tall string of hotels. She hugged her notebooks to the front of her as a shield. They helped balance the weight of her backpack stuffed to the brim with textbooks. As the only Carmichael without a vehicle, she was subjected to this torture routine at 5:55 every school morning.

Sure, her siblings didn't get their cars until college, but none of them had gone to a high school on the far side of town. While Sarah loved her international studies program, it came at the price of a looping bus ride that lasted over an hour.

Her parents had been none too pleased at her insistence to return to public school. After watching Allie's deterioration, they had wanted the rest of their children to receive a Christian education. Her brothers had loved their Christian school, and it met all their academic and athletic needs, but once Sarah heard about the international program offered by Virginia Beach Public Schools, nothing else would do. More than anything, she longed to be a foreign missionary, and it would be the perfect preparation.

At least it had seemed perfect. Now that her graduation approached, she questioned her reasoning. Not everything had turned out as perfectly as she planned.

She had promised her parents on their large stack of Bibles that the school wouldn't change her, and she went far out of her way to prove it, even dressing in conservative clothing that could pass for a private school uniform. Besides, she felt safe covered in her modest clothes, set apart from worldly influences, and her parents had been placated by her gesture.

If only they knew the truth.

Sarah continued to trudge along the sidewalk, wishing she'd woken in time for coffee. Only a few more months and this would be over. As she crossed the last half a block to the bus stop, thoughts of Fatima flitted through her mind. She had no right to complain. At least she had her freedom, her safety.

Against a street sign ahead leaned the only bright spot in her morning—Jesse. She took a deep breath as a fluttering sensation filled her stomach and warmth flowed through her veins to drive away the cold. Jesse. The tall, dark-haired young man with hooded eyes and a neatly trimmed beard nodded her way in that too cool manner of his. At nearly twenty, he should have graduated long ago, but family troubles during elementary school had put him behind schedule, despite his obvious intelligence.

For four years they'd caught this bus together morning after morning and headed off to the same international studies program. Her parents felt safe knowing she wouldn't wait on the dark street alone. If only they knew that Jesse might be the biggest danger of all.

"Hey, gorgeous," he drawled as she came close.

She just rolled her eyes. His philosophical banter and joking flirtation had turned to patient seduction since she turned eighteen in the fall, but Sarah remained determined to treat him, as always, as a fun—if slightly annoying—buddy. "Yeah, right. I barely had time to brush my hair, and I think I still have sleepers in my eyes."

Jesse took her chin in his strong, warm hand and turned her face to the streetlight. He ran a finger down the corner of each eye, sending pleasant shivers through her. "You look fine to me. More than fine. Absolutely delicious."

He dipped his head, but Sarah twisted away in time. "It is too early for that, Jesse."

"Get back over here, silly girl. It's cold."

Unable to resist, she obeyed his bidding, and he wrapped his arms around her from behind. Her backpack and notebooks kept the embrace in the platonic zone, although he nuzzled her hair in a way that pushed the boundaries of friendship. Sarah couldn't resist breathing in a long draught of his heady cologne, which made her knees grow limp.

She relaxed against him and her eyes began to droop as he hummed a pop tune in her ear with his deep bass voice. A love song, she assumed, although she didn't follow secular music.

Nope, no secular music for Sarah. She had enough sin in her life as the matter stood. Surely nice Christian girls had no right feeling the sensations that coursed through her at Jesse's touch—a touch she allowed again and again against her best judgment. Surely that alone qualified as sin. She'd read enough books on purity that seemed to imply as much.

Despite their longstanding, rather intimate friendship, she would never consider Jesse as a spouse. He had made it clear over the years that he would never share her beliefs. She had no right letting him hold her like he did, except that he felt so warm on cold mornings, and so amazing.

Tears sprang to her eyes. Sin like this separated people from God. She'd heard that again and again at church. Not that she'd ever felt close to God in any sort of personal way.

Almost able to see the flames licking at her feet, she wiggled out of Jesse's arms. He shot her an amused look.

Just then the bus rounded the corner, and he threaded his fingers through hers. The breaks hissed and the door creaked open. Jesse pulled her up the steps and to the far back of the bus. They settled into seats across from one another to satisfy the driver's rule about boys and girls not messing around, but as they lurched forward on their way, Jesse manually swiveled her until their knees met in the aisle.

"So what's the topic of the day?" Sarah would stick to philosophy. She'd have none of his sexual innuendo this time.

A slow smile spread across his soft full lips. "Is moral behavior necessary for happiness?"

Treading toward dangerous territory, but Sarah would go along with it. Above all else, she cared about Jesse and had attempted for years to use these philosophical topics to lead him closer to Christ. Jesse came from a rough background, but she knew he had the potential to be a great guy, if only she could make him see the truth. "That's an easy one. Sin leads to destruction. Therefore one must be moral in order to be happy."

"Says who?" His smile turned into a smirk.

"Says..." she was about to say the Bible, but that was against his rules. Jesse did not accept the Bible as absolute truth, only as one religion's version of truth. She'd have to come up with something better. "Says Immanuel Kant. 'Morality is not the doctrine of how we may make ourselves happy, but of how we may make ourselves worthy of happiness.' Our morals are developed by culture in order to help us earn happiness, therefore they're important. Alcoholism leads to sickness, violence, and accidents. Lying leads to internal distress and broken relationships. Immoral sexuality leads to disease, heartache, and unplanned pregnancy. Not to mention actual crimes, which hurt others and result in legal consequences."

"I'll give you crime, but otherwise a buffet of illogical arguments to destroy. Let's start with lying. It only causes distress if you feel guilt. You only feel guilt if you believe it's wrong. You only believe it's wrong if you follow a standard of absolutes like the Bible, which makes you feel bad. Ergo, it is the moral code itself and not the lack of morality that causes the problem."

Sarah stammered but had nothing concrete to challenge him with. Fatima suffered years of abuse after turning a legal adult. The girl feared leaving the house without a full veil. Surely her moral code was to blame. Sarah would never admit that to Jesse, though. She wished God would send her a miraculous answer. Wished that she could hear his voice the way Allie claimed to, but why should he do her any favors when she sat here longing for Jesse's touch? She checked the sky for lightning.

"Now as for broken relationships," he continued, "that only happens if you get caught. So the trouble isn't lying. It's lying badly."

Sarah laughed outright at that one. Jesse was too smart for his own good—too smart for *her* own good.

"A similar argument could be used for alcoholism. It's not the drinking itself, but doing so in an irresponsible manner that causes problems. And...the same could be said for sex."

Was it her imagination, or did he draw out that last word. Her lips felt suddenly dry, and she licked them before realizing the signal she sent. She looked down at the grooved floor.

Jesse would have none of her evasion tactics. He tipped her chin to stare at her with his dark brown, fathomless eyes. "I would argue that all the reasons you gave against sex are only in reference to irresponsible sex."

Sarah blinked against the intensity of his gaze. "What about heartache?" She twisted the white gold and pink topaz of her purity ring around her left finger. It caught a glimmer of early morning sunlight. On her thirteenth birthday when her father had given it to her, when she had made her vows, it had meant the whole world to her...but now?

"You mean heartache from feeling guilty?" he asked. "Again, I blame the moral code."

"No. I mean that sex creates intimacy between a couple on a much deeper level. Women are wired to emotionally imprint on their sexual partners, and without any promise of permanence, it amplifies the level of heartache when the relationship ends."

"I could argue whether or not sex leads to greater intimacy, but since I'm a romantic at heart, I'll give you a point for that one. But relationships don't have to end badly, you know, and some relationships are worth the risk." He took her hand in his and ran his thumb in circles across her palm. "Why don't you let me show you my world? You've been preaching to me about yours for years, and I've never complained. I even read that Bible for you."

Sarah smiled at the memory—tenth grade. She had traded the New Testament for Nietzsche.

"Let me take you to see the other side. How can you make an informed decision if you won't try the options? Remember John Locke? 'No man's knowledge here can go beyond his experience.' You're the one who said faith has to come from deep inside, but I know you better than anyone else, Sarah." He touched his forehead to hers. "And deep inside...you still question."

Sarah sucked in a sharp breath and pulled away. "Not true." Except that it was. Now she could add lying to the mountain of sins separating her from God. No wonder she didn't feel close to him. No wonder she questioned. Surely it was her fault, not God's. One of Jesse's favorite Socrates quotes flitted through her mind. *The only thing I know is that I know nothing.*

That wasn't quite true. She knew that deep inside she was empty, starving and thirsting for something. Wasn't God supposed to satisfy that need? But it had never worked that way for her. Only her relationship with Jesse had soothed that place. What was wrong with Sarah that she couldn't overcome this longing?

Jesse tugged on her hand, pulling her back close. "Come on. Let's hang out this weekend. My friend John is having a party at his dad's condo on the oceanfront. Let's get away together, dance a little. I'll introduce you to some quality beverages. You're eighteen years old. Your parents have no business controlling every moment of your life. 'If you would be a real seeker after truth, it is necessary that at least once in your life you doubt, as far as possible, all things,' Descartes."

Allie certainly hadn't let their parents call the shots once she turned eighteen. In fact, Allie didn't even think drinking was a sin, although being engaged to a pastor, she chose to refrain. And to see the way Allie and Andy clung to each other even at church... If it was good enough for Allie, it was good enough for her.

Still, Sarah wavered. Could she spend time with Jesse and remain pure? Sure, Christians claimed that sin was sin, but their actions spoke louder than their words. Some sins were joked away, others frowned upon, while still others led to discipline and even ostracizing.

Then again, if sin was sin, she was already in big trouble.

As she dealt with her own internal struggles, Jesse's eyes swept her lips, and before she could stop herself, she was imagining what it might feel like if he pressed his lips to hers. Jesse knew it. His eyes told her as much.

Why fight it? She was tired of playing things safe.

He leaned in, his lips passing within millimeters of hers and onward to her ear. His warm breath tickled her skin as he whispered, "Come on. One night together, away from Mr. Thompson."

Sarah's eyes traveled to the mirror where their attentive bus driver observed them with a frown even now. For once it would be nice to be alone with Jesse, to see what she'd been missing over the last four years of playing little miss Goody Two-shoes. She was exhausted from trying to live up to her parents' standards, and still she fell short.

Jesse leaned back. He trailed his finger down her cheek and then let it trace a line along her thigh. The assault of tingles and shivers grew more than she could bear. Other than her plaguing guilt, his touch felt like heaven. Maybe he was right. Maybe her own misguided concept of sin was making her miserable, not the very natural feelings between them. Maybe it was time she gave normal life a try.

It wasn't as if her own moral code was working at the moment. "So what do you say?" He leaned back lazily against his seat. "Where and when?"

SEVEN

"Ugh!" Several days after Fatima's arrival, Rain slammed cold food items against the wall of the freezer in a desperate search. "Must—find—ice cream!"

From behind her came Fatima's giggle. "Organic soy ice cream?"

"No way. Aha! Success." Rain pulled a small container of ice cream from the far back and held it high over her head in victory. "I'm talking the real stuff, baby, Chunky Monkey extraordinaire!" But the tub felt terribly light in her hand. "Uh oh, hold the celebration." Placing it on the counter, she lifted the lid with much trepidation.

Her gaze fell upon white cardboard with only a small chunk of the food of the gods in one corner. "Eeek! Disaster. Call 9-1-1!" She displayed the pitiful contents to Fatima with an exaggerated frown.

Fatima's giggles turned to a full-blown belly laugh. "Ouch! Rain. Do not do this to me. My ribs, they still hurt. I am your wounded butterfly. Remember."

"This calls for a grocery store run. Come on, you're flying with me, butterfly girl. No excuses this time. I need your moral support. I'm a pregnant woman craving junk food. Things could get ugly."

"Oh no, please."

"I'm serious, and you need to get out of this house." Now was the perfect chance. What Fatima wouldn't do for herself, she might just do for Rain.

"Perhaps when James is with us."

Rain raised an eyebrow. "You seriously think that sweet guy can protect you better than a hormonal female bent on ice cream? Get real, girlfriend."

"But Layla has not yet brought me a headscarf." Terror lurked in Fatima's eyes.

"Oh, sweetie, you can't wear a veil. You would be too conspicuous. As long as you dress normally and don't speak too loudly, no one will suspect anything. It will be fun. No more excuses."

Rain tugged Fatima toward the coat closet.

Fatima pulled on her arm from the other side like a tug of war, digging her heels into the carpet and thrusting her rear backward to leverage her small bit of weight against Rain's ample proportions. "No! I would feel so exposed. I cannot. Truly."

The girl's strength and tenacity caught Rain off guard and nearly toppled her. Fear did strange things to people, but Rain managed to regain her footing and drag Fatima to the closet.

"Listen to me." Rain held up a pointer finger. "I have a plan." While Fatima couldn't wear the veil, there were other ways of covering up on this side of town.

Rain pulled the item she needed from the closet—James's giant black hoodie emblazoned with a gold leaf logo. She shoved Fatima's arms into the sleeves, zipped it with a flourish, and thrust her in front of the mirror by the door.

With a quick yank of the strings the look was complete. "Et voilà!"

Fatima examined her reflection and turned her head from side to side. Between the hoodie and Sarah's loose hand-me-down jeans, Fatima's figure was completely disguised, her face shadowed and barely visible.

Rain clasped her shoulders from behind and peeked into the mirror. "What do you think?"

"You are good, my friend. I am more covered than the girls like Layla who wear the headscarf."

"Wore the headscarf."

"Yes, I still forget. It is hard for me to understand she is no more a Muslim." Fatima shook her head.

"But you are the chicest veiled woman around."

"I don't know about chic. Layla was chic. I'd say I'm more street thug." Fatima hit a hip-hop pose, hugging her arms across her chest.

Rain sputtered a few times before she burst out laughing.

"I am...what do they call the crumpers on the dance show?" Fatima hit a new pose with both fingers pointing to the ground. "Buck. I am buck, no?"

Oh, how Rain loved this woman, so funny and so strong in spite of it all. Tears of laughter streamed down her face now. After a moment, Rain regained her composure enough to talk. "You are so buck. Since when do you watch *So You Think You Can Dance*?"

"Oh, my father, he paid little attention to me if I stayed in my room and did as I was told. One of the Lebanese satellite stations played the show with Arabic subtitles, but there was no translation for this 'buck.' If Father had noticed the ballroom costumes, *Allah* forbid. I will not say what he would have done to me."

Rain sobered. She had seen firsthand how Fatima's father "punished" her wayward behavior, like refusing to be dragged to a foreign country to marry a stranger who was likely even more abusive. No, she didn't want Fatima to speak of it. "But your sense of humor must help. I'm sure you could joke your way out of trouble at least some of the time."

Fatima's head disappeared further into the recesses of the hoodie. "One does not joke with Father. He would think it disrespectful. No, I joke only with other women and not for a very long time. It is good to joke again."

This was too sad. Better to focus on their outing. Rain grabbed her own olive wool coat from the closet and opened the front door while donning it.

"Let's go, butterfly girl." They passed through the hallway.

"You make me sound like a superhero. Batman! Cat Woman!"

"Na na na na na na na..." Rain intoned as they headed down the stairwell.

"Butterfly girl!" Fatima declared with panache, leaping down the last few steps to the landing. "Can I have a mask?"

"Then your veil would be complete, but you'd probably get arrested or something. You need a superpower." Rain tapped her temple as they stepped into a cool, crisp Virginia winter. The bright yellow sun lent a cheerful air to the barren trees and dusty street. Before long the branches would be bursting with life.

"Superpower?" Fatima twirled toward Rain, and Rain could see her excited face through the narrow opening of the hoodie. "I know. I will capture my enemies in my silken cocoon."

"Wouldn't that make you a moth?" Rain quirked an eyebrow.

"Hey, work with me. I came outside with you against my will. Do you not think this earns me silk?"

"Okay, okay. Silk cocoons. And naturally you can fly."

Fatima did a little skip. "Oh, yes, I will flutter beautifully with my colorful wings."

"Nice." Rain nodded.

"But who will you be? You must be superhero as well."

"Are you kidding?" Rain pushed her belly forward and pointed to it with both hands. "I am Preggo Woman. I'll melt anyone who stands between me and Chunky Monkey with my laser beam stare, and I can sit on my enemies and smash them."

Fatima's lips tipped upward, but then she turned and walked down the street. Her chuckle sounded forced.

Rain thought back through her last words. What had she said wrong? She was trying so hard to keep things light and fun for Fatima. Finally she just asked. "What is it? Did I say something that brought up a bad memory?"

"No, it is not that..." Fatima's voice came softly from the shadows of her hood.

"Did I frighten you?"

"Of course not."

"Did I..." Rain ran through the words a third time. Then it hit her. "Did I offend you somehow? Is it a cultural thing?"

"Yes. I suppose you could say this. Yes, our cultures, they are very different, but we know this already."

"Please tell me what you're thinking, Fatima. We're friends. I want to understand so I won't make these mistakes." They stopped at the corner, and Rain pressed the button for the streetlight.

"It...it is hard for me that you joke about being...about being..."

"Pregnant? Do people not talk about pregnancy in your culture? It used to be that way in America in the 1800s." Rain wrinkled her nose at the thought of such a repressive society.

"Oh no. Among women we are fairly pragmatic about pregnancies and babies. We look forward to them with much joy. Only, they are only made in...I mean, we only have babies..."

Understanding clicked in Rain's head. "When you're married. I see. So you're uncomfortable that I'm pregnant and unmarried."

"Yes, this is hard for me."

"Hard?" What on earth did her pregnancy have to do with Fatima?

"Yes, hard for my mind to accept that such a nice girl as you would do such a...thing."

Rain fought down a spark of anger. "So you don't approve."

"Of course not!" Fatima's hand flew up to cover her own mouth.

The light turned green, and they continued forward. Two young men passed them and shot appreciative grins at Rain, but Fatima's hoodie rendered her invisible as they had planned.

Fatima took Rain's hand in her own. "I am so sorry, Rain. Layla has told me in this culture I should not 'judge,' but surely some things we must all know are wrong, deep in our hearts. Doesn't everyone understand this? Could I truly be so different?" Fatima's words sounded of compassion and humility and a sincere desire to understand.

This time instead of sparking anger, Fatima's comment sparked some deeper awareness that Rain had hidden for months, a weighty lump deep in her abdomen that she had managed to thrust aside once James came home. All last semester Rain had been inundated with Christian teaching as she helped Allie search for a church that fit her needs—too much talk of sin and blood sacrifices and atonement. Surely Rain would never believe such things.

But she had felt odd twinges of...conviction...after James moved back in. They would strike her at the strangest times, like when she looked at their rumpled sheets by the light of day.

"Rain, are you angry with me? Truly, I am sorry. I should be learning to close my mouth. I am so thankful for all you do to me. You are a good person, even if it is hard for me to understand it all. I...I love you, Rain."

Rain melted at the words and stopped to gather the girl in her arms. "I love you too, Fatima."

She let go, and they continued walking. The grocery store loomed ahead now, like a golden city on a hill.

Rain could hardly believe Fatima would judge her like that. She should probably drop it, but she wanted to understand why the girl would feel that way. After all, Fatima wasn't a Christian like Allie and now Layla. Maybe in contrasting the religions, Rain could discover something important. "So can I ask you a question?"

"Of course, anything, my friend."

"I assume you think that...being with James is a sin."

"I am sorry if I offend you, but without marriage this is my belief."

"Because it is the Islamic view?"

Fatima paused and turned to Rain. "Yes, but it is more. Although it is hard for me to leave my culture behind, I must confess I doubt the teaching of Islam. Islam says a man should beat his wife for the good of her soul. Yet this I question. In my heart of hearts, I do not know this is true. I believe we should treat one another with gentleness and kindness, with respect and dignity. Islam says we must kill the infidel. Again, I wonder. Why do I wonder? Because deep in here..." She thumped her fist against her chest. "I know killing is wrong. This is a knowledge deeper than religion. I always was thinking it must be somewhere inside of everyone."

Rain pressed her lips tight together as she digested the implications of the statement. Fatima wasn't spouting dogma, she was sharing her soul. Rain cleared her throat. Needing to hear the truth, she attempted to mute the hurt in her voice. "And this deep conviction, this sense of inner conscience, it tells you that being intimate with a man you love and are committed to is wrong?"

Fatima blinked in surprise. "When you say this way, I am confused a little. But, this voice inside, it tells me children belong in families and families should be forever. To me, this means children should come in marriage. It is a gift to women and to children, I think. It is a promise, a safety. Divorce should not be so easy as it is in Islam. This is wrong as well. But marriage...yes, I believe this is right."

That deep place inside of Rain grew from a twinge to a thump, a heavy lump throbbing in her gut.

"What about your god, Rain? I do not understand what god you follow. What does he say?"

"My god is very big and broad." Rain gave the pat answer from her interfaith congregation. "He or she is everywhere and in everything."

"This, it makes no sense to me." Fatima cocked her head. "To me this sounds like no god at all."

Rain swallowed hard. To her as well sometimes. She had met a real God last fall, a God with a face and a voice, a personal God who knew her as a friend. Yet she turned him away in favor of James. She thought she could have them both, but it wasn't working like she planned.

She kicked at a stone with her foot. "You should come to my church sometime. We have a few Muslims who attend along with some Jews, Christians, Hindus, and Buddhists. It's a place where everyone can be accepted and pray side by side in love."

"Maybe someday. I cannot attend mosque. I am not sure that God...Allah...whoever he is...is liking me right now, though. I might be afraid." Fatima stared at the ground for a moment but then turned her face to Rain. "You still did not tell me what your god of everywhere and everything says about relations outside of marriage. I would very much like to know."

The god of everywhere and everything said nothing at all. And what did the personal God she had pushed away have to say? She'd never had the courage to ask.

Fortunately, they arrived at the sliding door of the grocery store at that moment.

Rain took the opportunity to change the subject. "Yes! Watch out ice cream. Here we come."

"Please, Rain, be melting no one with your death ray."

Rain laughed. "Okay, I'll lay off the superpowers. Innocent bystanders are safe enough in my pursuit of Chunky Monkey."

But would her relationship with James survive her ongoing quest for truth? At least they had finished their English diversity projects that stirred so much conversation between Allie, Layla, and her last semester. Soon they'd be grouping up again for the philosophy class they had together, though, and this time the Christians would outnumber her two to one.

EIGHT

"Hey, Pastor Mike, wait up," Layla called to the African-American man she had come to think of as a brother. He stood near his large SUV in the parking lot of an old church in a needy neighborhood where the folks from their own church, The Gathering, manned a soup kitchen every Thursday.

Mike's beautiful wife Serena, weighed down with supplies and their youngest child, nodded and smiled to Layla but otherwise continued leading their gaggle of stair-step kids bundled in warm winter outerwear toward the building. She seemed happy to allow Layla and her husband a private moment to talk. That said a lot about their relationship.

Layla jogged toward Pastor Mike. He placed the heavy Crock-Pot back in his trunk before turning to her. She hunched deeper into her jacket against the chill.

"Layla, my newest little sister." He extended his arm, and she gladly settled into a side hug. Although the affection poured on her from the men at this church had taken her aback at first, she quickly adjusted. Today she leaned into Pastor Mike's strength, blinking back tears within the protective shelter of his arms.

Stepping back to take a better look at her, he asked, "Is something wrong?"

She had so badly wanted to talk to him all week but had been nervous to share the news over the phone. Who knew what sort of connections Fatima's family might have? They'd gotten to her with a threat in less than twenty-four hours. Although she and Mike appeared to be safe enough in the open parking lot, suddenly the words escaped her. She had no idea how much she should share.

"Layla, what is it?"

"I don't know how to ask for help with this." She bit her lip. "Would you understand if I shared a little but begged you not to ask too many questions?"

"Not a problem. A pastor is kind of like a therapist...only better. I don't charge an arm and a leg." He chuckled with his deep, rich laugh. "Any secret you have is safe with me."

Looking into his caring brown eyes, she knew he spoke the truth. She was so glad to have found this congregation and this pastor so quickly. And if she caught a glimpse of Mo every week, well she could hardly help that, could she?

"I have a friend," she began, carefully weighing her words. "She's a Muslim from Saudi Arabia." Yes, that was common knowledge. "Her family is very radical. She wears a full veil and can't leave the house without a male chaperone. And..." Layla pressed her lips together.

"It's okay. You don't have to go on if you don't want to. I'll be happy to pray for your friend."

"No, I want to tell you." The words flowed freely now. "It's just hard. Her father beats her terribly. He was going to drug her and send her to Saudi Arabia and force her to marry a complete stranger."

Pastor Mike emitted a low whistle and shoved his hands into the pockets of his baggy jeans. "That's some rough stuff."

"So she ran away." Layla's voice caught. "And now she's in terrible danger." Salaam and Ahmed knew all of this information. There was no reason the church people couldn't. "That's really all I should say for now. But yes, please pray for her, and you can share that much with the church too."

"Absolutely, I will pray, and I'll ask the church to join us. I firmly believe that God will send his angels to watch over this innocent girl."

He paused in the gray winter twilight and rubbed his chin. "And for the record, if the need ever comes for me to be a human angel to her, I would be honored."

Layla covered her face with her hands as tears filled her eyes. Mike pulled her into his arms again, and she rested her head against his thick winter jacket. "I'll get you all wet." Layla hiccupped.

"It's all right. Everything will be all right." His mellow voice soothed her to her core. In that moment, it sounded like the voice of Jesus she had once heard in a dream.

For the first time in a week, Layla dared to hope that everything might turn out okay. A picture of Fatima at Rain's kitchen table, happily chowing down on Chunky Monkey ice cream while giggling about the new American TV shows she'd discovered popped into Layla's head, and then Fatima demonstrating the latest dance craze. New tears filled Layla's eyes, happy tears this time. For now she would push away the scary images of Ahmed and Salaam blocking the stairs and find a moment of respite in the arms of this incarnate version of Jesus.

Finally, she pulled back and wiped away her tears.

Pastor Mike gathered his Crock-Pot and led her toward the building. "Come on. Let's get to work. If serving these people doesn't perk you up, nothing will."

How true. She'd discovered again and again during the past few angst-ridden months that following Jesus's command to serve the "least of these" brightened her day and gave her hope more than anything else.

Layla's cell phone chirped out one of her favorite new praise songs. It always put a smile on her lips. "Excuse me, Pastor Mike, I'll be in in a minute."

"Sure thing."

Layla headed toward the church's front stairs, fumbling to pull her phone from her purse. When she examined the screen, her smile faded. Mom. This would never get easier. What would be today's tactic? Tears? Yelling? Or Mom's favorite—stony silence? Which was admittedly difficult to achieve over the phone, but Mom was a master at her craft.

After a moment of hesitation, Layla forced herself to tap the screen and accept the call. "Hi, Mom."

"Marhaba," Mom answered a flat hello in their native Arabic tongue despite the fact that they typically spoke English at home. And so the subtle reminders began.

"How are you?" Layla asked, sinking heavily onto the stairs, still leery of what turn the conversation might take.

"Hmph."

Aha! Stony silence. The manipulation tool of champions. Since their Lebanese traditions required a lengthy string of scripted niceties upon greeting and saying goodbye, Mom's grunting response spoke volumes.

"I'm doing fine. School's going well."

Mom said nothing.

"How's the weather in Detroit?"

"Cold."

Cold in Detroit in winter. No, really? But somehow Layla managed to maintain a respectful tone. "It's chilly here too. It's a different kind of cold—wet and rainy—but I heard it might snow next week. That would be a nice change. I miss the snow, and if we don't get some soon, the window will be passed."

"If you miss the snow, come home."

"Mom."

"Hmph."

Layla sighed. She knew she would regret this next question, but experience had taught her that she might as well get it over with. "Is something wrong?"

Another long span of silence spread across the phone. Layla

couldn't decide whether or not she should fill it with more mindless chatter, but finally her mother spoke. "I don't know what to say to you anymore."

"I'm still the same Layla. I'm still your daughter. You've known me since I was born."

"The same Layla? My daughter? Some days I feel I have no daughter anymore."

"That's not fair." Layla pressed her eyes closed. She had thought they were past the disowning phase. Although, as she paused to consider, she realized that wasn't what her mother was saying this time, and in truth, the Layla she had known was gone in many ways. Dead to her old self. She knew it must feel like a betrayal. Good thing she hadn't used the actual term *born again* with her mother. It would just give Mom more ammunition.

"You dare to speak to me of fair? I spit on fair!" Mom said. "Nothing is fair about this. You can't even wear a little bitty headscarf. Can't even look like my Layla so I can find you on the street."

There was no sense in arguing that ninety percent of the time her mother saw her was at home, where she never had worn a veil to begin with. All she could think to say was, "I love you, Mom."

"Hmph! What kind of love is this? To turn your back on your family, your traditions? I do not know this kind of love."

So Mom would maneuver into the guilt lane now. Layla had better change the subject before she veered into full blown yelling or sobs. She might as well take this opportunity to stake out the situation at home. "Hey, Mom, I've been meaning to ask—have you seen Fatima lately? She hasn't called me in a while." That was true enough. They'd always had an email sort of relationship.

"Probably she's not knowing what to say to you too. Oh, my baby. I miss my little *farah*, Layla. Where did she go?" A sniffle came through the cell line loud and clear. Childish nicknames, great, but Layla had no desire to be a shy little mouse anymore. She wanted to develop into a strong, independent woman like Allie and Rain.

"I'm so sorry. Right now she has to serve food to needy people at a soup kitchen, but she still loves you, Mom. She really does." Layla stopped short of saying she missed her. In fact, she was so thankful to be a thousand miles away from her mother right now.

Just as a wail came through the speaker, Layla hit the end button.

She tossed the phone into her purse, sagged like a deflated balloon, and dropped her chin into her palm. This new role of family rebel didn't suit her. She had always been a diplomat, a peacemaker. Wasn't that a good thing according to the Bible? She'd have to ask Pastor Mike. Surely there must be some way to live out her newfound faith without tearing apart her family.

At least Mom hadn't known anything about Fatima. Layla could be thankful for that much. It seemed like Salaam and Ahmed had spoken the truth—Fatima's family was keeping things quiet and trying to find her before their honor was destroyed. Maybe they wouldn't kill her if they could find her in time. Maybe Layla was making a mistake by keeping Fatima here. Maybe she shouldn't have mentioned her to Pastor Mike.

But Fatima's family most assuredly would ship her off to Saudi Arabia, strip her of her freedom, and destroy her life if they could get their hands on her. No, Layla could never let that happen, just like she could never let her mother talk her out of her newfound faith in Christ. Right now, prayer was just about the only thing she could think of that might help. Or better yet, an army of prayer warriors. They needed God's supernatural intervention in this situation.

She headed into the warm church in hopes that blessing others for a few hours might help her shake off the doldrums that seemed to follow her everywhere these days.

NINE

On Saturday night Sarah checked herself in the mirror of her bedroom one last time before her date—or maybe she should just call it a get-together—with Jesse. Perfectly demure makeup in pastel shades. Check. Straight blond hair neat and tidy with the sides pulled back into a barrette. Check. Clothes modest enough to make it past the front door but not conspicuous enough to stand out at the wild party he planned to take her to. Ugh! What had she gotten herself into?

But she had to admit, her lilac sweater set that she usually wore over a long skirt looked rather appealing paired with simple, straight-legged jeans. At least she still appeared a reasonable facsimile of herself and hadn't turned into some sort of tramp just to please a man. She sighed. Would she regret this evening? Maybe, but Jesse was right. She had no business judging his lifestyle from a distance. How could she ever really know what she believed until she saw the other side?

Her purity ring caught her gaze and held it for a moment. Nothing would change, she promised herself. She didn't intend to go diving head first into sin. Tonight would just be research that would prove the Christian straight-and-narrow path the best choice. Layla had taken a huge risk in her search for the truth. Shouldn't Sarah be willing to take a few risks herself?

She needed a greater appreciation for her own belief system. If she was going to continue down this path, she needed to believe it from deep within her heart. Jesse had been right about that as well. Maybe seeing the ugliness of sin firsthand would do the trick.

Hoping to avoid Mom, she jogged lightly down the steps, but no such luck. Her mother sat knitting in an armchair within sight of the front door. Sarah hated deceiving the good-hearted woman, but if her parents weren't so ridiculously smothering, she wouldn't have to lie to them. She bet most of the kids in her youth group could slip out the door with a quick mention of a party without getting the third degree.

Besides, she was legally an adult! It really was none of Mom's business anymore. Allie had been off trotting the globe at Sarah's age, probably enjoying giant mugs of ale at some pub in England or Germany where Christians thought nothing of it. Sarah armed herself with those facts as she approached the coat rack in the foyer. She went to grab the keys from their well-organized hanger and dash out the door with a quick good-bye, but no luck there either.

A jingling from the formal living room caught her ear, and she turned to see Mom shaking the keys. A perfect June Cleaver imitation, right down to her long skirt, worn for no other reason than to look nice for her husband when he came home from a late night at work. "What are the rules again, sweetie?" she asked in her Southern accent, with a sugary smile pasted in place.

For heaven's sake, Sarah had been borrowing the family minivan for two years, but she took a deep breath and recited the rules dutifully. "Be considerate of others. No speeding. No boys in the car without a chaperone. Run from the presence of cigarettes, alcohol, and drugs. And of course, fill the van with gas before coming home. I've got this, Mom, really." She snatched the keys from her mother's hand and leaned over to give her a kiss on her stiffly sprayed brown hair. Gulping back her mounting guilt, she attempted a grin.

Eighteen. Allie in Germany. Research. She chanted the words in her head.

"You know it would be a lot less gas if you would just hang out with your church friends instead of running off to the far side of Virginia Beach. My goodness, that school of yours might as well be in Chesapeake. You'd think your study partners could meet you here sometimes."

"Mom!"

"I know, I know. You're just trying to get good grades."

If Sarah could thank Allie for one thing, it was that Mom had lightened up on her lectures since her older sister returned home. "I love you, Mom. I'll come home early...if I can."

"Well, you might as well stay until you're finished with the project."

"Great. It will save an extra trip." Guilt gnawed at her stomach.

Eighteen. Allie in Germany. Research.

Though flustered, Sarah remembered to snatch up her backpack along with her purse. She shot her mother one last wavering smile before heading to the van. By the time she reached Jesse's house a few blocks away, she'd managed to compose herself.

Jesse walked to her door, opened it, and without so much as a word of warning, crushed his lips to hers. Her whole world shattered about her. He had never dared to do that before. Though quick, the pressure of his thorough kiss set her lips aflame. She couldn't think straight—could barely see straight. She blinked a few times and pressed a hand over her branded mouth. His cocky grin told her he was perfectly aware that he had just claimed her as his own in the most ancient sort of way. Her blood heated, and those forbidden tingles sprang to life.

"Hey, gorgeous. Glad you made it. I thought you might chicken out."

Was it too late? Her foot itched to slam the gas and drive away right now, but something in her expression must have warned him.

He pushed her sideways with his hip, practically sitting on top of her for a moment. "Scoot over and let me drive."

Without a word, she slid past the center console and into the passenger seat. He led her down the street like a lamb to the slaughter.

Allie slid into the pew next to her mom as the organist was still warming up in the beige and cream sanctuary circa 1970. Mom's gaze traveled slowly down Allie's long fuzzy sweater to her jeans and boots. Somehow, Mom managed to keep any expression from her face. After a moment, she took a deep breath. "Nice to see you today, Allie." She pasted on a smile.

Choking back a laugh at the obvious effort required for Mom to avoid mentioning her casual attire, Allie kissed her cheek. "You too." And she meant it. Thanks to Andy's advice last semester, she had learned to see her mother in a whole new light. While she still found the woman amusing, she could love her the way she needed to. Allie settled in beside her family.

"Aren't you sitting with Andy?" Mom asked.

"No, I have to slip out early. We have a big dance rehearsal at school today."

"How's that new troupe of yours doing?"

"It's going great. It really was a God thing, you know?" Allie's group for a dance composition class last year had centered around worship as a theme. Their performance had earned rave reviews. After traveling the piece to a number of area churches, it had only seemed natural to form a small worship dance team.

"Don't I know it, sugar. A God thing for sure." Mom's smiled looked genuine this time. "You all were just too beautiful. I know the congregation loved it when you did that wonderful piece here."

If someone had told Allie a year ago that the congregation of the First Church of the Stick in the Mud would welcome her dance group, performing to a heavy metal worship song no less, she would have had them committed to a mental institution. But things really had changed around here.

Andy, her gorgeous fiancé, waved to her from the stage, where he was making last minute preparations with the pastor. He had a lot to do with the changes for the better at this place, and he hoped to continue leading the church into the twenty-first century now that he had moved from youth pastor to assistant pastor.

Allie leaned past her mother. "Hey, Dad. Hey, Rob."

"Hey, sweetie." Her tall blond dad leaned over her mother to give Allie a kiss. Today he was sporting one of his many ties covered with a graphic design formed of crosses and scriptures.

Her brother Rob waved. No tie for him, although he still wore a collared shirt and khakis. Since Allie had initiated the casual dress craze, he had toned down his Sunday spit and polish look as well.

"Where's Sarah?"

"Oh, she didn't make it today," Mom said. "Poor thing."

Allie's stomach lurched for a moment. Sarah never missed church. "What is it?"

"Poor thing has just been working herself to a frazzle with graduation coming up. That International Studies program of hers is a lot of extra work. I sure do hope it's worth it."

"Oh." Allie twisted her lips. Something was wrong with Sarah, and it wasn't too much homework. God had really put Sarah on Allie's heart lately, and she'd been praying for her. She needed to find more time to spend with Sarah. Last Monday night had gone well, but the whole situation with Fatima had kept Allie from having an in-depth conversation with her sister the way she intended to. "I wish I could see her at lunch today, but I really can't get out of this rehearsal."

"Don't worry, she'll be just fine with a little rest. You know our Sarah. S stands for strong and stable, as I always say." Mom patted Allie's knee.

S also stood for snap and shatter. Sarah was so brittle, Allie feared she'd been on the verge of falling apart for months.

"Oh, and Allie..." Mom lowered her voice and ducked her chin. "Sarah apprised us of the situation with that *friend* of yours."

Allie wasn't positive Sarah should have done that. Although Mom would never "gossip," she was active in at least five prayer chains.

"Now don't you worry. I just told everyone we had an unspoken request. I won't say more unless you ask me to, but I want you to know that our house is available. She can sleep in your old bed anytime she needs to."

"Thanks, and if you really mean it then please don't bring it up to anyone at all. If we need to move her from Rain's place, it will mean someone's after her. So we wouldn't want anyone connecting her to us."

"Mum's the word, sugar." Mom twisted an invisible lock on her lips.

The Fatima situation seemed stable for the moment, but something kept whispering to Allie that Sarah was the one truly in danger.

Sarah huddled against the biting wind as she stared over the Atlantic Ocean to the horizon beyond. When would the weather let up? She was tired of cold and gray. Surely they were due for a typical Virginia Beach warm winter spell soon.

Behind her sat the condo where she had partied with Jesse last night, but she couldn't bear to face it, so she gazed out over the surf instead. She had begged off church, claiming to be sick, and for once in her life she had told the complete and utter truth. Nausea roiled in her stomach to match the churning ocean, and her head pounded like the waves on the sand.

She regretted that third beer, but did she regret last night? She just didn't know. The question had plagued her all morning and had made it impossible to face her church and the friends she had judged over the years for their "worldly" behavior. A part of her wanted to talk to Allie about this. Allie would understand.

In fact, Sarah realized, in her own way Allie had tried to warn her that this could happen, but Sarah wasn't ready to talk to her yet. She needed to figure things out on her own first. She'd grown tired of other people telling her what to believe, what to do—bone weary to the depths of her soul.

Images and impressions from the night before flickered through her mind—the fire of Jesse's lips on hers, the fuzzy haze that settled over her as she sipped her first ever beer. Though it had tasted bitter against her tongue, it had saturated her body with velvety warmth that felt so good. Her stiff limbs had softened at its magical touch. The room full of partiers took on a dreamlike quality. The lights swirled. The colors blurred. The sounds grew muffled in the nicest sort of way. The pounding music she normally hated somehow made sense as it seeped into her being.

When Jesse pulled her tight against his taut form and began to sway to the beat, for once in her long, tedious life, she didn't resist. She didn't fight. She just gave way to the mesmerizing flow.

How many times had he pressed his lips to hers? She could hardly remember. The entire evening had turned into one mystical haze. She had giggled and sighed as his lips traveled down her neck and over her collarbone.

Why had she never noticed how brittle and cold her existence was? How bland? Jesse had tried to tell her. Life could be so much more—teeming with energy, pulsing with rhythm, flowing with heat. She had lived her first eighteen years as some sort of zombie, a walking dead person. Not that she'd ever seen a zombie movie, of course. Mom and Dad would not approve.

Sarah sighed.

It wasn't until Jesse pushed her into the backseat of the van and began to fumble with the buttons of her sweater that the haze faded and everything shot into clear focus. She shrieked and grabbed at her top. She wasn't ready for that.

He just leaned back with that sexy chuckle of his and apologized for misreading the signals, then kissed her soundly one more time, leaving her in a daze yet again.

But what did it all mean in the light of day? Had she ruined everything? Could God forgive her? Did she even believe or care anymore? Something in her life had been way off the mark. She had no desire to be that cold, rigid person anymore. But where did she go from here? Nothing in her perfect, orderly, organized existence made a bit of sense anymore.

She hugged her knees to her chest as loneliness pressed at her from every side. Only able to think of one solution, she pulled her phone from her pocket, scrolled to Jesse's name, and hit dial.

TEN

Layla craned her neck to check the back door of the cheerful old theater for the tenth time since she'd entered the place. Although she'd lost track of the words on the large overhead screen, she managed to keep pace clapping to the up-tempo worship song. She sat with a few girls she vaguely recognized from Old Dominion University, but she wished Allie or even Rain might show up. Especially since the person she kept searching for, Mo, was never this late.

He'd been the one to bring her here last semester after she moved away from her uncle and in with Allie. The peace and joy in her heart told Layla right away this was the church for her. That was before she'd gone home for Christmas and vowed to never see Mo again, but she assumed that meant "see" as in boyfriend, not "see" as in across a crowded sanctuary at the weekly Sunday evening service. She wished so badly that she could talk to him for just a few minutes tonight.

Sharing her burden with Pastor Mike and with her girlfriends had helped, but she longed to share it with Mo as well. Perhaps it was just an old habit she needed to shake, but he had taken up residence in her heart and mind, and she still didn't know how to evict him from the premises.

She continued to scan for familiar faces and caught sight of Rain's friend Vanessa, with her pale curling hair, romping about with the children to the praise song. Vanessa offered a big grin and waved for her to join them in the back.

"Me?" Layla mouthed, pointing to herself, and laughed at the thought. She had gone from formula prayers on the women's side of the mosque with her face pressed to her prayer rug to this hip church with its hugging and singing and "words from the Lord" in just a few short months. Now this woman wanted her to dance during a religious service! She laughed again, shaking her head.

Vanessa nodded yes in an exaggerated manner and waved her back again.

Layla tuned into the rhythm of the music. It had a Hebrew beat. Most Muslims hated all things Jewish, but the style reminded her of her Middle Eastern roots. Her feet began to twitch in time. She turned to Vanessa and the kids again. They were having so much fun dancing in a circle with their simple, repetitive steps. Layla had always loved to dance. She mostly knew the belly dancing variety, but surely if the children could catch on to the choreography, she could too. It reminded her of the Lebanese *debke* she had taught Rain and Allie last semester. Besides, she was tired of sitting here searching for Mo.

Just then the worship team shifted into a new song. This one Layla knew. She'd been listening to it almost daily on her iPhone. The words exploded across the sanctuary. "There's a place where I love to run and play..."

Vanessa and the children began running and clapping their way around the periphery of the theater. Oh, how Layla wanted to experience this! During her amazing dream that changed everything, she had felt God's overwhelming love—the touch of his hand—and had gazed into the unfathomable depths of his adoring eyes. And now she felt a new prompting in her heart: her Daddy whispering to run and play, to dance with him through his fields of grace.

She thought of the scripture she'd read during the week—Jesus's instruction to have faith like a little child. Dare she try it? She could hardly mess up running and clapping, unless, of course, she managed to trip and fall on her face. As if on cue, one of the tiny girls with bouncing curls tripped and tumbled down the aisle, but she quickly gathered herself together and continued running and giggling with a huge grin spread across her chubby face, not in the least embarrassed. If the child could do this, Layla could too.

She'd made the mistake of wearing heels tonight, but the impulse hit to slide off her shoes. Without waiting, without letting her more rational mind talk her out of that wonderful prompting, she pushed off her shoes and stepped into the aisle. Vanessa winked at her as she danced, laughed, and clapped her way past. Layla joined in at the end of the line of children.

The rhythm filled her, blossomed from her core straight to her hands and feet, and she lost herself in that moment. All the fear and tension from the week was crowded from her being by the ecstasy bursting from her center and bubbling through her. She could almost see it flowing out from her and filling that room. How did Allie explain it? As if the kingdom of God within her was flowing through her fingertips and toes.

"I love my Father…" she sang along with the words. Oh, how indeed she loved her new heavenly Daddy, a Daddy who knew her heart. This Daddy wanted the very best for her, not just what culture and tradition demanded, not just what would make the family appear impressive to others.

Suddenly another scripture she had read that week came to mind, the one about leaving your mother and father. It had upset her at the time. So far it had been the aspect of Christianity that most diametrically opposed her upbringing, but as she danced with her heavenly Daddy through his grace-laden fields, it began to make sense. She had to find her identity in him now, to love him more than anything…or anyone…here on earth. Even her own family.

Just like the song said, nothing could take that away from her. She continued singing with all of her heart.

Yet she had let her parents take Mo away from her, and didn't she know somewhere deep inside—in that same place that had made her question her Muslim religion and had drawn her to Christ—that they belonged together? They had found each other and fallen in love at the tender age of five, and it seemed nothing short of a miracle that God had brought them back together at this pivotal moment in their lives. Surely it would work out eventually—the timing just wasn't right.

She pushed thoughts of Mo from her mind so she could enjoy the euphoria of God's presence a few minutes longer. She would need it to get through this week.

After the song ended, she gathered with the other dancers in the back, taking a moment to rest her hands on her knees and catch her breath. She hadn't exercised like that in a long time, and she had never poured her whole being into movement in such a manner before.

Vanessa offered a high five. "That was awesome!"

Layla giggled, just like the little girls. "It sure was."

"You going to stick around for a while?"

"Just try to drag me away," Layla said between panting breaths.

As a new tune began, the girls taught her one of their circle dances, and she quickly picked up the steps, enjoying the unity of moving in community as one body. It seemed to her there was a scripture about that somewhere too, although she was still figuring out the intricacies of her new Christian faith. Thank God that he accepted, even encouraged, her childlike attempts.

As she rounded the circle and caught sight of the back door again, finally, the face she had searched for all night appeared—Mo, with his strong bone structure, olive skin, and dark, rumpled curls. Oh, how she wanted to run her fingers through them.

But he wasn't alone. Two guys entered behind him. She vaguely remembered the one—Farid something or another, an Egyptian who occasionally hung out with the Muslim Student Union crowd. Of course, she'd met Mo at an MSU party, and he had turned out to be a Christian. Maybe it would be fine. She didn't know the other guy, but he looked Middle Eastern as well.

Why would Mo bring them here? Didn't he know she was in enough trouble already? But of course, she hadn't said a word to him about Fatima. She could hardly blame him for not taking that into consideration, and she of all people knew Mo dreamed of freeing Muslims from their chains. She had been the first, and he had shared his secret hope of doing it full-time someday.

She shouldn't be surprised, yet cold fear threatened to overtake her again. Part of her wanted to dash for the ladies room and hide, but she couldn't hide forever. Just like she'd found the courage to step into the aisle and dance, she mustered the resolve to face Farid. With Muslim females you could gauge how devout they were by their dress, but the guys gave away no such clues. Nonetheless, she gulped and waved.

He looked frightened as well as he waved back but managed to offer a shy half-smile. Perhaps he was taking the same risk she was by being here tonight. As he raised his eyebrow, she understood. He would keep her secret if she would keep his. She smiled her reassurance across the room.

Letting out a breath, she attempted to pay attention to her dancing. Why must their religion be fraught with so much danger and fear? So much coercion and control? Then she corrected herself—her *former* religion. She wasn't a Muslim anymore, yet so much of that culture and mindset still clung to her. She wasn't quite sure which parts she should hold onto and which she should cast off to enter fully into that freedom she knew God wanted her to experience.

She turned her heart back to prayer and breathed in the peace of this place again. A part of her longed to bring Fatima here, longed for her to experience this freedom as well, to revel in the music, the teaching, and the love that permeated this makeshift sanctuary, but she knew she never could. The price was high enough for her, but for Fatima it could mean death.

It was all so confusing still. She had been cut off completely from her favorite aunt and uncle. A restraining order made certain of that. But what about her parents—her poor parents? She was their baby. They had devoted their whole lives to their children. Surely she must owe them something.

When she had told her parents of her dream and of coming to Jesus, they had tried to understand, she could tell they truly did, but they just didn't get it. She saw such sadness in their eyes, such heart-wrenching disappointment. It broke her heart as well. Would it be so awful to wait a while before telling people? Couldn't she give matters a while to calm down before she picked things up with Mo again? They'd waited seventeen years for each other. What were a few more?

Shway, shway, as they said in Arabic. Little by little.

Of course, her parents might still reject her when she stopped playing by their rules. Maybe she only delayed the inevitable by meeting their demands.

The song ended, and she returned to her seat to slip on her shoes. Mo's gaze caught hers across several rows of people. Her heart clutched in the most bittersweet sort of way. Her stomach turned that flip, as it always did at the sight of him. She bowed her head and began to pray as the praise band switched to a slow worship tune. She had no idea what else to do, but surely this powerful new God of hers could make a way where there seemed to be no way.

As he caught Layla's eye across the colorful sanctuary, Mo's heart strangled in his chest. Tonight she wore skinny jeans with a long flowing white shirt over her nicely curving figure, an outfit she might have worn last semester—yet without her headscarf, she looked like any other American girl...only prettier.

He didn't think he could take much more of this. Last semester had been hard enough. He could hardly believe that day on the beach when he found her again after seventeen years apart, but he quickly realized he could never fit an Islamic wife into his newfound Christian faith. And after years of searching for the truth, he wouldn't sacrifice his relationship with Jesus.

He had tried to push her away, but she wouldn't let things rest until he confessed. In that moment when he shared that he had become a Christian believer, he had seen it in her eyes. She wanted to be one too. She was just too afraid. Fear—the motivating factor of his former religion.

But now his wildest dreams had come true. Layla had accepted Christ. Everything should be perfect—so why was she further away from him than ever before? His future had slipped through his fingers like water, and he had no idea how to get it back.

Maybe he should find a different church. He couldn't bear to see her week after week if they couldn't be together. Then he turned his attention to Farid and Franko, peacefully swaying to the slow, sweet worship song. He couldn't imagine taking his new friends anywhere else. He supposed for now he should attempt to thrust Layla from his mind and focus on his new mission.

Determined to get out from under the control of his parents, he had taken a job waiting tables at the local Arabic restaurant. After this semester, he hoped to break financial ties with his parents entirely, maybe even switch to the Christian college across town to study theology. Although he had a natural knack for it, engineering had been his parents' dream, not his, which was why he wouldn't be graduating on schedule this spring one way or the other. He had put off choosing a major well into his second year.

If only Layla would find the courage to break ties with her parents as well, everything would be perfect. But this was all so new to her.

She had grown up as a pampered princess, and she had sacrificed so much already.

The good news was that his job had paid off with unexpected dividends as well. He found himself surrounded by members of the local Arabic community, and he had discovered a ministry field ripe for the harvest. Farid had come from a nominal Muslim family like his own, and Franko had given up on the rituals of his parents' Catholic religion years ago.

Both were ready for something new, for something authentic and life-changing. Of course, Mo knew plenty of devout Catholics, and he respected their faith, but for Franko, the religion had grown cold. He needed somewhere pulsing with real, live Christianity—real to the tips of your fingers and toes Christianity. No, Mo couldn't imagine taking these searching young men anywhere else.

Turning to take in their faces, he attempted to turn his mind to what really mattered—Egyptian Farid, with his dark, brooding looks and contemplative nature, Lebanese Franko with his sandy hair, shockingly blue eyes, and boisterous personality. Americans, even those with the best of intentions, didn't understand the vast cultural landscape of the Middle East, which was precisely the reason Mo dreamed of ministering to his own people.

If only he could manage to keep one magnetic Miss Layla Al-Rai from his thoughts, he might actually succeed.

The last worship song faded away. The acoustic guitarist continued strumming gentle chords. During this part of the service members sometimes went to the microphone to share a word or a testimony, or one of the leaders might feel led to open the altar for a specific need.

But today Pastor Mike, almost dressed up for once in a button-down shirt worn loose over slacks, took center stage. He pressed his lips together and scanned the audience before he spoke. "I feel led to have a special time of prayer for a young Muslim woman who ran away from her abusive family. I can't tell you all the details. I don't even know all the details, but I know that she is in terrible danger, and I know that God has placed her on my heart today."

Mo's chest constricted. He hadn't mentioned anything like this to Mike. Only one other person could have. *Dear Lord, say it isn't so.* Mo's eyes shot back to Layla, despite his recent round of resolve.

"Please reach out your hands and join me in praying for this young woman."

Fatima! It had to be Layla's best friend. She'd shared so much with him about the battered young woman. Who else could Mike be talking about? *Please God, don't let Layla be involved in this.* Hadn't Layla faced enough danger last fall when her uncle tried to kill her?

For one brief second his gaze caught hers. She quickly closed her eyes and turned her head downward. Forget what he decided just moment's ago. This changed everything. He had to talk to her! The situation must be serious, dangerous even, if it hadn't made it to the Lebanese gossip chain. He hadn't heard even a whisper of it at the restaurant. Unbelievable!

Mo tried to focus and pray, but his thoughts scattered in a thousand directions. He could barely register the peace permeating the place as the body of Christ joined together in intercession. When Mike finally closed and invited the parishioners to meet and greet one another, Mo's first impulse was to run to Layla.

A hand caught his arm and turned him toward the row behind him. His friend John smiled. "Hey, Mo, introduce me to your friends."

Mo had nearly forgotten about them. This girl did awful things to his concentration. She'd cut different lengths into her long flowing hair. He liked the way it framed her big, beautiful brown eyes, but he managed to peel his gaze away from where she stood with a group of girls from ODU.

He forced himself to pay attention to the issue at hand. John was a great guy, and Mo wanted his friends to feel welcome. "Sure, John, this is Farid and Franko."

"Nice to meet you. Are you both from the Middle East too?"

"My parents are from Egypt, and Franko is Lebanese like our buddy Mo here," Farid said.

"Cool. Have either of you lived over there? I've spent some time in Kuwait on business."

Just when the conversation started flowing and Mo tried to extricate himself, Pastor Mike joined them, and he had to start the introductions all over.

He fought down a growl and managed to remain polite. Layla might be in horrible danger, but now that he was thinking more rationally about it, he realized rushing over to her immediately after the prayer might draw suspicion her way. He shot up a quick thanks that God had kept him from that mistake. Pinching the bridge of his nose to fight off tension, he took a few deep breaths to calm himself. However, he would not leave this place until they had a chance to talk.

ELEVEN

Layla scooped up her purse and leather jacket from the deep red carpeting beneath the folding, theater-style chairs after the final prayer of the evening. Mike had preached on incarnational Christianity, on being Jesus to everyone we meet. An apropos subject, as he had been such a prime example to her just this week.

When she stood, a set of warm hands covered her eyes. Her stomach sank to her pricey high-heeled shoes—paid for by her parents, just like everything else she owned. Surely Mo wouldn't get her into trouble by flirting with her in public for everyone to see.

When a female voice said, "Boo!" Layla let out a breath she hadn't realized she was holding.

"Allie Carmichael?" She removed the hands and swiveled to her blond roommate. "What are you doing here?"

"Shondra and I had a dance rehearsal that ran late." She indicated a pretty, young African American woman who sported long waving hair with maroon streaks that looked almost as expensive as Layla's shoes.

Allie continued, "There was no way I was going to make it across town in time for Fuddy-Duddy Chap—"

Layla raised an eyebrow, cutting her off.

"Oops, I promised not to call it that anymore, didn't I?"

"You are engaged to the assistant pastor. I think you should make an effort," Layla said.

Shondra giggled. "And they do have that drum set now."

Layla laughed as well. She knew this sassy girl from somewhere. Of course! Allie's gorgeous worship dance last fall, the one that had moved Rain to tears. Shondra had been in it too, and now they had that new company together. No wonder she knew Allie so well. But something else rang familiar about her.

"Do we have a class together?" Layla asked.

"Yeah, I'm in philosophy with you guys. Only I tend to come late and dash out early. I've been crazy busy this semester. School, church, dance, work... It gets a little nuts sometimes."

"I've been trying to get her to visit here for a while." Allie gestured to the theater that served as a home for The Gathering. "Her family church is in Portsmouth, and they expect her out there for three services a week."

"Plus, I'm just not sure it fits me anymore. Don't get me wrong, it's great, but sometimes I feel like I need to work out my own relationship with God separate from them. You know what I mean?"

Layla reached out and touched Shondra's arm. "Absolutely. If anyone knows what you mean, it's Allie and I."

"Oh my gosh!" Shondra put a hand to her mouth. "You're Allie's Muslim friend. I didn't put two and two together. Man, do I feel stupid."

"And my roommate. I can't believe you two haven't met yet." Allie shook her head.

"Well, if I were wearing a veil, I'd give you full permission to feel stupid," Layla said. "I was raised here in the States. It's kind of cool just blending in with a crowd for the first time in my life."

"Hey, Layla." Allie nudged Shondra with her hip. "You think there's any chance this *chica* can join you and Rain and me for the group project coming up? She really doesn't know anyone else in that class."

Shondra frowned. "I kind of dread getting stuck with a bunch of atheists or pagans or something. I have some strong opinions and a little bit of a temper when you get me riled up. I don't think I'm the right person for that sort of challenge."

"Ha!" Allie said. "A *little* bit of a temper?"

A rosy blush tinged Shondra's brown cheeks, giving them a charming glow. "Okay, a lot a bit."

"It's fine with me if you want to join us." Layla had a good feeling about this girl, and it would be interesting to add an African American to their group. Rain was far more hippie flower child than black. "But you realize we're going to seriously outnumber Rain. I'm not sure she's going to like that."

Allie shrugged. "She'll deal. She can expound on the many paths to God, or the goddess, all she wants. No harm, no foul. At least she won't convert any of us to her New Age beliefs."

Shondra's brown eyes grew round. "Sounds...enlightening."

"She's a hoot. You'll love her. There's never a dull moment with that one." Layla couldn't hold back a smile as she recalled some of Rain's kooky antics.

Which reminded her, they needed to powwow about Fatima. Nearly a week had passed. "Hey, Allie, I was hoping you and I could head over to visit Rain tomorrow night, to work on that *other* project. See if Sarah wants to come too."

"Yeah, sure. We definitely need to do that, and I've been wanting to spend more time with Sarah anyway. I'm kind of worried about her."

"What's going—"

A hand on her shoulder interrupted Layla's train of thought. There was no chance she could dodge the same bullet twice in one night. Something about the strength, the familiarity of the grasp told her immediately it was Mo. If that wasn't enough, the concerned look on Allie's face said it all. Layla paused for a moment and collected herself.

She turned and stared for a minute at his chiseled features and scruff of a beard, at the curls falling over his brow. Her fingers itched to push them away from his deep, melting eyes, but she didn't move a muscle.

"Hey, precious," he said. "I need to talk to you for a minute. Can we go outside?"

Warmth flowed through her at the rich sound of his voice with its touch of a Lebanese lilt. She wished he wouldn't speak to her in such an intimate manner. She was trying so hard to respect her parents' wishes. Must he make matters even more difficult?

His gaze searched hers, probing, begging. He must have suspected Pastor Mike was talking about Fatima. She needed to explain, and she had been wanting to share the situation with Mo anyway. But why tonight? Why with his Middle Eastern friends here?

"Layla?" he whispered.

She shot a look to Farid and the other guy.

"They won't say a word. I promise. They probably won't even notice."

True enough, the duo appeared caught up in conversation with one of the small group leaders. "Fine, but just for a few minutes." She twisted back to Allie and Shondra. "Please excuse me. I'll be back."

"No worries," said Allie, although she looked plenty worried.

"Don't mind us," Shondra said with a wiggle of her eyebrows, clearly having no idea about the issues that cast a dark cloud over Layla's relationship with Mo.

"Thanks," she mumbled as Mo put a too familiar hand on the small of her back and led her outside.

Once through the door, a frigid blast of wind slapped Layla across the face. Thank goodness, just what she needed. She shook off Mo's hand and replaced his warmth with her jacket, although it wasn't at all the same. "I wish you wouldn't do that."

"Wouldn't do what?"

"Act like I'm still your girlfriend."

"No one here cares, Layla. They're all rooting for us."

"I care."

He sucked in a sharp breath and tipped his head up to examine the dark sky. The overcast clouds blocked any stars from view. Only a nearby streetlight cast a cold, bluish glow over them. "I don't want to fight. That's not why I brought you out here."

Layla shivered. "Well, hurry up then. It's freezing." She tucked her hands in her pockets and bounced from foot to foot, as much from nervousness as chill.

Mo looked as if he wanted to gather her into his cozy arms, but he shook himself and continued. "That was your friend Fatima that Mike mentioned. Right?"

"It was. It's all so complicated. I guess we do need to talk." Layla's stomach tied into knots, as it often did these days.

"Is she here?" Fear flashed through his eyes.

"Yes, but she's not staying with me."

His gaze darted about before he asked, "Where is she?"

"With Rain and James."

He seemed to relax at that. "Good. Not many people would make that connection, and they'll take good care of her. I'm glad there's a man around to protect her if needed."

"You should have seen her when she got here. She was bruised and bloodied and terrified. Oh, Mo, it was so awful." A sob escaped Layla.

At that they both crumbled, and Mo drew her into his arms. She breathed in his masculine woody cologne, and for one brief moment, everything was right in the world.

"I'm sorry, baby. This must be so hard for you. But I'm worried about you too. You were in enough trouble without adding Fatima to the problem."

"Fatima, yes." Layla pressed her hands to his muscular chest but cuddled closer rather than push away. "And this."

If only Mo could hold Layla close like this forever. If only he could keep her safe in the fort of his arms. He hated that her parents stood between them even now. He wished they would have agreed to meet him and talk to him over Christmas, but they didn't even give him the courtesy of opening their door. He had stood on her icy porch for hours before he gave up.

How could he possibly help her through this thing with Fatima if he wasn't even supposed to speak to her? This was like last semester all over again. It made him sick to think she had faced her knife-wielding uncle without him.

I was there, and I will be there.

He sensed the whisper well up from his heart. Of course, God could do a much better job protecting this precious creature than he could, but he still wanted to be there for her, so much that he ached.

At least he could talk it through with her. "Does anyone else know about this?"

"Rain and James and Allie, of course. And Allie's sister was there when Fatima arrived. But the awful part is that Salaam and Ahmed cornered me in the stairwell at school and tried to scare me into telling them where she was."

He felt the blood draining from his face and rubbed his hand down it in frustration. He hated this—all of it.

She cupped his cheek. "It's okay. I convinced them I didn't know where she was, and I think I managed to sway at least Salaam to my side. I told them about how her family abuses her and begged them to help if they find her."

A deep whoosh of relief escaped his mouth. "That was smart, actually. Salaam's a pretty good guy, and I don't think Ahmed is too radical or anything."

"I was praying the whole time."

See, the whisper came from his heart again. He chuckled. "I guess you and God have things under control for the moment. But seriously, don't shut me out, okay? We need to monitor this closely. I'll keep an ear out at the restaurant."

"Yeah, if the gossip gets around, you'll probably catch it first. I guess you can call me if you learn anything specific, but otherwise we should stick to quick conversations here, or maybe at the soup kitchen."

Mo rarely made it to the outreach anymore with his work schedule, but he would find a way if needed. Another thought hit him. "Do your parents know anything about this?"

"No! Thank goodness. I can't even imagine what they'd do." She shivered, although she must be warm now, nestled as she was in his arms.

"I'm just thinking that if they did know, they'd be okay with me advising you. I don't want you to feel like you're deceiving them on my account." He nuzzled her silky hair scented with tropical fruits.

They stood like that for a while, drinking in the sacred moment. She leaned her head into the crook of his arm and gazed at him with a dreamy expression. "Maybe you're right. Let's not push things, though."

"Fine. But, Layla, how long are we going to go on this way?"

She appeared to shake off her hazy cloud. "I don't know."

Unable to stop himself, he pulled back a few inches. Part of him understood her need to please her family, but anger burgeoned in his chest nonetheless.

"Please don't be mad at me." Liquid pooled in her eyes.

"I'm n..." But he was. He shouldn't lie to her, so he said nothing.

She extricated herself from his arms and took a few steps away. Nothing had changed. Blast their former religion. Blast their culture. Blast her controlling parents.

"Anyway," she said, "we'll keep in touch if anything changes."

"Of course."

"And you'll pray for me, won't you?"

That melted his anger along with his rigid stance. "Of course I will, baby. I do all the time." He supposed that would have to suffice in place of what he really wanted to say. *I love you, I miss you, and it's killing me that we're apart.*

TWELVE

The teapot on the old gas stove whistled, signaling to Rain that the water was ready for her loose-leaf lavender. She figured tonight would be tense enough without adding the jitters of caffeine to the situation. Soothing herbal tea seemed more the ticket.

She put it in the pot to steep just as the doorbell rang. Presumably Allie and Layla, prompt as usual. Fatima hopped up from the couch where she was watching an entertainment news show with James and nearly skipped to the door with excitement. Rain smiled. She loved seeing the young woman so happy. Layla hadn't wanted to overdo the visits and raise suspicions. Allie had only come by once due to her busy schedule. And their last group gathering, when the battered Fatima had first showed up at their door, had ended up anything but fun.

Fatima opened the door and offered each girl the three standard Middle Eastern kisses on the cheek. "I am so glad you are coming tonight. I have so much to tell you. This week, it has been wonderful. Rain and James are so good to me. They are like very young, very hip parents." Fatima laughed and led them to the counter separating the kitchen from the living room.

"Welcome, ladies." Rain pulled some cups from the cabinet. "Tea's almost ready, and I have some real cookies tonight. Miss Fatima Fussy Bottom turns her nose up at my healthy ones."

"Yes, real ones I picked from the bakery." Could Fatima's grin possibly get any bigger? "White chocolate macadamia. My favorites." She fetched the plate from the kitchen and placed them on the counter.

"Whoa, wait a minute." Layla held up a finger. "Fatima, you went to the store? Please tell me you did not wear your veil."

"Oh, you must see. Rain, she is soooo smart." Fatima scurried to the closet and extracted James's big black hoodie. She put it on and struck one of her hip-hop poses. "I am so buck, right?"

Layla shook her head as if she didn't believe her eyes. "It's kind of perfect. Like the urban version of a headscarf. You are indeed ingenious, my friends."

Rain was glad Layla approved. She certainly didn't want to put Fatima in any danger, but she didn't think it was a good idea to keep her cooped up in the house either.

Allie picked up a cookie. "And even if someone saw her, they'd never recognize her in a million years."

"No one looking for Fatima the veiled Muslim woman would suspect a thing." Fatima tugged the strings a little tighter and dug her hands deep into the pockets. "But they might be mistaking me for a street thug."

"You're funny." Allie giggled. "I had no idea."

Layla reached to pat Fatima's hand. "Oh, this one is hysterical."

James came to join them. "And you should see the two of them together. I'm afraid we might have a Lucy and Ethel situation on our hands here."

Layla eyed Rain and Fatima, clearly amused. "I was afraid of that too. James, I'm trusting you to keep an eye on these two."

"Woman, if you think I have the power to control these forces of nature, you greatly overestimate my abilities." James plunked himself on a stool. "So should I leave you to your girl talk?"

"We should probably all discuss our game plan for Fatima before you take off," Layla said.

"As long as you don't expect me to drink any of the fru fru tea. I'll take a cookie, though." He helped himself to one.

"Isn't Sarah coming?" Rain asked. Allie mentioned today in class that she wanted to spend more time with her sister.

"No. She made some lame last-minute excuse about homework." Allie's mouth twisted in concern.

"Oh, it is okay. I do not wish to be a bother," Fatima said, breaking her cookie into small pieces and taking a dainty bite. The girl ate like a bird. No wonder she was so tiny—pretty much the opposite of Rain these days.

"It's not that. I really think she wanted to be here," Allie said.

"And she sent me such lovely clothes." Fatima unzipped the hoodie and brushed a hand over her long, loose creamy sweater worn over modest beige pants.

"She's concerned about you, I know she is. She called to check on you several times this week, but she just hasn't been herself lately." Allie took a bite of her cookie.

Rain put the finishing touches on the tea and began handing out cups.

"Yeah, you mentioned at church that you were worried about her." Layla took a cup from Rain and took a whiff of the lavender. "This smells awesome, Rain. Thanks. So what's up with Sarah?"

Allie fiddled nervously with her cup. "I'm trying not to worry, but she's really been on my heart lately. You know how uptight she can be, and it's hard living in that house with my parents. They really pile on the pressure to be perfect."

"I know how that is," Fatima said. "I like your sister. Maybe she will visit another time."

"I'll tell her you suggested it."

Rain's parents never cared what she did, as long as she followed her *own path*. Sex, weed, wild parties, nothing had been off limits... except church, maybe, and the Republican Party. Rain snickered into her tea. She imagined things must be tough for Sarah, but Allie had managed to maneuver the situation with the Carmichael parents. Maybe Sarah just needed to sow some wild oats or something, needed to find herself.

"So, about Operation Hide Fatima." Layla set her tea onto the counter. "Seems like you guys have the wardrobe situation under control. How's everything else going?"

"All's quiet on the Western front." James nodded to Fatima and Rain. "Except when these two get the giggles. How about you, Layla? Any news?"

Layla bit her lip. "Well, the good news is that my mother hasn't heard anything in Detroit, and until I talked to Mo last night at church, he hadn't heard anything either. That means the Middle Eastern gossip chain hasn't latched onto it yet."

Layla was holding something back. Rain could tell. "But?"

"I didn't want to say anything earlier because I really don't think it's a big deal. But...some guys from the Muslim Student Union cornered me at school one day. I guess they're friends with a cousin of yours from D.C."

"Dani?"

"Maybe. I didn't ask too many questions." Layla recapped the tense encounter on the stairwell for them.

The thought of sweet, innocent Layla facing those guys gave Rain the chills.

"But they did say your cousin just wants to help," Layla said. "Do you think it's true?"

Fatima paused to consider that. "He is more moderate than my family. Maybe he would help to protect me, but eventually he would have to leave. I don't want him to find me."

"Yeah, I agree," Allie said. "Layla told me all this last week, but I still don't understand why no one else seems to know about it."

"It means they aren't wanting to kill me...yet," Fatima said in a flat tone of voice.

Layla picked it up from there. "If this becomes public knowledge, a radical family like Fatima's will believe they have no choice but to kill her."

Fatima just stared down at her cookie and broke it into smaller and smaller pieces.

"How could they do a thing like that?" James's mouth gaped. "I mean, I saw the injuries, but I still can't understand it."

Layla took a deep breath. "It's hard to explain. So much in our culture is based on a system of pride, honor, and shame. Family identity means everything. If she shames them..." She didn't seem inclined to go on.

Rain supposed in her own way, Layla had shamed her family too.

After a few moments of silence Layla added, "And her brothers are some pretty scary guys. I think they would do it."

"I hate to be the one to ask the obvious," Allie said. "Would it be safer for her to go home before people find out? I mean, should we even consider that?"

James and Layla both shouted, "No!"

Fatima's head shot up, and she practically hissed the word, "Never!"

"They would still find a way to drag her to Saudi Arabia and marry her off."

Fatima shook her head robotically from side to side. "I can never go back. Not now that I have seen what a real life is like."

"I'm sorry," Allie said. "I just want to make sure we've thought through every possibility. And Fatima, are you still sure you won't talk to the authorities? Layla took out a restraining order, and it seemed to help."

"I do not wish to. Please do not make me. Only if there is no other way."

"Besides," Layla said, "my uncle isn't in the same league as her brothers. They wouldn't care about restraining orders. They'd find some way to make her disappear if they really wanted to."

Everyone stared at one another for a few minutes. Rain took some bracing sips of her tea. The scent and sweet flowery taste soothed her. She was glad she had thought ahead and prepared it.

But she didn't want to get stuck in this dreary mode. Fatima had been doing so well. "Okay, let's talk about where we go from here. By every indication, Fatima is safe enough right now, and I think she needs to get out a little more. James and I want to take her to a few safe places, maybe to our new church. There are a few Muslims, but they're the black American variety and incredibly peace-loving. We don't need to worry about them."

"And maybe to the soup kitchen," James added. "I think she'd enjoy a chance to help others in need."

Fatima rallied a little bit at that. "Yes, I do not want to always be the victim needing help. I want to be a strong American woman for once in my life."

Rain took in Fatima's diminutive form. There was strength under the surface though. Not many people could have survived her background and kept their sense of humor, their love of life.

"And we prayed for you at The Gathering," Layla said. "The whole congregation is keeping you in prayer. I wish I could take you there, but Mo and I both go, and he brought some other Middle Eastern guys this week. I don't think it would be safe."

Rain missed that place. She loved it there, but James didn't want to go to a hardcore Christian church. Something tugged at her heart as she considered it. Last semester she had felt so close to God, but she had such a difficult time buying the whole sin and atonement thing. However, the more she talked with Fatima, the more she wondered about that deep inner conscience Fatima spoke of.

Hadn't Rain grieved that place in her heart time and time again?

Perhaps she wasn't as blameless as she liked to believe. Allie had told her that sin wasn't just about being evil. That it meant *missing the mark*. Hadn't everyone done that a time or two? Rain had been raised to see all humans as inherently good—that rules warped them—but she was starting to see things differently.

"My mother has all her prayer groups on the case too." Allie smiled to Fatima. "She's calling it an unspoken request. We don't want anyone linking you to my family in case we need to move you there at some point, but God knows everything. I'm sure he knows you're the one they're praying for."

"This is so very kind of all of you, but I hope this is not true about God knowing everything." Fatima sighed. "I am afraid Allah must be cursing me right now, hating me even, if he is real. This I am not so sure of anymore. I'm thinking sometimes that maybe I am better with no God. I hope you will all understand."

Allah sounded nothing like the loving God Rain had met last year. How could it be true that there were many paths to God, when the very nature of the God at the end of the path was not the same?

"I get you. I feel the same way." James put a protective arm around Fatima's shoulder. "How about we don't worry about God for a while? If he or she is actually out there, and is actually worth worshiping, then I'm sure she'll understand how hard this all has been on you."

It was kind of James not to mock the idea of God completely. He had changed during the last months too.

Fatima rested her head against James's shoulder and visibly relaxed. "I hope you are right, my brother."

Rain hated to hear Fatima say these things. In that moment, she doubted her interfaith church would ever help Fatima find peace. It certainly hadn't helped her, except to make her mind grow hazy with too many options.

Like Layla, she too wished Fatima could visit The Gathering and see what a truly good-hearted, loving religion could look like, but maybe Fatima wasn't ready for that anyway. She had been burned pretty badly by her Muslim faith, and now, at least according to her parents' radical version, her religion might want her dead.

"So," Rain said. "Do we have a plan for now? Small outings to safe, controlled places. Keep our ears open for any developments."

"Sounds good," Layla agreed.

"And my family is on standby if we need to move her," Allie reminded them.

"I've been bringing home a gun from work," James added as if it were no big deal.

All eyes in the room grew huge.

"What?" He lifted his free hand into the air with the other one still secure around Fatima.

"I thought you guys were pacifists or something." Allie looked confused.

"I hate violence." James gave Fatima's shoulder a squeeze. "But I love this new little sister of mine, and I promised I would do whatever it takes to keep her safe."

"I'm glad she has you, James, and you too, Rain," Layla said.

"And I'm glad she has her new street thug look." Rain attempted to lighten the mood. "She really is kind of buck. Don't you think?"

"Oh yeah, oh yeah." Fatima moved away from James and hit a few more of her favorite hip-hop poses. "I am so buck."

Everyone laughed at that. Fatima proceeded to demonstrate her newest, hippest dance moves for the girls. Rain joined in the merriment as best she could for Fatima's sake, but the whole evening really had her mind spinning.

She didn't want to think about how empty her new religion left her—so different than the personal God she had discovered last semester. And she couldn't shake that other thing Fatima had said either, about babies belonging in families and families being forever.

That's what Rain wanted for her child. Maybe the Bible wasn't just a set of rules to suck the fun and spontaneity out of life. Maybe those rules were actually meant for their good.

She rubbed a hand over her belly. How did she want to raise this child? What version of the *truth* would she teach it? She had a lot to consider.

THIRTEEN

Layla managed a somewhat normal Tuesday. She focused on the droning voice of her engineering professor, on the world of science, math, and formulas, a world where everything made sense—so unlike the crazy one she lived in lately, where her sweet friend's life had been threatened. In this mixed-up world, she and Mo had somehow ended up apart. Layla Al-Rai, gentle, obedient daughter, had just about torn her family to shreds. She pushed all that from her head and glued her attention to the complex equations on the board.

Once the class was dismissed and Layla exited the door, a hand covered with dark curling hair snaked around the corner and pulled her into a dim alcove before she could even register what was happening.

Her face grew oddly cold and prickly. Her vision began to swirl, and although she wanted to scream, she thought she might faint instead.

"Layla, calm down. It's just me." Salaam's face appeared before her as her sight began to clear and her eyes adjusted to the lighting.

"Salaam! What are you doing?" Her heart pounded frantically, but as she peered into his eyes, she saw no malice. Her breathing grew steady again.

"I'm sorry. I didn't mean to scare you, but I need to speak to you in private."

Of course, Salaam didn't realize she no longer shared his faith. Normally, such conversations didn't take place between a lone man and respectable woman in their culture. "What is it? Must be awfully important to go through all this."

"We need to talk more about your friend Fatima. You really need to do something."

"But..."

"I know, I know. You don't know where she is. Listen. I need to tell you things Ahmed didn't want to say. This cousin in D.C., he really is a good guy. Tell her Dani is looking for her. If he can get her home safely without too much fuss, he thinks they'll let her live."

The cold fear of moments earlier was replaced by seething anger at the whole ridiculous situation. Layla pressed the back of her head against the wall, smashed her eyes closed, and took a deep breath. "Listen to yourself, Salaam. You're talking like this is normal—as if we should just accept it as part of life. You're an intelligent, civilized man for crying out loud. You have a college education. Don't you get how crazy this is?"

"Crazy or not, it's reality. People like you and me and Dani can make a difference. Right now they're telling people she's sick in her room, so we still have time. Once word spreads that she's run away, it will be too late. You know how these people are about their honor."

"Honor?" Layla glared and resisted an odd urge to spit the nasty taste of the word from her mouth. "They have no honor. It's their self-inflated pride they want to protect."

"And they will protect it. If they send someone here searching for her, it won't be Dani. It will be her brothers. I can't say for sure, but I get the impression these guys have killed before."

As she recalled the harsh glint in the eyes of the Maalouf men, Layla's stomach twisted, threatening to expel the contents. "Probably. But what can I do? I have no idea where she is."

"Yeah, that's your story and you're sticking to it. I don't blame you, but if you have any way to get word to her, tell her Dani's just trying to save her life."

"They'll send her to Saudi Arabia to marry a stranger."

"Better that than dead. And seriously, could a stranger be any worse than what she's dealt with her whole life?"

Layla sighed in defeat. "For the first time in this ridiculous conversation, you might have a point. But who knows, it could be worse. And besides, a husband is different than a father. Look, if I hear from her, I'll tell her what you said. Okay? I can't do any more than that."

Salaam gripped her upper arm, a forbidden touch that drove home the seriousness of his point. "Try, Layla. Try hard. No one wants a tragic ending. And whatever you do, don't go to the police, or it could turn out tragic for you too."

With that warning, he left.

Layla's heart sped, and her breath came in shorter gasps. Dizziness overtook her again. She had lived through a murder attempt once. Could she survive another? These men weren't misguided but kind, like her uncle.

They were truly and epically evil.

She didn't want to go through all of that again, and she certainly didn't want it for Fatima. How on earth did mousey little Layla Al-Rai get herself into this awful mess?

Maybe she should call Mo, but Salaam really didn't tell her anything she hadn't known before. He had simply brought matters into startling clarity. She would keep it to herself for now and keep praying for the best.

Noah Dixon entered the stale-smelling old police precinct with its stained linoleum floors and searched for any friendly face. At this moment he wished he'd spent more time getting to know the area officials rather than just immersing himself in the Islamic culture of Detroit, or that he'd spent more time at some of the normal churches instead of attending a traditional Middle Eastern service, but he would do his best for his angel on the balcony. Over a week had passed since he had spotted her. Surely there was something the police could do to help.

The woman at the counter sized him up with cynical brown eyes—not promising at all. He glanced around the room and noticed a beat cop digging a jelly filled donut from a white paper box. Although a bit cliché, the guy had a jolly Santa Claus vibe that boded well. Surely he must have daughters around the age of Noah's missing angel.

Man, how he wished he had asked for her name, not only to keep him from sounding ridiculous for calling her "angel" in his head all the time, but so that he wouldn't sound like an imbecile when he tried to report her missing.

He shot up a quick prayer and kept his gaze on the rotund cop until the guy turned his way. Noah smiled at him and tipped his head. The cop smiled back and tipped the donut in return. Perfect. Trying not to appear too obvious, Noah followed him toward his desk and somehow managed to slip past the nazi at the counter who was busy filling out a form.

When he arrived at the cop's desk, the guy sized him up, but not in the same heartless manner as the woman out front. "Can I help you?" The cop sat down and took a bite of his donut while he awaited Noah's reply.

Noah tried to gather his thoughts. He probably should have rehearsed this speech to avoid sounding like a lunatic. "Sorry to just barge in like this, but I had a feeling the lady at the counter wasn't going to give me the time of day."

Santa Cop chuckled. "Good character assessment. Maybe you should take up a career in law enforcement."

"Actually, I'm a minister. Noah Dixon." He reached out his hand. The cop set down his donut with clear reluctance and shook it. "But people skills come in handy in my line of work too."

The cop nodded and scooped up his donut again. He took another bite and somehow managed to talk around it without seeming rude. "What brings you here today, Minister Dixon?"

"I was wondering what the rules are about reporting a missing person."

"There isn't actually a waiting period, that's just a made for TV thing. But you do need to know the person well, be able to verify that they're missing, and provide us with some key information. It's best when the family reports it."

"What if the family might be the reason she's missing?"

Santa Cop raised a graying eyebrow. "Interesting. Go on. Are you a close friend?"

"No, actually, I'm not, but I get the feeling she doesn't have many friends. It looks like her family keeps her shut in her house."

"Do you suspect abuse?"

"I do."

"Is she under eighteen?"

"I don't know. I...I think she looks more like a young adult."

The cop set down his donut now—on purpose—and leaned toward Noah, his attention clearly piqued. "How did you say you know this girl?"

"I didn't say, but I walk through her neighborhood every day. Every day I see her on her balcony, and she waves to me, but she's been missing for the last week."

"Okay, Romeo. So you wave to her on the balcony."

The cop at the desk across the aisle—a younger, wiry fellow—snickered.

Great. Noah sounded as ridiculous to them as he did to himself, but for the sake of the girl, he managed to maintain his composure. "Yes, sir. I wave to her."

"And...she waves back?"

"Yes, sir, every day."

"Now, son, I don't think you can help us verify if she's actually missing. She must at least have some neighbors who would know her. I'm sure they would report if something was wrong."

"She's a Muslim, and she wears the full *niqab* veil. I'm not sure if people would know whether or not she left the house."

"So you don't even know what she looks like? Are you even sure it's the same girl every day?"

Oh boy, maybe Noah should just legally change his name to Raving L. Lunatic. He sure hoped this cop wouldn't lock him up. Taking a deep breath, he swiped a hand down his cheek. "I've seen her face actually. She shows me her cuts and bruises, and I pray for her."

"Dang!" Santa Cop clutched his chest. "Just rip my heart out, why don't you? It's tough to do anything over in that part of town. They're a pretty closed-mouthed bunch where we're concerned."

The young cop who snickered at Noah slapped his desk. "That's where I know you from. You're the white dude who walks around Little Arabia every day. I always did wonder what you were doing there."

"I'm prayer walking," Noah answered.

The young cop laughed outright at him now. "Prayer walking, as if they don't have enough prayers over there."

"I guess...I guess I'm just trying to bring a little light into a dark place."

"You like some kind of Christian spy? An undercover superhero?" the young cop teased. "You got a purple cape under that parka?"

"Cut it out, Schwarz!" Santa Cop shot Schwarz a glare. "Sounds like he's doing a good thing. Someone needs to find a way into that place." He gestured to the chair across from him.

Noah sat down with a sigh of relief. It seemed in spite of, or maybe because of, Schwarz's mocking, he was finally getting somewhere.

"I don't think I introduced myself. I'm Officer Jensen."

"Nice to meet you, sir."

Officer Jensen, a.k.a. Santa Cop, folded his arms over his

protruding belly. "Now here's the thing, son. I can't file a report based on what you told me, but there's a chance some of her neighbor ladies might know something. Thankfully there are moderates in that area, and sometimes we can find out a thing or two from them."

He pushed a pad of paper and a pen across his desk to Noah. "Write down whatever information you have, including her address, and we'll poke around and see if we can get anything more substantial."

Noah pressed his eyes closed for a moment. *Thank you, Jesus.* He wished he could do more, so much more, but at least it was something. And at least he wasn't getting thrown into the loony bin.

James dropped a heavy box of canned goods onto the floor of the food pantry. He enjoyed helping out here with the folks from The Gathering. They really were a great bunch of people. He sliced through the packaging tape with a utility knife and started stacking cans onto the shelves. It was cool the way various churches pitched together to offer three free meals a week to the people in this needy neighborhood.

A set of gorgeous brown eyes surrounded by ebony skin peeked over the open window from the dinner area. "Hey, James," said the adorable munchkin who came almost every Thursday.

He still could hardly believe that before long he'd have a little girl of his own. It blew his mind but filled him with more joy than he'd ever experienced in his life. "Hey, Nae Nae. You liking that spaghetti?" He assumed so from the tomato sauce covering her face.

"Yeah, it's real good. And I was real hungry."

"Well, you make sure your mom stops by on the way out for some food to take home."

"Oh! Are those Pop-Tarts?" Nae Nae pointed to the top shelf.

"Pop-Tarts? How about something healthy like…" He held up a can.

"Spinach. Yuck!"

He chuckled. "I'll make a deal with you. I'll give you some Pop-Tarts if you promise to eat the spinach too."

She wrinkled her nose. "You drive a hard bargain, man."

He held out his hand. "So is it a deal?"

"I guess." She shook it reluctantly.

"For now why don't you get yourself some nice homemade oatmeal cookies from Rain?"

That cheered her right up. "Okay." She grinned and ran to Rain and Fatima at the dessert table. Layla manned the spaghetti station nearby, but Mo wasn't here. The guy was working his tail off these days.

Fatima had decided a hoodie might be too much for indoors, so she modified her street thug look with a bandana hiding her blondish hair and a turtle neck sweater under a plaid flannel. James had to nix several bandanas before they found a patterned one that wouldn't be confused for gang colors. He had to admit, those girls were pretty ingenious about coming up with ways for Fatima to feel comfortable in American clothes.

She had told him how she'd always dreamed of being one of the trendy Muslim girls in Western clothes and a headscarf like Layla, how she'd fantasized about driving herself to the mall.

James had been itching to teach her to drive ever since, but he couldn't figure out how to get her a permit. He supposed he could take her on some back streets just for kicks, but the issue was a reminder that she couldn't stay in hiding forever. Eventually they would need a long range plan, but he had no idea what that might be.

He had a hard time wrapping his head around her whole situation. Since puberty she had only left the house covered head to toe, and only then for short trips escorted by a man to the mosque or occasionally shopping. Oh, and she'd gone to parties and social gatherings with other women. She hadn't said it outright, but he got the impression her family had some major money.

Either way, she'd obviously been sheltered. He had hoped tonight wouldn't be too much for her, but she had made herself right at home. Her face glowed as she handed cookies to a smelly, old guy in funky clothes. Yes, this was just what she needed—a chance to feel useful.

Rain didn't look nearly as happy. Although she hadn't brought it up since December, he knew she still wanted to visit The Gathering. He had started helping here after Pastor Mike found him some free counseling, but maybe it was time to find an outreach opportunity at their new interfaith church.

He walked outside toward the truck to grab another box to unload in the pantry.

As much as he appreciated the sense of love and unity in this place, at the end of the day it was a Christian ministry. Only churches that believed in a literal interpretation of the Bible were involved, and there was always a pastor hanging around trying to get people *saved*.

Admittedly, he had come a long way over the past few months. At least he was willing to consider there might be some sort of divine force, but the Christian mindset was still way too narrow for him.

Besides, if Rain wanted to follow a more traditional style of Christianity, their new Unity Light church made space for that too. He had even agreed to hold a dedication ceremony for the baby, but they both needed to stay open minded, allow for all sort of beliefs, lots of truths. Personally, he wanted to look more into the Buddhist side of things. At Unity Light, he had the freedom to do that. Even Fatima, the agnostic Muslim, could feel comfortable at their new church.

Wasn't that what really mattered? Diversity? Acceptance? Love?

James hoisted a box onto his shoulder and took a moment to enjoy the mild Virginia weather that had returned this week—looked like they never would get the snow the weather man had promised—then he headed back inside before the box dug a hole in his shoulder.

Rain would get over The Gathering sooner or later. She just needed to make more friends at their new church. Right? As he entered the dining room, he searched her out. She stood in a corner talking to Serena, the pastor's wife, while Fatima manned the cookie station alone. Rain was gazing at the woman like she had something that she desperately needed.

As much as James loved this place, maybe it was time to say good-bye.

FOURTEEN

Layla reveled in the silence of the cottage sans teenyboppers. They all had their young adults group at the church on Friday nights. She sat for a moment in the middle of the empty living room on the cozy couch just drinking it in. Her mind touched briefly on Mo, who hadn't shown up last night at the soup kitchen, but it was for the best. As much as it did her heart good to see him, in other ways it was easier not to see him at all.

She snuggled deeper into the couch and smiled at the empty living room with its vanilla candle flickering on the coffee table. And then, as if the universe was playing some sort of cosmic joke on her, her phone jangled in her purse. She had set up the especially clanging ring just this week to serve as an early warning system.

Mom.

Reluctantly, she went to the kitchen island and dug her top-of-the-line smart phone from her designer handbag. Until she'd moved in with a bunch of middle-class Americans, she had never realized how much her parents spoiled her...but maybe not for much longer. Layla braced herself and hit accept.

"Layla! *Habibti*! You will never believe it," her mother squealed like a teenager.

What in the world? Layla had certainly not expected this. "Mom?"

"You were right. Something is going on with Fatima. I just know it. The police knocked on my door today, and they asked about her."

Darn. This would complicate matters.

"I couldn't believe it," Mom chattered on. "We've never had the police at the house before. Praise be to Allah, I had some fresh *kanafeh* and coffee to serve them. You should have seen how they ate! I sent some back to the station with them."

Despite the tense situation, Layla couldn't help but grin. Leave it to Mom to worry about feeding Lebanese desserts to the entire police department. Layla pulled the conversation back on track. "What did you say to them?"

"Oh, I told them you have been her best friend since childhood, and of course how you have always worried about her. That you haven't heard from her in a long time, and that you asked about her last week."

Layla supposed the police involvement could be helpful if things turned ugly, but for now she didn't want the police or her mother to have a clue where Fatima really was.

"I think I will take the Maaloufs some sweets and ask about Fatima," Mom said. "The police seemed hesitant to go to her home."

"I'm sure they don't want to cause any unnecessary trouble. I think you should keep out of it."

"I don't know. Of course, I don't like the police poking into Middle Eastern matters, but this is your sweet Fatima. Someone should look out for that girl."

"Please, Mom. Just let the police handle it." Layla didn't want anything to draw suspicion her way.

"I suppose you are right, but I'm going to see if I can learn anything from my friends."

Layla saved her breath on that one. The Middle Eastern gossip chain was an unstoppable force. "Let me know what you hear. I'm really worried about her."

"I know, *habibti*. I'm so glad you are safe and happy in Norfolk."

"Yeah...." Was this some kind of a trick? "Me too. You stay safe, though."

"I will. I need to go now and prepare dinner."
"Okay, thanks for calling."
"I love you more than life."
"I love you too, Mom."
"I miss you."

Layla hesitated for a minute but realized with her mom in this mood, she could easily reciprocate. "I miss you too. The semester will be over before you know it, and I'll be home for summer. Okay?"

"Yes, I will be fine. Goodbye."

"Bye."

So the police were suspicious but it seemed like they really didn't know anything either. Her fingers itched to dial Mo, but with Mom in such a good mood, Layla stopped herself. She didn't want to do anything to drive a wedge between them again. More and more these last weeks, she'd realized how much she needed her family. How much she depended on them.

Whatever little bit of information she had for Mo could wait until Sunday.

On Sunday morning Rain glanced to Fatima as the choir on the stage sang an uplifting number about being your own light in gorgeous four-part harmony. Fatima looked particularly adorable today for the interfaith service at Unity Light. Since the street thug look wouldn't do for a Sunday morning service, even at this inclusive church, they had tried a completely different direction.

Fatima had picked out a long flowered pink skirt and sweater set from Sarah's bag of offerings. She coupled it with a sheer white scarf to cover her neck, and Rain had stopped at the nearby thrift store for an old lady church hat in pink, complete with a mesh veil. It provided the modesty and anonymity Fatima needed while letting her femininity and beauty shine through.

That morning before they left the house, Fatima had studied herself in the mirror for a long time, running her fingers across her cheeks like a blind person, as if truly seeing herself for the first time. Clearly this outfit better suited the way she had always dreamed of looking than her comical street thug attire.

Fatima smiled at the singers on the stage. Rain couldn't wait to hear her impressions of the service after a lifetime of attending a radically conservative mosque. S.F.A., Fatima called her old congregation. Straight from Arabia.

And how would Rain describe this church? She almost hated to ask herself. Soothing, to be certain, full of peace and happiness, which surely must be good things, but something always felt off. It was too peaceful, causing her to feel ever so slightly dazed when she entered the place, like she was on some weird sort of drug.

It was hard to explain. Yes, the church contained beauty, but the beauty of a soap bubble—all iridescent with rainbow swirls, shiny in a way that made you forget it was hollow in the center and could pop and fade into the ether at any second.

When she attended churches with Allie last year, she left feeling nourished and satiated deep in her core. But here? It was more like trying to live on hot fudge sundaes, a sweet treat to tickle the taste buds. You'd feel full for a few minutes—until your blood-sugar dropped and all that junk made your stomach sick.

Maybe she was being too hard on the place. James seemed happy here. She had told him it was important to her to raise her child in church, and he had found one that worked for both of them.

Her mother had taught Rain to have an attitude of gratefulness to the universe in all situations. So why couldn't she shake this dissatisfaction?

The officiant stepped to the pulpit in her clerical robes. It looked like church, sounded like church—almost. "In God we find our most intimate essence." Reverend Sherry spoke in mind-numbing, hypnotic tones. "Our inner light. And in this way, we become our own deity. Christ served as our perfect example, and through following his teaching, we find spiritual fulfillment. We are creators with God. Creating with our minds and expressing those creations through our daily affirmations."

Almost like church, but fundamentally different at the core. More and more Rain doubted her own innate divinity. She had chosen a path that grieved the personal God who knit the universe together, who held it in his hands.

Fatima might be struggling with her own crisis of faith, yet her honest evaluation had helped Rain sort truth from fallacy. Everyone knew right from wrong deep down, and no one could ever be good enough. They could never live up to God's standards on their own.

Layla had said it so perfectly after Allie's big dance performance last semester. *But Jesus, he speaks of love and of peace with no contradictions. He lived by these principles. With humility and compassion and sacrifice. He gave his life for me. Me. A woman. I can barely fathom it. But I have felt the touch of his hand. I have seen love emanating from his face. I know it's true.*

This church never spoke of redemption, never spoke of Jesus paying the price. Finally all that blood and atonement made sense to Rain. She needed someone to take the punishment for her sin. She wasn't sure that she wanted to be in charge of her own life anymore. More and more she was convinced that she wanted to invite Christ, the very son of the living God, into her life to fill her with his light and his presence, to lead and guide her and make her a new creation.

"Let us pause for a moment of silence and search out the inner light before I launch into our topic for the day. Rest in the peace of your own divinity."

The peace that settled over the sanctuary was not the same peaceful place of stillness where Rain had met God last year. It rolled in like a fog, heavy and thick. Like pink, sticky cotton candy clouding her thoughts. She couldn't seem to find God there at all, not his deep, loving eyes, not his strong arms, not his wise counsel. But sure enough, all her concerns disappeared. Like that bubble. Pop, into nothing.

She opened her eyes to examine James. He looked so happy. Surely she was making a big deal over nothing. She let her gaze run over the congregation, a rainbow of shades and styles, just like Allie's dance last year. Their family would fit so perfectly here. No one would pressure them to marry just to prove their love with a piece of paper. They would be applauded for being exactly who they were, for following their own paths like her mother always taught her. No one would try to change them here. It couldn't be all that bad.

FIFTEEN

Mo carried a large tray laden with hummus, tabouli, rice, stuffed grape leaves, and a number of Middle Eastern dinner specialties to a family of five in the otherwise dead restaurant. Thursdays were always their slowest night. He wouldn't hold his breath for too many tips, but it was a pleasant place to hang out nonetheless. Between the spices wafting through the air, the warm lighting, and the cozy yet trendy décor in browns, blacks, and creams, he always felt at home here. As he passed the steaming plates to the family, he brushed past a college-aged woman with silky black hair and noticed how much she looked like Layla. Even the stylish purple sweater she wore reminded him of something Layla might choose.

Of course, everything reminded him of Layla these days. There were three words for guys like him. *Pa-thet-ic!* But there had been something so magical about the whole relationship. Almost two decades had passed since he first told a beautiful, brown-eyed little girl named Layla that he loved her as he pushed her on the swing set in the playground—the same day he'd given her the bouquet of buttercups. To find her again after all these years had seemed nothing short of miraculous.

Even then, he had been willing to shut Layla out of his life last semester when she wasn't a Christian believer. But now he had let her fully into his heart, and she had turned him down—not for lack of love or attraction, not because they'd had a fight—because of her parents. What was he supposed to do with that? According to Layla, they were "on a break." What did that even mean?

He could probably date other girls if he wanted to, but he had zero interest. Maybe this was a good time to focus on himself and his spiritual growth like Pastor Mike had encouraged him to do last semester, which would be a great idea, except that he couldn't seem to focus at all. At church this week she had consumed his thoughts, although she had managed to avoid him the entire service.

Rounding the corner to the kitchen, he nearly ran into the plump, motherly figure of the owner, Mrs. Katan. "Whoa! Sorry about that."

"What I tell you again and again? You must watch where going, Mo!" She gave him a swat, but the twinkle in her eye said she considered him a member of the family now.

"Sorry," he said again, twisting his face into an expression of apology. He might lack focus at times, but his friendly personality and hard work had won over the staff, and when business was good, they earned him plenty of tips as well.

"Is okay." She peeked around the corner. "Dead tonight, *aye*? You want to go home? You have any papers due? Tests to study?" She always worried about his school work.

"Not really. I'm all caught up. I can stay and make sure we don't get a late rush."

"Just a little longer then. *Maalesh*?"

"Sure thing."

"Hey, Mo, I was wanting to ask you. You are from Detroit, yes?"

"Yes, ma'am, originally, but my family lives in Ohio now."

"Oh, never mind then." She shrugged her shoulder and went to turn away.

He'd promised to keep an ear out for any news. "Wait. Mrs. Katan, is something going on there? I still have a lot of family in the area. I visited over Christmas."

"Just some gossip. I thought you might know more."

"About?"

"The police are snooping around the Arabic district. They looking for some young woman, asking too many questions, but no one knows anything. Maybe she runs away. I heard she has friends in Norfolk, but she must has friends many places."

"If she's a young woman, why do they say she's run away?"

"I guess she is from conservative Muslim home. You know how this is."

"Unfortunately, I do. I hope she's okay."

"Nobody knows anything at moment. That is probably good thing for now." The Katans were a mixed family from Jordan, a nominal Christian husband and a moderate Muslim wife. That could have been him and Layla, except that he took his faith very seriously, and he had been determined to set Layla free of the chains of her old religion. Now she was. Almost. Not quite.

Hold up! He had news from Detroit. It wasn't much, but at least it would warrant a visit. He could hardly wait to see her again. Pulling off his white apron, he chased after the waddling Mrs. Katan and caught her near the bakery display featuring baklava, ma'moul and other Middle Eastern favorites. "Actually, I just remembered something important I need to do tonight. Can I take off early after all?"

"Of course, *habibi,* just pass your table to Joe." She offered him a wink and a smile.

"Thanks so much."

Within five minutes Mo had handed off the needed information, dashed to his car, and zoomed from the artsy section of town to the nearby ghetto with the soup kitchen.

He hurried inside. The crowd had thinned, and church members were wrapping things up. It only took a moment for him to find the face that haunted him night and day. His heart rate kicked up a notch as he watched her conversing with a homeless woman. Layla laid a hand on her shoulder and gave it a warm squeeze as she listened to the woman's story with sympathy emanating from her beautiful features.

She must have felt his eyes on her because she looked up to catch him staring—and instantly stiffened. His heart sank at the sight. He had been overjoyed to see her. She was supposed to be in love with him, so why did she seem unhappy that he had come?

After giving the woman one last pat on the arm, Layla headed his way. "Hi, Mo."

No hug. She didn't even reach out her hand to him. Instead she crossed her arms protectively over her chest. "What's up? Did you get off work early?"

"I have some news. I wanted to catch you before you left."

Her eyes sparked with interest, but she maintained her closed-off posture. "Really? About Fatima? She just left with Rain and James. Rain had a big paper to work on."

"Yeah, I finally heard some news at the restaurant. It seems the police have been questioning people in her neighborhood, but I couldn't find out anything else."

Layla sighed and relaxed only a bit. "My mom called and told me about that. You're right, though, they don't seem to know much."

"Wait! You heard about this already?"

"Yes. I would have told you on Sunday, but you seemed busy. It was really nothing, though. I mean, my mom was pretty excited. I'm worried she's going to try to play amateur detective or something, but no links to us at the moment." She glanced about nervously.

Somewhere in the depths of his broken heart, anger began to bubble. "So you've known for the better part of a week! I thought you were going to keep me posted. I thought we were working together on this."

She bit her lip and ducked her head in that shy manner he had found endearing not long ago. Now it just annoyed him. He couldn't take her evasiveness much longer. "Like I said, it was nothing, really.

Please don't be mad at me. That's the last thing I need right now." Tears glimmered in her eyes.

He swiped his hand down his face and attempted to stuff his anger. She was going through a lot—her new faith, her tense relationship with her parents, and now this dangerous situation with Fatima. He took a few deep breaths and managed to find his patience. Truly, he understood, but it hurt. "Then don't shut me out, Layla. That's all I ask."

"It's just..." She dabbed at her eyes. "It's just that my mom talked to me like everything was normal—between us, I mean—when she called. Like nothing had ever happened, and I was still her beloved daughter. You don't know how much that meant to me, how good it felt."

He took her hands in his. "I do understand. But what you don't understand is that in time things will change. You'll begin to adjust, and you'll want a life of your own. Living out your own dreams and destiny will become more important to you than pleasing your parents."

She snapped her hands away. "You don't think it does now? What about all the sacrifices I've already made? Don't those count with you? I'm just trying to keep a little peace. Keep everything from blowing up in my face. Getting a degree is my dream too, you know. It was my dream long before you were."

Mo realized too late the mistake he'd made. "I'm sorry," he whispered. "Let's not do this."

"My parents are right about one thing. Everything in my life is a mess right now. This isn't the right time for a relationship. I need to figure out who I am on my own first, me and Jesus. I need to understand that relationship before we continue ours, Mo. I don't want to confuse the two."

She made too much sense, but it didn't make matters any easier. Maybe if he hurried back to the restaurant he could at least make a

few dollars tonight. So far...
guess I should go then."

"I guess you should."

"If anything happens with Fatima, though, I hate waste. "I

"Of course." She folded her arms across her chest again.

He gave up and turned to leave. Why did it feel suspiciously like they had just broken up?

James helped Rain and Fatima place steaming Middle Eastern dishes on their small dining table. Fatima had insisted on cooking for them tonight. He couldn't wait to dig into the main course of *kabsa*, a Saudia Arabian specialty of lamb, veggies, and rice topped with fruits and nuts. The spices smelled out of this world.

They all sat and joined hands. Since they'd started attending Unity Light, Rain insisted on a moment of silent meditation to focus on their gratitude before any formal meal, and he certainly wanted Fatima to know how much they appreciated her efforts.

He dug into his first bite, and the sweet, spicy flavor was just what he had dreamed it would be. Fatima had mentioned cinnamon and saffron for sure. He also picked up on cloves and some other spices in the mix. "Oh my, that is incredible."

"Thank you, James. As good as your oatmeal?"

He chuckled. "Way better."

Fatima grinned. She seemed to be adapting well to their culture, but it was fun to experience a piece of hers tonight. He'd noticed she seemed much more comfortable in her American clothes as time went on, and he hadn't seen her praying at regular intervals as he knew most Muslims did. Then again, she had been questioning her faith lately. "So I had to rush right out to work on Sunday, and I didn't get to ask you what you thought of Unity Light."

She paused with her fork midway to her mouth. "Hmm...it was

...d. It was peaceful...and beautiful. People say ...slam means peace, but I have not seen this side. The Arabic translation is *surrender*. This is what I have seen, ideas and orders being forced on people, on wives and children especially."

James thought for a moment that she might go on, but she stopped and blinked back tears instead.

Rain gave her hand a squeeze. "I think any worthwhile religion should focus on love and peace, don't you, Fatima."

Fatima rallied. "Yes. Absolutely. Some of the teachings about love at your church surprised me, though. They seem to accept love in all sorts of packages, like the minister and her...wife? I've heard of such things. Still it is a shock to me. And I know this is a multi-faith church, but I wondered if this is what Christians believe. Is this Layla's new belief?"

James smirked and focused his attention back on his food. He'd let Rain field this one.

"I think the traditional understanding of the Bible is that God does not approve of homosexuality." Rain took a big gulp of water before she continued. "Of course, there are varying views on the issue, but I've read the Bible, and I would have to agree that it is not encouraged. It's referred to as a sin in a number of places, but you also have to understand that according to the Bible, Jesus paid the price for our sins on the cross. He doesn't hold them against us."

James glanced from Rain to Fatima and back again. He hadn't realized how much of this Christianity stuff Rain understood. She seemed kind of impressed with the whole concept.

"Do you mean he doesn't curse us for our sins? He doesn't hate us when we do wrong?" Fatima stared down at her plate.

Her words turned his stomach sour, but he kept eating for Fatima's sake.

"Goodness, no!" Rain looked ready to spring from her seat. "Is that what they teach you in Islam?"

"It is what my parents always say." Fatima's voice seemed to stick in her throat for a moment. "Every time I am bad. Every time I disobey. If it is true, Allah, he must be hating me more than ever right now. I will never be able to do enough good to erase this. But your talk of love, of Jesus paying the price...this is so different to me. Remarkable, really. I don't remember hearing about this cross at your church, though, Rain."

"No, they focus more on Jesus's teachings. I'm not sure they really believe he was God's son and that he accomplished something supernatural on the cross. I mean, it's a multi-faith church, so it really wouldn't be right to focus too much on that kind of stuff."

James couldn't miss the disappointment in Rain's voice. Man, this did not bode well.

"But Layla believes this?"

"Absolutely. She told you about meeting Jesus in a dream."

"Of course. And you, Rain? Do you believe this?"

Rain didn't seem inclined to answer.

James tried not to stare, but he wanted to hear the answer more than Fatima.

"Please, Rain, be telling me."

"Maybe," Rain whispered. "Like you said, it certainly is a remarkable idea."

"And you, James?"

His head shot up. "Oh no. Not me. I like to discuss all sorts of religions and philosophies. I find them interesting, but I don't believe in any specific one. Real Christianity can be very limiting. It's pretty insistent that you follow only one God and obey his rules, and those rules don't always make sense in this culture. You know what I mean?"

Fatima nodded. "I'm starting to. And so you choose a church that follows some of the Christian teaching that works for you, but not the parts that could be difficult. This I do understand. So many Muslims do the same, especially in the West. They don't follow the true teachings and examples of Mohammad, even though Allah instructed clearly in the Qur'an that we must. Layla's family is like this. They follow parts of the Qur'an but ignore the sections that don't work in a progressive culture like America."

"But Islamic experts always say that it's a religion of peace and love." James rubbed his chin. "I think you might misunderstand, Fatima. I think that is the true religion, and your family is what we would call radical."

Fatima started to laugh, softly at first and then with gusto. "Oh, James. I should not laugh. It is not funny, truly. But you have not read the Qur'an. Even if you did, you would read a softened English translation. You have not been to the Middle East. Yes some, maybe even many, Muslims in America believe as you say, but this is not the true teaching of Islam, and it is not how it looks in the Middle East. Of course there will always be good-hearted Muslims who follow a path of peace and love, but this is not the example the prophet set."

"I don't buy that." Rain thumped the table with her fist. "Most Muslims are wonderful people. Surely you see that."

"Because they follow this inner conscience we've been speaking of. Not because they follow the foundations of the faith." Fatima crossed her arms over her chest. She didn't seem about to back down.

"So you're saying they have us duped?" James's mind reeled. He wondered what Layla would say about all this. Surely it was just Fatima's extreme background that made her view things this way.

"Pretty much. Americans are so politically correct, they don't dare to challenge these so-called experts. Did you know in our religion we are permitted to lie to the infidel for the sake of Islam? That's you and your entire country. You are the infidels. We are free to lie to every one of you, and you are naïve and trust because this is what your culture tells you to do."

"Why would they want to trick us?" James asked, confused.

"Because they are bent on world domination. This has been the goal for centuries. Allah will accept nothing less. They would establish Sharia law in every nation, and they would gladly trick you to do it."

That sick feeling that had hit his stomach earlier strengthened.

"This is hard to take in," Rain said.

"Why do you think they call them radicals and fundamentalists rather than crazy renegades? Because they are radically following the fundamental teaching of Islam. This should not be difficult to understand."

James took a deep breath. "I guess we want to think the best of people. I mean, look at you. You're awesome."

"Yes, and they beat me and imprisoned me in my own home for the sake of Allah."

Rain put a protective arm around Fatima. "But never again."

"No, never again." Not if James had anything to do with it.

"I know it is so horrible to say." Fatima pressed a hand to her mouth. "But it is not a good religion. I am just so afraid still that it might be true."

"Well, at least two people at this table are convinced it isn't." James attempted to return to his *kabsa* and some sense of normality. He felt like he had entered the twilight zone during that conversation. He didn't want to believe what Fatima said. Surely she had just been brainwashed by some bad people.

"I think Unity Light is the perfect place for you to learn about all different ways of thinking, Fatima." Rain leaned her head on Fatima's shoulder. "You've lived in a very small world, and it's time for you to experience the rest of it. Once you expand your horizons, you won't be so afraid. I mean, only twenty percent of the world population is Islamic, and only a portion of that twenty percent believes like your family. Everyone else can't just be wrong. At our church they teach there are many paths to God."

Now that was the Rain he knew and loved.

"But if you do want to learn more about true Christianity, maybe we could have Layla or Allie lead us in a little Bible study here," Rain suggested.

And there she went morphing into a stranger again. He might not be too worried about the off-chance of Muslim world domination, but he sure as heck was worried that Rain was turning to the dark side.

"Oh no! I am not ready for a Bible study. I think you are right. I will try to open my mind to many new ideas right now, anything to take away this nagging fear." Fatima rested her head atop of Rain's.

James wasn't sure Fatima should completely abandon her fear yet. They still had no idea what might be in store with her family. He didn't believe in the wrath and judgment of Allah, but he did believe that at least some radical Muslims were twisted, violent people. He had seen the evidence firsthand.

SIXTEEN

Layla shuffled through her backpack and neatly stacked her thick, heavy engineering texts atop the green and lilac comforter of her bed. No wonder she needed her parents' help so badly. Her books alone cost a small fortune. Another week had flown by with school, worries for Fatima, concerns about her parents, and angst-ridden thoughts of Mo, but she would try her best to focus on studying for the next few hours.

Studying on a Friday night. Kind of pathetic, but such was her life.

Almost immediately, she stumbled upon the distraction of watching Allie examine herself in the full-length mirror. She exchanged her beaded necklace for a looping scarf. Allie wore her standard fitted T-shirt and skinny jeans, but she appeared to be dressing up the ensemble for date night with Andy. Layla had briefly experienced the fun of Friday night dates, but that felt like a distant dream now.

"I like the scarf," Layla said.

Allie held the necklace beside it and examined both for a moment. "I agree. Not that I would dare to challenge your most excellent Lebanese fashion sense."

"Ha! At least we get a few things right in my culture." Food, music, dance, fashion. Of course, Middle Easterners were known for their strong families and hospitality too, but lately Layla had been contemplating how those concepts were sort of skewed, linked as they were to the whole system of shame and pride, of honor and control.

Ugh. She really needed to reign in her thoughts tonight.

Allie came over and plopped onto the bed beside Layla. She gave her a long, hard look. Then reaching out, she gently tucked Layla's dark hair behind her ear—a sisterly caress that brought tears to Layla's eyes.

Still studying her, Allie asked, "How are you? Really? I don't want the polite answer."

"How am I? Really?" Layla sighed. "I'm a mess. I'm terrified for Fatima. I miss Mo. I don't know what to do about my parents." She swiped her palm down the side of her face. "I sound like such a whiner. I hate that."

Allie took Layla's hand in her own. "I wouldn't have asked if I didn't want to know."

"I have so much to be thankful for. You and Rain, this house, my amazing new relationship with God, the fact that I'm still in school. I don't know what's wrong with me."

"Hey, life's hard. Yes, God is there for you and you can trust in him. But that doesn't mean you won't still have ups and downs. That doesn't mean you don't get to feel anymore. You know? That's what having a spiritual family is for, to help share each other's burdens."

Layla leaned her head on Allie's shoulder for just a moment. "Thanks."

"We'll figure this thing out with Fatima. So many people are praying for her now. Seriously, she's probably never been this safe in her whole life. And you said your mom was cool on the phone the last time you talked. Right?"

"Yeah, this Fatima thing is giving her something new to focus on. That's helping, but I can't stop wondering how it all will turn out."

"Try to focus on one day at a time. Worrying is a wasted emotion. All that time spent imagining the worst outcomes that might not even happen. It's the opposite of faith. Try to picture things working out instead of worrying that they won't. Imagine a good future and focus on that."

Layla tried to imagine her parents accepting her new religion. As hard as it was right now, she supposed in time, they would probably figure out a way to deal with it. For a moment she pictured herself and Mo at her parents' dinner table. A child on her lap and another one seated next to him, with her mom and dad relaxed and smiling nearby. Yes, with time it could happen. But then her mother started yelling and Mo yelled back. Both of them had such tempers. The Layla in her imagination started to cry and buried her hands in her face.

Allie must have picked up on her tension. She turned Layla and took her by the shoulders. "What now?"

"You're right. I can picture things working out with my parents if I really try, but it's Mo. He's not being very patient with me through all this. I mean, this is a huge transition for me. I think he logically gets it, but he's having a hard time controlling his reactions. I've noticed hints of an angry side to him that I don't like. It's completely normal in my culture, but I thought Mo would be different."

"That is kind of concerning." Allie gazed at the wall past Layla's head for a moment, then she smiled. "But he's young, and he's in love, and he's hurting. And he's still a new Christian too. It's good that you aren't rushing into anything."

"Yeah, and Mo really does keep his anger under control."

"Good. The biblical view is that it's okay to feel anger, but it's not okay to let that anger lead to sin."

"I guess his anger just reminds me too much of my uncle, of Fatima's family, even of Ahmed cornering me on the stairs. It's not a nice feeling to see even a glimmer of it in his eyes, but maybe I'm not being fair."

"Maybe your bad experiences are making you read too much into it. It really does seem like you're meant to be together, but you might both have some learning and growing to do first. I know those years apart made a world of difference for me and Andy." She gave Layla a long, warm hug.

Then Allie stood and picked up a paperback from her desk. "I just finished reading this book about boundaries in Christian relationships for my premarital counseling with Andy. It's helping me to see how my parents used guilt to control me. They didn't want to let me think for myself or form my own opinions. That's not healthy, and that's probably what made me hypersensitive to any criticism or control from Andy."

Allie paused for a moment and bit her lip. The memories must still hurt. "Christians can get the wrong impression that they should let other people push them around and call the shots, but it's just not true. God designed us to take responsibility for our own lives. Someday each of us will stand before him and give an account, and we won't get to shift the blame for our choices to anyone else. You should check the book out."

Allie tossed it onto Layla's bed, and Layla turned it over. The title was simply *Boundaries*. Warmth filled her heart, and she somehow sensed that the book would help her. Although she wanted to lean on Mo, she could probably become dependent on him in unhealthy sorts of ways if she let herself. Maybe it would help with her parents too. Even in the best of homes, the Middle Eastern culture was rife with guilt and manipulation. She wanted to understand the type of relationship God would want her to have with her family.

Allie picked up her bright red woolen coat and pulled it on. "I wish someone had given me that book a decade ago. It should be mandatory reading for new believers, and I think it would be extra helpful for dealing with a guy raised in a patriarchal system. You need to grow in your own identity in Christ right now."

"That's exactly what I tried to tell Mo."

"If he's worth your time, he'll figure it out. Like I said, just give him some grace right now. He's really hurting."

"Thanks."

Allie dropped a kiss on Layla's head before heading out for her date with Andy. Layla attempted to focus on her homework, but her mind spun with so many thoughts. After about ten minutes, her phone rang its early warning system. She picked it up from her nightstand. Hopefully Mom would be in a good mood again.

A second after she hit the accept button, her mother hollered across the line, "You won't believe it!"

"Won't believe what?"

"I tried to wait for the police and let them do their job like you said. But days go by and they do nothing, and I can't take it anymore. You know me. I have to find things out. So what do I do? I bake cookies of course." Mom paused from her chatter to take a breath. "And I take them across the street like a good neighbor. And I ring the doorbell, but they don't come and they don't come, and I ring and I ring. Can you believe it?"

Uh oh, this did not sound promising. "So what happened?"

"Finally, the door opens and it's their servant from Africa, and she says no one is home. So I say, what about Fatima? Is she home? And she says no, she's out. And I say, but is she well? My daughter was wondering about her. She hasn't heard from her. And she says Fatima is getting over the flu, and she's busy. Well, I don't believe this. Not for one minute, but I left the cookies. What could I do?"

"I don't know, Mom. I told you it wouldn't work."

"Ahh, but you are wrong. Later, the servant, she comes and she talks to our maid, Dalia. They are friends, you know. And she says she must tell the truth, and Fatima is missing, and she is so worried. That the men are searching, and that she's afraid they might kill Fatima. Oh, it is so terrible, *habibti*!"

Of course none of this was news to Layla, but it still stabbed to hear it. She reminded herself to act surprised. "*Haram!* Oh, my poor, sweet Fatima. That is so terrible. I wonder where she could have gone."

"I wonder if maybe they killed her already, and they are lying, even to their own servants. I am so worried for her, but I am so glad you are far away and not involved." A sob caught in Mom's throat.

"Did you tell the police?"

"Of course. This is too big to cover up. They have to know. Maybe they can help her still."

"Since they were already searching, it's probably better that they know the facts. But I can't help wondering if she will be in more danger if it becomes public knowledge."

"Eee! You are right. But I did not think of that. I told all the ladies at the mosque already. We never have such excitement as this."

Layla imagined the walls crumbling about her, but she could do nothing to stop them now. This situation had never been within her power to control. The longer Fatima went missing, the more people would figure it out. "I hope Fatima found somewhere safe to stay," Layla said.

"*En sha'allah,*" Mom whispered. *As Allah wills.* Layla had hated that phrase even when she was a Muslim. It was such a cop out. "I hope she is safe too, *habibti.* Maybe I should try to learn more."

"Please, you have to promise me this time. Let this go. Her brothers are more dangerous than you realize." Now that Layla thought about it, her mother's snooping would probably steer Fatima's brothers off her trail for now, but they wouldn't tolerate anything beyond neighborly concern. Their pride wouldn't stand for it.

Mom sighed loudly into the phone. "Your father says the same. I know you are right. It is so hard though, when I know she is in danger."

"You did your part. Sounds like you gave the police enough information to start an investigation, but you can't let the Maaloufs figure out it was you. You could put our whole family, not to mention their servant, in jeopardy."

"Fine, I will stop. And you too, Layla. You must promise me you will keep out of this."

She paused to consider her response. Holding back the truth from Ahmed when he threatened her was one thing, but this was her mother. "Mom, I will try. But if she comes to me for help, I can't turn her down. Is that fair?"

Mom sighed. "Yes, this is fair. Of course you can't turn her down. Only be wise, and get her somewhere else just as soon as you can, to someone they would not suspect."

"That's a smart idea. Thanks."

They chatted for a few more minutes about school and relatives before they said good-bye. Afterward, Layla held the phone in her hands and stared at it. Matters were heating up by the second, and she couldn't do anything to stop them.

Sarah savored the swirl of sweet and tart in her mouth as the strawberry daiquiri slowly melted. Tonight's beverage selection was much tastier than the beer at the last party she'd attended with Jesse, and she had promised herself two drinks max. She'd regretted that hangover more than anything else and had no intention of reliving it. Pounding music, flashing lights, and the relaxing liquor enveloped her, melting her into a pleasant haze all over again, not to mention Jesse's heavenly touch. She could get used to this.

"Hey, babe. There you are." Jesse nestled beside her on the overstuffed chair in a dim corner and rested a familiar hand on her thigh. With his other hand, he took her drink and placed it on the stand beside them.

"I never left this spot." From beneath her drooping eyelids, Sarah gazed at his handsome features. She had been more than happy to stay tucked away into her cozy little corner while Jesse socialized. These really weren't her kind of people. She was here for him alone.

"How about one last dance before you turn into a pumpkin, Cinderella?"

"Sounds divine."

He pulled her to her feet, and her arms felt as if they floated loosely at her sides. Her head tipped back languidly until he pressed her against his taut form, and then she tucked her head beneath Jesse's chin and rested it on his well-muscled chest covered by a soft knit jersey.

"You like that, huh?" Jesse nuzzled her head with his chin. His hands wandered downward, and he tucked them into the back pockets of her jeans.

Sarah didn't bat an eye. She'd become so accustomed to his touch. Those addicting tingles and shivers sprang to life again. She ran her hands through his dark, tousled hair, messing it into a new arrangement.

A part of her wished she could spend her entire life in this pleasant, fluid haze. She'd adjusted quite nicely to these outings with Jesse, even managing to ignore her guilt. If anyone was to blame for her new lifestyle, it was her parents who had pushed her here with their stifling restrictions. She hadn't done anything so horrible. Although she hated lying to them, what could they expect under the circumstances?

Jesse danced her deeper into the shadows and pressed her against the paneled wall. He caught her mouth in a searing kiss, a kiss that had grown so familiar to her over the past mornings at the bus stop and seemed so right, as if she'd been designed to fit in his arms and meet his lips and wandering caresses with her own.

Sarah neither knew nor—in this glorious moment—particularly cared what she believed anymore. One thing she knew for certain. She was falling deeper and deeper in love with Jesse each day. Surely if his lifestyle, his agnostic beliefs, were good enough for him, they couldn't be all bad. From the second she'd opened a crack in her heart to him, he'd completely engulfed her thoughts and emotions.

"So is it official?" he asked in a low, husky voice.

"Is what official?" she asked in a whisper to match his.

"Are we a couple? Can I tell people you're my girlfriend now?"

Sarah's heart soared so high and with such force, she thought it might crash right through the ceiling. "Of course I'm your girlfriend. I just don't want my parents to find out yet. Okay? Oh Jesse, I can't believe I avoided this for so long."

"You're here now, in my arms. That's all that matters. You were worth waiting for." He trailed kisses down her neck and over her exposed collarbone.

As a new wave of pleasure washed over Sarah, she pushed away any thoughts that said this was not the right time or place, let alone person, to be experiencing these sensations with. She brushed past her concerns that the alcohol might be impeding her judgment and heightening her reactions. She ignored any worries over what would happen when her parents and church friends discovered her deep, dark secrets. Most of all, she pushed God far, far from her mind. Instead she relaxed into Jesse's touch and determined to live in the moment with no regrets—for as long as she could.

SEVENTEEN

Rain arrived to the coffee shop late on Monday night and couldn't help but recall the meeting last year when she had really bonded with Allie and Layla. Maybe they should make up some cheesy little name for their group. Or not. Today she would get to know their newest member, Shondra Livingston. She had seen her dance during Allie's soul-stirring worship piece last semester but had never actually talked to her before.

She waved to the girls and quickly ordered a chamomile tea from the counter before joining them. This week was technically spring break, but they all had responsibilities in town and plenty of school work to catch up on.

Sliding into the available chair, Rain said, "So what did I miss?"

"We were just getting to know each other. Families, majors, stuff like that." Layla took a sip of her typical fancy coffee concoction.

"Short version?" Rain pressed a hand to her chest. "Only child raised by aging flower children. Now studying writing and expecting a little girl with my significant other, James."

"Succinct." Shondra offered a fist bump. "I like that in a woman. Me, middle child of five siblings, raised in a traditional black gospel household, double major in physical therapy and dance. Got to pay the bills somehow."

Rain had a feeling Shondra was going to fit in just fine.

"We're supposed to choose some deep philosophical issue that we basically agree on but find some subtle differences in our views." Layla always served as the gatekeeper of the group. She loved to be organized and stay on task.

"This should be interesting," Shondra said.

Layla nodded her agreement. "It's similar to the English project that brought us all so close last semester."

Rain recalled those conversations. They had meant so much to her, but for the past few months the girls had kept things pretty light.

Shondra gestured to Layla. "And you ended up coming to Christ. That's so crazy. In my culture it seems to be the Muslims converting people from Christianity."

"That's because they water everything down and present a pretty picture here in the States," Layla said. "If Americans understood Arabic, if they saw how the religion looked in the Middle East, I don't think they'd be so easily persuaded."

"But black Muslims have their own version of the faith." Rain felt compelled to present the other side of the argument. Layla sounded like Fatima, but she wasn't being completely fair. "You can't say that their beliefs are less valid just because they aren't the originals. They have some beautiful beliefs. I've met a few at my new interfaith congregation."

Layla raised a brow. "But what are those beliefs based on? Certainly not the life of Mohammed. Barely on his teachings. They just pull out the nice stuff about love and peace and disregard everything else."

"Their beliefs are based on their own inner light." Rain tried to maintain her patience. "Fatima gets it. We all have a deep sense of inner conscience. Why can't it be enough to follow that?"

"Because there has to be—"

"Whoa!" Shondra slapped the table and cut Layla off. "I came here trying to avoid a big fight. Rain, I really don't know much about your beliefs. Can you share a little?"

Rain blew on her tea longer than was warranted. Did she even know what she believed anymore?

"Well, for years I was just sort of an agnostic. James was a hardcore atheist, so we kind of avoided religion. But last semester things changed for me, and for him too I guess. I truly believe in God now, and James is more open to the possibility."

Shondra looked shocked. "Wow, Allie, you are quite the evangelist."

"It's hard to stay the same when you bring such diverse people together." Allie gave Layla's shoulder a squeeze and smiled across the table to Rain. "But it wasn't just me influencing them. I changed too."

Rain continued her train of thought. "My new church, Unity Light, is basically a Christian church. A lot of the messages include biblical teaching, and we believe that Christ embodied the perfect way to live." How could Rain explain the differences? "But there's a lot about finding your own inner divinity. And boy do they stress the positive affirmations and denials. Every day we're supposed to put away the negative and embrace the positive. On one hand I see their point, but I'm not convinced that a lifestyle of denial is healthy."

Shondra shivered. "That kind of spookily sounds like my church."

"Oh yeah," Allie said. "You mentioned your church was really into positive confessions. I don't really know much about charismatics. They were kind of lumped in with Catholics and Presbyterians when I was growing up. You know, the *deceived* Christians. Not that I think that way anymore. I believe we should all be one body in Christ and set aside our doctrinal quarreling to make a real difference in the world."

"Amen to that, sister," Rain said.

"Ha!" Shondra giggled. "And people at my church seem to think they're the ones with the market on truth. It's not that I disagree with everything. The Bible has so much to say about the power of our words, the authority we have through Christ, the supernatural gifts, and the promises of God to the believer. I don't mean to undermine any of that."

"But..." Allie said.

"You saw that but coming a mile away, did you? But...in my particular church I feel like they take some basic charismatic teaching, add in a cup of 'word-faith' as we call it, and mix it with a dash of black liberation theology. It all becomes about being royal and wealthy. I mean, to people who've been oppressed for hundreds of years, that can be some pretty heady stuff."

"Hey, no one's more for black empowerment than me. I've lived with James for eight years and my hippie father before that. But what about all the taking up your cross and denying yourself stuff?" Rain was confused now. She thought she had finally pinned down this whole Christian message. "What about blessed are they who mourn? Blessed are the poor in spirit?" The beatitudes were some of her favorite verses.

"Exactly." Shondra shook her hands in frustration. "I do believe all that stuff too. You have to find a balance. God is just so vast, you know? If you focus on one part of his personality and ignore the other parts, you can easily veer off course. Visiting other denominations with our dance troupe really brought that back to me. Each one has something that they specialize in, and often they're areas that my church is lacking in."

"Really?" Allie gaped. "Even Fuddy-Duddy Chapel?"

"Allie!" Layla chided.

"I know. It really has changed. But lately I've been listening to the sermons through Sarah's ears. I can see where she got her perfectionist, judgmental tendencies. I'll be really happy when Andy takes over for good."

"But you need to look at it from my perspective, Allie," Shondra said. "You don't see my church raising money for kids to go build houses and dig wells in third world countries this summer, or sending medical professionals to help out with refugees, or running a soup kitchen like the financially strapped students and young families at The Gathering. No. We're too busy being *overcomers*, glory to God!" She raised her hands over her head and stamped her feet gospel style.

Then she twisted her lips in annoyance. "We need an even bigger and better church building, maybe a private plane for the pastor to buzz around to speaking engagements. Not that there's anything wrong with those things, but I think if you pushed the members, they'd tell you that if people want to be blessed and experience provision, then they should go to church. And trust me, there's plenty of perfectionism and judgment involved in that too. No need to go out and be Jesus to people when they can come to learn about the promises of God for themselves."

"But who does that?" This whole mindset was starting to rile Rain up.

"Hey, don't kill the messenger! After getting out and meeting other Christians, I don't think that way anymore. Although there's a lot of good in my family's church, it's really hard for me to drag myself there Sunday after Sunday for their little insiders club."

"Do they speak in tongues?" Allie wiggled her fingers around her head. "We visited some churches with my old troupe, Alight, that were really into all that supernatural stuff. Even though I hadn't been raised that way, I found it kind of cool, just like in the Bible days."

"Yeah, I believe in the gifts of the spirit for sure, but they manage to get a little weird with that stuff too. It's like they barely believe you're saved until you prove it by speaking in tongues, which results in a lot of pressure, which, in my opinion, results in a lot of faking. Same with the whole 'falling out under the Spirit' thing. I've experienced it. God's presence is incredibly powerful, but more often people just do their 'courtesy falls' so that the minister will move on to the next victim."

"I hate fake." Allie made a face. "That was my biggest complaint about church when I was growing up."

"There was a lot of falseness in my culture too," Layla added. "That's what really drew us all together last year. We all wanted something real."

"Me too," Shondra said. "I'm still trying to figure out what authentic Christianity looks like. The Gathering seems pretty close."

"I'm sure that there are a lot of good churches." Rain had felt God's presence in all different sorts of churches last semester. Just not in hers now. "It's not really about how they dress or the music. It's more about the heart."

Layla reached over and took Shondra's hand in hers. "Seems like you found the right group."

Shondra smiled. "I've really been praying that God would surround me with fellow truth seekers. I never talk about this stuff. I just keep it all bottled up inside. Tonight is an unexpected blessing."

Fellow truth seekers? Rain felt like a fraud. Deep down she knew the truth. Just like Layla, she had met truth face to face. And she had rejected him in favor of James.

"So do we have anything to base our paper on here?" Layla brought them back to the business of the day once again.

"Well, it seems like we're all some sort of Christian, but we all interpret the Bible differently," Rain said. "Maybe we can start there. Use that Sir Francis Bacon quote. 'A little philosophy inclineth man's mind to atheism; but depth in philosophy bringeth men's minds about to religion.'" At least, Rain hoped they were all some sort of Christian. She had yet to make any real commitment to Christ. Was she just fooling herself?

"Good idea." Layla typed that into her word document. It was kind of crazy to think they had gone from three diametrically opposed religions to all being *some sort of Christian* in just over six months, and that was the first time she'd heard Rain claim to be a Christian at all. Although Layla had been so sure Rain would accept Christ after Allie and Shondra's powerful dance performance, Rain seemed to talk herself out of it by the time they got back to the apartment.

"That's cool." Shondra scribbled into a notebook. Thank goodness, another organized person in their group. Allie and Rain were both hard workers and always came through, but they made Layla nervous in the process. "I didn't realize Rain was a Christian too."

Was she? What Rain had described didn't sound that much like Christianity to Layla, more like Christianity-light. "Allie has been discipling me, though. So we might have a hard time finding subtle differences there."

Rain tapped her chin. "You know, I've noticed a lot of your culture is still a part of you, Layla. That must influence how you interpret things. Has there been anything in Christianity that is hard for you to accept? Areas where you find yourself having your own take on things?"

Layla hated to admit it, but maybe it would help her process her thoughts. "The hardest thing for me so far is Jesus's teaching about leaving your mother and father. It just doesn't sit well with me. Family has always been the most important thing in my life."

"The most important?" Rain eyed her skeptically. "I seem to recall you saying something about it not being the most important thing, but the *only* thing."

Layla bit her lip. "I suppose I did say something along those lines. I have a new appreciation for freedom and individuality, but my parents mean so very much to me. In whatever ways I can, I still want to honor them."

Allie looked to Shondra and nudged Layla. "It's hard. Her parents have taken care of her for her whole life. They're paying for college, not to mention her convertible and designer clothes."

"Hey, don't make me sound like some sort of spoiled princess." Although, hadn't Layla had the same thoughts herself over the last weeks? Was she really ready to give up her Louis Vuittons for Jesus? "I could do without the stuff. Really I could, but I've waited so long to get an education."

"So work for it, girlfriend. That's what I'm doing." Shondra flipped back her hair with its reddish streaks. "You think my momma and daddy can send five kids to college? And debt is a four-letter word at my house."

"She's kind of right," Allie said. "Not that your rent isn't appreciated, but the teenybopper's parents all offered to let you live there for free if needed, and you could get your food from the pantry that The Gathering runs. Mo could probably find you a waitressing job for tuition. We could even help you establish residency so it would be cheaper."

"And of course, if you got married...let's just say there'd be lots of perks." Rain wiggled her brows suggestively.

Layla's mind spun and threatened to explode. She wasn't raised to be independent like these girls. In her culture men provided for the family or everyone worked a business together. Girls didn't just go off and live their own lives.

But she didn't feel like going into all that right now. "Wow, we veered off subject. You made your point though, Rain. It would be interesting to examine how my culture colors my interpretation of Scripture."

They were off to a good start on the project, but it seemed this subject was going to force Layla to look at some areas she'd rather avoid. Hadn't she lived enough of her life avoiding uncomfortable issues? She wanted truth, right? Authenticity? The price was so high though.

Did she really have the courage to seize it, or would she end up caving in the end?

EIGHTEEN

Layla took a moment to watch the ping pong war being waged nearby in the student center—back, forth, back, forth, much like her thoughts these days. She had come here to escape the craziness of the bungalow. Most of the time it was pretty quiet here, but spring break fever had hit the students remaining on campus.

Once the raucous cheering settled down, she focused back on her engineering paper. That was the whole reason she was here, after all, to focus on her education. Soon she'd need to pick an engineering specialty. She was leaning toward mechanical at the moment since it was such a broad field, and it was Mo's major as well.

Now that she thought about it, he would thrive in systems engineering since he was such a people person. Maybe that would give them something positive and relaxed to discuss the next time they met. She hated all the tension between them lately.

Her conversation with the girls last night had left her with a lot to think about, but it had somehow soothed her as well. She hadn't realized how much she missed those talks. Imagining positive outcomes like Allie suggested had helped improve her state of mind too.

Plus, she'd started her day in prayer, a habit she had almost fallen out of in all the craziness of Fatima's arrival. She thought of that quote she'd liked from philosophy class: "The function of prayer is not to influence God, but rather to change the nature of the one who prays." Who had said that? Kirkegaard?

She wrangled her thoughts back from philosophy to engineering and typed the last few paragraphs into her laptop before packing to head to the bungalow. Her backpack weighed a ton, and it took considerable effort to sling it over her shoulder. As she started toward the exit, she noticed Salaam coming her way. She waited for her gut to clench in fear, but nothing. He merely raised an eyebrow and inclined his head toward the alcove nearby.

She followed him into it. "Hey, Salaam. What's up?"

"I'm really glad I found you. Have you heard anything new?" He cocked his head to the side endearingly and raked his fingers through his curls. Mo did the same thing, and in that moment Layla sensed that she could trust Salaam, at least a little.

"Things are heating up in Detroit. My mom says the police are investigating now. She's really worried. She's afraid the Maaloufs might have killed Fatima already."

"I heard the same thing about the police. And Dani said the family's searched all over Dearborn and Detroit. They can only think of a few people she knows out of town. Her uncle in Canada, you, of course Dani, and there's another old friend from elementary school out in Oregon."

Fatima's buddy Sabia, but Fatima hadn't mentioned her in years. "So what now?"

"Seems your mother's been poking around for you. Did you know that?"

"I told her not to." Layla shifted her heavy backpack. "But she never listens to me."

"It turned out okay. Until then they'd planned on heading here first, but they figured if she was with you, there'd be no reason for your mother to snoop. I guess the dad is on his way to Canada and the brothers are going to visit Dani even though he's been cooperative.

Seems they don't trust him, and they really don't think she'd be brave enough to go to the west coast all by herself."

"That's good, I guess. I'd rather not have to face those guys." She felt oddly calm as they discussed it, bolstered somehow by her prayer time that morning.

"But here's the thing. Dani hasn't seen her, and we're only a few hours from D.C. So it's a matter of time now."

That managed to speed up Layla's heart rate a bit. She took a deep breath, hoping to recapture the sense of peace. "What do you suggest?"

"If they're looking for you here, maybe you should go home for a while. Make up an excuse."

Layla's jaw literally dropped, but she managed to close her gaping mouth. "I can't leave school!"

"Just for a week or two, until things settle down. Talk to your professors. A lot of classes are online these days anyway."

He was right, of course, but how could she leave Fatima? It might be smart to cast suspicion away from the whole Norfolk area, but it felt so wrong to abandon her friend. "I don't know, Salaam. I'll think about it. I really hope it doesn't come to that. Why can't they just leave her alone? Disown her? Say she died, went missing, whatever? That's what they're going to have to tell people if they murder her anyway."

"I'm sure Dani has tried to reason with them, but I think you know these aren't reasonable people."

"Maybe we should call the police here. Keep them on the alert."

"It would just make things worse."

She blew her bangs from her eyes and shifted her backpack again. "I hate this."

Salaam grinned. "Me too. Were you heading out?" he asked, indicating her backpack.

"Yeah. I finished my paper. Plus, it was getting too noisy in here to study."

He reached and snatched her backpack from her, easily swinging it over his own shoulder. "Let me walk you to your car. You've had a hard enough morning."

"Thanks. That would be nice." She fell into step beside him, grateful for the reminder that there truly were many wonderful Muslim men in the world. Salaam wasn't a bad guy, and neither was Mo, despite his occasional well-controlled anger. Eventually this would all be over, and she and Mo would figure out a way to be together. She had to keep believing that.

Rain snuggled into a corner of the couch after tucking Fatima safely into bed. She picked up her soft leather Bible from the coffee table. Although it was far from worn, she ran her hand over the supple binding that had been broken in with her frequent reading. She took a whiff of the peaceful, earthy scent she associated with this book. Opening it, she thumbed through the crackling pages, soothed by the sound as well.

She'd read through the whole thing once already. Now that she understood more about this whole Christianity thing, she wondered if she should switch to a more literal translation than her beloved *Message*, but it was an old friend now. She was working her way through Matthew again...and she felt it coming. There was no way she could read about Jesus's crucifixion, death, and resurrection one more time without surrendering to him.

She brushed her hand over the book again and sighed. What would James think? A part of her wanted to throw the book out the window and keep her life just as it was, but she couldn't.

She traced her fingers over the mound of growing babe. It wasn't fair to jeopardize the stability of her family, but it wouldn't be fair to withhold the truth from her child either. Wasn't this ongoing battle within her proof enough that sin was real? That she needed a savior?

She knew deep inside what she was supposed to do, yet here she was still resisting. Tears slipped down her cheeks at the thought.

Caught in her mental meanderings, she almost missed the jangle of keys in the door. By the time it registered, James had entered the room. She brushed off her face with one hand and tucked the Bible between her and the couch cushion while James shook off his coat and threw his bag onto the table. Pasting a pleasant smile on her face, she called, "Hey, babe. You're home early. Did the study session go well?"

He sagged next to her on the couch. "Yeah. As good as can be expected. How was your evening?"

"Fine. We edited a chapter of my book, watched one of Fatima's reality shows, and then she headed to bed early."

"Nice. And are you going to tell me what you just hid in the couch cushion, Lucy, or am I going to have to fish it out for myself?"

Rain's cheeks heated. "I didn't hide it. I just...put it away. I know you're not really a fan, and I wanted to greet you properly." She dug out the Bible and sat it on her lap with a sheepish grin.

He picked it up and turned it over in his large, strong hand. "Why am I starting to feel like you're cheating on me with this thing?"

His word struck a chord in that place deep inside of her. She wasn't cheating with a Bible, but with its author. Or maybe the reverse was true. She felt like she was cheating on Jesus by putting James first.

"James, I don't want to have to choose between you and Jesus. Promise me that you'll never make that ultimatum."

James tapped the book against his leg. "I'm not going to leave you ever again, and I'm not trying to control you anymore. My therapist says it's bad for the psyche. But...it would change things. You know it would. We've been so simpatico all these years. It would create a division that we've never experienced, especially when we're raising our child. Isn't it enough to stay open? To take the good and leave the spooky, scary stuff behind?"

Dare from Deep Within

A thousand thoughts spun through Rain's mind, but only one tumbled from her mouth. "I want to go to The Gathering again."

James laid down the Bible on the coffee table slowly, deliberately. He rubbed both hands down his sculpted cheeks and tugged at his goatee. "I know you do, baby. I can see it in your eyes every time we visit the soup kitchen, every time it comes up."

"I need to do this. Can you understand?"

"Not really, but I love you." He looped his arm around her and pulled her to his chest. In that moment her resolve nearly crumbled. Hadn't she fought, prayed, cried all last semester to get back to this place?

So he wouldn't leave her, but what would be the long term ramifications if she accepted Christ? Allie always said that Jesus took people just as they were, but Rain had learned enough to realize that things changed once a person made him Lord of her life.

At least she had a few more chapters before she faced the crucifixion scene all over again, and The Gathering was still days away, but she had spent too much time around this slippery slope. She wouldn't be able to keep herself from tumbling head first into a relationship with Jesus much longer.

James pressed a kiss against her forehead. "You'll be going to The Gathering this Sunday, won't you?"

"Yep."

"I don't suppose I can convince you to leave the baby home with me."

She chuckled, causing the mound of her belly to bounce between them. "Will you go with me?"

He didn't answer for a moment. Then finally he said, "We'll see."

Noah surveyed the Arabic congregation surrounding him. Although they were polite and welcoming each Sunday morning, he felt like an outsider. Maybe because his discount-store khakis and polo didn't add much to the weekly fashion show that seemed to be an essential part of Middle Eastern church, or maybe because this wasn't his sort of service. He had chosen the biggest Arabic congregation in the area—a mixed group of orthodox, Catholic, Maronite, and Coptic Christians—hoping to find support for his ministry, but it hadn't worked out too well.

The priest on the raised dais lit some candles and wafted incense toward the congregation before returning to his liturgical ramblings. Not that there was anything wrong with candles or incense, and he'd never found anything in the liturgy that particularly bothered him. It's just that most of the people seemed to zone out. Like this was a mandatory weekly obligation to suffer through, not a life-giving oasis.

And he hadn't met a single person in this congregation who shared his passion for reaching Muslims. They seemed to think it would be better to leave well enough alone and not rock the boat. They were thankful enough to worship freely here in America without bomb threats and government persecution. He understood that, sort of.

Whenever he tried to hang out with the young men in the congregation, they devised convenient excuses. If he ran into them at the hookah bar, they were always just about to leave. They must be afraid to be associated with a rabble-rouser like him—or maybe they just thought he was weird.

The priest held a huge, gilded Bible over his head and invited the children to gather in the front. They followed him and the Bible in a procession around the sanctuary, smiling and giggling as they went. Precious little souls. Once they made it back to the front, the priest lowered the holy book and allowed each of them to kiss it before returning to their seats. Noah loved this part of the service, and he enjoyed seeing the children free of the bondage their parents had suffered in the Middle East.

But didn't they realize that unless someone stood up and spoke the truth, before long the Muslims could infiltrate this part of the world too? Already they had prayers blasting over the loud speakers in public places and were introducing Sharia law on a municipal level.

And no one here seemed to care. Nor did anyone seem too concerned about the disappearance of a girl he now knew to be named Fatima Maalouf. He'd overheard parishioners chatting casually about her before the service. They seemed to find the situation gossip-worthy but had an attitude that there was nothing they could do about it. Radical Muslims would be radical Muslims, and no one wanted to stand up to them.

At first Fatima's family had lied and covered for her, but when their story didn't check out, they relented and told at least part of the truth. So far all the police had confirmed was that she was missing. The brothers had mentioned that her passport was missing, and she might have traveled back to Saudi Arabia, but that story didn't check out either.

Although he now had a name and a context for his angel on the balcony, he was no closer to finding her than he had been weeks ago. Thankfully at that moment, the congregation slid to their knees upon the adjustable prayer rails. While they all mumbled their rote petitions, Noah clutched the back of the pew in front of him so hard that his knuckles turned white. *God, save her!* He screamed the words in his head. *Keep her safe. Find her. And please, oh please, God, let me know that she's all right.*

After several months his plan to blend with this congregation and inspire them to reach out had clearly failed. He determined to find a new church soon, one where he could be fed spiritually, one where people cared about his mission and would join in his cause. Enough was enough.

NINETEEN

Rain slid into the folding theater-style chair next to Layla and offered a smile. Only five minutes late, and the band still seemed to be warming up with the first fast paced tune. She took a deep inhale, breathing in the fresh, sweet air in this place. Although she couldn't quite put a finger on it, something felt different to her here than at any other church she had visited, as if the air vibrated with energy, so alive, so free.

She shook off her coat and situated her belongings, then faced front and clapped along to the beat. Before long her toes were tapping and her body swaying as well. Layla moved to the rhythm beside her, even raising a hand and waving it along with the music. She had come so far in such a short time. Allie had told her how Layla practically sank into the chair like a shy little mouse the first time she'd attended The Gathering. Rain wished she had been there to see it, but she hadn't dared to visit church so soon after James returned to her life.

She couldn't let James hold her back forever. Nor could she let fear stand in her way any longer. That's what it came down to, really—fear of living without him, fear of raising this baby on her own. She fancied herself such a strong, bold, courageous person, but where had that courage been last semester?

Maybe she wasn't being fair, though. She had managed to find the huge store of courage necessary to protect her child, and she hadn't been convinced about the whole Christianity thing yet. While deep in her heart she had suspected it was true, had felt its power, she'd needed these past few months for her thinking to catch up.

But now? She had no excuses left. What was that verse that meant so much to Layla last semester, something about Jesus knocking at the door of your heart? She sensed him at that very moment. Poised. Waiting. Gently tapping. Longing to enter.

The band switched to a song about dancing like a child, and Layla's features lit like sunshine. Rain watched as her friend scanned the room. Her searching gaze found its target as a group of young dancers began running through the aisle. As they dashed past Layla joined them, laughing, clapping, running, spinning her way around the church.

Rain contented herself with bouncing from side to side in her spot and waving her hand as Layla had done. Her huge mound of baby might tip her off balance if she tried dashing around the sanctuary on slanting floors. She giggled at the thought and threw herself into her own little dance with increasing gusto.

Warmth washed over her in ripples like heated honey. Goosebumps rose on her arms. Tingles and shivers ran down her spine, a pleasure that was holy, pure, and light in a way she had never felt before.

Rain lost herself in that moment, swept up by passion's flame, burned by the touch of that sweet, sweet spirit, forever changed. She stopped focusing on the screen filled with lyrics and allowed her thoughts to soar heavenward in prayer.

After a few minutes spent reveling in God's presence, oddly, thoughts of Allie's sister Sarah popped into her head. Had the girl ever experienced anything like this? Rain suspected not, or she could never be the cold, rigid person that she was. She offered up a prayer for Sarah, then delved into that glorious light once again.

The next song about God's great dance floor continued to fill her with bursting brightness. She joined the congregation in their rousing fist bumps, feeling like a part of something so much bigger than herself. In her mind's eye, she caught a glimpse of thousands of worshipers before the throne of God, shouting and praising.

Then it hit her—that intimate friend she had met last semester was the king of the entire universe! She nearly swooned at the thought. A king, a father, a friend, a savior, all wrapped up in one amazing being. Surely serving him would be worth any price.

Rain floated on a cloud through the remaining worship songs, the announcements, and even the brief meet and greet. This was not a dull, numbing haze like she'd felt at Unity Light, but rather something more vibrant, more real than she'd ever experienced before. As if she was lost in a luminous sphere and the transient world around her had grown vaguely dim. A pale, illusory shadow compared to the vivid wonders of eternity.

Although Sarah's sermon notes appeared as impeccable as ever, her mind wandered far away from the cream and brown sanctuary where she had spent nearly every Sunday morning, Sunday evening, and Wednesday evening of her entire life. Pastor Jenkins continued droning on about predestination versus free will, but she couldn't focus on his message. Her thoughts wandered off to the results of her own free will instead.

Assuming she hadn't wasted her whole life and God had indeed created her, she must be far away from his plans at the moment. She had lived a predestined existence up until now, predestined by her family and this church—a perfect, squeaky clean life, right down to her navy jumpers. A neat and orderly sort of existence, predictable and structured, the way she liked it. She had stuck to the news, sports, Christian programming, and of course old black and white reruns on the television just as her parents demanded.

No wonder she felt like she'd been living in black and white, caught in a 1950s sitcom.

A hot flush of anger washed over her, and the muscles throughout her body tensed. She'd missed out on so much, stuck in that cold, rigid existence—shallow even—in her focus on rules and outward appearances. She needed to figure out how to live from deep inside like Allie did, even like Jesse did in his own heathen sort of way. The problem was, deep inside of her was a mess.

As she filled in the next blank in her bulletin outline, Mom patted her hand and smiled. She looked so proud of her perfect daughter. If only she knew. Sarah might be wearing the proper calf length skirt and stockings, but it was Allie on the other side of Mom in a wildly patterned minidress with leggings who had things together in the areas that mattered.

Sarah felt more like a failure than ever. She didn't regret taking charge of her own free will, but she hated this angst-ridden place she was stuck in. After all these years as a Christian, she couldn't fathom a harsh, random universe without a God. She still believed in basic Christian values. She still wanted a traditional family. On matters of politics, she still thought like the hardcore conservative she had been raised to be.

She just needed to figure out what she truly believed concerning the Bible and the more specific rules for living, and she needed to figure out if she wanted Jesus to be the lord of her life, and what exactly that meant. Good old Socrates had said the unexamined life was not worth living. Well, mess or not, at least she'd been examining the heck out of her life.

There were all sorts of Christians, right? And goodhearted agnostics like Jesse. It was time for her to figure things out for herself. Pastor Jenkins always said that God didn't have any grandchildren. But what about her plans to be a missionary? She didn't know how to give up on her dream, but if she couldn't get it together soon, she might have to shift directions—perhaps work for the Peace Corps or in some other form of foreign service. This was all so new.

Might there still be something here for her in this church? Perhaps in Andy's messages more so than Pastor Jenkins's? She had always filtered everything she learned through those strict core beliefs instilled in her by her parents. Maybe she needed to reverse the system around before it was too late.

That subtle nudge in her heart reminded her that she should talk to Allie about this, but despite Allie's more freedom-loving style of Christianity, she would never approve of Sarah dating an unbeliever like Jesse. What if Allie felt obligated to tell Mom and Dad? Sarah couldn't take the risk.

In this moment, Jesse was the only part of her life that made any sense. She thought about him night and day. The memory of his touch, his scent, his handsome face eclipsed everything that used to matter to her. Even in her current state, she had enough common sense to know that being this ridiculously caught up in a guy could only lead to trouble, but she couldn't seem to stop herself from barreling head first toward the train wreck that was sure to lie ahead.

Rain roused back to the realm of the five senses, the world of time and space, as Pastor Mike began his sermon in a booming bass voice reminiscent of Martin Luther King.

Her mind shot to sharp focus as he put in words the experience she'd been having for the past twenty minutes. He spoke of God as a father but also as so much more. "Paul says we receive a spirit of sonship and can cry out, '*abba* father!' That word *abba* is what a child says when they are first learning to speak. We come to God like a toddler, with infantile dependence, and yet with confidence and abandon in his unending love."

Mike spread his arms wide and crouched down like he might for his child. "We throw ourselves into God's arms. We crawl onto his lap. The lap of the king of the entire universe. Our *abba*, our dada, our papa. And there we are safe and at rest. There we feel no fear, no worry, no insecurity. There we trust him with our decisions and our lives."

Rain's father had insisted she call him George and make all of her own decisions. No wonder she clutched to James with such clinging dependence. James was more than happy to call the shots.

But she wouldn't let James call the shots anymore. That would be God's job now.

Mike paused for a moment. He appeared to be praying under his breath. "God is knocking at the door of someone's heart at this very moment. I can feel it. You want to let him in. Let's not put this off one more second. Come up and let us officially welcome you into the family of God."

Nothing could hold Rain back any longer. She had felt God's touch. She craved his presence, wanted so badly for him to be her very own *abba*. Without any conscious decision on her part, she rose to her feet, heading down the aisle and into a whole new existence.

Allie checked her phone one more time on her way to class. Nothing. She wanted to throw the stupid thing on the concrete. Why wouldn't Sarah call her back? Why did she ignore every single one of her texts? Probably the same reason she had disappeared mere seconds after the church service on Sunday night. Something was going on with her, and she knew Allie would get to the bottom of it if she had a chance. Grumbling in frustration, she shook her phone. How could she help Sarah if the girl avoided her like the plague?

As she tucked her phone in her purse, she noticed clusters of blue and red pansies lining the walkway. The first blossoms of spring—new life, hope, exactly what she needed at this moment. Between Sarah, wedding planning, school, work, and her busy new dance performance schedule, she'd let herself get stressed out. She took deep breaths of the fresh air to calm herself and focused her thoughts on God.

When she arrived to class, Allie entered the room to the sight of Rain waving frantically to her from a desk in the back. Rain, early? The anticipation bursting from her face gave a clue to the reason. The last time she'd looked like that was when James moved home. She was glowing as bright as the sunshine that flowed through the windows and back-lit her curly puff of golden brown hair like a halo.

Allie wove her way through the desks and hurried to Rain, waving with excitement as well. "What is it? Good news?"

Rain squealed like one of the teenyboppers. "The best. I just had to tell you in person."

"Tell me what? Spit it out."

"I accepted Christ last night at The Gathering."

The twinge of excitement Allie had felt upon entering the door switched to a peaceful sense of awe. After Rain had shied away from becoming a Christian last semester, Allie had begun to wonder if she ever would. Rain's new interfaith church had seemed like a detour in the wrong direction. Allie had continued praying but decided to otherwise leave matters in God's hands and just focus on being the friend that Rain needed.

She should have caught the euphoria of a new believer a mile away. She had seen it often enough during her years spent as a dancing missionary. It was so unexpected this time though.

"Are you just going to stand there gaping? Aren't you going to say anything?" Rain asked.

Allie grabbed her in a crushing embrace. "Oh Rain, there are no words. This is so incredible. I am so happy, just a little shocked. It's almost unbelievable."

Rain pulled back and grasped Allie by the shoulders. "I know, right? Who would have guessed when we started that diversity project that in less than a year we would all be Christian believers? It's crazy."

Allie's head grew a little swishy at the wonder of it all. "It is crazy. I mean, I prayed for you guys, but I never expected this. Things like this just don't happen."

"I guess God had a pretty special plan in mind for our little group." Rain beamed.

A picture of Professor Robinson with his wire rimmed glasses and tweed jacket flashed in Allie's mind. "You know...now that I think of it, I know one person who would have guessed."

"Really?"

"Yeah. It didn't seem right to bring it up before, but Professor Robinson is a Christian. After the semester finished, he told Andy and me that God laid that project on his heart a decade ago, and that around thirty people have gotten saved during or shortly after taking his class."

Rain let go of Allie. "What? He never said a word about religion."

"That's what I said."

"That really is crazy."

"It kind of makes sense, though. According to him, all you need to do is get people talking and asking the right questions. He trusts God to bring the truth to the surface."

"That's cool."

"I thought so, and Andy's pretty much made the good professor his new best friend." Allie giggled, recalling the unlikely duo.

"Hey, I think he's teaching a few doors down. Let's go tell him." Rain bounced and clapped like a little girl despite her huge belly.

"He would absolutely love that. We need to hurry, though."

"No worries. Everyone's used to me being late, and they'll just figure I was a bad influence on you."

"You are!" Allie said as they rushed toward the hall.

"Dork!" Rain bumped Allie aside with her ample hip and beat her through the doorway.

Allie smiled after her zany friend, still in awe. Of course, in all the excitement they hadn't discussed James, or the baby, or Rain's living arrangements. Allie had been the one who told Rain she could come to God just as she was and trust him to clean her up, but she had a feeling that this situation was likely to get messier before it improved. She grimaced and shot up a prayer for her new Christian sister—and an extra one for Sarah while she was at it.

TWENTY

Layla floated into her bungalow where she was met by pulsing Christian rock music and giggling teenyboppers, which fit her current mood just fine. Ever since Rain accepted Christ earlier in the week, Layla's feet had barely hit the floor. She even managed to stop worrying about whether or not she should go home for a while. Instead, she had put the issue in God's hands and was staying open to his guidance. After checking with her professors, getting away for a week or two seemed feasible, but she didn't want to rush into anything.

"Hey, Layla!" Britney, Cara, and Chelsea all managed to shout at once, and then they fell back into giggles over the coincidence.

"Jinx, you owe me a soda," Britney shouted, pointing to Cara with her free hand.

"No fair! I was just about to say that, but I was choking laughing," came back Cara.

"I want grape. No, Dr. Pepper. No, wait, it's coming to me. Root beer! But I want Barq's with the bite." Britney raised her arms over her head in triumph.

Cara turned to Chelsea. "I think you owe the soda."

"Sorry, I'm broke," Chelsea snatched a few Cheetos from a giant bowl on the coffee table.

Britney huffed, pushing wild red tresses from her heart-shaped face. "Don't give me that. You just brought home three pairs of jeans and a purse from the mall."

Chelsea snapped her blond razor cut hair with way more drama than the situation warranted. "Exactly. And now I'm broke."

"You owe me a soda anyway. And you too. A case each." Britney jumped up on the couch cushions and began to bounce.

"Do not!" the brunette Cara yelled, planting her hands on her slender hips.

"Do too!"

"Do not!" Chelsea agreed.

"Sounds like you're outnumbered, Britney, and good thing." Layla laughed. "The last thing you girls need is more soda. You all have way too much energy. Maybe you should go jogging or something."

"I have an even better idea!" Britney yelled in a singsong voice, holding her hands over her head as she bounded off the couch and back to the floor.

"Dance party!" her partners in crime shouted in unison.

Cara ripped Layla's backpack from her shoulder and threw it on the counter dividing the kitchen from the living room. Then she whisked Layla into the raucous fray.

Layla allowed herself to revel in the moment and in the joy of her new Christian sister Rain, which had buoyed her spirits this week. From what she'd heard, most Christian converts floated around in a fanatical sort of euphoria for months on end. In Layla's case, though, she had struggled from the beginning to keep her thoughts focused on God in order to maintain her joy and peace. Her life had been at stake, her future. She risked so much to accept Christ. Of course it had been worth it—incredibly, wonderfully worth it—but it had been a challenge too. She had paid, was still paying, a huge price to come to Christ.

Not that it felt like it at this moment as she bounced and wiggled to the Christian rock music with her new friends in her own home down the street from her college. She just didn't want to accept that it might come at the cost of her family's love.

But watching Rain walk down that aisle...witnessing the joy and wonder on her face...listening to the sincerity in her voice as she followed Pastor Mike in a prayer of commitment to Christ in front of the whole congregation... With startling clarity, it had all brought back that night Layla first met Jesus.

As she thought about it more, she realized Rain might have to pay a price too. Layla was well aware of the Bible's restrictions on sex outside of marriage. She had respected that about Christianity even before she had understood much about the faith, but what would that mean for Rain and James? And how about the instruction not to marry an unbeliever? It kind of seemed like a no-win situation.

Maybe each Christian had to take a risk to follow Jesus. Maybe everyone had to give up something along the way. No one ever said the Christian walk would be easy. How had Allie put it last year? Something about God being more interested in their character than their comfort.

Swiping her now damp bangs from her forehead, she paused a moment to take a breath. Chelsea bumped her with a hip to get her dancing again. She managed to keep up the pace for another whole song. These girls were way younger than her, though, and she was beginning to feel the difference.

When her phone called out Mom's special ring, Layla was happy to head to the quiet of her room to answer it.

She clicked the accept button and pushed the door shut to block out the deluge of noise from the living room at the same time. "Hi, Mom."

"Layla, my love! Oh, I am so glad to hear your voice. I have missed you. But what is all that racket?"

"Those are my roommates. Well, three of them. I guess the other two are at class."

Mom paused before continuing. "You sound so happy."

"I am."

"If you are happy, I suppose I will be happy." Mom chuckled. How Layla had missed her throaty laugh.

Layla plopped into the pale-green spherical chair she had bought to replace the pink one she loved so much while living with her aunt and uncle. She tucked her knees to her chest and hugged them with her free arm. "And I'm very happy that we're getting along so well these days."

"Me too. All this trouble with Fatima." Mom tsked. "It makes me remember what matters in life. So sad. All of it. The police, they find nothing still."

"That means there's still hope. Right?"

"Yes, I suppose we can be looking at it like this. Hope is always a good thing. But..."

Layla fought to keep her muscles from tensing at the foreboding tone in Mom's voice. "But what?"

"Please don't misunderstand. I know I've been harping on you about coming home all year, but this is different. We're so worried. Oh my baby, my Layla, my love, *habibti*." Mom spun out into a string of Arabic endearments.

Layla heard a scuffle in the background. "Give me the phone," came Dad's voice from a distance. "Layla?"

"Hi, Dad."

"Is everything okay down there?"

"Of course."

"What your mother was trying to say is that we're worried about you. Both of us. We're concerned the Maaloufs might show up there looking for Fatima, and if that happens, we want you far away when it does."

It's time. The words echoed in Layla's heart.

"I know you don't want to miss your classes, but I really wish you'd come home for a week or two until this blows over. Aunt CiCi hasn't been feeling too well, and she's asking for you. You can use that as an excuse. What do you think, princess?" She could tell he was trying not to beg, yet his desperation came through loud and clear.

Despite his obvious fear, peace settled over Layla like a comforting cloak. "I already cleared it with my professors, Dad. Go ahead and book me a flight."

"Praise be to Allah!"

She heard her mom squeal in delight in the background along with some chatter about tabouli, hummus, and baklava. No doubt the menu for Layla's welcome home dinner. Her mouth watered at the thought of homemade Middle Eastern food.

She only half listened as Dad worked out the plans. He would take care of it for her. He always did. She would receive a detailed itinerary including weather and packing instructions by the evening. She would just have to be careful not to get too comfortable with this homecoming. It would be easy to be sucked back into the controlling, albeit secure, world that was her old life.

Sarah struggled past the haze of sleep, but when she realized the rumpled sheets and bed were not her own, she bolted up, clutching the fabric to her chest. Her heart rate sped, and she could barely catch her breath.

Beside her stretched Jesse Kinsella.

She calmed only a bit—at least that explained where she was. At least she was safe in the garage apartment attached to his aunt's house where he'd lived for the past five years. But as memories from the night before filtered through her mind in shadowy tableaux, she pressed a hand to her mouth. Bile rose in her throat, from too much liquor or regret—she couldn't quite say which. All she knew for certain was that she felt dirty all over and far too grown-up.

She resisted the driving urge to dash for the shower and wash herself clean. What time was it? The clock on the nightstand read 6:05.

The sun filtering low through the blinds from the east confirmed that must be morning. She had a vague recollection of calling her mom and saying the study session had gone so late she would have to stay at her friend Erica's house, which meant she wasn't in trouble, but she couldn't go home either.

Still, she needed to get away from this place. She needed time and space to sort everything out, to sift through the hazy details of her memories. Spotting her clothes in the corner, she hurried and pulled them onto her shivering form. The shower would have to wait until she got home, until she whiled away at least another hour or two at a coffee shop, despite the filthy feeling that threatened to overwhelm her as she remembered the horrible things she'd once thought, once said, about girls...like her.

This wasn't supposed to happen. She thought she'd had everything under control. Yes, she loved Jesse. Yes, she had been enjoying these new experiences, but she hadn't meant to take a step she couldn't undo. Once her shirt was safely buttoned, she took a moment to twist her purity ring in a circle around her left ring finger. She had promised herself to Jesus and to her husband alone. This ring was meant to be a present to him on her wedding night. Now the pink heart sparkled at her with a mocking glint. Worthless. Ruined. Just like her.

She tore it from her finger and stuffed it into the back pocket of her jeans. As much as she couldn't bear to look at it, if she threw it away, how could she ever explain its loss to her parents?

Of course, the ring was the least of her losses. She studied Jesse's sleeping form again, and the reality of the situation struck her like a bucket of cold water.

He must have sensed her staring because he stirred and rose lazily to an elbow. "Hey, gorgeous, where you rushing off to? Your parents aren't expecting you for hours."

"I don't feel good. I need to go."

"You didn't drink that much last night." He got out of bed wearing pajama bottoms and headed toward a small kitchenette where he pulled a clear bottle from the cabinet. "Nothing cures a hangover like a little more liquor." He poured the liquid into a Redskins shot glass and walked it to her.

Suddenly she realized nothing would ever make her feel quite right, quite like herself again. No matter what, she would take this night with her wherever she went. But at least a shot would take the edge off and soothe the tension about to burst through her skin.

She whisked it from his hand and downed it in one gulp. Heat flowed through her, loosening her muscles.

Jesse scooped her to his chest. "And this helps too." His mouth settled against hers, and for the moment all thoughts of leaving vanished from her cloudy mind.

TWENTY-ONE

Rain could barely wait to head to The Gathering this evening. She scooped her Bible and coat from the kitchen table and headed for the door. She'd been antsy like a child all day, giddy with anticipation to go to church and learn about her newfound faith, to meet more of her new brothers and sisters in Christ.

Not that she had let her excitement show too much during the week. Although she'd been buoyed on that spiritual cloud, she'd done her best to behave normally around James, only allowing her enthusiasm full reign when she talked with Allie or Layla. Fortunately, between their house guest, the paper-thin walls of the apartment, and the growing swell of her belly, Rain had been able to avoid physical intimacy with James.

She wasn't sure how to deal with that. There just wasn't an easy, obvious answer. Although she'd prayed, she hadn't gotten any clear instructions from God yet either.

"Dear sister? Rain?" The soft words came from Fatima's bedroom, but Rain barely recognized her voice. "Could you maybe come here for a moment?"

She hadn't heard that broken, timid timbre from Fatima since their first few days together. Not hesitating for a moment, she hurried to her.

As she entered the room, she spotted her friend curled in upon herself in the corner where her bed met the wall. Fatima's skin displayed a pale, unhealthy tinge. Sweat beaded at her brow.

"Oh no! What's the matter, sweetie?"

"I'm scared about my brothers." Fatima eyed Rain's belongings. "Oh, you are leaving for church. I forgot." Her eyes grew wild with terror.

Tossing the items onto the foot of the bed, Rain said, "I was hoping to go. I really enjoy my time there."

"But James is gone too?"

"He is. He had to work. I think you'll be all right for a little while." She reached out to take Fatima's hand. In Rain's anticipation about The Gathering, she hadn't realized Fatima might be upset to be left alone. Of course she'd been by herself at the apartment over the past month—Fatima wasn't a child—but not since matters had changed this week.

When Layla came over yesterday to say good-bye, Fatima had put on a brave face. But although Layla never specifically mentioned Fatima's brothers, Fatima must have put things together and realized they would be headed this way.

After a moment clearly spent trying to collect herself, Fatima clutched to Rain's sweater and began to shriek. "Don't leave me! Please don't! Rain, you cannot leave me here alone!"

Fatima's shrieking turned to screaming despite Rain's shushes and soothing pats. Then Fatima began to wheeze as if she couldn't take enough oxygen into her lungs and to shiver all over, deteriorating into a full-blown panic attack. Rain pulled her hard against her chest and could feel the pound of Fatima's rapid heartbeat through the layers of fabric separating them.

Without warning, Fatima tugged away, clawing at her chest and dashing for the window. She threw it open and tried to gulp down the fresh air, but she couldn't seem to drag it into her lungs. Rain caught her from behind and supported her, fearing she might faint and tumble out the opening.

It felt like forever that they stood next to the window, but eventually Rain managed to settle Fatima enough to coax her back to bed. Fatima's raging emotions mellowed into a steady cry. It seemed she cried for hours. Years and years of tears, every heartache, every beating, every ugly word that had been flung at her during a lifetime with her abusive family poured out in a healing flow onto Rain's nurturing chest.

So much for going to church tonight. Right now Fatima mattered most. Her fear and desperation filled the room with a presence as palpable as God's had been just last week at The Gathering. Jesus had consumed Rain's thoughts ever since, but she hadn't paused to give much consideration to the concept of Satan, God's enemy. If asked, she wouldn't have been able to say for sure that she even believed in him, but she sensed him in the bedroom with them right in that moment, a tangible evil, clawing at Fatima's soul.

Rain wiped damp hair away from Fatima's beautiful brow and began to pray under her breath. She might not know much about this new Christian faith, but she had witnessed the power of prayer. Allie took authority over Satan on that night that they faced Layla's knife-wielding uncle, and they had all come out unscathed. In her own faltering words, Rain attempted to do the same.

Although Fatima was not a Christian, Rain felt certain deep in her heart that God would reach out to her precious friend in this way. And sure enough, she felt his supernatural comfort falling over them like the softest fleece blanket.

Fatima's sobs melted into soft whimpers and sniffles. Before long she would probably fall asleep, but there was no way Rain would leave her tonight. While the young woman had found her humor and strength, that wounded butterfly Rain had seen on their first night together was still closer to the surface than she had realized.

Rain nuzzled her chin against Fatima's silky hair. Her friend's chest rose and fell now in a rhythmic manner that suggested she had indeed fallen asleep, but Rain stayed put and continued praying for this priceless soul in her arms.

Mo tapped his foot and crossed his arms over his chest as he impatiently awaited his turn to talk to Pastor Mike. Was this lady's latest knitting project really that important? Weren't there already more than enough infinity scarves in the world? He caught himself before he growled aloud.

A boy of about eight shot a look of censure at Mo. Great, even a child realized he was behaving badly tonight. He stopped his foot mid-tap and managed to relax his stance a bit, but he didn't bother trying to fix his attitude. This was far too important.

The woman droned on about colors and types of yarn. He resisted the urge to push her aside. More than a week had passed since he'd caught a single sight of Layla. Sure, it was his fault he'd missed church last week to pull an extra shift, but he usually saw her at a distance once or twice during the week at school. He had wanted to stop by the soup kitchen but couldn't get away from the restaurant. Now Sunday was here and no Layla, no Allie. Not even Rain, although she had accepted Christ just last week. The woman should be here!

A twinge of guilt niggled at him. Rain should be in church for her, not for him. He let out a slow, controlled breath. On Monday when she'd caught him to tell him the good news about her conversion, he'd been thrilled for her, and already he was thinking of no one but himself. This whole situation had proven that he wasn't yet as strong of a believer as he'd imagined.

By the time Mike gave him his full attention, Mo was about to explode with worry.

"Layla's missing," he blurted.

Mike grasped his shoulder in that brotherly way of his. "I'm great. Thanks for asking, and you?"

Mo grimaced.

"Relax, buddy. She's fine. She went home to visit her parents for a week or two."

All of the tension and worry Mo had experienced during the past week crystallized into red-hot anger. "And she told you, not me?" He was so mad he could spit. "Are you for real?"

"Calm down. I get that it hurts your feelings but—"

"My feelings! Forget my feelings. She's being completely unfair, and ridiculous, and stupid, and—"

"How about I stop you before you say something you regret?" Mike's voice turned firm and low, no doubt the one he used to correct his kids. "Mo, I am her pastor, and she had every right to tell me. You are not her boyfriend, and she had no obligation to inform you."

Unsure whether to aim his mounting anger at Layla or at Mike, who was treating him like a naughty child, Mo took a minute to collect himself. "Why did she just take off like that?"

Mike glanced around before continuing. "Her parents are worried about the situation with Fatima. I guess they don't know where Fatima is, but they suspect her brothers are on their way here to look for her."

And at that his anger diminished by half. "Oh... She did the right thing, but she should have told me. She was supposed to keep me updated."

"I don't know what to say. She must have forgotten."

The woman was supposed to be in love with him. How could she just forget? Not cool, Layla. His looping emotions of the past half hour made their way back to worry— but a different sort of worry.

In his struggles to win her back, had he finally managed to push her away?

"Layla, *habibti*, dinnertime!" Mom's voice filtered through Layla's bedroom door.

She pushed herself up to sitting on her satin quilt and closed her book—not a textbook for once, not even the nonfiction book Allie had given her or a Bible. For the first time since the summer, Layla had been luxuriating in a novel. Mom had met her at the door with the newest Khaled Hosseini offering, no doubt hoping to remind her of her Muslim roots and her love of Muslim literature.

But Layla hadn't resisted. Hosseini might have been raised a Muslim like her, but he certainly had his own take on the world. He always helped her filter through culture and tradition to find what really mattered and made sense.

So far this novel had helped give her the perspective she'd been needing, as if she'd sat down and had a good long talk with someone who understood, the sort of talk she used to have with Mo. This author never disparaged his Islamic brothers and sisters, and he honored the positive aspects of the religion, but he never hesitated to ask the tough questions either.

Layla had asked those tough questions last semester, but now she was home, in her very own room, on her very own bed. She ran her hand over the satin patchwork comforter in shades of purple and cream. She examined the plush pale carpet contrasting with the deep plum walls.

Her gaze trailed over the white crown molding to the patterned ten-foot ceiling. She stood and meandered to her sitting room with its Victorian settee. The suite featured a spacious bathroom and a walk-in closet larger than the room she shared with Allie. In fact, the entire bungalow would probably fit in Layla's private part of this house.

She was glad the girls had no idea how rich she really was. It would make them uncomfortable, which was exactly why she'd made Dad get her that slightly used Mustang convertible and left her Lexus here at home. She remembered how the girls had been blown away by her uncle's more modest house in Virginia Beach.

What would they think of this one? Like the Maalouf's, her parents owned an entire floor of a condominium complex, and while both buildings might show some wear on the outside, they were immaculate once you entered the ornate doorways.

"Layla! *Ya'allah!*" Her mother's voice came more sharply, hurrying her along. "Your father is waiting."

Layla headed down the long hallway, her slippered feet padding against the marble floors. Last night's dinner out had been tense with all of her older brothers and sisters and their many children in attendance. Mom had forced her to wear the veil, as she had over the winter break, so as not to confuse her nieces and nephews.

She wished she could speak the truth to the kids about Jesus and about love. They were all still pretty young, though. At this point, their parents had every right to guide their spiritual educations. She supposed eventually a time would come when she could talk to them, maybe when they were teenagers and questioned her on their own.

She passed the enormous living room with its two-story domed ceiling. That area alone broke into the floor above her, taking about the space of a small apartment. Then she trekked by the formal dining room that sat twenty and onward to the more casual section of the house. Mom and Dad were already seated in the cozy, rounded booth in a corner of the eat-in kitchen. Although they had a full-time maid, the kitchen was Mom's domain alone. To the other side of the kitchen lay the family room, attached game room, and patio-sized balcony.

"There's our girl." Dad's face glowed as he smiled to her.

"Oh, it is so good you are home." Mom bustled over to give her a hug, showering her with warmth.

Dad stood to embrace her and drop a kiss on the top of her head as well. Layla felt like a little girl again, safe, loved, and cared for.

She slid into the booth between them and bit her lip. She could hardly believe she had stirred up so much trouble for these wonderful people. God had blessed her with amazing parents. This house, this family—it would be a lot to give up. Of course her Christian faith was well worth it, but hopefully she would never have to choose.

That image of Mo and their future children seated at this very table flashed in her mind. She needed to keep believing for a positive outcome. Guilt jabbed at her. She hadn't even told him she'd come home. She convinced herself it would be better if he appeared confused if the Maalouf brothers questioned him—that Salaam would keep her posted if they showed up—but the truth was, she just couldn't bring herself to dial Mo's number. She really should at least text him after dinner, but she probably wouldn't.

An uncomfortable moment passed as they settled down to dinner. Layla longed to bow her head and bless the food, but her mother passed around plates and her father began stuffing his mouth with pita bread before she found her courage. Of course, they had already prayed before dinner and saw no need now.

Tonight's meal of eggplant covered with meat, pine nuts, and thick tomato sauce was one of her favorites. The unique blend of Lebanese pepper scented the air with cinnamon and other spices. She heaped her plate with rice then smothered it with the main course, adding plenty of pita and hummus on the side.

She silently offered up a quick thanks before she took her first mouthful of the delightful concoction. "Oh, Mom, this is amazing," she said with a groan. Layla never had time to cook meals like this at college, and she didn't have the best culinary skills anyway.

"You see how good it is to be home." Mom's grin spread from ear to ear. Nothing made the woman happier than cooking compliments.

Layla couldn't help but return the grin. "It's wonderful."

"And you got plenty of studying done today?" Dad asked.

"Yes. It went really well. I didn't realize so many of the lectures and resources were available online."

Mom's eyes sparkled at that. Layla caught a wordless exchanged between her parents, concluding with a sharp glare from her father that piqued Layla's curiosity.

"You can't blame a woman for wondering." Mom snapped her linen napkin and laid it over her lap.

Although she knew she'd regret it, Layla couldn't resist asking. "Wondering what?"

Dad frowned.

"What?" Mom raised her fork in the air. "I said nothing, just like I promised. She's the one who asked."

Layla's normally longsuffering father emitted a low groan.

"Dad, what is it? Just tell me."

Dad took a deep breath. "Ever since we talked about you coming home, your mother has been wondering about these online classes you mentioned. She didn't know much about distance education. She hadn't really heard of it outside of those cheap trade school classes they advertise on television."

Mom nodded her support, encouraging him to continue.

"She wondered if you might be able to earn your degree this way."

"And live at home where you belong," Mom stated the final conclusion that Dad had been avoiding.

Layla managed to catch her sigh on the inhale before it escaped. Why hadn't she seen this coming? Now more than ever, she needed the space from her family. If she lived here, she would never be able to grow in her new Christian faith.

"I don't know, Mom. I think they mostly just have general education type classes online, maybe some introductory stuff, but engineering is a tough major. I need that face-to-face time with my professors." In all honesty, Layla didn't know whether or not engineering was part of ODU's growing online program, and she had no desire to find out.

"But perhaps?" Mom persisted. "There might be a chance?"

Dad shrugged apologetically.

Layla had brought this on herself by mentioning the whole online issue. Tension caught hold of her neck and began to work its way down her shoulders and back. "Let's not start all this again. Okay, Mom? I thought we were finally getting along. I thought we found a system that was working for all of us."

Mom huffed and stabbed at her eggplant. "Did we?"

Despite their cease fire, the issues between them still brewed. As much as she hated to ruin this lovely dinner, Layla supposed this was as good a time as any to deal with them.

TWENTY-TWO

Layla slid her plate aside. "Now that you mention it, I regret letting you push me into wearing my veil when we went out for dinner last night. I felt dishonest. I don't want to pretend that I'm someone I'm not."

"Your brothers and sister know the truth," Mom said.

"Trust me." Dad shook his head. "Your mother has given them all an earful on the subject. Many times."

"What?" Mom stabbed at her food without actually scooping up a bite. "I need someone to talk to. It is a lot to deal with."

Layla had wondered about that. No one had brought up her conversion with so many children always around. Over the holidays, and then again last night, Layla had waited for one of her siblings to pull her aside and give her a lecture. "So what do they think about it?" Layla dared to ask.

"Saeed is not happy. He is worried about the children being confused. This is why we insisted you wear the *hijab*," Mom said.

At thirty-five, Saeed was the oldest brother of the family. Layla had been a late-life surprise for her parents, and Saeed had left for college when she was still a small girl. These days, he had his own business and home, along with an Islamic wife and three perfect children. "He never said anything to me." Of course Layla had never really been friends with him. He was just part of that big collection of people called family.

Dad tapped the butt of his knife on the table. "I asked him to let me handle this. You know his temper, and you don't respond well to it."

That was probably the reason they had never forged much of a relationship. She was closer to Yasmeen, who was married with four children of her own, and to Abdul, who had recently gotten engaged to a nice girl back in Lebanon. "And the others?"

Mom stood from the table and stomped to the giant refrigerator, where she buried her head and shoved food items around.

Finally Dad answered, "They're on your side. They think you should be allowed to be an independent adult and make your own decisions about religion."

Something crashed in the fridge.

"As you might have guessed, your mother is not pleased." Dad went back to his meal.

It made sense that they would support her. Yasmeen's husband was not very devout, and Abdul had minored in religion in college. He was fascinated by other belief systems. Suddenly she longed to talk to him about everything. Might God be reaching out to him as well?

Mom plopped back into her seat. "Hmph. You will wear the *hijab* in public and that is final, when we go shopping and to parties and to the mosque."

"To the mosque?" Layla's words came out with a squeak. Her fork fell to the table as her appetite fled. She hadn't gone to mosque over the holidays and had assumed her parents would honor her wishes in that area again. They hadn't forced her to join them in family prayers either. Why now?

Dad put a warm hand over hers and gave it a squeeze. "Settle down, princess. The whole reason you are home is to remove suspicion from you and keep you safe. Now is not the right time to declare your new Christian faith. People must believe that everything is normal. We need to get you out in public as much as possible to remove all doubts."

She could hardly argue that logic. Picking up her fork again and fiddling with it, she debated her response. It wouldn't hurt anything, she supposed. Dad was right—this was not the time to bring negative attention to herself.

And she wouldn't have to lie. It wasn't as if anyone would ask. She could attend mosque and fake the prayers. Her face would be down often enough that she wouldn't have to say the words. "Okay, Dad, but just until things blow over. I don't feel good about living a double life."

"I understand." He smiled that warm, glowing smile again. Despite their disagreement, she still spotted the pride in his eyes that always made her feel so special.

Just a little longer. What could it hurt?

Allie forced one foot in front of the other as she made her way through the hall of the bungalow. She felt as though she was swimming upstream through a thick sea of noise. The teenyboppers had thrown another one of their sleepover bashes. It was barely 7:00 a.m. and already—or was it still—the stereo was blasting with Christian rock music. Although she had been exhausted enough to sleep through it last night, this morning she stood no chance. She needed to get up for a performance at a women's brunch anyway. Piercing giggles split the air as she stepped into the living room.

Coffee. She needed coffee, and quick.

In that moment she envied Layla, wishing she could be a thousand miles away with disgruntled parents. Anything was better than this. Then again, if that were true she could always move home with her own parents. Scratch that thought. She'd stay right here, thank you very much.

Girls in colorful pajamas and spongy curlers draped across the furniture much like their clothes and slippers strewn about the room.

Sleeping bags covered the floor, although Allie doubted much sleeping had occurred.

She stumbled to the kitchen and pulled out her favorite fuchsia oversized mug. Deciding instant would get her out of the room faster, she filled the mug with water. As she searched out the instant coffee, she thought she heard a rhythmic thud, but it was hard to tell for sure over the clatter of the music.

Tugging aside the yellow chintz curtain, she peeked out and froze in place. She wanted to shout, to warn the girls, to grab a knife, a lamp, anything! But her mouth wouldn't open. She couldn't even crack a sound. Her feet felt like lead, superglued to the kitchen floor.

The scene on the front porch could easily be mistaken for an episode of *The Sopranos*. Three tough-looking guys in black leather coats and with slicked back hair and sunglasses pounded on the frail wooden door. It bent with each crash.

Although she still felt stuck in freeze frame, she watched her favorite mug slip from her fingers in slow motion and crash to the floor, shattering in hot pink shards across the black and white checkerboard tile as water splashed everywhere.

No one seemed to notice over the din. Although, she finally heard someone shout, "Door!" and watched Britney bounce in that direction.

While she dreaded the innocent young girl facing the mafia outside, Allie still couldn't find her voice. She sucked in a breath to try and yell to her, but it stuck in her throat. Maybe it was for the best. Britney knew nothing about Fatima. She would honestly be clueless.

Allie began mumbling scriptures about protection that Andy had collected and e-mailed to her after Fatima arrived.

He will give his angels charge over you to keep you in all your ways.

On her way to the door, Britney knocked over a soda. "Shoot!" she hollered and grabbed a robe to wipe her foot and sop up the liquid.

No evil can come near you, no harm can come through your door.

The pounding repeated.

"Chill out!" Britney said. "I'm coming."

Then Allie's own prayer came to her lips. *Father God, confuse their minds. Confound the enemy.*

It seemed that years had passed between the moment that Allie spotted the men and the moment when Britney finally opened the door. Allie sidled her way to the opening between the kitchen and living room to watch the exchange, avoiding shards of fuchsia.

"Hi," Britney said in her normal perky tone. "Sorry I took so long. I spilled a soda. Nasty."

The shortest, although toughest looking, of the three men leaned into the doorway, but he seemed hesitant to cross the threshold. He glanced about the room and his eyes, hazel eyes just like Fatima's, grew huge. "I think, perhaps, we should not be here." He scanned Britney in her shorty pajamas. "Would you, maybe, like to cover up?"

Britney giggled. "You must be new to the beach area. This is covered up around here. Can I help you? If you're selling stuff, you're out of luck. We're all broke."

Squeals erupted as a pillow fight broke out.

"I am...we are..." The spokesman of the group attempted to compose himself. "Is there a woman named Fatima here?" The look of horror on his face clearly said he hoped she was far, far away from these heathen infidels.

Britney shrugged. "I've never heard of her."

The pillow war waged on. The tall guy craned his neck to get a better peek at the insane scene.

"How about a Layla Al-Rai?"

"Oh yeah. She lives here." Britney leaned flirtily against the door. "You friends of hers? I was wondering when she'd bring some grown men around this place. Allie is our other older roommate, but she's engaged."

"Can I speak to Layla please?" Impatience tinged his voice as red crept to his cheeks.

"Nah, she went to Detroit for the week. Her aunt's sick."

"What about this Allie?"

"She's here."

A pillow went flying into a giant bowl of popcorn perched on the corner of the couch. The bowl flew into the air, flipping several times before raining yellow puffs across the room. All the girls shrieked again.

Britney shook her head. "Hold on. I'll get Allie."

As she walked to the kitchen, one of the guys said, "This was a bad idea."

Then another one elbowed him. "Dude!" He pointed to the hallway.

Allie glanced at the hallway but didn't see a thing.

They all tensed and stuck hands in their coats.

Guns?

Allie was about to scream a warning when teenybopper Chelsea shot up from the couch in a green goopy mask with cucumbers over her eyes and did the screaming for her.

The three guys jumped at least a foot. "They're crazy," said the leader of the pack. "Let's get out of here."

"Allie, some guys want to talk to you." Britney bounced from foot to foot.

"Not anymore." Allie pointed to the empty doorway and sighed. They were gone.

She surveyed the chaotic scene before her again and began to crack up laughing. God had answered her prayers in the most hysterical way possible. Falling against Britney and hugging her, she said, "You girls are so awesome! I don't know what I ever did without you."

TWENTY-THREE

A few nights later, Layla curled up on a butter-soft leather couch in the family room and tuned into *The Muslim Woman's Show* on the huge flat-screen TV. Middle Easterners sure did love their technology.

Sister Amani's encouraging face popped onto the screen. A different program, *Daring Questions* with Brother Rasheed, had initially prompted Layla's quest for the truth, but since she'd come to Christ, this show seemed to better address her concerns. Although Layla didn't have Arabic satellite reception in Norfolk, she often streamed the programs on her laptop.

Amani welcomed the viewers and opened the very hard topic of sexual abuse toward women in the Middle East. Thank goodness Fatima had never dealt with anything like that, although if she were married off to some stranger in Saudi Arabia, the possibility would become all too real. Layla found the topic depressing, although important. As it didn't apply to her, she considered changing to a more relaxing show, but Amani always brought every issue back to Jesus, hope, and healing. Who knew, maybe Mom would pick up on something as she fussed in the kitchen that would speak to her heart. Or better yet, maybe Mom would join her and leave the dishes to the maid.

The past few days had gone well enough, other than the disturbing report from Allie back in Norfolk. Salaam didn't get word to Layla until it was too late this time. It seemed the Maalouf brothers had dragged cousin Dani along with them and were keeping a close eye on him. At least everyone was safe for the moment. Rather than focus on her frustrating inability to help, Layla stared at the television again.

After a while, Dad joined her. He sank into the couch on the other end and observed the program for a moment without saying a word. She noticed he had changed from his dress slacks and tie that he wore to the engineering firm into a worn pair of jeans and a soft polo. Like so many Lebanese men, he kept his dark hair cropped short so that you hardly noticed his balding head. Unlike most Muslim males, his gentle, barely lined face was clean-shaven, other than his evening shadow of course.

Finally, he held out his hand, palm up, and nodded to the remote control. Layla tossed it to him, and he clicked off the television set.

"Can we talk for a few minutes instead?" he asked.

"Sure. It was a sad episode anyway."

"Layla, *habibti*, winter break was a rough time for all of us, but I want you to know that I'm trying to understand things from your perspective." He indicated the TV. "I've been watching the program you suggested, *Daring Questions*. This Brother Rasheed speaks with much truth and love. I've been studying more about the prophet, *Isa Masi*, as well."

Dad used the traditional Islamic name for Jesus. Surrounded as she was by American Christians, Layla had never really thought of him that way. Even Rasheed opted for the Arabic Christian term *Yashua*, but she appreciated that Dad was making an effort.

"And?"

"What can I say? Isa's teachings are beautiful. He was an amazing person, and this is why he is mentioned in the teachings of Islam as well. You cannot forget that you were raised in a Muslim home full of love and peace."

Layla pulled her knees to her chest, forming a shield for her vulnerable heart. "Exactly, Dad. You raised me with those values, but I didn't see them in Islam. I don't see nearly enough of them in the Muslim community around me, and I certainly don't see them when I visit Lebanon."

Dad turned a knee toward her. "But that doesn't mean they don't exist. I have showed you those verses in the *Qur'an* since you were a child."

"And you've ignored so many others. If a religion is true, then all of it is true. You shouldn't just pick and choose. Besides, Brother Rasheed teaches that those verses of love and peace are from early in Mohammad's ministry and that they were abrogated, superseded, by later ones of war and hate."

"I've heard this as well." Dad rubbed a hand down his face. "But it is not simply about religion. It is also about culture, heritage, identity. You are Middle Eastern. You are Lebanese. And you are Muslim. You can't simply change these facts."

"I'm still a Muslim in a way. I'm a Muslim background believer now. That's what we call ourselves."

"Who is this *we*? Mo? I thought you broke up with him."

Layla resisted the urge to pound her head against her knees.

Mom peeked around the corner, but when Layla shot her a look, she scurried away.

"I did break up with him. The *we* is all the people who have faced the ugly truth about Islam and turned to Jesus instead."

Dad stood and shoved his hands in his pockets, pacing a few steps away from her. "You can't let someone fanatical like Brother Rasheed ruin everything you've been raised to believe. Just because the Middle Eastern culture is backward and hasn't caught up with the twentieth century doesn't mean you need to throw away our whole religion. Surely the Bible contains some archaic ideas. Didn't the Jews slaughter entire races?"

"That's in the Old Testament, Dad. Jesus brought a new covenant of grace and forgiveness."

"You cannot just deny who you are!"

Layla allowed his words to hang in the air for a moment as she sent up a prayer. Perhaps God was working on Dad's heart as well. Once a Muslim started asking the hard questions and facing the truth, it grew difficult to remain unchanged.

Dad took a deep breath and turned to her. "I didn't mean to start an argument. Actually, I wanted to present you with an idea that you might not have considered."

As his demeanor shifted, Layla relaxed and stretched her legs out from her curled position.

"Have you heard of something called the insider's movement?" Dad returned to the couch.

"A Muslim movement?"

"No, a Christian one."

Layla scanned her mind but came up blank. "I'm still pretty new to all of this."

"They speak to Muslims, but they have a different sort of approach. Unlike these new friends of yours, they don't think you have to stop being Muslim in order to become a Christian."

"I'm not sure that makes sense. I mean, no one actually told me that I had to stop being Muslim, but the two belief systems don't fit together. While we both say we worship the one God of heaven and earth, even the character of God in the two religions is very different."

"All of that aside, the point is that it's fine to stay culturally Muslim while still embracing Christian teaching."

She weighed this new idea. "I actually have been struggling with how to reconcile certain aspects of my culture that I love with Christianity."

"You see. Maybe you should read their literature. They say there's no need to stop attending mosque or prayers and that women can continue to veil. There's no reason to rip families apart or put people in danger over this. You can incorporate your Muslim traditions together with your new belief in Jesus."

Dad's suggestion sounded kind of like Rain's former multi-faith church. A little of this tossed in with a little of that. Forget the weird, radical stuff. Don't worry about truth. "I don't see how I could do that, Dad. Some of the Islamic prayers directly contradict my new beliefs."

"I'm sure they offer ways around that."

Ways around that? "I spent all last semester, my whole life really, searching for the truth. I don't want to compromise that just to keep the peace."

"It all depends on how you look at it. Does it really hurt to wear a little scarf around your head? Does Christianity forbid it? It would mean so terribly much to your mother."

What would Mo think? He had always encouraged her to follow her own heart on the issue of the veil. "For one thing, I've come to realize that the veil was a symbol of bondage for me. In my dream, Jesus took it from my head and set me free. I don't want to go back."

Dad reached out and patted Layla's knee. "But this time you would be doing it willingly, with a new understanding and a new purpose. You would be doing it out of love, not bondage. Christianity encourages modesty, right?"

Thoughts swirled in Layla's head, and she grew confused. How easy it would be to embrace this idea. How much simpler it would make her life. She struggled to straighten her reasoning and prayed that God would give her clarity. "You know, I see modesty differently now. It's not about hiding yourself. If it was, then all women should wear the *niqab*. Modesty is more about not drawing undue attention to yourself, and I can tell you firsthand that nothing draws attention in this American culture like the veil."

"I really don't care if you wear it at school, but here in Detroit the opposite is true. You draw attention from our Muslim friends when you don't wear it."

Layla could think of no argument for that, except that she longed to live a life of authenticity and integrity.

Dad smiled at her, but she noticed tightness around his eyes. "Like I said, you make some good points, but please consider my points too."

She stared at her hands clutched in her lap. "I don't know, Dad."

"All I'm asking is that you think about it. Your mother and I would be so happy if you could accept this way of combining Islam and Christianity. Who knows, this might even be a middle ground where we all could come together."

Those were indeed good points, and if Layla's parents would take even one step closer to Christ, might that be worth her taking a step backward? She had grown so tired of disappointing them. Although this situation with Fatima had minimized the tension, she could still sense it at times, simmering on low and ready to boil over at any moment. It would be wonderful to have this thing settled in a way that pleased everyone. To be a dutiful, respectable daughter as she'd always considered herself.

But something still felt off about the whole idea. Layla sighed. "I'll consider it. That's all I can promise right now."

"Good." Dad stood and walked out of the room, but he returned a minute later with a stack of books in his hands. "Here is the literature I mentioned. Investigate it for yourself."

She chuckled. Wasn't that what got them into this trouble? Despite their religion and background, Dad had always encouraged his children to investigate issues for themselves.

Layla took the books. They felt like Judas's kiss against her palms.

***

James observed Fatima as she sat watch at the window, her typical perch ever since they'd received Allie's bad news, but surely her brothers would never find her here. He couldn't think of any obvious connection, unless they tracked down every one of Layla's friends.

Today Fatima had on the same jeans and purple T-shirt she'd been wearing the first time he saw her, but her cuts had healed and her bruises had faded. The girl belonged in a painting with her quiet beauty—so fragile but so strong. She twirled golden hair around one finger as she watched the cars passing by.

When she showed up in his kitchen last month, he never expected to grow this attached. She really had become the little sister he always wanted. He recalled dreaming of a sibling to brighten his dreary childhood home, someone to love and who would love him back. But as he got older, he realized he would never wish his parents on anyone else. That was around the time he had decided that he would never bring a child into this cold, harsh world.

Of course that was before his counseling, and before Rain. Their home would be different. His gorgeous woman sat knitting on the couch, warming the room with her presence. The resulting blanket spread over her baby bump displayed what an awesome mother she would make. His gaze returned to Fatima. The way this broken girl had mended and blossomed under Rain's touch over the last few weeks proved it as well.

Fatima caught him staring at her. She giggled and gracefully fluttered her fingers in his direction, reminding him of the butterfly Rain so often called her. Then she turned her attention back out the window. What did she think about as she sat there? She used to pray to Allah on her balcony in Detroit. That's how she'd found her praying man. The poor guy must be torn up worrying about her. James didn't even want to imagine how he would feel if their situations were reversed.

He would do anything for this girl, fight for her, maybe even die for her if needed. His hand reflexively moved to his gun still in its holster from work the night before, although for now things seemed calm and safe enough.

No sooner had that thought flashed through his head than Fatima stiffened and gasped.

Rain was closer and still surprisingly nimble. "What is it?" In a flash, she ran to Fatima and put an arm around her shoulder as James traversed the room to join them.

For a moment Fatima didn't answer—seemed unable to answer. James followed her line of vision and found a fancy silver BMW that clearly did not belong in this neighborhood. As he watched, three rough looking men stepped out wearing black leather and sunglasses.

James sized up the men. Drug dealers maybe?

Fatima pointed to them and began to shiver. Her breathing turned to panting.

"Is that them, Fatima? You need to tell us." Rain wrapped both arms around her now.

The men stood huddled around the car for the moment. One short, compact guy was talking on a cell phone. Something about him struck James as oddly familiar. Darn it! It couldn't be.

"Bro...thers." Fatima finally managed to get out between her panic-stricken breaths.

"Dear God, no!" Rain whispered.

James sprang into action. "Step back from the window," he barked as he ran to the spare bedroom. He grabbed Fatima's purse and *niqab* and hurried back to the girls. Nothing else would give her away. From the kitchen counter he grabbed Rain's purse and keys as well.

"Here's the plan," he said, pressing himself to the wall by the window. "The second they enter the building, you two head down the fire escape. Rain, get her in the car and take her far away from here. You can come back for the rest of her stuff later."

"James," Fatima whispered. "I am so scared."

With a glance out the window, he went to her and pressed a kiss to her head. "Don't worry. We've got this." That protective instinct welled inside of him. No matter what, he would keep her safe, just like he would protect his own daughter someday. "You girls go to the bedroom now, in case they get up here quicker than expected."

James pressed himself to the wall again and peered out the window. The short guy got off the phone and nodded toward the building. He shared Fatima's profile and golden-brown hair.

In a loud whisper, James called to the girls in the other room. "Wait a minute...wait a minute."

TWENTY-FOUR

The three guys made their way toward the front door of the apartment complex. In that moment, James wished he and Rain had forked out the extra cash for a place with a security system.

He needed some sort of plan. Suddenly it hit him. He tugged off his work shirt and rumpled his dreadlocks. Then he pulled his gun from the holster, stuck it into the waistband of his jeans, and let his wife-beater undershirt fall over top. Adjusting his belt, he let his pants droop low on his hips. He wished he had some liquor to splash on himself, but even if he did, he wouldn't dare leave the window.

When Fatima's brothers entered the door downstairs, James called, "Now." He heard the window creaking and saw the girls climbing onto the fire escape. Hopefully they could get down the three stories quicker than the men could climb up.

The girls hurried as much as they could without making a ruckus. Rain checked the area before they ran for the beat up, old Volkswagen. Pride swelled in his chest. Those were his girls.

Low voices came from the hallway, followed a moment later by a threatening knock.

"Hold your horses," James called in a slurred voice. "I'm comin'."

The girls were ten feet from the car. He waited.

The pounding started again. "Open up! Now!"

"I'm comin'. But the stuff's gone. Ain't gettin' more for days."

The girls made it into the car.

Pound! Pound! Pound! Then some nasty cursing made its way through the door.

The faithful old VW started on the first crank and the girls tore off down the street.

James took a deep breath and opened the door. The three guys looked poised and ready to attack. He didn't like these odds.

"I told you. I ain't got no stuff," he shouted, allowing his voice to squeak. "Come back Friday." He went to slam the door in their faces.

One of the guys shot out a hand to stop him. The other two shoved their way in.

"Hey, hey!" James continued shouting. "That ain't cool!"

The biggest of the three said, "Sorry, man."

One of his companions elbowed the big guy in the gut. "Don't apologize." His Middle Eastern accent came through loud and clear. He pulled off his glasses, revealing a hard, cold version of Fatima's hazel eyes.

"I ain't got no stuff!" James flat out shrieked this time, bugging out his eyes to look as psychotic as possible. He pulled up his white undershirt to reveal the pistol tucked into his jeans.

The big guy jumped back, but the other two remained unfazed. They opened their jackets, revealing their own guns.

"How about we don't make this ugly," said the one who looked so much like his sister. "We don't want *stuff*. We're looking for a woman."

"Shoot, I don't deal in women. That's some messed up crap. No way. Not me. I just sell stuff. Don't hurt nobody."

"Not that kind of woman. Listen to me, you fool. Her name is Fatima. She is very small with golden hair, or maybe she's wearing a long black veil. I'm not sure. Tell us where she is, and we will be giving you no trouble."

"I ain't got no women, I tell you. Well, I got my woman. Her junk's all over this place. I ain't got that kind of woman. But a veil...man. Bet they make a fortune on her."

The other short guy turned bright red. He took off his glasses now too. A vein throbbed in his temple. "For the last time, not that kind of woman. A respectable woman. At least, Allah willing, she had better still be if she wants to survive the day."

"Well, I ain't got no woman. I don't hurt nobody. Just sell some stuff." James broke into an impromptu howling musical version of his refrain. *"Don't hurt, don't hurt, don't hurt nobody. Just sell me some stuff to earn me some cash. Mo' money. Mo' money. Mo'—"*

"Shut up!" snapped the Fatima lookalike.

"He's nuts," said the tall guy. "Maybe we should go."

"He's high as a kite," said the angry one. "He barely knows what's going on. Let's check the place out."

The Fatima lookalike, who seemed to be in charge of the mini-mafia, led the way through the apartment as James continued to sing. They checked in Fatima's room, the bathroom, and then ducked into James and Rain's room. He heard them whispering, but several moments passed and they didn't come out. He was tired of singing and tired of them creeping around his house.

Getting quiet so they couldn't follow the trail of his voice, he tiptoed through the hall and pulled out his gun. With one swift move, he stepped into the open doorway, cocked his pistol, and held it in front of him in a strong, two-handed firing stance.

They all turned from the window they had been peering through. Thankfully, the girls had thought to close it. The tall guy looked like he might pee himself.

James stared down the sights, aiming directly at the chest of the leader. "I think you better go now. I'm startin' to feel a little upset, and you don't wanna see me when I'm upset. Oh no. Oh no, you don't."

"This is ridiculous. She'd never be here. He'd scare her to death." The Fatima lookalike pushed past the other two and stalked out of the bedroom. James kept the gun pointing at him until all three exited the front door and slammed it.

Then he sagged against the wall and began to shake. That had been close. Way too close. Fatima's brothers must be well connected. This was going to be rougher than he'd expected.

Rain rang the doorbell at the Carmichael house. Good thing Mrs. Carmichael had invited her and Layla to dinner back when the semester started, otherwise she could have never found the house on such short notice. She rang again and offered Fatima a reassuring grin. The girl stood beside her and seemed sunken to half of her normal diminutive size. "Don't worry. Everything will be okay."

Finally she heard a scuffle from inside. Allie's mom opened the door, wiping flour from her hands onto her apron. She patted her perfectly sprayed, helmet-inspired hairdo. "Rain, sweetheart, what are you doing here?" But she droned on in her southern simper without giving Rain the chance to answer. "I almost didn't hear y'all. I was back in the kitchen baking bread for dinner. There's nothing like homemade bread, you know. Sarah's taken to blasting that awful rock music lately. I don't understand what's gotten into the girl, but I guess kids will be kids, right? I try not to interfere. This last year at home is always a rough one. I should know. She's my fourth to graduate high school. Well, Rob still lives at home, but he's a boy and he just sort of does his own thing. Am I right?"

Rain shook off her confusion at the unexpected deluge of information. "Mrs. Carmichael, I'm so glad to see you. I believe Allie and Sarah talked to you a few weeks ago about a young Muslim woman."

"Yes, they did. Now y'all come in out of that chill. Where are your coats for heaven sakes?"

Her commanding tone brooked no argument, and the girls dutifully entered the house.

"You know, I always say, Virginia has two seasons. Summer and fal-win-spring. I for one am ready for summer." Mrs. Carmichael stuck her head out the door. "Is she here? I mean the Muslim girl. Is that why you came?"

Finally, they were getting somewhere. Rain wrapped her arm around Fatima. "She's right here. This is Fatima Maalouf."

"Dear me." Mrs. Carmichael pressed a hand to her heart then reached out and lifted a strand of Fatima's blondish hair. "I never would have guessed in a million years. Why, you could be the all-American girl next door. And so pretty too!"

Fatima huddled deeper into Rain's side.

Rain tightened her hold, hoping to reassure the girl. "Let's not overwhelm her. She's been through a lot today. Her brothers—"

"Fatima! Are you okay?" Sarah came dashing down the stairs, and Fatima pulled away from Rain to greet her with a hug.

Huddling into Sarah's shoulder, Fatima whispered, "It is so good to see a friendly face."

Fortunately, Fatima missed the *well-I-never* look that crossed Mrs. Carmichael's features before she caught herself and fixed it.

Rain continued her train of thought. "Sarah, I was just telling your mom that Fatima's brothers showed up at our apartment today. We really weren't expecting them to find us. I mean, what are the odds?"

"Oh my goodness!" Sarah took Fatima by the shoulders and held her at arm's length to examine her. "You're okay, though?"

"I'm fine now, thanks God." Fatima folded her hand over Sarah's.

"But how did you get away?" asked a flustered Mrs. Carmichael.

"Fortunately, Fatima was watching out the window as their car pulled up. When they headed into the building, we headed down the fire escape."

"Fortunately nothing!" Mrs. Carmichael cried, clapping her hands together. "That was God's protection plain and simple. It's all those prayers, I tell you. Oh, I can't wait to share this testimony with my girlfriends."

"I don't think..." Rain said.

Sarah spoke at the same moment. "Mom, you can't tell a soul. This is serious. You promised."

"I don't mean now. I mean eventually when things are safe. Good gracious, I do have a brain in my head."

Rain's purse began to vibrate, and a second later an R&B tune rang out. She stepped into the living room and searched through the bottomless mess of her bag while the Carmichaels continued bickering.

"Hello?" The number indicated James, but she couldn't hear him over the ruckus. "Shh!" she said, pressing a fingertip into her free ear. This was the third time he'd called since she left the apartment.

"No news yet, babe," she said.

"Cool." James answered. "But I was thinking. If they found us, they might eventually find Allie's family. I mean, the school might have her parents' address on file. They must have inside connections to have figured things out so quickly."

"Shoot! I didn't consider that." Everything around Rain fell silent. She looked up to see six eyes focused directly on her now.

"Didn't consider what?" Sarah asked.

James continued talking, "We can't ignore the possibility. These are some scary dudes."

Rain held up a finger for Sarah to hold on a minute. "So what do you suggest?"

"I don't know. But I don't think she should stay there too long."

"Okay. Let me see what we can figure out, and I'll get back to you." Rain clicked off the phone. "He doesn't think Fatima should stay here for too long."

Sarah turned Fatima toward the couch. "Let's all sit down for a minute and think about this. Mom, maybe you can get us some coffee."

"Sure thing, sugar." She bustled off, appearing excited to have a duty.

"Wow, she's something else." Rain shook her head.

"Mom? Don't get me started." Sarah sat down next to Fatima.

Fatima giggled softly.

Thank goodness. Rain sighed with relief at the glorious sound. She had been afraid Fatima would shut down completely when she spotted her brothers.

Rain tucked herself into a plush, oversized chair. A fire blazed in a nearby glass-enclosed fireplace, casting the dim room in a warm glow. Like Mrs. Carmichael, she was ready for spring to hit in full force and kick out this dreary weather once and for all. At least inside the house was pleasant enough. This cozy room should help Fatima relax.

Just then someone opened the front door, and Fatima jumped a good six inches. She stifled a scream.

A startled young man walked into the living room. "Sorry. Didn't mean to scare anyone. What's all this?"

"Don't worry, Fatima." Sarah took her hand. "It's just my brother. Rob, you remember Rain, right? And this is Fatima, the girl from Saudi Arabia that we told you about."

Rob tossed his backpack in the corner and turned his full attention to the girls. "Rain...right, I met you at church last semester."

No wonder his tall form and blond good looks struck a familiar chord with her.

"And Fatima..." He paused. As he studied the beautiful young woman, a glimmer lit his blue eyes.

Uh oh. Rain had seen that look before, but the last thing Fatima needed right now was an admirer. This was the first time she'd been in public uncovered, and already it was starting. Fatima ducked her head in that way Rain had seen Layla do hundreds of times last semester.

"Remember," Sarah prompted, "Layla's friend who ran away. It seems her brothers have come looking for her."

That snapped him out of his goofy trance. "I do remember. Man! Is everything okay?"

"For now," Rain said. "We're trying to think of somewhere safe for her to go."

"Whew. That's no small order. Whoever takes her in will be taking a big risk," he said.

Rain shrugged a shoulder. "I was willing."

"And so are we," Sarah reminded him.

"But you guys knew her already. It's going to be hard to convince someone who hasn't even met her."

Fatima dared to look up at Rob with huge, haunted eyes. She quickly turned to Sarah. "I do not mean to be a burden. I am so sorry. I should be going."

Too late, Rob realized his mistake. "No, no, no!" He hurried over to kneel in front of her and reached to take her free hand.

But she pulled it away and tucked it into Sarah's arm.

Rob glanced from Sarah to Rain and back again.

"Like I mentioned, Fatima is from Saudi Arabia." Rain hoped he'd figure it out from there. She didn't want to embarrass Fatima any more than necessary. The girl was on the verge of another breakdown.

"Right." Rob ran his fingers through his thick, sun-streaked hair. Oh yeah, this was the surfing brother, which was probably why he'd stayed in town for college.

"Anyway, Fatima," Rob continued, "forget what I just said. I'm an idiot. Anyone who took one look at you would be dying to help...I mean...okay, scratch that. I'm sure we'll find someone who would be honored to help a gor...sweet girl like you."

Something about his bumbling speech must have struck Fatima's resilient sense of humor. She laughed but didn't answer him.

Mom bustled back in with a tray of coffees. "Rob's home? Why didn't someone tell me?"

Rob took the opportunity to stand to his feet and put an end to his awkward knight errant routine. Rain wasn't surprised that Fatima had drawn out his protective instincts with her fragile femininity.

"I'll get yours in just a minute, sugar," Mrs. Carmichael said to Rob as she handed out steaming mugs.

Rain stifled her own laugh. Allie always hated when her mom called people sugar. Allie! "Hey, can you all excuse me a minute. I should call Allie and fill her in."

"Before you go," Mrs. Carmichael said. "I was praying in the kitchen, and I had a thought about where Fatima could stay. My dear friend Donna Fletcher, she's such a wonderful woman of God. She lives in Chesapeake and goes to a different church, and I rarely even talk to her these days. She's an intercessor, and she has a real heart for the Middle East. I just know she would do this." She handed a coffee to Rain, but Rain sat it on the end table and leaned forward to gauge their reactions.

Sarah raised her brows and looked to Rob. "It might work. What do you think?"

He nodded his head. "Mom's right, Mrs. Fletcher would love to do something like this. And…what's her husband's name?"

"Doug," Mom said.

"Doug, right. You guys should see him. He's a retired Navy SEAL with the crew cut to prove it, and he's as big as a house. I used to love to go over there. He'd show me all his guns and knives. They'll come in handy."

"Sounds like a great idea," Rain agreed. Who would have guessed that Mrs. Carmichael's brain had survived thirty some years of aerosol fumes? But now that Rain considered it, Layla had mentioned how Allie's mom once spoke words to her that must have come straight from the Holy Spirit. In her own way, Mrs. Carmichael must have a real connection with God.

Fatima fidgeted on the couch but kept her eyes turned down and didn't say a word.

"What is it, sweetie?" Rain asked.

"I must...go alone...to the strangers?" Her terror came through loud and clear. "To this big man with his big knives?"

Rob smacked himself in the head with his palm. He'd managed to do it again, poor guy.

"They'll take good care of you. The very best," Mrs. Carmichael said.

"Rain, there is no way you might be going with me?" Fatima's hazel eyes pleaded with Rain.

"I really can't. I mean, maybe for a day or two. But I can't be driving back and forth from there to school. Your brothers know who I am, and they might follow me."

"Wait, I can stay with you!" Sarah sparked with enthusiasm and nearly spilled her coffee. "It's closer to my school than here. I think it would work, right?"

"I don't see why not," Rob said.

"And you could keep the van for a while. I really don't need it. I'll just go shopping in the evenings when Dad's home." Mrs. Carmichael sat down on the arm of the couch next to Sarah.

For reasons Rain didn't understand, Sarah's eyes rolled at that comment.

Fatima just listened to the whole exchange.

"What do you think? Would you feel better if Sarah was with you?" Rain asked.

"We could work on my Arabic," Sarah reminded her.

"And my English." Fatima cracked a shy smile before burying her face in her coffee mug.

"It will be fun." Sarah patted her knee. "In fact, I can't wait."

"You don't have to rush," Rob said with too much concern. "I mean...she just got here. She should like...maybe take a nap and...and have dinner first. Both of you should stay for dinner. Mom always cooks enough for an army."

"I never did adjust after the older kids moved away." Mrs. Carmichael's tinkling giggle brought to mind Scarlett O'Hara and all the other great Southern belles who'd gone before her. "Of course you'll stay for a while. I need to get a hold of Donna and make the arrangements anyway. Maybe until tomorrow."

Rob's relief was comically obvious.

Rain's naughty side took over. "What do you think, Rob? Does that sound like a good plan?"

Pink crept up his neck as he answered. "Yeah...um...I think that's a great idea."

"Okay then," Rain stood. "I have some phone calls to make."

She needed to fill in James, Allie, and Layla about everything that was going on. Between the new living arrangements, Rob's obvious crush on Fatima, and Sarah's odd behavior, things were about to get pretty interesting. Now that Fatima would be moving out, Rain would have to make some tough decisions about her relationship with James and their living arrangement as well. Suddenly she regretted turning down the offer to stay with the Fletchers. It would have bought her some time.

TWENTY-FIVE

Allie, why must you always be late for dinner? Mom's voice sounded in her head. Probably because she had to trek across two cities following her after-school dance classes, but her hyperstructured mother seemed unable to budge on the official 6:30 dinnertime. At least Allie had given up trying to fix the woman long ago. Instead, she had fixed her own attitude and no longer took any stress or guilt over being late.

Nonetheless, she pressed harder on the gas pedal and swung around the slow car in front of her. She really wanted to see how Fatima was doing. Today must have been awful for the sweet, broken young woman. Allie would do all she could to help soothe her tonight.

As she drove, she took a moment to picture Fatima in her mind with her golden hair and delicate features and held her up before the Lord—imagined her being bathed in his Holy Spirit light. Then she poured out her heart in words as well.

Before long she pulled up in front of the house. Although she'd made certain she wasn't being followed when she left the studio, she circled the block once to double check. When she felt confident all was clear, she headed inside. She hung up her coat and slipped off her shoes. Fortunately given today's chilly weather, she had on yoga pants and a wraparound sweater over her leotard. Mom hated when she showed up in dancer's shorts and flip flops.

Following the boisterous sounds to the kitchen, she found the full troupe gathered there. In all the chaos, they didn't notice her at first. Mom smacked Dad's hand as he tried to snitch a finger full of mashed potatoes. Although he towered over her and firmly held his place as head of the home, Mom would put up with no funny business from the jovial man.

Allie hoped her mom and dad would both take it easy on Fatima tonight. Mom was too quick with the lectures, and after years of his shouting on the street corners about hell and damnation during tourist season, she never knew quite what to expect out of Dad. At least Andy had had a fruitful talk with him about his evangelism approach recently. Dad seemed to respect Andy's opinion since he was, after all, his assistant pastor, as well as a divinity school graduate.

Rob, Rain, Fatima, and Sarah sat at the kitchen table. Fatima laughed out loud at something Rain said. Thank goodness. But what was that moon-eyed look on Rob's face? Good grief, Allie had realized Fatima was beautiful, but she hadn't suspected she would have quite *that* effect on men. Probably the whole damsel in distress thing. Fatima's gentle helplessness must be too much for a guy like Rob to resist.

Mom finally caught sight of Allie. "There you are. What took you so long? You know we eat at 6:30 sharp."

Allie ignored the reprimand and crossed to her mother to give her a kiss on the cheek. "Hi, Mom, everything smells great. Hey, Dad, how's the insurance business?" She kissed him as well.

"As steady as death and taxes."

"Allie!" Rain cried. "Get your skinny rear over here. We have a debate for you to settle."

"Not now." Mom used her don't-mess-with-me tone. "Dinner's already getting cold. You girls help me get the food on the table."

Allie, Sarah, Fatima, and Rain all stood to help while the men filed through the door without lifting a finger. Only Rain shot Allie a questioning look as they marched platters and serving bowls into the dining room and placed them on the immaculately set table. Allie just shrugged a shoulder. At the Carmichael house there was still a strict division between men's work and women's work, another issue Allie had given up fixing long ago. Fatima must be used to such antiquated ideas because she never batted an eyelash.

Mom surveyed the results and nudged the food items around until the table appeared ready for a photo shoot in *Better Homes and Gardens*. "Now, are we waiting for that fiancé of yours or not?"

Nice how Andy became Allie's fiancé rather than Mom's pastor when he was misbehaving. Allie bit back a grin, thankful that she now found her mother more amusing than frustrating. "He had a counseling session and wasn't sure if he could get away or not. He said to go ahead without him."

"Perfect. Boys, please come join us," Mom called.

Dad and Rob sauntered into the room.

"Is this it?" Dad asked.

"Andy might join us later," Allie said.

"And James had to work," Rain offered.

"All right then." Dad moved to his throne at the head of the table. Okay, so maybe that wasn't so bad, but something about his demeanor, along with his lack of help setting said table, rankled Allie. Thank goodness Dad's chauvinistic attitude was next on Andy's list of little *talks*. It really wasn't a very good testimony to people from Allie's generation, as attested by Rain's earlier response. Fortunately, it hadn't rubbed off on Rob too much, but Mark had embraced it full force along with Mom and Dad's uber-conservative Southern Christian alma mater. Thank goodness Rain had never brushed shoulders with him. That could get ugly.

"Almighty Father, please bless this bountiful dinner of which we are about to partake. We thank thee for thy many provisions and thy grace. Thank you for Rain and Fatima here with us this evening. Please offer to them thy protection and guide all of our steps as we must make weighty decisions about Fatima's future. In thy holy, heavenly name we pray. Amen."

Despite the fact that her King-James-only father's prayer could have been uttered by a pilgrim at Plymouth Rock, the sentiment had been lovely. Allie whispered amen and took her seat.

As they passed around roast chicken, potatoes, salad, corn, and homemade bread, Allie studied Fatima. Although a bit nervous, Fatima was smiling and laughing along with the conversation, and while she continually averted her eyes from Rob's probing gaze, she didn't seem disturbed by it. In fact, that rosy blush to her cheeks seemed to indicate she might be enjoying the attention.

Allie turned her gaze to Sarah. Although she spoke excitedly about spending time with the Fletchers, she seemed to clam up at the oddest moments, like when the topic of the veil came up and Mom complimented Fatima's modesty. Usually Sarah would be the first to chime in, but she just bit her lip and focused on her food. Now that Allie thought about it, Sarah's jeans and sweater set were much more casual and—in an odd sort of Sarah way—revealing than she'd seen the girl wear in years.

Although Allie had been praying for Sarah to unwind a bit, she still couldn't shake her bad feeling about the whole situation.

"So, Fatima." Dad broke through the din with his booming voice. "What was it like growing up in such a conservative family in America?"

At that, Allie, Rain, and Sarah all caught one another's gazes and bit back giggles. Only compared to Saudi Arabians would the Carmichael house *not* be considered conservative.

With all eyes on her, Fatima shrank in her chair, but then she took a breath and pulled herself up straighter, seeming determined to be polite in this American home. Her voice began as a whisper but grew stronger as she spoke. "Everything is different. For example, this dinner. If we had guests, the women would be serving the food first and then eating separately later. I would not be asked to speak in such a mixed group. Of course, if I were with men who were not part of my family, they would see only my eyes and hands, so it would be strange to speak to me anyway."

Rob gaped. "And you're okay with that?"

"No." She looked down at her food. "I am not."

Silence ensued as they all attempted to digest such an existence. It in fact did make the Carmichael home seem progressive.

"At least not in theory," Fatima continued, "although, this new life is much for me to adjust to. I always dreamed of being like Layla, a girl who wore only the headscarf and was not afraid to state her opinions or speak to men." She looked back up and managed a small smile. "I suppose I am getting there."

"You're doing great." Rain gave Fatima's shoulder a squeeze. "You've made friends with James, and now with Rob and Mr. Carmichael. You'll do fine with Doug Fletcher too. I'm sure of it."

"With his guns and knives. Perhaps a few contraband grenades." Fatima giggled.

Allie sighed with relief as the banter continued. Fatima's resilience never ceased to amaze her, but she supposed that spoke to how hard Fatima's life had been before. In her own quiet way, she was a fighter. Until this moment, Allie had not completely understood how much courage it had taken for Fatima to break free. She put her life in jeopardy, sure, but she also had to face a huge, unknown world all on her own after a lifetime cloistered away.

The doorbell rang.

"It's probably Andy," Mom said.

"I'll get it." Allie hurried to let him in.

Andy entered and kissed her on the cheek, causing those familiar butterflies in her stomach. Only a few more months until the wedding. She could barely wait.

"Sorry I'm so late. How's everything going?" He hung his coat on the rack and took off his shoes as Mom demanded out of consideration for her light beige carpeting.

"Pretty good. Fatima is doing better than I expected. She was sharing how challenging this new life is for her, but she's tougher than you'd think."

"That's a relief."

"Yeah, just don't offer to shake hands or hug her or anything."

"I know. I had to take cultural sensitivity classes before I did that summer mission trip."

"Right. Actually, it's Sarah I'm worried about. She hasn't been herself lately. Have you noticed?"

"Since I'm not leading the youth group anymore, I don't see her that much, but she has seemed kind of subdued."

"Bring up a topic she would usually jump all over and see what I mean."

"Like modesty?"

"Mom already covered that one. Maybe purity. Or rock music."

Andy chuckled. "That's kind of evil."

"Hey." Allie swatted him then looped her arm through his. "This is serious. I'm worried about her."

"There's the lovebirds," Rob said as they entered the dining room.

Perfect opening. Allie eyed Andy.

He got the message and dropped a kiss on Allie's lips.

She noticed both Sarah and Fatima turn a pinkish tint.

Andy pulled Allie even closer. "You're right about that. I know love is supposed to be a decision and all of that, but boy do I like this feeling." He looked directly at Sarah.

Allie knew they'd argued over this very subject in youth group. They all waited for Sarah to give her scripted response about feelings having no place in love, but she just continued eating.

"Well, I always think a nice balance of decision and feelings are healthy," Mom said.

"I'm all about the ooey gooey and the shivers and tingles." Rain laughed. "You people crack me up. I've never lacked for feelings with James, but I guess now that I'm a Christian and all, I'll have to reconsider that."

"I think you need those feelings in the beginning," Rob said, his gaze flitting again to Fatima. "But once you make a decision to join your life to someone else's, you need to commit to it no matter how you feel in the moment."

"Well put, son." Dad gave Rob a proud slap on the back.

Andy pulled out Allie's chair then sat beside her and shook out his perfectly folded linen napkin. "You're awfully quiet, Sarah. I know you have some opinions on this issue."

Andy filled his plate in the time it took for Sarah to respond, but no one seemed inclined to fill the silence, and she finally relented.

"I don't know anymore. I mean, if you fall in love, you fall in love. What are you supposed to do about that? The heart wants what the heart wants, right? I'm starting to realize that it's all kind of complicated."

"Firsthand experience?" Mom asked with her eyebrows raised high.

Sarah's pink tinge turned to a bright fuchsia. "Of course not! But I do have friends. I try to offer wise counsel and stuff. Boy, am I glad I'll never have to deal with all of that." Her voice trailed off toward the end.

Andy shot Allie a significant look and continued to watch Sarah as they finished the meal. He polished his heaping helping of dinner before Fatima managed to clear her birdlike portion. Mom shooed the men and guests to the family room where she would serve apple pie and decaf. Allie and Sarah cleared the table and joined Mom in the kitchen. They scraped the plates and dumped the dishes in the sink.

Mom was busy with the coffee, so Allie took the opportunity to pull Sarah into the hall for a moment. Sarah hesitated but didn't seem inclined to cause a fuss.

"What?" she asked.

"Why are you avoiding me?"

"I'm not. I'm just super busy. Graduation is just around the corner. You remember what it's like."

"Something's going on with you. Don't bother denying it. Andy sees it too. Just talk to me. You keep stuff all bottled up inside, and it's not good for you. I want to help."

Sarah turned and moved toward the kitchen. "Nothing's wrong."

Allie caught her back by the elbow. "Sarah!"

Sarah jerked her arm away. "Just drop it." She disappeared through the door into the kitchen, where she immediately opened a conversation with Mom.

Allie lingered in the hallway, more certain than ever that something was wrong with Sarah. If the girl insisted on shutting her out, there was nothing she could do about it—at least until Sarah hit rock bottom and was ready to reach out for help. Allie hoped it would never come to that.

TWENTY-SIX

From the moment they walked into the restaurant, Mo hadn't liked the look of the three shady characters in black leather jackets, especially not the two short guys with their cocky preening. And he certainly didn't appreciate the way they leered at their blond waitress, Katie, as she took their drink orders.

When Katie headed toward the kitchen, Mo approached her. "Hey, why don't you let me take those guys, and you can have the next table that comes in."

"Gladly. Thanks, Mo. You've always got my back. I thought it would be a good tip, but those two lighter-haired guys give me the creeps."

"I can handle them." He patted her on the shoulder.

"Here's their drink order. You can take over."

Mo fetched the sodas and *arak* and headed to the table. As he approached, the guys split up their low, mumbling circle. Mo didn't like the suspicious looks on their faces. He placed the drinks on the table.

One of them picked up his shot glass full of the anise-flavored liquor known as *arak* and held it in the air. "Here's to being far away from the prying eyes at home."

"Cheers." The other two clinked his glass, and they all took big gulps of the stuff.

Muslim men out on the town? Alcohol was clearly forbidden

217

by Islam, but Mo remembered that sort of mindset. Guys arrogant enough to assume the rules were meant for everyone but them. The types who were only radical when it suited them, like when repressing women or hating Westerners. Mo pushed past his disdain. Tucking the serving tray under his arm, he pulled out a pencil and pad. "Are you ready to order?"

The smallest and toughest looking of the three craned his neck to scan the room. "Where's that blond chick? I thought she was our waitress."

"Yeah," his cohort said. "With that short skirt, she's maybe serving up more than just dinner." He elbowed the biggest, mildest-mannered member of the group.

Mo managed to keep his expression neutral. These were the types that were likely involved in some sort of illegal activity. Although he hadn't been raised that way, he suspected the insane sense of entitlement foisted on many young Middle Eastern boys was to blame. That combined with a touch of verbal, and in some cases physical, abuse was the perfect recipe for a narcissism that bred criminals and terrorists alike.

Collecting himself, he pulled out his pad and pencil. "I was backed up, so she took your drink order."

At least the third guy had the decency to look embarrassed. As Mo checked the guy's full glass of *arak*, he realized he had never swallowed.

"I'm Mo. I'll be serving you tonight."

Something sparked in the eye of the smallest guy, whom Mo deduced must be the leader of the pack. "Mo," he seemed to draw out the name, "what's good here?"

"You guys new in town?"

The small one glared at him. "Something like that."

So they weren't feeling chatty anymore. "The stuffed zucchini is really good tonight."

The leader shrugged. "Sure. Be bringing us three plates of that along with the appetizer sampler."

Mo wrote down the order and tapped his pencil on the pad. "Got it."

When he looked up, the leader was examining him with a hard glint in his eye. A chill washed over Mo. "I'll be back with that sampler." He rushed away, turned a corner, and leaned hard against the counter of the waiter's station while he collected himself.

What if these were Fatima's brothers? He wished he'd suspected sooner. He never would have mentioned his name. Might they have connected his name to Layla's?

As he typed the order into the computer, Katie entered the serving station to refill some glasses with soda. Mo had never paid much attention to her looks, considering he'd been head over heels for Layla when they met. She appeared cute and innocent with her bouncing blond ponytail and little pink tennis shoes. Her *short* skirt hit just a few inches above her knee and wasn't a bit tight—perfectly modest by normal standards.

He hated to risk putting her in the line of fire, but she was the only other person on duty, and he really needed her help. "Hey, Katie, can you do me a favor?"

"Always."

"Don't be obvious or anything, but keep an ear open when you pass those guys. I have a feeling they're up to no good. And whatever you do, don't make eye contact. They might take it the wrong way."

She twisted her face. Being only half Jordanian with Christian parents, she wasn't used to worrying about that sort of stuff. "I was hoping to steer clear, but since they're smack dab in the middle of my section anyway, I'll let you know if I overhear something."

Not five minutes later, Katie came flying into the kitchen. "Mo, you're right!"

"What is it?" He put down the appetizers to give her his full attention.

"They're looking for some girl. It all sounded really sinister."

Mo's senses sharpened to high alert. He knew it! "Did you hear anything else?"

"Sounds like they've been at ODU. I heard something about a sister and a lot about crazy infidels." She giggled, being one herself.

It had to be them. "Thank you so much, Katie. You have no idea what a huge help this is. I think they might be looking for a friend of mine. Stay far away from them for the rest of the night, and don't leave until I can walk you to your car."

Fear flashed in her eyes, but she blinked it away. "I'm sure it will be okay."

"Well, I'm not taking any risks."

Mo picked up the tray and delivered the food. The guys were deep in conversation, speaking Saudi Arabic and discussing soccer. If he'd had any lingering doubts, their accents chased them away.

It took every ounce of his self-control to keep a pleasant expression on his face and to mute his seething anger. He wanted to punch the snide bullies in the face, but he was outnumbered three to one. Besides, he didn't want to give himself away.

Instead, he hurried back to the kitchen and texted Layla. Since she had been avoiding him for weeks, he wrote, "Call me. 9-1-1. Info on Fatima's brothers."

He danced about nervously, waiting for her to call. He delivered food to a different table. He was about to beat his head against the wall when the phone finally sounded the sappy love song assigned as her ring tone. Trembling now, he hit accept.

"What took you so long!" he snapped and instantly regretted it. He needed to get his temper under control once and for all. She never responded well to it. "I'm sorry. I'm just really worried about you and..." Covering his mouth he whispered, "Fatima."

"Hey, Mo. What happened?"

"There are three guys here at the restaurant right now. I'm almost positive they're her brothers. Sounds like they've been snooping around campus."

She sighed. "Two brothers, one well-meaning cousin. Yeah, they already stopped by the bungalow and Rain's house."

The entire restaurant seeped to red. A volcano threatened to explode right out of the top of Mo's head.

"But try not to worry. God's really been watching out for us every step—"

"You knew!" He somehow managed to whisper and yell at the same time. "You knew and you didn't even bother to tell me! And you didn't bother to tell me you were leaving town either. I had to find out from Mike. This is a new low, Layla Al-Rai. I am sick of your crappy treatment. I... You..." He somehow managed to stop himself before he said something truly ugly.

"I'm sorry. I...I...didn't want you to worry. I...I thought it might be better if you didn't know much in case they questioned you."

"You thought wrong. If I'd known, I wouldn't have offered my name on a silver platter. I might have gotten some useful information out of them. Stupid." He mumbled the last word, unsure if he referred to her, himself, or the whole crummy situation.

"I don't know what to say, Mo. I made a mistake."

"Yeah, so did I. I made a big mistake trusting you. I made a mistake believing that you loved me. I've had it. I've had it with all of this." Mo clicked off the phone.

He took several moments to try to calm down and settle his breathing. The cook rang the bell and put the three steaming plates of zucchini stuffed with meat, pine nuts, rice, and tomatoes on the rack. Mo slapped more rice on the side and flung them onto his tray. He rubbed his hands hard over his face, attempting to erase his fury, and headed out to deliver the food.

The guys were still bickering about soccer teams and seemed inclined to ignore him once again. Just as he turned to leave, the leader called him back, "Ah, Mo."

He kept his features calm. "Do you need anything else?"

"I just had a question for you. Are you by any chance Mo, the boyfriend of Layla Al-Rai? She's a friend of ours."

"Layla?" He let some of his anger burn through his tone and his snort of disdain. "Try ex-boyfriend. That girl was more trouble than she was worth." Sadly, it was true.

"Women! Am I right?" The guy chuckled, seeming friendly enough, no doubt an act. "Do you know where she is? We were hoping to visit her, but this idiot lost her number." He shoved his brother.

"Hey! I thought you had it." The brother continued the act. Nice touch.

"I don't know. I heard something about her visiting a sick aunt in Detroit, but I really don't care what she does. I wasn't going to say anything because I didn't want to embarrass you, but I'm dating that blond chick now." Mo gestured toward Katie with his head.

"Nice." The guy smiled, baring his teeth. No wonder he'd given Katie the creeps. Although a woman would probably consider him handsome, there was no missing the slime around the edges. At least he seemed satisfied with Mo's answer. He must have heard the same story from someone else.

Mo continued his own nonchalant role in their elaborate charade. "I'll be back to check on you. Make sure you save room for dessert. Our baklava is out of this world."

It wasn't until he returned to the kitchen and sagged against the wall that everything hit him. He'd hung up on Layla—probably broken up with her. The woman of his dreams. The future mother of his children. Someone around here certainly was an idiot, but to his chagrin, he suspected it wasn't Layla.

"Say good-bye, Rob," Sarah said as she attempted to shove his towering frame out the Fletchers' front door.

"Good-bye, Rob," he answered dutifully as he waved to Fatima one last time. "Be safe."

Sarah pressed on the door.

"I'll be praying for you," Rob shouted through the crack before the door clicked shut.

Sarah leaned on it and started to giggle. Fatima joined in the laughter.

Even Doug Fletcher looked over his newspaper from his recliner in the corner of the living room and smiled. "Sorry to be the one to tell you, but that boy's got it bad."

"A part of me wants to worry," Fatima said, "but he is just too funny."

Sarah had noticed how Fatima had taken to Doug Fletcher from the moment she set eyes on the behemoth. He had the calming sort of energy that soothed babies and animals, and he'd spent enough time fighting in the Middle East to understand how to approach her.

"Don't give Rob another thought." As Sarah heard his car starting up, she stepped away from the door. "He's harmless. Hopeless but harmless."

"I know, this is exactly what I am thinking. It is nice, though. I never had a man treat me like this, with so much attention but also so much respect."

"How do men treat you in your culture?" Sarah asked.

She noted that Doug listened intently.

"Mostly they don't. They don't even see me or know me. But I know how my brothers speak of women, especially Western women." She blushed. "It does not bear repeating."

"Why don't you girls get settled in your room?" Doug suggested.

They turned down the hallway.

"Oh, wait! Sarah, come here for just a second," Doug called.

Fatima continued toward the room and Sarah headed back.

"Hey, Mr. Fletcher," she said, using the manners her mother demanded despite his insistence that they call him by his first name. "What's up?"

"I just wanted to warn you that the third drawer in the short dresser gets stuck sometimes. You might want to just skip that one." He lowered his tone. "And I wanted to encourage you to get Fatima to open up without me around. She's so wounded. That much is obvious. This is an amazing opportunity for you to minister to her."

Sarah's heart sank in her chest. Her stomach turned sour. She knew he was right, except that she was in no condition to help anyone, and for the first time in the past month, she completely and utterly regretted her relationship with Jesse. "This is a tough situation, but I'll do my best."

He nodded and contemplated that as he picked up a coffee mug from the holder in the arm of the recliner. When he brought it to his mouth for a sip, his bicep bulged, causing the waves under the ship tattooed on his arm to ripple. Sarah smiled at the effect. She'd always believed tattoos were a sin, but these days she'd been rethinking just about everything. The scripture scrolling beneath the ship, *"Peace, be still,"* certainly put a different spin on the whole situation.

He nodded again. "I'll be out here interceding in prayer for you. I think the Holy Spirit wants to do something special."

Goosebumps rose on Sarah's arm. She rubbed them away. Just the thought of the Holy Spirit in the room with them—which she had an odd sense might be true—made her want to run far, far away. She eyed the wine rack in the corner. She could really go for a drink right about now.

Somehow she managed to pull herself together to answer. "Thanks, I appreciate that."

Being a man of few words, he just nodded one last time and folded his newspaper. He leaned his head back and closed his eyes, and she knew he meant every word he had said.

Not quite ready to face Fatima, she stopped by the kitchen for a drink of water. How could God possibly use her—dirty, messed up Sarah—to minister to Fatima? She'd had so many doubts, committed so many sins. Was she even a Christian anymore? She'd always been the first to judge that people like herself were *backsliders* and no longer worthy of God's grace. Except that she needed it more than ever. Assuming, of course, that any of this was true.

She took a few sips of cool, clear water. Whether or not Christianity, or at least her parents' legalistic version of Christianity, was true, she longed to help Fatima. She had spent her life wanting to bless the Fatimas of the world—had trekked across town for four years to her international studies program. She would be a friend and somehow reach out to her.

The thought of Doug's prayers bolstered her courage. Even if her connection to God had been cut off lately, she didn't question his. If the Holy Spirit was in this house, maybe he could manage to flow through a dirty, clogged up conduit like her for Doug's sake and for Fatima's. Maybe that's what Andy had meant all those years when he kept harping that it was God's job to flow through us, and that we didn't have to do things in our own strength.

Goodness knew, Sarah had no strength of her own.

TWENTY-SEVEN

Sarah entered the nautical-themed bedroom she would be sharing with Fatima and shut the door. Fatima was sorting through her pile of hand-me-down clothes, mostly given to her by Sarah.

"Now that we're staying together, you can borrow whatever you like. I always wanted a sister to share clothes with, but Allie's four inches taller than me, and she was gone for half of my life."

"A sister." A shy smile split Fatima's face. "I always wanted a sister. James, he said he was my big brother, but Rain seemed more like a nurturing auntie. I would love to share clothes with you like a sister, but I wonder if this makes Rob my brother. He would be so, so sad." Fatima giggled.

"I think Rob would like to make you my sister-in-law for real right about now, but he'll get over it. In fact, I suspect you're going to have that effect on guys. You're very beautiful, but it's more than that. When you're relaxed, you light up the room. I imagine lots of guys will want to take care of you and keep that gorgeous smile on your face."

"It is nice, I suppose. But..." Fatima bit her lip.

"But what, Fatima?"

"It is just so hard. So different." She picked up a pink T-shirt and stared down at it longer than warranted.

"Different I understand, but explain hard to me?" Sarah sat on the bed and gave Fatima her full attention.

"Men." She took a deep inhale. "Men have always been so frightening to me. They yell. They hit. They mock."

Tears pricked Sarah's eyes. But this moment wasn't about her. It was about Fatima, so she blinked them away. "Did you have any kind men in your life?"

"Only my uncle. My mother's brother. He did not visit often. Father never liked him."

"But of course you want to get married and have children someday. Right? You just need to find a man like your uncle. There are plenty of them out there. You've just been in the wrong circles." Now that qualified as the understatement of the year.

"I don't know." Fatima pulled the T-shirt to her mouth and stifled a little sob.

Sarah moved closer on the bed but didn't want to startle her. "What don't you know? If there are kind men? You've met James, my father, Rob, Doug. It's not just an act. They are truly good people."

"No, no. This I see. This I believe. But I do not know if I can ever trust. Ever love. Ever...marry." With that she sat beside Sarah and began to weep. Between sniffles she continued, "It is all anyone ever expected of me. I wasn't a person. I was a baby machine. I had no choice. I never thought to actually pick a man."

"How did you feel about that?" Sarah asked.

"For many years I accepted it. I did want a home and children. But the husband..." Her voice squeaked. "I was so scared, and now that I must choose one on my own—I don't think I ever can. But I don't want to be alone either. It is too much, too much that I never even considered before. This life is hard."

Although Sarah was not normally demonstrative, something deep inside urged her to wrap an arm around Fatima. Fatima snuggled into her side. Sarah heard Andy's voice again, telling her to be the incarnational form of Jesus. She had always found that silly before, thinking her role was to blast people with the truth, not to coddle them, but in that moment she almost understood. "Someday things will change."

"But..." Fatima began, then disintegrated into deeper sobs.

Sarah sensed Fatima was holding something back but didn't feel inclined to push her.

After a few seconds, Fatima calmed herself. "What about you? How is it for you with men?"

Fatima was not the only one holding things back. Sarah liked her, she really did, and she knew that she could trust her, but she didn't want to unpack her ugly baggage all over this innocent girl.

She defaulted to the answer she would have given a few months ago, which was true in its own way. "I'm not like most American girls. I don't believe in dating lots of guys, and I certainly don't believe in sex before marriage. But my parents are very happy together. My father protects my mother, not just her body but also her feelings. I look forward to having that in my life someday."

"It sounds lovely," Fatima whispered.

"It is." Guilt washed over Sarah again in a filthy deluge of sludge. She would never have that idyllic life now. She no longer deserved a man like her dad, and she couldn't imagine marrying someone like Jesse. She was caught in no man's land. Not quite a Christian, yet unable to walk away.

At least she had put some geographical distance between herself and Jesse. Just one of the many reasons she jumped at this chance to stay with the Fletchers. She wouldn't have to stare into his hypnotic eyes morning after morning on the hour-long bus ride. She might even be able to avoid the press of his lips long enough to unravel her thoughts.

Dirty. Filthy. Whore. Those were the words that filled her mind these days. But then, from a deeper place, somewhere in the core of her abdomen, came a string of different words. *Forgiven. Worthy. Mine.*

Shut up! She silently screamed at the voice.

Disentangling herself from Fatima, she ran toward the bathroom. "I'll be right back."

She sagged against the door and collapsed to the cold, hard floor. No, she didn't want to hear that voice. Not now. She thought of Doug Fletcher on the other side of the wall deep in prayer. Maybe coming to the Fletchers' had been a huge mistake after all.

***

Layla put her cell phone down on her nightstand. She had just hung up with a cheerful Fatima, who was all settled in at her new home. Fatima sounded excited about her budding relationship with Sarah as well. Layla should be ecstatic—thrilled that Fatima was safe and happy—and a part of her was.

But an even bigger part struggled with loneliness and confusion. She still could hardly fathom that Mo had hung up on her—had broken up with her, or something along those lines. Of course, it was her fault that they hadn't actually been dating, but they'd had an understanding, and now he was through with her.

She had been crazy to think that Mo would just stand by patiently and wait for her, indefinitely, with no promises whatsoever. No wonder he'd gotten angry with her. What did she expect? Her trust in their mystical bond, in a destiny that began with whispered words of love on a swing set in kindergarten, had been nothing but fanciful dreaming.

Mo was just a regular old, real life guy, and she had pushed him too far. The problem was she didn't know what she could have done differently. As much as she loved him, as much as she had believed God wanted them together, her family and her education had been her first priorities for years. How could she just walk away from either of them?

It wasn't even as if her parents had asked her to deny Christ or to turn from her faith. They were wonderful people who understood that she must follow her own heart. They simply asked that she keep quiet about things, perhaps find a way to weave her new belief system together with her Muslim traditions. Was that too much to ask?

She picked up the books that her father had given her from her nightstand. They made so much sense and seemed to solve everything. Surely that disquiet she felt in her heart was just her own difficulty in digesting the new ideas. She always had been one to take her time with change, but perhaps this would be worth it.

Her father had been watching the Christian television shows with her. Mom had even stopped from her incessant bustling to listen a few times, without any groans or huffs. Perhaps this was the plan God had in mind all along. Hadn't he been the one to confirm in her heart that it was time to come home?

Mo wouldn't understand. He had taken a radical stand for Christ, and he would never compromise. Maybe it was for the best that he had broken up with her. Layla needed a new vision for the future.

In this vision, God had brought Mo into her life so she would have a fellow Muslim to help her in her search for Christ. In this vision, God was calling her to be a missionary to her family—the people who meant the most to her in the world. In this vision, she might even transfer to a distance-learning program and move home where she belonged. It was time to face facts—Layla had no idea how to take care of herself.

Where love and husbands and children fit into all of that, she had no idea. What sort of husband would be suitable for a sort-of Christian, sort-of Muslim, sort-of didn't-know-what-she-was kind of girl?

Then it hit her! Ryan Hassan, the mostly American, somewhat Muslim, with a Christian mother who had halfway converted to Islam kind of guy. She had been drawn to his insightful, laid back, and—let's face it—downright cool personality when her aunt tried to fix her up with him last semester, not to mention his dark tousled hair and deep blue eyes. But she had been in love with Mo, and she and Ryan had decided their timing was off.

In need of any hope as a life preserver in the confusing morass of her thoughts, Layla pulled out her phone and dialed Ryan's number. They hadn't even spoken since fall, only exchanged comments on Facebook a few times. This was silly. If he didn't answer, she wouldn't leave a message.

On the fifth ring, he picked up. "Hello?"

"Hi, Ryan. This is Layla."

He didn't respond.

"Layla Al-Rai."

He chuckled. "I know who you are. I'm just surprised to hear from you."

"I'm sorry I didn't call sooner. Things have been really crazy in my life."

"What about your boyfriend? Or non-boyfriend as the case may be?"

"Mo." She took a deep breath. "It's been a mess with my family. I think he finally gave up on me."

"So that's why you called."

"No…yes. I don't know. Maybe." She giggled. "Actually, I have no idea why I called. I just sort of did it on impulse."

"Well, I for one like your impulses. You should follow them more often." His chill voice came across the line, sounding unbelievably attractive.

"There's just so much going on with me, and with Mo out of my life, there's no one to understand. My American friends don't get it, and I can't talk to any of my hardcore Islamic friends about it. My best friend for most of my life is going through a lot right now, so I can't burden her with this."

"Then it sounds like you called the right guy."

Had she?

She so badly needed to talk to someone, and Ryan was here for her. For the next hour and a half, she poured her heart out over the phone as Ryan listened patiently and gave her the best advice he could, gently encouraging her to follow her instincts and not give in to outside pressure. She knew he was right, but she still felt conflicted as to which of the many voices in her head was the true Layla...and more importantly...which was God.

TWENTY-EIGHT

Rain pushed damp corkscrew curls from her brow as her feet pounded along the cracked pavement of her rundown Norfolk neighborhood. With Fatima safely deposited at the Fletcher house, she had more free time on her hands than she wanted to deal with. She had promised herself she would take up jogging once the morning sickness passed, but she had gotten caught up with other projects. Now that she was well into her third trimester, she had a feeling this might be a mistake.

The baby bounced in front of her, banging hard with each step. Muscles at the base of Rain's belly already cried out in complaint, along with her oxygen deprived lungs. But if she stopped running, she would have to think, and that was the last thing she wanted to do.

For another whole block she kept placing one foot in front of another, but when a stitch tied tight in her side, that was the final straw. She relented. Pacing in a circle, she massaged her side while sucking in deep breaths.

At least today the sun was shining bright and warm overhead. It didn't seem to seep through her skin to affect her mood though. Inside she was gray and dismal. She turned back in the direction of home. While she had run less than a mile, that still meant a good fifteen minutes alone with her thoughts in order to get there.

Great!

She really couldn't put it off anymore. She had to talk to James. If only she had clarity about what exactly to say. There were a few things she knew for certain. One, she was thrilled about her decision to accept Christ. Two, she loved God with all her heart, and she would not turn back. Three, she wanted to please him with how she lived. Already she knew enough to understand that did not include cohabiting with a man out of wedlock. But what about the instruction not to be—what did they call it again?—unequally yoked with an unbeliever? It seemed like a no-win situation.

Then there was the baby growing inside of her. Surely God would want her to stay with the father, to raise their little girl in a family.

Dear God, please speak to me!

There had to be an answer. Spotting a bus bench just ahead, she decided to sit for a moment and catch her breath. Clearly there was no point in trying to outrun her thoughts. They followed her everywhere.

Instead, she closed her eyes and tuned to what she'd come to think of as her God-o-vision—that sort of inner, spiritual television—and took a moment to seek his face. She captured it for only a moment when a different picture took over. Clear as day, she read the message emblazoned on the back of her eyelids: I Corinthians 7:13-15.

What the heck? Did God do stuff like that? Allie had certainly never mentioned it, but Allie was still growing in the more spiritual aspects of the faith. Whereas Rain, with her mystical upbringing, seemed to have an open window to the heavenly realm.

She stood to rush home. She'd have to check out that scripture. Maybe it was nothing, but maybe it would contain the answer she needed.

James only had time for a quick stop home between his classes and tonight's shift, but the thought kept spinning through his mind that with Fatima gone, maybe he could catch a rare moment alone with his gorgeous woman. He kind of liked her new voluptuous form.

But he did not like the sight that met his eyes one bit as he entered the apartment. Rain sat at the kitchen table with her purse on her lap.

"What now?" This did not look to be a *Lucy, you got some splainin' to do* kind of moment. In Rain's golden-green eyes, he read sadness and regret.

She twisted her hands in her lap. "James, we need to have a serious talk. Let me start by saying I moved my stuff out today."

His stomach lurched. He couldn't lose her again. "You what? Why? Everything's been going so well."

"Just listen. I needed to say that first because I want you to understand that what I'm about to say next is in no way meant to be controlling or threatening or manipulative. That's why I already took the initiative. No matter what you decide, I'll be staying with Allie and Layla for at least a month or two."

His jaw dropped. What was going through her crazy, beautiful head now? "But the baby's coming."

"I accepted Christ."

His jaw tightened. Although he had suspected that would be coming for a while, it was the last thing he wanted to hear.

"I should have done it months ago. I wanted to, but I put you first. I know I said nothing but the life of our child could ever come between us. I guess I was wrong. I love you as much as ever, except I realize now that I can't put you before God."

He pressed his fingers to his eyes. How could he argue with logic—or rather, lack of logic—like that? "Listen, baby—"

"No, let me finish. I need to be able to go to church, a real Jesus-following church, not the anything-goes one we've been attending. And I need to take my child there with me."

He slumped into a chair beside her and dug his fingers into his hair. "I said you could do all of that. What more do you want?"

"And..." She looked down at her toes.

"And... Spit it out. What could be worse?"

"And...I need to be married to the man I live with. I need it to be forever and right in the eyes of God. I know we're committed to each other in our own way, but that's not enough for me anymore. I need it to be official."

James shook his head as thoughts spun through it at lightning speed. *This changes everything* was the only one that stood out clearly. Nothing would ever be the same. "I don't know what to say."

"I don't want you to say anything right now. Like I mentioned, the last thing I want is for you to feel pressured or coerced. I just want to give you time to think about this. It isn't about you. I love you with all my heart, James. You're the man I want to be with. I just hope and pray that you're the man God has destined me to be with. If not, I don't know how I'll go on, but I'll have to. I need to put God first."

He yanked at the dreadlocks at his scalp, as if that would somehow pull the magical answer from his head, but there was no magic to fix this. How could he stand a chance against her perceived reality? How could he take on her God and win? Should he even try? But this affected him too. "I...I...I guess you're right. I need time to process this, but you don't have to leave."

"I do. I need to leave...for me. Otherwise we'll fall right back into the way things always were. I need to make a radical change."

"You're going overboard. Yes, this is a big adjustment, but we'll figure something out that works for both of us. We always do. James and Rain together forever, right?"

"James and Rain together forever? If you mean that—really mean that—then 'to death do us part' isn't such a stretch. Just think about it. But for now, we need some time apart."

James pounded the table in front of him and swore. "We've had too much time apart. This is not what I want."

"It's the only way. I'm sorry. I love you." And with that she slipped out the door.

Noah seriously didn't know how much more he could take. Before long he would wear holes in the area rug of his little efficiency apartment from all the pacing and praying he'd done over the last weeks.

"God, I'm at the end of my rope here. Even if she's dead, I just want to know. I hope you preserved her. I so badly hope that my angel is safe and I can find her soon, but I need to know the truth. I can't go on like this much longer."

He hated the whiny tone of his prayer. He'd always been taught—and believed—that Christians should pray with power and authority, but his heart was too broken for that right now. God knew that more than anyone, so there was no point in hiding it. Even David had cried out to God in despair, and God called David a man after his own heart.

After all, God had created this bizarre, illogical thing called love. Surely he must understand. Noah had given up hiding that as well. He was bona fide, head-over-heels in love with the girl, and he couldn't help it.

The police didn't have any leads, but God knew the truth. Noah just wished so badly that God would share it with him. If Fatima was dead, Noah would find the strength to move on, but if she wasn't, he had to see her again. He had to tell her how he felt, and most of all, he had to rescue her from her family.

Noah turned a few more paces before his landline rang. That was weird. No one ever called him on that phone. He had been planning to cancel it.

"Hello?"

"Hi, my name is Pastor Mike Washington. Is Noah Dixon there by any chance?"

"Yeah, I'm Noah." That was weird too. Noah hadn't ever heard of a Mike Washington.

"You're a hard dude to track down." The man's intonation and deep rich chuckle gave Noah the impression that he was young and African American.

"I'm sorry. Do I know you from somewhere?"

"No, I'm the one who's sorry. This is a weird, out-of-the-blue kind of phone call. Let me start over. I pastor a contemporary, artsy little church in Norfolk, Virginia, near Old Dominion University. It's called The Gathering."

"Nice name." Noah had a good feeling about this guy.

"Thanks. For whatever reason, God has been sending all these Muslim college students to my church. We had three new visitors just this Sunday, and the university has a huge Muslim Student Union. It's kind of crazy."

"Kind of crazy awesome." What was God up to now?

"Right? So I went on a pastor's forum looking for someone who might be able to help me. A guy there suggested your name. A Ron Johnson that you went to Bible college with, except he'd lost track of you, so I looked you up on my own. I sure hope I have the right guy after that big, long story."

"Yeah, I would be the person you're looking for. I'm very invested in Islamic ministry. What did you have in mind? Prayer support? Advice? I'd be happy to help you however."

"Actually...okay, now this is going to really sound crazy. I was praying about it, and I felt led to invite you to move down here. I can only offer you a part-time salary, but the cost of living here is pretty low, and we have plenty of singles you could room with."

Only a part-time salary! That sounded a lot better than the no salary Noah was earning here. He'd been living on a combination of donations and odd jobs. Surely they had odd jobs in Norfolk.

"And the church is growing really fast," Mike continued. "I'd be open to expanding your role if it works out."

"Yeah, that does sound crazy." Noah laughed. "But we serve a pretty crazy God."

"Exactly. I knew you were my guy. Not that I'm trying to pressure you."

Noah paused to digest everything. "It's strange. I'm unhappy at the church I've been attending, and I was thinking of looking for a new one. But a new one here, you know? I've invested a lot in this area, and I'm in the middle of a big issue with a woman I've been ministering to. I don't think I could get away, at least not for a while."

"Hey, that's cool, man. I'm just tossing it out there. Who knows? Maybe it wasn't God. Maybe my wishful thinking got ahead of me, but would you at least pray about it?"

"Absolutely! The last thing I want is to miss out on God's plan." The words sounded right, but he knew in all truth the *last* thing he wanted at this precise moment was to lose Fatima Maalouf for good.

He sighed. He needed an attitude adjustment. He'd never even spoken to the girl, and she wasn't even a Christian. "I don't know. Maybe a fresh start is exactly what I need, but I can't just jump into anything. Let's both pray and think about this for a while."

Noah wrote down Mike's number, discussed logistics, and said good-bye. He'd been dreaming of an opportunity like this for years, but how could he leave Fatima behind and in trouble? He couldn't begin to wrap his brain around the possibility, not even for the best opportunity in the world. Maybe if he could find Fatima and talk her into leaving the area, they could go to Norfolk together. Him and the veiled Muslim woman.

Sheesh. Now he wasn't making any sense at all.

Man, whose bright idea had it been to assign James kid duty? He sat on the curb watching some of the children from The Gathering play hopscotch with the street kids at the soup kitchen while the other adults prepared the meal. He shouldn't have come. He promised himself he'd find a new ministry at his multi-faith church, but what was the point?

Rain didn't even go there anymore. She went to this church now—yet another reason he shouldn't have come, but he'd been way too lonely in the empty apartment. He wondered where Rain was tonight.

A few rough youths passed by with trouble sparking in their eyes, but one hard look from James turned them in the other direction. Okay, so that explained why Mike's wife, Serena, chose him for this job. Still, it was hard—too hard—to sit here watching the kids giggle and hop when he was on the verge of losing his own family. His own child.

Mike came out and joined him on the curb. "How are my babies doing?" He studied the two immaculate little girls playing with obvious contentment side by side with the grubby children.

"I'm taking good care of them. Although, I have a feeling that any child of Serena's could take care of herself."

"True enough, but let's let little Malcom get more solid on his feet before we turn him loose in the big bad world. Okay?"

With images of his own baby—his baby he might or might not get to raise—flashing through his mind, James said nothing in response.

"Sorry, buddy. You're upset about Rain and the baby, aren't you?"

James hadn't even been sure if Mike knew about all that. But of course he did. Mike, his church, and his God were the whole reason Rain had left. James clenched his jaw.

Mike gave his shoulder a firm clasp. "I want you to know, this marriage ultimatum wasn't my idea. It was hers."

James flinched away. "Seriously, man? You're going to feed me that crap? The one thing I respect about you is that you keep it real."

"I'm serious, James. Usually in these cases I stick with standard biblical wisdom, and standard biblical wisdom says not to marry an unbeliever."

The words slapped against James like a frigid wave, taking his breath away for a moment. It wiped out the heat of his anger and left him with something cold and empty— more like despair—in its place.

Mike allowed him a moment to process.

James swallowed and tried to recapture his anger, anything to fill this empty, helpless void. "So you would tell her to break up with me? Just like that? Leave me in the dust and take my child." His hands clenched hard against the jagged sidewalk. "You of all people know how much I sacrificed, the huge risks I took, to get them back."

"It's a tough situation, and I care about you, man. I do. You're my bro, which is why I didn't say much at first. I suggested she pray about it. But that girl has a real connection to God, and she heard something I wouldn't have guessed. She mentioned that you're the only guy she's ever been with, and she believes that you're already married according to the Old Testament way of doing things, not to mention by common law standards. So that changes the issue. If you'll still have her and commit to taking the vows you should have long ago, she feels she should stay with you, especially now that you have this child together." Mike shrugged.

"What did you have to say about that?" James's hands began to unclench, although he still thought this religion with its crazy book and its crazy laws was seriously messed up.

"Who am I to argue? It's obvious she's deeply in love with you, so I hope she's not letting that cloud her judgment. On the other hand, maybe that deep love is the point. Even though you guys have skipped some technical issues that are important for this world, you're more intimate and connected on a spiritual level than half the married couples I know. Do you really think a piece of paper can make that go away?"

"It's not the paper...or the ceremony. If that's important to Rain, maybe I could deal with it. I planned to be with her for the rest of my life, so it isn't a huge step. The problem is this whole change in her. What if we don't connect like we used to? What about our kids? I don't want to raise my kids with all this bologna."

Mike turned his eyes to his daughters still playing hopscotch with the street children, smiling and laughing while bringing joy to the outcasts of society. "Like my kids?" he asked. "Would that really be such a disaster?"

An odd peace washed over James. "Unfair." He smiled. "Pulling the cute kids card. How can I fight that?"

"Just think about it, man. You have a lot on the line here, and that woman really does love you."

James did have a lot to think about. He hated to cave. Despite the fact that Rain insisted she wasn't trying to manipulate him, he felt coerced nonetheless. He hated this out-of-control, helpless feeling. This same feeling had sent him into a rage last semester and ultimately sent him to the counselor. Now it was being triggered all over again.

But he wouldn't bully Rain. He didn't want to control her. At least he'd come that far. He just needed more time to sort this out. He didn't want to jump into any decision that he'd regret.

TWENTY-NINE

On Friday afternoon, Sarah gathered the books she needed from her locker and tucked them into her backpack. All week she'd luxuriated in the wonder of having her own car here at school, not to mention the freedom from Jesse's mesmerizing pull that she always dealt with on the bus. Thankfully, since she didn't have any classes with him this semester, she'd been able to dodge him. While she couldn't deny she'd fallen in love with him—at least on some instinctual, biological level, which probably wouldn't qualify by any biblical definition—this distance had given her the perspective she needed.

Sure, he was handsome and intelligent. Admittedly, they had a lot in common but not nearly enough. He had wreaked havoc on her spiritual life and her family dynamics. She could barely stand to look her parents in the eyes these days.

Just one of many reasons she was glad to be ensconced at the Fletchers'. Doug and Donna might gaze at her with penetrating eyes that missed little, but she never felt judged, never sensed that she was letting them down, only that they cared.

For once she didn't rush but stopped to talk to a few friends on her way out the door. She didn't even leave the building until long after the buses departed. Thoughts of Jesse flit through her head again. Okay, so she missed him, a little, but she didn't miss all the confusion he wrought in her life. Things were much simpler and calmer without him.

And much lonelier and more boring too.

When she reached her light-blue minivan, concealed behind a big SUV, her stomach fell to her feet, where butterflies—make that bats—commenced fluttering in it.

There was Jesse, suave and sexy as ever in his skinny jeans and slim T-shirt, with arms crossed over his chest as he leaned against her van. The spring breeze whipped strands of chestnut hair over his hooded brown eyes. "Thought you'd never come."

Her voice caught in her throat.

"You haven't answered my texts all week," he continued. "I had to go ask your parents what was up."

"You didn't," she choked out. What did her parents think? Did they see it all in his eyes? Did they know her humiliating secrets? Her disgusting sins?

"Of course I did. Every time they see me they make me promise to keep an eye on you at the bus stop. Got to protect their virtuous little angel, you know. I could hardly let them down."

"Yeah, you've done a great job." Sarcasm dripped from her voice.

"Well, I admit I had my own spin on the subject." He sidled up to her and scooped her into his arms. His tone fell to a throaty whisper. "But you're no worse for wear. In fact, you're looking hotter than ever."

Sarah's blood started to heat. Those sensations she loved but hated started all over again. Her mind grew foggy. Halfheartedly, she pressed against him. "Don't, Jesse. I need some space. I need time to think. That's why I've been avoiding you."

"Since you took your time getting out here, what I need is a ride home."

Shoot. She could hardly make him walk seventeen miles, and the public bussing system in this city was next to useless. Besides, she'd wanted to pick up a few things from home. She couldn't think of any way around it, especially since she was the reason he missed his ride. "I guess," she muttered.

"And you know what else I need?" He leaned in to take a taste of her lips. "This." Then he nipped at her ear. "And this." Next his mouth settled hungrily against her neck, driving those awful, amazing sensations into overdrive.

Before she knew what she was doing, Sarah found herself tangled in his embrace as their lips engaged in a frantic dance. She ripped herself away. "People will see."

"Then we better get back to my place for some privacy." Jesse fished the keys from her purse and moved toward the driver's seat.

Sarah dredged deep inside of herself but simply could not find the will power to turn him down.

※

After so much time spent in the company of her various protectors over the past month and a half, Fatima had enjoyed having the last two days mostly to herself. Sarah had spent last night at a friend's house and continued studying all day today, but Fatima expected her home anytime. With Doug and Donna in the house, that peace and contentment they seemed to bring into a room had flowed her way all night. She'd read half a novel from the Fletchers' bookshelf, a favorite hobby she hadn't found much time for at Rain and James's house.

While she loved the "me" time, she also needed something to keep her thoughts focused, otherwise they were sure to take a dark turn toward her haunting past or her perilous future. For tonight, she escaped into the wild west of 1848 for a sweet romance that soothed her heart and gave her just a bit of hope that someday even Fatima Maalouf, abused Muslim woman, might find a happy ever after.

Wheels crunched in the gravel outside. She glanced at the clock—*1:15*. Goodness, she'd gotten too lost in the ranches of west

Texas. Sarah should have been home long ago, and Fatima hadn't even noticed.

She tiptoed to the door and peeked down the hallway. The lights were off other than the dimmed one in the dining room and the outside flood lights. Soft snoring came from the Fletchers' room down the hall. Of course, they'd only been living together for five days, but Fatima hadn't thought Sarah would be the type to stay out so late.

Sarah came in the front door and weaved her way toward the bathroom without noticing Fatima peeking through to the hall. However, Fatima noticed Sarah had not shut the door securely or locked it. She must be exhausted. While Fatima slept in each morning, Sarah rose before dawn to get ready for school, and she often stayed up late doing homework as well.

Fatima took care of the front door situation. Checking out the window, she noticed Sarah's van parked at an odd angle. Yes, exhausted for sure. The girl really shouldn't be driving so late. Perhaps Fatima would have a "big sister" type talk with her. She hated being the victim and loved to nurture others whenever possible.

She headed back to her room and heard retching as she passed the bathroom. Fatima stopped and pressed her ear to the door. "Sarah, sweet sister, are you sick? Do you need something?" she whispered, not wanting to wake Doug and Donna.

"I'm okay," came weakly through the door.

Fatima returned to her bed but sat cross legged, waiting to make sure Sarah was indeed okay.

Sarah stumbled into the room, eyes half closed, wearing only an unfamiliar man's T-shirt and her panties. Her jeans, shoes, and jacket were no doubt strewn across the bathroom floor. She smelled of masculine, musky cologne. "Are you sure you are all right? You do not look so good. You are pushing yourself too hard."

"I'm fine. So tired. Good night." Sarah's speech was garbled. She collapsed onto her bed.

Finally, something computed in Fatima's brain and she put two and two together. She had seen enough American teen movies to know what this was. She just never expected Sarah, of all people, to turn up drunk out of her mind. Fatima's cheeks burned from embarrassment for the girl, since Sarah was too far gone to be embarrassed for herself.

Alcohol was strictly forbidden in Fatima's Muslim culture. She had always considered it sinful, heathen—and no wonder. Such an out-of-control state of mind could lead to all sorts of trouble…many more mistakes…all kinds of evil. Anger filled her veins as Fatima realized Sarah had driven home this way. She could have killed herself, not to mention someone else's mother or husband or even an entire innocent family.

Sarah wiggled in her bed, and Fatima gasped at an even more disturbing sight than her friend's intoxicated state. Across the exposed outer edge of her left buttock, in black cursive surrounded by angry red skin, was tattooed a single word.

Fatima hoped Sarah hadn't had the permanent mark emblazoned on her rear while drunk. Although knowing Sarah even a little, she couldn't imagine the girl doing it while sober. Fatima had a feeling Sarah was about to be in for quite a shock.

Sarah awoke to the awkward realization that it was Easter morning. She cracked her eyes open to the sight of a still slumbering Fatima and her heavy breathing that didn't quite attain to snoring. The clock displayed 7:04, still early. Sarah pulled the covers back over her head.

Today she'd be expected at church and at home for an elaborate dinner of both ham and lamb—a gentile and Jewish celebration extraordinaire—but she had little to celebrate this morning. All day yesterday she had harangued herself about her despicable behavior. She didn't even remember driving home drunk and couldn't recall if that had been her idea or Jesse's. But since he always had looked out for her physical safety, she assumed she snuck away from him while he slept.

This had to stop! Christian or not, she could not continue living such a reckless lifestyle. Beyond being a goody-goody evangelical, Sarah had always been practical, reliable, and responsible. There was simply no excuse for her erratic behavior. If being around Jesse turned her into this awful person, then she'd have to make a change.

Except that these days he was the air that she breathed, the life's blood that flowed through her veins, his mouth the only food she desired. It was truly, utterly horrible.

Seduction. The word welled up from somewhere inside of her. Of course he had seduced her. That had been his goal since fall when she turned eighteen, and she had been well aware of it. Yet she played along...stayed friends...toyed with fire. She should have shut down his attempts long ago.

Perhaps it went even beyond that. He had seduced her away from God, seduced her from her life's goals, and she had let him do it. It was no one's fault but hers. As soon as she moved here, Sarah had tucked her purity ring away in a drawer—that sham piece of jewelry that had no place on a nasty, dirty woman like her.

She shook her head at the thought. It made no sense. Logically, she was no longer convinced that premarital sex was wrong, and yet from years of habit she couldn't stop judging herself as harshly as she would have judged anyone else.

Add to that the fact that she still hadn't confirmed for college in the fall. She supposed it would be Old Dominion University by default since Christian school no longer made sense. Maybe she'd be bunking with Layla and the teenyboppers after all. She certainly couldn't face her parents day after day. Plus, she had no idea what she would study. Maybe she needed to take some time off to "find herself." She had always thought that saying was so stupid, but she had never in her wildest dreams imagined becoming as lost as she was right now.

Today was Easter. The day of new life. She needed that more than ever. If only she felt sure that Jesus was the answer. Her world had been so simple, so black and white, for eighteen years. Maybe too simple, maybe too rigid, but a part of her longed for those good old days.

The nagging burn on her rear that she vaguely recalled from last night started up again. Surely she hadn't gotten some sort of disease from Jesse. She couldn't fathom the embarrassment. He'd used protection every time, right? But considering her drunken state during a number of their encounters, she couldn't say for sure. This was too much, too far. She couldn't keep going like this. She was on the proverbial highway to hell, bent on self-destruction, and she had to find a way off.

Needing to relieve herself, Sarah stumbled from bed toward the bathroom they shared with the Fletchers down the hall. When she sat on the toilet seat, that spot on her rear screamed in protest. As soon as she could, she stood and turned to check it.

She pulled up Jesse's long, faded T-shirt and angled her slim bottom toward the mirror. To her horror, there it was emblazoned across her rear, a single word, branding her, mocking her.

Jesse. As if he owned her very soul.

She sank to the floor as the final remnants of her carefully constructed life crashed in upon her. She clutched at her chest, unable to catch her breath, then at her stomach as nausea overtook her. Maybe she could just sit here on the cold, linoleum floor until she died.

Dirty. Filthy. Whore. Fitting words to match the one on her tattooed rump. She would not listen to any crazy contradictory voices this time. This time she was too far gone for forgiveness and grace.

The Fletchers' wine rack flashed in her thoughts. She wanted to drink this all away, all the ugly memories, all the dirty deeds, but she couldn't bring herself to do that to the Fletchers. She was a guest in their home, and that wine was intended for modest consumption at fancy dinners only. Besides that, she was underage. She didn't even know how to get her hands on alcohol without Jesse's help.

Instead she turned on the shower and set the water to scalding, hoping against hope that she might be able to wash the sludge off her skin and down the drain.

THIRTY

Layla picked at a bowl of nuts, popping a few in her mouth, as Mom stirred a pot of chicken and rice soup—complete with garlic and the requisite Lebanese spices of course. The scent reached her nose across the huge kitchen.

"We have friends coming for dinner. Did I mention that? Go get ready, and be sure to wear your veil."

"Mom." Layla sighed.

"No arguing. We discussed this."

"How long until dinner?" Layla dug past the Brazil nuts to her favorite pecans. She deserved to have exactly what she wanted right now, even if just for a few seconds.

"In about an hour."

Layla retreated to the quiet of her room. After traversing the mammoth apartment, she settled on her bed and toyed with the books on her nightstand. She'd finished most of them in the last two weeks, but she picked up the *Boundaries* one Allie had given her.

She'd felt so drawn to it when Allie first placed it in her hands, but since then something had held her back. Instead, she'd pored through the Hosseini novel, which she enjoyed. Then the manuals from the "insider's movement" her father had given her, but none of those left her with the peace she needed. If anything, they just brought up more questions and confusion.

While in Norfolk, Layla had skimmed through the beginning of

Boundaries, but nothing really stood out to her, except that the life of the woman being depicted was seriously out of control. Layla had always been so structured and organized. She didn't relate.

But as she paused to consider the matter further, she supposed she did relate. She had so little control over her own life lately. Her parents had been calling all the shots, and it wasn't right. She'd been a breath away from agreeing to drop out of school for the semester and apply to an online program in the fall, even to keeping her Christian beliefs quiet and living out a Muslim life. Crazy! How did her parents get her to that point in two short weeks? She must be the weakest-willed person alive.

Layla picked up the book and began skimming through it once again. Almost immediately she found what she was looking for. She had thought boundaries were about keeping people out, putting up walls, but that wasn't the heart of the issue.

Boundaries were about knowing what you were and were not responsible for. God gave each adult responsibility for their own life and their own spiritual and emotional wellbeing. He wanted their yes to mean yes and their no to mean no. He wanted them—rather her, Layla—to stand up for what she truly believed. She shouldn't callously wound her parents, but at the end of the day, they were responsible for their feelings and decisions, and she was responsible for hers. In the past two weeks, ever since redonning her veil, Layla had felt awful.

She saw more clearly than ever the power of her mother's manipulation and guilt. For the first time in her life, instead of just feeling anxious and annoyed, she got a glimpse into how truly wrong it was for her mother to control her like that, and how wrong she had been for allowing it as an adult.

After poring through three chapters, she pressed the book to her chest. Of course one quick read through wouldn't be enough to undo a lifetime of training, but it bolstered her courage, and she would continue to study and memorize the words if needed. She had to head back to school in time for two big exams next week. Tonight she would inform her parents, and this time she would not let them talk her out of it. That would be enough for now.

Once in Norfolk, she would still have a lot to figure out, but at least she felt confident she was on the right track.

She stood to leave her room, then paused to snatch up a veil. This was her parents' home after all, and the visitors their friends, not hers. Okay, so she still had a long way to go, but she headed for her dad's study with a renewed sense of determination.

Opening the door, she pulled herself up as straight as possible and entered. No little mouse today.

"Hey, princess, what is it?"

"Dad, I'm going back to school this weekend. I need to get back for some important exams. Things should be safe enough now with the Maaloufs, and we'll discuss the online issue again this summer, but I'm not wasting all my hard work. Please book the ticket, and please don't bother arguing with me."

"Yes, ma'am." He bit back a chuckle, but his eyes sparkled with amusement. "You know your mother won't be happy though."

"Mom will adjust. Whether or not she's happy is her choice."

"I see."

Layla raised her chin. Nope, no more little mouse. She would take charge of her own life and her own destiny.

"Layla!" her mother hollered from the next room. "They're outside. That veil had better be on your head."

She smiled sheepishly to Dad and wrapped the scarf over her hair and neck.

He just raised a brow. "Choosing your battles, I see."

"For now." But someday Layla hoped she would dare to live life on her own terms.

A little over a week had passed since Rain moved out of the apartment, and already her resolve was slipping. She flopped onto her side on the bed that belonged to Layla and picked at the lilac and pale green of the comforter. Before long Layla would be home, which would mean Rain was moving to an inflatable mattress on the floor, but which also meant more company, thank goodness. Outside her bedroom door the never-ending slumber party from hell raged on. The fact that she'd even considered hanging out with Allie's crazy teenyboppers this evening spoke volumes.

Although Rain loved to be with people, she'd never been uncomfortable with being alone either—unless she was sad and already lonely, like she was today. From the depths of her soul, she missed James, the love of her life, the father of her child. Yet when she stopped to think about the euphoria of accepting Christ into her life, she knew it was worthwhile. She'd loved every second of the past two Sundays she'd spent at The Gathering. This had been the first time in her life that Easter, rather *Resurrection Sunday,* had meant anything more significant than eggs and bunnies.

Yes, this new life was worth any sacrifice, any risk, but when she considered the possibility that James could still turn her down, her stomach turned sour.

She picked up her cell phone from the nightstand and turned it over in her palm several times. Clicking it on, she scrolled to James's name in her contact list. Actually, he was listed under "My Man." Her finger hovered over the call button for several seconds, then she removed it, then put it back again. Finally, she tossed the phone to the foot of the bed far out of her reach.

Ugh! This was no good. She couldn't just let herself get mired in depression, and she couldn't cave either. The tone of the rest of her life depended on her remaining strong. Rain was a fighter. Gathering every ounce of courage and resolve she could find, she forced herself to her feet, shook off her funk, and headed directly into the face of her greatest fear.

If she could tackle the teenyboppers, she could tackle anything. Rain took a deep breath as she reached for the doorknob. Once she turned it, a cascade of noise tumbled into the room, but it was giddy and fun compared to the mournful silence of the bedroom.

She followed the squeals and giggles into the living room. Britney, Cara, Chelsea, Anna, and three of their friends from school perched at odd angles on sofas and ottomans as they played a frantic-looking board game.

"Rain!" Britney yelled. "Come join us. This is so, so fun. You are not going to believe it."

Rain would have to crank her energy level up several notches to match these girls, but even as they smiled and waved her over, she felt her mood lifting.

"Come on, Rain, but don't plan on winning," Chelsea cried. "Britney is stupid good at this. No wonder she thinks it's so fun."

"Yeah, I'd think it was fun too if I won every single time," Cara protested.

Rain held back a giggle. Britney reigned as the barely benevolent dictator of the teenybopper squad. Maybe Rain would stage a coup, just for fun. "Okay, but beware, I'm a little competitive." She rubbed her hands together.

Truth be told, Rain enjoyed seeing others win as much as she enjoyed winning herself, but games were so much more entertaining when she threw her whole effort into them. "So what's the general idea?"

"Basically, you pick a card and follow the directions, but they're pretty nuts. You might end up singing, or drawing, or dancing, or doing something completely nonsensical."

"Sounds perfect. I think I can give Britney a run for her money tonight."

"Oh, you think so?" Britney stood perched on the ottoman with her hands on her skinny little white girl hips.

"Oh, I know so." Rain followed her proclamation with a set of snaps and a head toss that set her corkscrew curls bouncing with sass.

The girls might be a little wacky, perhaps even a touch shallow for Rain's taste, but their youthful exuberance was just what she needed right now. Tonight she would laugh and play and let herself live in the moment. James had a decision to make. She couldn't make it for him, and pining over it would help nothing.

Noah trekked through the streets of Little Arabia as he did every morning. Most of the snow had melted, leaving only dirty mounds formed by plows and patches hidden away in shadowy corners. The call to sunrise prayers rang out from loudspeakers as always, but he kept his mind focused on his own prayers. A week had passed since Pastor Mike from Norfolk had called. Still the police had no real news about his angel on the balcony, Fatima Maalouf.

Noah might be new to all this love stuff, but he had learned years ago to hear God's voice and answer his call. Day after day as he prayed, he sensed his mission here was done, and when he contemplated the move to Norfolk, the quiet peace in his inner being told him that it was in fact the plan. As he passed the storefronts and turned into the residential area, the words *it is finished* resounded in his head.

But all that assurance did not quite reach his gut, which still felt sick at the thought of leaving Fatima. He'd veered off course, and he knew it. Had God called him to fall in love with the girl, to consider marrying a Muslim woman he'd barely met just to get her away from an abusive family? Of course not. His logical mind understood how ridiculous that sounded. A decision like that would undermine his ministry, everything he'd been working toward.

Sick as it made him, he needed to move on. God was right to call him away from this place, to set him on a new, fresh path. His work here had grown stale and jaded. His anger with Fatima's family had caused his heart to grow cold toward Muslim men in general. Now as he passed them on the street, he saw nothing but prideful, callous abusers. He no longer desired to share the water pipe with them at the hookah bar. All he cared about was Fatima. She had taken over his soul.

Turning the final corner, he forced himself to face his worse fear. For one second he dared to hope against hope, but her balcony lay empty once again. Without any pomp or circumstance, Noah quietly whispered good-bye in his heart. A tear slid down his cheek, and he swiped it away. Likely she was dead or shipped off to Saudi Arabia. He had done his best by praying and going to the police. Now he had to put her to rest.

Today he would take action. He would cancel his month-to-month lease and contact Mike about the move. Sadly, no one would even miss him here. Of course, it would take a week or two before everything was settled, but he would not walk down this street again. He would allow himself to wallow in the loss of Fatima Maalouf no longer. Noah tipped his hat in final tribute to the angel with the golden hair and set off in a new direction.

THIRTY-ONE

"Thanks so much for coming over." Layla met Ryan Hassan at the front door of the bungalow. The moment seemed to call for a hug or a handshake or something, but given their Muslim backgrounds, they just stood for a minute and nodded to each other. He turned his gaze down to his shoes and back up. Then she waved him in.

Ryan brushed his feet on the welcome mat and entered. He ducked under their low doorway. How had Layla failed to notice just how tall and striking he was during his visit to her aunt's house?

"Let's sit in the kitchen. A few of my roommates are here, so we don't have to feel awkward or anything. They're all studying, which is a small miracle. I say we enjoy it."

Ryan smiled and situated himself at the kitchen table. "You were such a mess the last time we talked. I couldn't just leave things like that."

"Coffee?" Layla picked up a mug from the counter.

"Sure." Ryan pushed his hair from his brow.

And how had she forgotten how deep and blue his eyes were?

Layla poured two cups and put them on a tray along with cream and sugar. What was she doing here, basically alone, with this handsome young man? Mo was still the love of her life, right? But in this moment, she longed for the comfort and understanding she knew Ryan would offer. She wasn't ready to deal with an awkward scene with Mo or with the very real possibility that he was still angry with her. Ryan's laidback attitude was just what the doctor ordered.

Ryan was not a Christian, though, she reminded herself, and she'd decided to boldly live her Christian faith. Well, sort of. Not quite. She'd even let her mother bully her into wearing a veil to the airport, but she took it off the moment she walked through security. That had to count for something.

She placed the tray on the table, and Ryan scooped up a mug with his long, tapered fingers. He added cream and sugar. Layla liked the way his long black eyelashes contrasted with his light skin.

He caught her staring. "Okay, enough of the requisite hospitality stuff. What's up with you, Layla?"

She took a sip of her still black coffee to mask her expression. Yuck! But she was stuck with it now.

"Come on. Talk to me."

"Fine. I'm still kind of a mess. After we talked I made a decision that I was going to live life on my own terms and not let my mother call the shots. I guess now I'm wavering on what those terms will be. All these decisions can be overwhelming when you're not used to them."

"Okay." Ryan set down his cup. "Let's start from the beginning. You told me about your dream. That was a decisive moment for you. Right?"

"Definitely."

"So on that morning when you woke up, how did you picture your future?"

Layla ran a finger around the rim of her mug. "I mean, it was a little scary and confusing, but I guess I pictured making a clean break with Islam and giving up the veil. I pictured finishing my education here in Norfolk, and...once things calmed down, I pictured myself with Mo."

"Has any of that changed?"

"Not really, but my dad made some good points, and the literature he gave me was pretty convincing. It was awful when my mom was mad at me. I did okay at first, but over time she wore me down."

He quirked an eyebrow. "And you want to make decisions based on being worn down?"

"Of course not. My American friends think I should just strike out on my own, but they don't realize how much my parents have coddled and pampered me all my life. I'm not sure I'm strong enough to do it. I'm not sure if I have the courage."

He took another sip of coffee as he considered her answer. "It must have taken a good dose of courage to accept Christianity in the first place."

"True, but I was so sure it was the right thing to do. As far as wear the veil, don't wear the veil...go to mosque, don't go to mosque...I'm just not certain."

Ryan tapped his chest. "What does your heart tell you?"

Mo had asked her the same thing last semester. Before that moment she had never thought to consider her heart. Layla sighed. "You had to go there, huh?"

"We could argue the logic in circles for hours, but in the end..."

"My heart says to take responsibility for my own choices. It says to live a life of integrity and to not pretend to be someone that I'm not."

"There you go." He shrugged.

"But I'm scared."

"Have you read Kierkegaard?"

"A little for philosophy class." She'd liked Kierkegaard fine, but she couldn't recall anything that would apply.

"He said, 'To dare is to lose one's footing momentarily. Not to dare is to lose oneself.'"

"Ouch." Layla winced. "I think I resemble that remark."

"Look, I'm perfectly content identifying as a Muslim. It doesn't bother me that I pick and choose from different religions. In the end, it means a lot to my dad, and it doesn't cost me anything, but it's different for you."

"Yeah, it is." She ducked her head, an old mousy habit she couldn't seem to shake. "But can I make it on my own?"

"You're stronger than you think. Plus, you'll never know until you try."

That was true. She'd never fathomed standing up to her parents over anything, let alone religion.

Ryan grasped her hand on the table top. Though warm and inviting, his touch didn't thrill her like Mo's—didn't call out to her to join her life with his and become one forever.

He gave her hand a squeeze. "So what does this mean about you and Mo?"

She offered a wry grin and gently extracted her hand. "Things aren't as easy with him as I expected. He's a pretty passionate guy. Part of me would prefer someone laid back like you, but my heart still says that Mo's the one. I can't deny that."

He returned his attention to his mug for a moment. "Then I guess you'll need to take a risk with him too."

"I guess so."

He drank down a few gulps of coffee and then pressed his lips together. "I don't know what else to say."

"Oh, Ryan, you are a wonderful friend, the best. I don't want things to be awkward between us."

He took a deep breath. "Good. Friends then?"

"Always."

And Mo would always be more than a friend. She didn't want to sneak around behind her parents' backs, but soon, very soon, she would take a strong stand. Just as quickly as she worked up that courage and strength that Ryan claimed she had.

Mo whipped off his waiter apron and took two Arabic coffees in demitasse cups out to the table where Pastor Mike waited for him. "Hey, buddy, thanks so much for meeting me here. You didn't have to, but I appreciate it."

Mike waved the comment away. "I remember how crazy things get with school and work. No worries."

Mo sat down across from him. "I just wanted to say I'm sorry for how I've been acting lately."

This time Mike didn't dismiss the words with a casual gesture.

Mo pressed on. "I need to get ahold of my temper."

"Honestly, you surprised me. I always considered you such a cool guy. I didn't realize you had that side."

"I hadn't seen it in a while either." Mo frowned. "I thought I was doing such a great job growing in Christ. I've even been considering dropping out of ODU and switching to seminary, but this whole thing with Layla and her family brought out a part of me that I thought was gone."

"It's a lot to deal with. I get that." Mike took a sip of his coffee. "This is good, by the way."

"Thanks." Mo wasn't quite sure what to say next.

"Are tempers normal in your culture? Do you think that's part of it?"

Mo paused to consider. "Anger is probably the most accepted emotion. You can be sad if someone dies, I guess, but after you mentioned about my feelings being hurt, I realized that we're a pretty tough people. We don't cop to being wounded. We just get mad and get even."

"Makes sense." Mike nodded.

"Except that it's not very healthy, huh?"

"Nope. Jesus said blessed are they that mourn, and that they'll be comforted. It's easy to help someone when they're hurting but almost impossible to help an angry person, even for God."

"Wow, I never thought of it like that. I guess I never wanted help. I wanted to do things for myself, but I get that I need to let God in."

"Let me ask you this. What's at the bottom of your anger?"

At the bottom? Mo tried to sift through his feelings, to take a deep look inside his heart. "She's driving me crazy, you know? I want to take care of her. I want to marry her. She doesn't need her parents anymore. She has me, but she won't let me in. I don't know how much of this I can take. I don't even know if she wants me anymore."

"It's rough feeling out of control like that."

"Man, is it!"

"But you have to let go of that control and turn the situation over to God."

His entire body went tense at the very thought. "That's easier said than done. I mean, I've been working on it for a year and a half, but I guess I'm not as far along as I thought. And I thought Layla would be thrilled to let me in and let me take charge of things for her."

"Layla needs to figure out how to stand strong on her own two feet before she can partner with someone else."

Although he knew Mike was right, that statement didn't sit well in the feeling place Mo had been examining. "But what do I do until then? I've got to get this anger under control, or I'm going to scare her away completely."

"The Bible doesn't say we can't feel anger." Mike sat back and crossed his legs, looping his arms over his knee. "God felt anger, and so did Jesus. It says to be angry but not to sin, to be quick to listen, slow to speak, and slow to become angry. I think you need to listen more and pause to consider things before you respond. Peace, patience, gentleness, those are what need to come out of your mouth, especially with a tender-hearted girl like Layla."

"That's a pretty tall order."

"But she's worth it, right?"

Mo pictured Layla on the day they went swimming at the beach—

the day she struck a pose on the edge of the boardwalk in her first ever swimsuit, the day he rubbed lotion onto her shoulders, brushed sand from her nose, and floated with her on the rolling waves. All the old feelings came crashing back. Of course she was worth it. Fighting tears, he just nodded.

"Have you seen her yet?" Mike asked.

"What do you mean?"

"Since she came back? Have you seen her?"

"She's back?" Anger waged war with despair and regret in his chest. Once again, he was the last to know the most basic information about her.

"Sorry." Mike sighed. "I guess it's worse than I realized, huh? But she just got here yesterday, so try not to freak out."

Through the haze of his many emotions, one thought came through loud and clear. "I need to see her...now. I need to apologize for how I behaved."

"Are you sure you're ready? Don't go if you're going to lose it."

"If I don't go, I might lose her."

Mo got permission from his boss and rushed over to Layla's house in under ten minutes. He pulled up to the curb a few houses away. Her driveway was always littered with the cars of her many roommates. As he took a minute to gather his thoughts and plan what he was going to say, the door to the bungalow opened.

Out walked Layla followed by a tall, good-looking guy. What in the world? Why did she have a strange guy at her house? As they approached a black sports car, Mo made out his features. He'd seen that guy at the restaurant before. Wasn't he a Muslim?

No sooner had that thought crossed his mind than the man leaned over and gathered Layla to his chest. She didn't resist. Instead she wrapped her arms around his broad shoulders and rested her head against him. They stayed like that for the count of ten, still talking, as Mo's world seeped to fiery red, and hot lava shot through his veins.

In his mind, he pictured himself storming out of the car and ripping them apart. He burned with the desire to stuff his fist far down the guy's throat. He started to move into action, fingers twitching on the door handle, feet poised to dash.

Then he got a hold of himself.

It took every ounce of strength and self-control he possessed to deny his instincts. "Be angry and sin not," he whispered to himself. "Be slow to speak and slow to become angry." Drawing on a supernatural reserve he didn't feel, he managed to stay in the car, but he couldn't stop himself from pounding the steering wheel with his fist.

Maybe there was some explanation. Surely Layla hadn't pushed Mo away just to jump into the arms of this stranger. He took deep breaths and forced himself to think the best.

At long last, the guy got into his car and drove away. More than anything, Mo wanted to confront Layla and learn the truth, but he'd pushed himself to the limit already by not punching the dude in the face. If he tried to talk to her now, he'd blow it for sure.

Never even noticing him, she disappeared back into the house.

He shoved the gearshift into reverse and took off down the street, unsure of anything but the fact that he needed to get far away.

THIRTY-TWO

Fatima knelt on the big, plush chair by the front window, waiting for her guests. The Fletchers were both at work today, but she'd come to feel safe and relaxed in their home. Sarah should be here any minute as well, although Fatima wondered if she would actually show up.

Her girlfriends had limited their visits for her protection, but Fatima couldn't wait to see Layla again, and it had been too long since Rain or Allie stopped by. The old Fatima loved friends and parties, and she wanted to find that person again. She was tired of being a broken butterfly who'd spent too much of her life shattered in pieces across the marble floor. The time had come to pull herself together, perhaps even to look to the future and make long-term plans.

Layla's red convertible pulled into the driveway with a crunch of gravel. Fatima hopped up. She rearranged her long purple sweater over her skinny jeans, both gifts from Donna Fletcher and her clothing ministry. Although Donna didn't come right out and say it, she had hinted that Sarah's hand-me-downs weren't very stylish. Fatima giggled. Even a veiled Muslim woman knew that much. She was adjusting to regular American clothing and happy to look cheerful and trendy. Maybe once the danger passed, she'd even try going in public without a veil. If Layla could do it, so could she.

Rain, Layla, Allie, and a fourth girl with brown skin like James's all exited the car. Fatima wondered at her presence, but she trusted her friends and assumed the girl must be okay. However, her gut clenched at the sight of Allie. Her resemblance to Sarah caught Fatima off guard, dredging up guilt over the whole Easter weekend fiasco. Although she had considered talking to Sarah, or even conferring with the Fletchers, in the end she kept her mouth shut.

Sarah's face the following morning clearly displayed her shame and regret. Fatima saw no need to make matters worse. She didn't want a tense relationship with Sarah, as she had more than enough tension in her life already.

Fatima greeted the girls at the door with hugs, hellos, and standard Middle Eastern kisses.

"Hey, this is my friend Shondra." Allie waved toward the young African American woman. "I hope you don't mind that I brought her, but she keeps asking about you, and I thought you guys would get along."

Shondra took Fatima's hand in a warm clasp. "You've been on my heart ever since Allie shared your story with me. I can't even imagine."

Fatima ducked her head. "I am fine now. They are all taking such good care of me. The next step, I am supposing, is to learn to take care of myself."

"No rush." Rain wrapped her arm around Fatima's shoulder and ushered her into the Fletchers' blue denim and checkered flannel living room. "Right now just get well and be safe. Okay? We can worry about the rest later."

"I guess so." But when would later come? Fatima had lived as a phantom, a shadow, since puberty. Soon, she hoped to be a real human being and to contribute somehow. Not that she had any idea what that might mean, but if the rest of these young women could, surely she could too.

She had prepared cookies and tea on the coffee table, and she invited the girls to help themselves. This seemed to be the American way, this "help yourselves," and Fatima longed to feel like an American for once.

"Oh, yes!" Rain grabbed a handful of cookies. "This baby is demanding more and more calories by the day." Her belly poked far out in front of her now, but Fatima managed not to blush at the sight. She had almost adjusted to Rain's very different lifestyle. "How is James?"

Rain stared down at her cookie but said nothing. Allie and Layla shot glances to each other.

"What is it?" Fatima persisted.

"I'm not living with him right now." Rain took another bite, chewed, and swallowed. As all eyes remained focused on her, she continued. "I've started going to The Gathering, and I've realized you were right, Fatima. Babies belong in families, and families should be forever. Now I'm waiting to see if James will agree. I'm sorry if I made you uncomfortable with the way I was living before."

"No, no, no!" Fatima nearly jumped to her feet but managed to remain seated. Her heart sank in her chest. "I am so sorry. I did not mean to make you feel bad, and I certainly did not mean for you to leave James. Are you sure?"

Rain sat silently.

"She's as sure as she can be," Allie said. "Hey, I heard you visited your first real Christian church on Easter with the Fletchers."

Fatima smiled at the pleasant memory. "It was not what I expected. It was very small and met in a cafe. I wore my new jeans." She rubbed her hand over them.

"Nice," Shondra said. "Very chic."

"Thanks. It felt more like a party or something. There was a lot of eating and talking, some nice music, even dancing."

"Sounds like my kind of place," Allie said, "but they had prayer and a sermon too, I assume."

"Yes, but again, it all seemed very casual." Fatima had barely remembered to think of them as infidels or their teachings as blasphemy. "The praying sounded like talking to a friend. They didn't even bow, and people kept adding to the sermon. It was more of a discussion really, about Jesus's gift of love."

"Great topic," Shondra said. "Can't go wrong with that one."

Fatima had found it all surprisingly refreshing. "It was nice to be out around people. I'm finally starting to feel like my old self again."

"And I heard you're an incredible hip-hop dancer." Shondra hit a pose. "Maybe you'll show me your moves sometime."

"Oh yeah, oh yeah," Fatima joked, crossing her arms and opening them again. "I am buck, like the Little C."

Shondra laughed. "I heard about that too."

"Hey." Allie glanced around the room and then out the window. "When's Sarah going to be here?"

Fatima's merry mood fell flat. She bit her lip. "I don't know. She's usually here by now, and she planned to come."

"Man, I wish I knew what was going on with that girl." Allie dug her fingers into her scalp in obvious frustration.

Fatima's gaze darted about the room, looking for a safe place to land. She couldn't bear to face Allie, but Rain and Layla knew her too well. Finally, she looked to Shondra. "So, do you like hip-hop?"

"Definitely. I taught some classes to kids at my church last—"

"Hold up!" Layla cut Shondra off. "Sorry, Shondra, but Fatima knows something, and she's trying to deflect. What are you hiding, girlie? Spill it."

Fatima sighed. "I really shouldn't say with so many people here." She looked to each woman. Of course they would be kind and understanding, but she could not expose Sarah's shame to such a large group.

Allie's chest cinched tight. She pressed her hands deep into the blue denim couch. As she'd suspected, something was going on with

Sarah. She needed to get to the bottom of this. "Fatima, I could really go for some ice water. Would you come with me to the kitchen?"

Fatima appeared pale and tense, as if she were about to face a firing squad. Nonetheless, she stood and said, "Please excuse me," as she followed Allie to the sunny, yellow kitchen.

Allie dropped the pretense of wanting water the minute they passed through the swinging door. "Please, Fatima. You have to tell me. You don't understand how concerned I've been."

Fatima studied the hardwood floor. "Sarah has become like a sister to me as well. I do wish to help her, but I do not want to be getting her in any trouble."

"I won't tell my parents, I promise, but I have to know what we're dealing with here."

With a good bit of stuttering and hesitation, Fatima told Allie the awful tale of Sarah driving home drunk, puking, and passing out on the bed. When Allie continued to prod her, Fatima described the tattoo across Sarah's bottom. Allie's stomach tied in knots. Matters were far worse than even she had suspected.

"Jesse? Jesse? That name sounds familiar." She scanned her mind and finally stumbled upon a tough little boy who'd moved in with his aunt and uncle down the street shortly before she left home. "I wonder if it's Jesse Kinsella, our neighbor. I think he rides the bus with her. That would certainly give them time to bond."

"I don't know." Fatima clasped her hands together in front of her chest. Her knuckles showed white. "I wish I knew nothing. I do not want to hurt her."

Allie took Fatima's hands in her own. "You did the right thing. I can't even imagine what Sarah's going through. She must be completely falling apart."

"She puts on a brave face for the Fletchers and for me, but I think you are right."

"Don't you give this another thought. I'll deal with it."

Fatima nodded and Allie led her back into the living room.

She'd stick around all night if need be, but she wasn't about to leave this house until she and Sarah had a very long discussion.

Layla sat up as Allie ushered Fatima back into the living room, but neither of them said another word about Sarah. Of course, it was none of Layla's business, but she couldn't help her curiosity.

Rain picked up on the discomfort in the room and opened a new discussion. "So Fatima, when we came in you mentioned the next step. Like I said, I don't want you to rush or anything, but have you given any thought to the future?"

"Oh yes, I have been giving this much thought."

Thank goodness. They had been chatting about the Fletchers' casual interior design while the girls were in the kitchen, and Layla couldn't take much more small talk. "You know, the police are heavily involved now back home. I realize you didn't want to cause trouble, but maybe it's time to talk to them, and you could at least try a restraining order. Then you'd have some legal leverage if they come around. You wouldn't have to say much—just that there's been tension at home, and you're concerned that they'll force you to return."

Fatima flinched.

"Seriously, Fatima. She's right." Rain nodded with sympathy. "We need to start somewhere. You can't do anything right now. Like, James really wanted to teach you to drive, but he can't if you don't get a permit."

"You can't get a job or go to school or even get a credit card." Allie rubbed Fatima's arm. "But once we tell people who you are, everything will change."

"There's a whole big world out there." Shondra pointed to the window. "You can't hide away forever."

"But my brothers! I think they are still here."

"No one's seen them in days. Layla, have you talked to your friend Salaam?" Rain asked.

"Not yet." She hadn't really wanted to know if Fatima's brothers were still in town. It was easier to assume they'd given up, especially when she was talking her parents into letting her return. Hopefully they were far off in Oregon by now. "I guess I should do that, though."

"If you cooperate with the police, I'm sure they'll look after you," Shondra said. "I mean, think about it. We'll all be safer once your brothers are behind bars."

Allie shook her head at Shondra but too late. Fatima pulled away from Allie. "No! I will not. I will shame my family no more than I already have."

Layla had assumed as much. A restraining order was one thing, but indicting her family in any way was quite another. Shondra didn't understand, but at least she didn't seem to take offense. Layla crossed the room and knelt in front of Fatima. "Then what can we do? Tell us what you want."

"Do not they sometimes give people a new identity?" Fatima whispered, twisting her hands in her lap.

"Yes, my sweet sister. It's called witness protection, but that's for people who testify against criminals, and you would have to move far away from all of us."

"Oh." Tears filled Fatima's eyes. "Then maybe Rain is correct. We do not need to decide anything right now. I was thinking there might be another way." She grinned through her tears. "At this moment, what I want is to have fun and enjoy my new friends. Shondra, please be telling me more about these hip-hop classes."

The conversation turned to lively chatter as Layla's mind spun into overdrive.

There was another way, the Middle Eastern way, perhaps the only way to deal with Middle Eastern issues. If Fatima was still determined not to talk to the police, Layla could only think of one other possibility.

In Lebanon, a few greased palms could buy a new identity, but things weren't so easy in America. She wasn't sure if such tactics were even ethical in her new faith, although she'd never given them a second thought before. It was simply the way the government functioned.

There was only one person who could help her now, who could answer these questions. It was high time she broke the stony silence and talked to Mo.

THIRTY-THREE

Sarah meandered through the subdivision's winding streets in her mom's minivan heading toward the Fletchers' house. She had spent the afternoon at the park with Jesse to avoid her older sister, but she'd have to come up with a better excuse than that since Fatima had been the one to organize today's get-together. She'd been cheerful and energetic these past few days, and Sarah didn't want to be the one to bring her down. Sadly, lying was growing easier and easier. Like when they told that cop at the park they were just "looking for her cell phone" in the bushes.

As Sarah had planned, Layla's car was gone when she arrived to the Fletcher house. What she hadn't planned was that Allie was sitting on the front steps waiting for her. Maybe she could still turn around, but the stern look on Allie's face told her that she couldn't run forever.

Sarah blew out a breath as she put the van in park. Her mind riffled through possible excuses while Allie marched toward her.

Allie opened the door. "Sarah, enough is enough. What's going on with you? I'm really concerned."

She played dumb as she exited the van. "I am so, so, sorry. Was Fatima upset? Erica got sick, and I had to drive her home, and she lives way over by the bay. I should have called, I know, but my phone was dead, and I didn't want her to think she was putting me out or anything."

Allie took her by the shoulders. "Fatima's fine. This is not about

Fatima. This is about you. I know something's going on, and I'm not leaving until you talk to me."

Shoot, what did Allie know? "Did someone say something?"

"It's obvious that Fatima's worried about you. She didn't want to tell me much, but I've known for months that something wasn't right."

Darn. Had Fatima picked up on something? When she hadn't questioned her on Easter morning, Sarah assumed she was in the clear, but maybe not.

"And don't you dare go blaming that sweet, innocent girl. This is not her fault."

The fact that Allie would even suggest she would blame Fatima broke something open inside of Sarah's hard heart. She jerked away from Allie and looked down at the gravel. "I know it's not her fault. It's my fault—only mine. Everything is my fault." Tears began to stream, and Sarah could do nothing to hold them back. "Just please don't tell Mom and Dad. Please, whatever you do."

Allie pulled Sarah into her arms and rubbed her back. "Shh. Shh. I would never betray your trust. I thought you knew me better than that."

"I just..." Sarah hiccupped. "I wasn't sure."

"The Fletchers are out at their small group, and Fatima will give us privacy. Come sit down." Allie led her to the porch steps, where they cuddled side by side. "Now I want you to start at the beginning and tell me everything."

Sarah couldn't hold it inside any longer. She obeyed Allie's bidding, happy to turn over control of her messed up life, if only for a few minutes. She started with Jesse's patient flirtation and ended with the drunk driving and unfortunately placed tattoo. "I feel so awful. So dirty. So unworthy."

"You aren't, Sarah. God loves you, and he's been reaching out to you this whole time. You don't have to be worthy on your own.

No one is. That's why we need a savior. Yes, you had some attitude issues. Yes, you were uptight and judgmental, but that's over now."

"Now I'm a basket case."

"Now you're a precious child of God in need of his grace and forgiveness. It's not the worst place to be." Allie gave her a squeeze. "Sometimes things need to get messy before they can improve. It's one of those rules of life that no one wants to tell you when you're a kid."

"But here's the problem." Sarah bit her lip. "I don't know if I am a child of God."

"He said he'd never leave you or forsake you." Allie tucked a few wisps of blond hair behind Sarah's ear.

"That's not what I mean." Sarah picked at her cuticle and found the courage to continue. "Jesse was right about one thing. Deep inside, I doubted. I questioned. Maybe that's why I was so rigid. I didn't want anyone to know. I had to put on a good show and be the perfect Christian daughter. But, Allie, I've never felt God like you have. I've never heard his voice. All those years I claimed he was lord of my life, but I clung to rules because he's a stranger to me. Those legalistic standards were the only way I knew to be righteous."

"Oh, Sarah!"

"And now I don't even have those. I really don't know what I believe anymore."

Allie sat quiet for a few moments.

Sarah detected a few whispery breaths that indicated she must be praying.

Finally Allie turned to her. "You're right. You have to believe from deep inside. But are you positive that you've never sensed God's presence? Never heard his voice?"

Sarah's memory shot to that first night at the Fletchers' house, when she had feared the Holy Spirit was in the room with her. When some deeper voice had battled her inner demons with the simple words—*forgiven, worthy, mine.* "Maybe, once, a few weeks ago. But why would God reach out to me now when I'm such a disaster? Why not during all those years when I tried so hard to serve him?"

"I don't know. Maybe because you were so determined to do it in your own strength. Maybe you weren't willing to let him in. I can't say for sure."

Allie's words rang true. Other thoughts filtered through Sarah's head like *pride goeth before destruction, and an haughty spirit before a fall* and *judge not that ye not be judged.* If there was one thing Sarah knew, it was the Bible, forward and backward in perfect King James. Yet somehow she suspected she had missed the whole point.

Sarah sniffled again, although she was all cried out. Words tumbled from her mouth before she could catch them back. "I can never do anything right. If I were more like you, everything would be different. Mom and Dad always loved you more."

"What's that mean?" Allie's tone remained gentle despite Sarah's harsh indictment.

"I'm sorry. I don't know what I'm saying."

"I think you do. Please, Sarah, explain what you meant."

Sarah buried her face on her hands against her knees. "All those years you were gone, you were all they talked about—Allie this and Allie that. I could never live up to you. All I got was criticism. I was never quite good enough. You know?"

Allie pressed her eyes closed. "I do know. That's a big part of why I ran away, but I never stopped to think what that decision might mean for you."

"Then you came home, and they were tripping all over themselves to please you...buying you cars...renting you houses. Meanwhile, they kept bugging me to switch to Christian school and spend more time at home helping out. It wasn't fair."

"No, it wasn't. I'm so sorry, Sarah. Will you forgive me?" Allie pressed a comforting kiss to her forehead.

"It wasn't your fault."

"Maybe not but I'm sorry I didn't understand." She shifted to face Sarah. "Here's what we're going to do. We're going to pray that God will reveal himself to you in a very real and present way, in a way that will soothe your spirit and overcome your every doubt, in a way that will give you the strength to break up with Jesse. That guy's no good for you. You get that, right?"

Sarah had known Allie would tell her to dump Jesse, but hadn't she come to that same conclusion on her own? The rest of what Allie said about God's presence being real to her—she wanted that more than anything. Sarah closed her eyes and allowed Allie's fervent prayer to wash over her like sweet spring rain.

Layla sat outside the restaurant where Mo worked and watched him through the window, feeling like a stalker. Despite her trepidation, a shiver of delight washed over her at the sight of him. He looked as attractive as ever as he rushed back and forth, charming the customers. His biceps bulged beneath the sleeves of his knit shirt. How she longed to be wrapped in his arms once again.

She had made up her mind. She was going to talk to him tonight. In fact, she had spent much of the last twenty-four hours poring through her *Boundaries* book and having Allie give her pep talks, but here she was faltering again. She didn't want to disobey her parents, but she was an adult, and they didn't have any business setting demands on her life anymore, except that she'd given them the power by living off their provision. They no longer shared her values or beliefs, and she needed to take control of her own life.

Then it hit Layla—it was more than that. She'd given them her word, and she did not want to break it. In that moment, she knew exactly what she needed to do. She fished her iPhone out of her handbag, which probably cost more than several of the cars in the parking lot surrounding her, and she dialed her father. Not her mother, mind you, but since Mom encouraged the charade that Dad was the head of the home, she felt no guilt in bypassing her more difficult parent.

"Layla, princess!" Dad greeted her. "How is everything in Virginia?"

"It's good, Dad." That wasn't entirely true, or else she wouldn't be calling him right now. Salaam hadn't been able to tell her anything. It seemed Fatima's brothers were keeping too close an eye on Dani for him to pass along information. "Well, mostly good. I'm hopeful that Fatima's brothers have given up and left town, but no one seems to know for sure."

"You haven't seen them?"

"No."

"That's a relief."

"But I'm still concerned." She braced herself against the supple leather interior of her car for what she was about to say next. "Dad, I need to talk to Mo. He's my only friend in town who really understands what I'm dealing with." And who could take into account the variable of Fatima being here, she thought but didn't mention. "I need his advice, and I need his friendship. I'm not asking for your permission, but I didn't want to be dishonest with you either."

Dad inhaled sharply. "I see."

"I realize I gave you my word that I wouldn't see him, but we both knew that didn't mean forever."

"It seems that your mind is made up."

"It is."

"Do you plan to date him again?" Disappointment weighed down Dad's voice.

"I'm not rushing into anything, but I've had this whole semester to find myself and figure things out, and eventually..." Her mind wandered to the wondrous memory of his lips pressed against hers.

Heat seeped into her cheeks. "Eventually I want to marry him. That is, if he'll still have me after all the heartache I put him through."

The look on Mo's face as he stood shivering on her doorstep for hours over the holiday break still haunted her. She should have let him in. Seeing his relatives had only been an excuse, and he had come to Detroit for her. She should have forced her parents to meet him, but mousy little Layla had caved to their demands.

No more.

"I'm not sure what to say, Layla. We had an agreement. What about your education?"

"I promise you this; I won't date him this semester. Okay? I'll be home for the summer soon and then off to Lebanon. That gives us a few more months to figure things out. Is that fair?" But now that she'd let her mind slip to imagining Mo in a romantic light again, a few months sounded like an eternity.

"Your mother won't be happy."

"What else is new? If her happiness hinges on controlling me, then she might have to be sad for a while. I need to take ownership of my life and my decisions. Well, me and God, but I need to be faithful to his leading."

"My little girl is all grown-up. I feel like I hardly know you anymore."

"I'm trying, Dad, and I love you, you and Mom. Please tell her that for me."

"I love you too."

They said good-bye, and Layla clicked off the phone. That went as well as could be expected, but now she had to face Mo.

Mo typed the lengthy order from his twelve-top table into the restaurant's computer. The mandatory tip from this table alone would make tonight's shift well worth his time. With finals coming up soon, he really should cut back his hours, but he needed to save up every penny for when the time came to break financial ties with his parents. Now that he'd researched the issue more, he'd decided to go ahead and finish his bachelor's in engineering next semester after all. It just made sense, but once he started on his master's degree in theology, he'd be on his own for sure.

Layla had been against him dropping engineering. He wondered how she'd feel about this new plan, but Layla wasn't his anymore, and he had to accept that and move on. He had his whole life still ahead of him, and if he went to a Christian grad school, no doubt he'd have plenty of intelligent, beautiful women to choose from—even if they weren't his Layla.

Katie nudged him out of his reverie. "Hey, Mo, that girl is looking right at you. Do you know her?"

And there she was. Layla. The face he could never quite remove from the back of his mind. Did he even want to talk to her? Now that was a ridiculous question. A thrill shot through him as he gazed at her, drinking in every detail from the wisps of her dark hair to the shy smile on her luscious, berry-tinted lips. Of course he wanted to talk to her, and he promised himself that he would not let his anger get the best of him this time.

He rushed to where she stood like a lost little sheep by the entrance. "Layla! I'm so sorry. I said awful things. I didn't mean them. I just miss you so much." Without meaning to, he wrapped his arms around her and caught her to him. Oh, she felt so right there, as if she'd been born to be pressed against his chest.

"No, I'm sorry. I did everything wrong. I've been a wimp, a weak-willed mess. I should have stood up to my parents. I shouldn't have given up on you so easily. It was ridiculous to expect you to wait around with no guarantee."

Her words rang like sweet music in his ears. He hadn't dared to hope that *she* might apologize to *him*. As he looked down into her face, the image was blocked by the awful memory of her in the arms of another man. He stiffened. The warm haze that had suffused him dissipated.

"What?" she asked. "Am I too late?"

Mo dropped his arms and shuffled backward a step. "Maybe I'm the one who's too late."

"Please, Mo, don't be cryptic."

He stared directly into her eyes, needing to see the truth as well as hear it. "Who was the guy I saw hugging you outside your house?"

"Oh!" Her olive skin paled to ivory. "You were there? I didn't see you."

"That's not the point." Mo crossed his arms over his chest but managed to maintain an even tone. He felt a hard mask creeping over his face but swiped his hand over it, revealing his true hurt and disappointment instead.

"No, it's not the point." Layla agreed.

He expected her to duck her head, but instead she faced him head on. "I'm sorry you saw that. It must have been painful and confusing, but I promise, Ryan is only a friend. In fact, he helped me to see that I need to stop letting my parents bully me and follow my own convictions, and he helped me realize that my heart will always lead me back to you."

Warm joy fought its way through the cold of moments before, but he wasn't ready to give in to it quite yet. His mouth tipped up on one side. "I told you the same thing months ago."

Layla grinned. "I know. So did Allie. And Rain." She began to tick them off on her fingers. "And Shondra. And Fatima. And Pastor Mike. I just wasn't ready to hear it then. This time I was."

"What's so special about this Ryan?"

She shrugged. "He's a good listener. His dad is Muslim and his mom is a normal American. It gives him a unique perspective, you know?"

Mo relaxed his stance and raked his fingers through his hair. If this Ryan had helped, he guessed he shouldn't be mad. Boy, was he glad he'd come straight from his talk with Mike that day and hadn't jumped out of the car and started a brawl. That would have scared her off for good. "I guess I get it."

"I was struggling more than I admitted to you. My dad was trying to convince me to stay culturally Muslim and keep my new beliefs to myself. I'm embarrassed to admit how close I came to caving. I'm still a bit wobbly in my resolve, but I'm working on it, and I know that God wants me to live a life of integrity, even if it isn't easy."

So what did this mean for them? He was afraid to ask. "How were things at home?"

"On one hand I saw how wonderful my parents are and how much I appreciate them. They do so much for me. But I also realized that I can't live my life for them. I have to live my life for God...and for me."

Gathering his courage, he added, "And what about me?"

"I wasn't sure if you wanted me anymore." Layla did duck her head now.

This time it struck him as the most adorable gesture in the entire world. Oh, how he wanted her. He wanted to grab her and kiss her silly right here and now like people did in those American romance movies, but he couldn't do that to her in public, and a part of him still feared she'd push him away. "I do still want you, but maybe we rushed things last time. It just all seemed so magical. I guess we still have some issues to work out. We haven't exactly had a normal relationship."

She sighed. "I agree, and I promised my dad I wouldn't 'date' you for the rest of the semester, but after that I'm going to have a firm talk with him and my mom. If they cut me off, then I'll have to grow up and figure it out somehow."

"Come here," he pulled her back into an embrace, right where she belonged. Hope burst bright in his chest. He wanted to lose himself in this moment forever, but the clangs and scents of the restaurant called him back to reality. "I need to get back to work. I have a giant table right now."

He let go but caught her hand in his, not wanting to break contact.

"There's one more thing." Layla tugged on his hand to keep him from leaving.

Turning to scan the restaurant, he noticed Mrs. Katan leaning on the kitchen window with her chin resting in her palm. As she gazed at them with a moonstruck expression on her face, she waved. He chuckled. "I guess I can spare one more minute."

Layla lowered her voice and glanced around. "I need some advice about Fatima. It's been two months, and her brothers are still looking for her. She doesn't want to go to the police. I'm starting to think we might have to handle this the Lebanese way, but I have no idea how to go about that. I know as Christians we're supposed to honor the law, but I'm not sure what else to do."

"How about you take me to meet her? I've helped out the local FBI before, so I have some contacts there and I know the system, but I know how to do things the Lebanese way too. Let's just keep that for a last resort."

A look of utter relief crossed her beautiful features. "Thank you so much. I knew I could count on you."

He'd be happy to let her count on him for the rest of her life.

THIRTY-FOUR

Mo studied Fatima in the soft lamplight of the Fletchers' blue and red living room. After chatting with the fragile girl for the past half hour, he could hardly believe that she'd survived two decades of abuse. Glancing from Doug to Donna to Layla and back to Fatima, he decided the time had come to address the topic he'd been skirting all night.

He tapped his hands together a few times. "So, Fatima, Layla's mentioned that you don't want to go to the police for a restraining order, but I don't understand why."

A hard glimmer set into her eye. He would have sworn her backbone turned to steel right in front of him by the way she switched from curling into the sofa to sitting ramrod straight. "I can't. I won't, and no one can make me."

This girl had an inner strength he hadn't bargained for. "But why?"

She bristled. "You must ask me why? You should know how hard it is to turn on your family."

"But my family never beat me. They never tracked me down to murder me."

At that she softened a bit.

Layla nodded. He was on the right track.

"I just can't," Fatima whispered. Through her anger, he glimpsed the fear and brokenness beneath.

No one said anything for a while.

Doug Fletcher stood and brushed off his jeans. "Hey, Mo, are you engineering guys any good with cars?"

That was an odd and unexpected question, but by the pointed look in Doug's grayish-blue eyes, Mo realized he must have a purpose.

"I could really use some help with my old Vette," Doug continued.

"Sure thing. Would you ladies excuse us for a moment?"

"Of course." Layla patted his knee in a familiar manner that fueled him. He wanted to do all he could for her, and right now, that meant finding a solution for Fatima.

He stood and followed Doug out the door and around the side of the house to the garage. Although taller than average and solidly built, Mo felt short and scrawny next to the former soldier.

Doug leaned against an old Corvette up on blocks. "Look, here's the thing. I'm not sure how much that girl can take. She's been to hell already."

"I didn't mean to push her. I'm just trying to get a pulse on the situation."

Doug crossed his arms over his chest. Everything about him screamed experience and authority. "I respect that, but I've been watching her for weeks. I can tell you this much—if we get the police involved it might get ugly. It took every ounce of courage she had just to get away. If she has to face her family in a line-up or a trial...I think it might break her. She might just collapse, give up, and go home."

Mo blew out a long, low breath. "They'd ship her off to Saudi Arabia for sure."

"And that would be the end of Fatima as we know her. Whatever life, humor, spunk she has left would be snuffed out for good. Assuming they don't just murder her once they're out of the States."

Doug seemed to know what he was talking about. "You have experience with this kind of stuff?"

"I do. I spent a lot of time in the Middle East. Two tours in Iraq and one in Afghanistan. These women don't have much to cling to."

Mo had thought he'd be the one with Middle Eastern experience, but his few summers in the moderate nation of Lebanon didn't rank with Doug's expertise. "What about the FBI? I have some connections there."

"It would be the same thing. They'd need her to cooperate. They'd want some sort of legal proof."

Mo kicked at the gravel. "So what recourse does that leave us?"

Doug took a deep breath. "I think you know. Sometimes when dealing with Middle Easterners, you have to do things the Middle Eastern way."

"That's what Layla said, but the thing is, we're not in the Middle East. We're in America. We can't just set up a fraudulent life for her here. It would come back to bite her for sure, and things would be worse than ever."

"I know."

"Plus, I'm concerned about the moral issues involved, not to mention the legal ones. I haven't been a Christian that long, but I'm sure we're supposed to honor the law." Mo stuck his hands in his pockets.

Doug came over to him and grasped his shoulder. "Son, I've been a Christian for longer than you've been alive, and if there's one thing I know, it's that people come first with God. Jesus makes that clear. He said that the Sabbath was made for man, not man for the Sabbath. As far as the laws, our commanders in the military had to get pretty creative in order to help people the way they needed to over there, so I don't have any qualms about doing the same."

"What do you suggest?"

"I'm not sure yet. I've been getting some hazy impressions but nothing clear. She has distant relatives in Syria, but that would make her easy to track."

"We can't ship her off to another country just to put her in danger all over again."

Doug let go of Mo and kneaded his temple. "There's not a simple solution, but I feel like the time for action is coming soon."

"Maybe we need to get everyone over here for a prayer and brainstorming session," Mo suggested.

Doug closed his eyes for a minute. "Mmm, that's it. I sense that's exactly what we need to do. Maybe the reason I wasn't getting anything clear is that this needs to be a group effort."

"Great, let's do it then." A sense of relief flooded Mo now that they had a plan of action in place.

"How about Saturday night? That will give us a little time," Doug said. "Can you set it up?"

"Between me and Layla, definitely."

Doug closed his eyes again. He nodded his head a few times and then opened them. "Things are going to move quickly from here."

A shiver went down Mo's spine. Although he couldn't pinpoint why, Mo had a feeling Doug was right.

Doug opened the door of the Corvette and cranked up the engine. "What do you say we work on this car for a few minutes so we can go back into the house as honest men?"

Mo chuckled. This Doug was something else. Mo had assumed he'd have to handle this situation all on his own, but it seemed like God had other plans. After tinkering with the engine for a few moments, he and Doug wiped their hands on a rag and headed back to the living room. The women were relaxed and sipping tea, discussing possible new hair styles for Fatima. She giggled at Layla's suggestion of pink highlights.

Mo winked to Layla, his precious little mouse. He could hardly believe she was back in his life. More than ever before, he determined to grow into a man of faith she could depend on, a man like Doug and like Pastor Mike, who knew how to be both strong and gentle.

He wanted to learn to let God's strength flow through him as he led their home.

Noah stared out the window as the rich green scenery flew past him. Trees, birds, wildflowers...it was only the end of April but it already looked like summer. He'd shed his jacket the minute he stepped out of the airport in Norfolk, breathing deeply the fresh woodsy-scented air of his new home.

Now he sat chatting with Pastor Mike. They'd barely talked on the phone before today, both being just weird enough to follow their inner instincts on this whole issue. As it turned out, they had a lot in common—mission trips, outreaches, even the particulars of theology.

Noah had assumed Mike would take him to the church or directly to his new home with two guys named Mo and A.J., but it seemed God had other plans yet again.

"So this is Virginia Beach?"

"Yeah, the whole Hampton Roads area is one big sprawling suburb: Norfolk, Chesapeake, Portsmouth, Virginia Beach. It's hard to tell where one stops and the next starts, but we crossed the city line a few miles back."

"Cool. So it's really a beach, like with swimming and surfing and stuff?" Being from the flat expanse of the Midwest, Noah had secretly dreamed of surfing.

"Absolutely. It's a huge tourist attraction. Wow, you didn't do your research at all, did you?"

"Not much. I checked out Old Dominion a little bit, but I just sort of took it on faith."

Mike chuckled, a deep, rich sound that soothed any embarrassment Noah might have felt at the confession. "Is that your modus operandi? Faith?"

"Basically. You?"

Mike slapped the steering wheel. "Guilty as charged."

"What else should I know about the area?"

"We have a huge navy presence. They're a pretty conservative, family-oriented crowd. They also contribute to our multiethnic middle class. Oh, and the Christian Broadcast Network is in Virginia Beach, which might be the reason there's a half-decent church on every corner."

"Sounds cool but a little overwhelming."

"That's what I'm saying. I can hardly believe our little congregation is growing with so many churches for people to choose from."

"Is there a strong Islamic presence here like in Detroit?"

"Not really, which is part of what makes this so crazy, but Old Dominion University is the exception to that."

Noah just shook his head, still spinning from all the new information and from the sudden changes in his life. He clung to that peace in his heart that kept telling him he was on the right path.

"Now we're moving into Chesapeake," Mike said. He swung off the next highway exit. "We're almost there."

"Where are we headed again?"

"Two of the former Muslims in my congregation have a friend that needs some counsel. Mo, your new roommate, is one of them. This girl isn't a believer from what I can tell, but I figured we could be there to support them and pray with them. That seems to be what they wanted most. I figured you might as well jump right in with both feet. You might have some wisdom to add to the situation."

"I don't know about that." Noah shrugged. "But at least I speak Arabic pretty well. I have a feeling I'll just be watching and learning for a while."

"Smart man."

They sat in silence for a few minutes as Pastor Mike drove through a busy thoroughfare full of malls, shopping centers, and restaurants. Noah took the opportunity to pray over their upcoming meeting and his new job.

A few minutes later, Mike pulled into a middle-class neighborhood with brick ranch houses. He turned into a tree-lined driveway in front of a home with an inviting porch and an American flag waving in the breeze. Cars were parked at odd angles all around them. Mike slid off the gravel into a bare patch of grass. "Hopefully this will be okay."

"Looks like the owners aren't too picky," Noah said.

They both hopped out. Noah rubbed his hands together. He couldn't believe he was getting to work so soon, but energy pulsed through him at the opportunity. It seemed that despite his weakness, despite his stumble in losing his heart to an unbeliever, God remained on his side. His gracious heavenly Father had paved the way for him to escape that situation.

Did his heart still ache at the thought of his golden-haired angel? Sure it did. It ached like heck—he pushed the thought from his mind before it could overwhelm him—but maybe this fresh start would give him the closure he needed.

A Middle Eastern-looking young man stepped out on the porch to greet them.

"Hey, Mo!" Mike called. "This is Noah, my new assistant that I told you about."

"Awesome." Mo stuck out his hand. Noah detected the slightest lilt of an accent, although the guy otherwise seemed totally American.

Noah shook his hand. "Nice to meet you."

"So I guess we'll be bunking together for a while."

"I'm looking forward to it."

"Me too. We'll have lots of time to get to know each other." Mo gestured to the house. "But right now, everyone's inside waiting for us. Just remember, this girl has been through a lot. We're going to need to listen and pray more than we talk. There's no easy solution here. We really need God's guidance."

A hundred questions poured through Noah's head, but since Mike just nodded, he followed his lead. Noah supposed he would learn more soon enough.

Mo opened the door and ushered them inside.

The casual living room in blues and reds was full to the brim with expectant faces.

Mo began the introductions. "Everyone, this is my pastor, Mike, and his new assistant, Noah. Noah is somewhat of a Middle Eastern expert."

Noah resisted the urge to scuff his foot like a little boy. "I don't know about expert, but I certainly do have a heart for the Middle East."

"I'd like you to meet Doug and Donna Fletcher. They own the house. This is Layla, a former Muslim like me. She's from Detroit, by the way."

Noah nodded to the girl although he'd never seen her before.

"And her friends Allie, Rain, Sarah, and Shondra."

Noah took in the rainbow of faces, already impressed with the love and unity this group exuded.

"Over here we have James. He and Rain took care of our girl for most of her stay, and that's Rob, Sarah and Allie's brother."

"Yeah," Rob said, "and my parents decided we would be enough Carmichael representatives tonight."

Everyone chuckled at that.

"But where's the woman of the hour?" Mo asked.

"I think all these people made her a little nervous," the raven-haired girl named Layla said. "I'll go get her."

Noah took another minute to gather his bearings in this new group. He and Mike sat down on the ledge in front of the fireplace and made themselves comfortable.

"Here she is," Layla called from the hallway. She entered the room with a shrinking figure pressed against her side. "Mike and

Noah, I'd like you to meet my dearest and oldest friend, Fatima Maalouf."

The room began to spin. Noah's mind threatened to explode. It couldn't possibly be true.

Then the girl brushed aside her curtain of silky, dark golden hair and revealed the face he had dreamed of, had prayed for over these past months.

Unable to contain his excitement, he jumped to his feet. "I can't believe it!"

"My praying man," she whispered.

"Thank you, Jesus!" he whispered in return.

They stood staring at each other for a minute. Just when things were getting awkward, she tugged away from her friend and ran into his arms.

"I can't believe this either," she said, pressed tight against his chest. "It is too good to be true. I was dreading this meeting, but this is the best gift I have ever received."

Layla came forward and patted her back. "You see, I told you everything would be okay."

Fatima pulled back enough to gaze directly into Noah's eyes. She cupped his face in her hand in wonder. "I believe you now. It is a miracle. If he is here, then maybe God truly does hear prayers."

"He does." Noah's heart swelled to bursting. He couldn't let himself do something girly and ridiculous like faint, and he couldn't think of anything to say. Finally he came up with, "I'm Noah. Noah Dixon."

She ducked her head shyly now. "And I'm Fatima."

"I know." He could feel his crazy grin stretching from ear to ear, but he could do nothing to stop it.

God was more gracious, more loving, more forgiving, and more awesome than even he had ever imagined. What sort of orchestration, what insane planning had it taken to get Noah here for this moment?

The whole situation didn't quite compute in his head. All he knew was that she was alive and safe and in his arms like he'd dreamed.

No sooner had the thought passed through his mind than she turned away and blushed. She piled onto the couch with the many other young ladies and turned a bright shade of pink. Fatima covered her face with her hands. "Please be forgiving me, everyone. I should not behave so. I was only so shocked."

Her voice was as rich as her honey colored hair. He'd longed to hear that voice, dreamed of it telling him that she loved him. Instead, she was apologizing for offering a simple hug. Just as he'd always known, there was a whole world between them despite her new American clothing.

Everyone sat still and waited. Then Mo nodded to Mr. Fletcher, the senior member of the group.

"As I think you all know," Mr. Fletcher said, "we've come here to pray about Fatima's future. To our understanding, her brothers haven't given up their search. We need a permanent solution. She can't live in hiding forever. We're hoping that in the counsel of many, we'll find some wisdom and figure out a safe place for her to begin the rest of her life."

Noah's heart that had been about to burst with joy a moment earlier collapsed in upon itself.

Had God brought him here so that he could finally have a chance to win Fatima's heart? Or had God simply brought him here so that he could see she was safe before she was swept out of his reach forever? The second option seemed all too likely and all too depressing.

THIRTY-FIVE

Layla stared at Noah in awe. She'd been so concerned, terrified really, that they'd made a big mistake in encouraging this meeting. Fatima had been on the verge of another panic attack in the bedroom. Layla had a difficult time calming her and convincing her to return.

But here was Noah Dixon, a miracle in the flesh. Fatima had relaxed instantly upon seeing her praying man. Clearly he was the reassurance she needed right now. He looked so different than Layla expected—barely a man really, with his boyish freckles, blue eyes, and waving hair. He wore jeans and a striped T-shirt, not appearing at all ministerial or serious as she would have guessed. In fact, watching Fatima's reaction, she suspected her friend had noticed how attractive this young guy was, even if he could pass for a high school student like Sarah.

Doug filled everyone in on the details and answered questions, but Layla was well aware of the situation, and although she was thankful she could put her mind to rest over whether or not this meeting had been a good idea, other issues plagued her.

Mo caught her attention and winked. He pushed dark rumpled curls from his eyes in that manner she found so appealing. Before long, she would take a stand and they could be together, although she'd be leaving for Lebanon soon anyway. But surely he'd understand that.

She'd just talked with the head of the Muslim street children outreach. Everything was in order for her to help again this summer, and her parents were more than happy to get her out of the country for a while. Besides, Mo had to work and make money this summer since he wanted to cut ties with his parents soon.

Layla watched Fatima as Doug fielded questions about her past and her family. Fatima shrank into the couch, but then she glanced at her praying man and seemed to find her courage again. Layla tuned into the conversation. She needed to advocate for Fatima right now, not obsess over her own issues with Mo. The people in this room could not begin to fathom Fatima's situation. Even she could only understand so much.

Fatima had never before craved the anonymity of her *niqab* as she did in that moment. She longed to sink into the blue denim couch until she became invisible. Being the center of tonight's meeting had been horrifying enough, but now she'd made a fool of herself and behaved brazenly on top of everything else.

Her praying man—she still could not believe it, still could not force her mind to focus on the words swirling around her or to sort out her confusing thoughts.

As Doug answered questions from the group, she fought to compose herself. They could discuss her situation all night, but they would never find a solution. Matters had been so much easier when she'd been the wounded butterfly with no job but to heal. She'd been wracking her brain all week and could not begin to picture a future for herself. Her story was destined to end in one of two ways: either in murder or in being shipped to Saudi Arabia. She couldn't think of another option.

Never ever in a million years would she testify against her brothers, and even if she were willing, she knew nothing substantial. If her friends forced her to go to the police, her family would find her, and if she did nothing, eventually they would find her anyway.

Each time she considered it, something inside of her shattered to a million pieces.

"Fatima!" Rain reached over Sarah and poked her, waking her from her trance.

Fatima got the impression they had already called her name several times. "Sorry. What is it?"

Her praying man spoke up. "I'm new to all this, so please forgive me for bringing up a sensitive issue, but I wanted to understand why you won't go to the police. They're already involved in Detroit."

Fatima swallowed hard and managed to find her voice. "They would want me to speak against my family. This I can never do. I have brought them too much shame already."

So much so that she'd considered hopping a bus home several times this week. One way or another, her life was over. What did it matter now? At least her parents and Allah might not hate her so much if she turned herself in. At least her dear new friends would be safe.

"But you shouldn't look at it that way. They've brought this shame on themselves with their violent, narrow-minded thinking. Not you."

Although she liked the gentle sound of Noah Dixon's voice, and although it was just as she'd dreamed it would be, she would not, could not, concede to his words. "You don't understand. You did not grow up in my culture."

"I understand more than you think," Noah insisted.

"Not really," Mo said. "You studied the culture, sure, but you've never lived in it. You can never imagine the fear, the bondage that wraps itself around you and refuses to let go."

Relief washed over Fatima. Mo got it, but something about his words summoned a fight in her that she thought she had lost.

"She shouldn't give into that." Sarah patted Fatima's knee. "That's why we're here, right? To speak sense. To help her make a rational decision outside of that bondage. She can't let religion hold her trapped forever. She isn't even sure Islam is true anymore, but she continues to judge herself by it. She's not being fair to herself."

"I agree and I disagree." Layla gave Fatima a squeeze, and Fatima cuddled into her welcoming side. "We don't want her to be bound by her religion, but we must take into consideration her very real hurts and fears. Besides, she needs to take ownership of her decision. This affects her more than anyone."

Surrounded as she was by friends who truly loved and understood her, cocooned in their love and acceptance, Fatima felt a brief stirring of an emotion she hadn't experienced in years. Hope.

"That's what I said to Mo a few days ago." Doug's fatherly voice reached out to Fatima like a caress. "I'm afraid if we push her too hard, if we make her face her family, she might cave and give up. Just go back home and that will be the end of Fatima as we know her."

Fatima couldn't believe he'd seen that. She thought she'd hidden it so well. Yet to her surprise, she felt no embarrassment at his words. Instead she felt loved and understood. "This is correct," she whispered. "This is my greatest fear."

"We won't let that happen!" Rain pounded the arm of the couch.

"Fatima," James said from across the room, "I vowed to protect you with my life, and that's not going to change. So don't you make me drag my rear up to Detroit to haul you home."

A giggle welled up from deep inside Fatima and bubbled from her lips. "James, my brother, I will try not to do this to you." She was on to James's strategies now. He knew that while she might not find the strength to fight for herself, she would do it for someone else.

"I still think pushing Fatima to go to the police is the wrong approach," Mo said. He'd spent hours over the last few days getting to know her and understand her story. Fatima believed he had no agenda, but only wanted the best for her.

"So what are you suggesting?" Rain asked.

"We need to find her a safe place to stay where her parents will never find her and where she can start a new life," Mo said. "That would be the Middle Eastern way of dealing with this, and given the circumstances, it's the only solution that makes sense."

"But she'd need a new identity. How can she get one without going to the authorities?" Her praying man was clearly distraught at the idea.

"Doug, would you care to field this one?" Mo asked.

"Sure. I know most of you will balk at this idea at first. I would too if I hadn't spent so much time in the Middle East. As Mo mentioned, sometimes when dealing with Middle Easterners, you have to do things the Middle Eastern way."

"Exactly," Layla said, "and in the Middle East, it's not hard to get fake documents. A lot of the governments run on bribes. You want a visa, you give a bribe. You don't, your paperwork gets *lost* forever." She put air quotes around the word lost. "It's just the way the system works."

It was so true and so stereotypical of Middle Eastern culture that Fatima couldn't help but giggle again.

"Anyone who has lived over there knows it's the only way to get things done," Doug said. "We can't encourage Fatima to defraud the American government indefinitely, but we might have to think outside the box if we want to find a solution to get her far away and safe."

Sarah's brother Rob, who'd remained silent until now, stood to his feet. "I can't believe I'm hearing this, Mr. Fletcher. I always respected you. I always looked up to you. How can Fatima start her life based on a lie? It isn't right. God can't honor dishonesty. She needs to go to the police, and she needs to stay here where she has relationships. Anything else is just ridiculous!"

Rob's outburst surprised Fatima, although it probably shouldn't have.

Out of nowhere, Allie's friend Shondra stood to her feet to match him with a sassy flip of her hair. "Way to be predictable, Baptist boy."

"Who said I was Baptist?" Rob crossed his arms over his chest. "And what's that supposed to mean, anyway?"

She pointed her finger right at Rob's face. "It's supposed to mean, why use the brain God gave you when you can be legalistic, judgmental, and cliché?"

Allie wrapped her arms around Shondra's waist and pulled her back to the couch where the six girls sat huddled together.

Fatima sank deeper between them. Her stomach churned. "Please," she whispered, "do not be fighting over me." It was the last thing she wanted. Where was that *niqab* when she needed it?

THIRTY-SIX

"Okay, everyone cool down for a minute," the dark skinned man named Pastor Mike said.

His soothing tone took the edge off Fatima's nerves, but she continued to retreat deeper and deeper into the couch cushions nonetheless.

"Look," Noah said. "I try hard not to be legalistic, and I understand how things work in the Middle East, but I still agree with..." He gestured to Rob.

"Rob." He supplied his name.

"Thanks. I still agree with Rob. If Fatima is going to start a new life, she needs to do it with integrity and surrounded by people who love her." He looked directly into her eyes with so much warmth and affection that she could hardly accept it. "You need to break from the past and make a new start, not run from it."

"Exactly." Rob stared right at her as well, with the look of a puppy dog begging to be loved. "She could get a restraining order, right?"

Mo proceeded to explain why a restraining order wouldn't be very effective in this situation, while Fatima considered both Noah and Rob. Either of these guys would happily protect her, probably even marry her and give her those children she had always wanted. Her heart began to race. Cold fear sliced through her. She pulled her gaze away from Rob's and stared down at her hands. She could never be any man's wife. Not after all she'd been through.

And she could never go to the police.

And she could never go home.

And running away would never work. They'd find her and that would be the end of it. There was no solution. These wonderful, well-meaning people were wasting their time.

"Okay," Pastor Mike said, "we came here for two reasons—to talk and to pray. We could talk this in circles all night, but what we really need here is a direct word from the Lord. How about we all join hands and spend some time praying?"

"Excellent," Doug said.

Fatima wasn't so sure, but she wasn't about to argue with Doug after all the wonderful things he'd done for her.

Everyone joined hands. Noah spoke first. "Heavenly Father, before we even begin, I want to pray that your peace and comfort would fall over our dear friend, Fatima. Thank you for this miracle that has allowed me to find her. I know that you're leading us and guiding us right now. I know that your hand is on her life. We will never understand everything she's been through, all her heartaches, all her fears. But, God, you made her, and you know her. Heal her heart. Give her strength, and show us your plan for her."

Prayers continued around Fatima, but again, she couldn't focus, and this time she didn't even try. A warm, soft cloak of peace fell over her, a sensation she had never imagined to be possible. In the midst of everything, her fear and pain faded away. She didn't fight it but soaked it into the core of her being. Perhaps if this was real, perhaps if God did not hate her, did not curse her, she might just stand a chance.

Rain gave her knee a little shake again. "A few weeks ago," she seemed to be talking more than praying now, "I sensed a strong presence of evil while I was praying for Fatima, as if the forces of Satan were right in the room with us fighting for her soul, tearing her in pieces."

Fatima leaned forward to gaze into her friend's catlike eyes. "Yes, I remember. That is exactly how I felt. How did you know?"

Rain shrugged. "I can't explain it, but that darkness is gone now. Isn't it? I sensed it leaving the room."

Fatima couldn't find the simple yes to answer the question. Instead she sat there, dumbfounded, tears welling as warm tingles flowed over her skin.

"I sensed something too," Doug said. "I've been feeling it for a while, actually, but it grew clearer and stronger as we prayed together. Danger is heading this way, and we need to move soon."

The words should have sent Fatima into a full-blown panic attack, but she listened with detached curiosity, shielded by her cloak of peace.

Shondra, on the other side of Allie, mumbled words, catching Fatima's attention. Although she couldn't make out what Shondra was saying, the woman's eyes remained tightly closed as if in prayer.

"I'm picking up on something in the spirit," Shondra said, eyes still closed. "I don't understand it, so I hope it will make sense to someone here." She opened her eyes and glanced around. "I saw a map leading from here to Georgia, but where the city of Atlanta should be, I saw the word Sam. Then a little plane took off and headed over the Atlantic on the map. It landed in Lebanon."

Layla gasped and pressed a hand over her mouth. "Oh my goodness! I would have never thought of it, but it couldn't be more perfect."

"What!" Mo nearly shouted.

Everyone sat forward and focused on Layla now. Fatima's curiosity reached new levels, but still she remained swathed in peace.

"I've told most of you about the outreach work I did with Muslim street children in Beirut. We spent time with them in the summer to keep them away from terrorists, sort of like a summer camp."

Rain shook her hands. "Get to the point, woman."

"Please!" Shondra said.

Chuckles filled the room, breaking the tension.

"Sorry." Layla ducked her head. "The director's name is Sam, short for Samir. He lives in Atlanta. I just talked to him, and he's leaving in a few days to get things set up in Beirut. His sister was supposed to go with him, but she can't now. He was wondering if I could head over early since the plane ticket is already bought, but I have to finish my finals first."

"Whoa! Spooky," Rain said.

"This could be the answer. I have a good feeling about this," Pastor Mike added.

"But wait!" Layla clapped her hands together. "It gets better. I met Sam's sister last year. She could practically be Fatima's double, a little taller but amazingly similar."

"Crazy," Mo said.

"I'm not done." Layla stood up. "In addition to his work with the kids, Sam helps to relocate abused women within the Middle East to protect them, usually from one country to another. I probably didn't think of him because he doesn't do that in the States, and all along I've been assuming Fatima would stay. Like I mentioned, it's easy to get your hands on whatever documents you need once you're overseas."

Doug nodded. "Yes, yes. This is perfect, and he'll know how to get her over there safely. No one will connect him to us."

"And he won't have any qualms about it," Layla said. "This is his passion. He believes in saving people from the radicals at any cost."

Everyone sat considering the new information for a moment.

And Fatima knew...it was perfect. God did not hate her. He did not curse her. Somehow, despite all the odds, God had made a way.

She couldn't even begin to unravel the ramifications of all this, except that she wasn't going to die, and from this moment forward, her life was about to take a very different turn. She dared to dream of finding a safe, loving home like she'd experienced with Rain and James or with the Fletchers, only this time she would stay forever.

James couldn't take his gaze off Fatima. He'd never seen that look of utter peace and joy on her face before.

"But she won't know anyone. I still think she'd be better off here and better off working within the laws." Allie's brother Rob persisted in his annoying refrain from earlier.

James just shook his head in wonder. Although he felt sorry for the guy who was clearly smitten by Fatima's helpless beauty, he didn't know how much more of Rob's piety he could stomach. "Dude! Are you seriously going to pretend you didn't feel that? That this isn't a miracle? I mean, Shondra had no way of knowing any of that stuff. What do you think, this is some sort of set up?"

He hadn't meant to admit that he believed in all this ooey gooey mumbo jumbo. Once the words escaped his mouth, James almost wished he could take them back. Except that they were true, and just like Rob, he valued truth.

"No, man. I don't...I just...." Rob turned to Fatima, then buried his face in his hands.

"I think we *all* know what just happened." Pastor Mike shot James a pointed look.

Caught.

"We asked God for specific guidance and direction," Mike continued, "and he sent it. There's no denying that. So what's next?"

No, James couldn't deny it, not any more. Mike began hashing out logistics with Layla, but more pressing issues filled James's thoughts. He'd felt God's presence in the room with them, seen his touch, heard his voice speaking through the young woman Shondra. His mind struggled to accept it. He hadn't picked up on it with his normal five senses, but he knew it just like he knew his name...or that he loved Rain and his baby.

If God wasn't real, it would be necessary to invent him. He'd read that Voltaire quote years ago. It had stuck with him all this time, and it finally made sense. What he experienced tonight demanded an explanation. He didn't know yet if the Bible was true or which denomination was superior or any of that stuff, but it was time to stop being stubborn and open himself to finding out. Rain and Mike would both be more than happy to guide the way. That much he knew for darn sure.

He took a moment to study Rain. Her bouncing golden-brown curls, her greenish eyes containing the whole world, the baby poking out and resting on her lap, her gently curved lips that always tasted of apricots. His heart raced in the nicest sort of way. He couldn't live without her, and he had absolutely no desire to try. He'd needed the last few weeks to sort through everything, but tonight had solidified his decision.

Reaching into the pocket of his baggy jeans, he fingered the object he'd been carrying around for the last few days. The time had come to put it to good use.

James tuned back into the conversation.

"It seems like we have a decision," Doug said. "Is everyone in agreement?"

Nods and yeses filled the room, although James noticed Rob was grudging in his acceptance. James could hardly blame the guy. He knew firsthand what it was like to almost lose the woman of your dreams.

"We all want the best for you, and this is it." The new guy, Noah, looked like he might puke.

"Fatima, is this what you want?" Allie asked her.

"Yes," Fatima answered with quiet assurance. "I am not afraid. I can do this."

"Great. Now who wants to drive Fatima to Atlanta?" Doug asked.

Wow, James had missed quite a bit in his mental wanderings.

"Me!" Rob spoke up immediately.

"And me," Noah said with a hint of challenge in his voice.

"I'd love to go," Mo said. "But her brothers have seen me, so I don't think it would be smart."

"Same for me," James said. "But all my love goes with you, sweet sister." He blew her a kiss.

Fatima smiled and looked completely content. *Thank you, God*, James whispered in his heart, and he meant every word.

"I can go with these two and referee," Pastor Mike offered.

"That's a good idea," Doug said. "I don't think her brothers have been here and seen me, but there's no way to know for sure. Of course, Layla still needs to make the call and set things up, but everything should fall into place quickly now."

"Sure thing." Layla extricated herself from the press of girls on the couch and stood. "I'll go to the kitchen and give him a buzz."

"Hold on just one second, if you don't mind." Now was James's big moment. He wasn't about to let it pass. "I know we came to discuss Fatima, but since so many of my new friends are here in one room, I'd like to discuss one more issue, and I have a feeling Fatima won't mind." He winked at her.

Fatima gestured to him, offering him the floor, and so he went down on one knee in the middle of it.

Rain put both hands to her cheeks. "No."

"Yes." James scooched closer to her and pulled the ring from his pocket.

"Oh, James!"

"Hush, woman." He chuckled. "Let me have my moment. Rain Butler-Briggs, ever since I met you in geometry class eight and a half years ago, I have known you are the love of my life. I love you with all my heart, and I already love our child more than I can ever say.

Will you do me the honor of becoming my wife and making our love official before God and man?"

"Oh, James!" she said again. Tears streamed down her face. She reached a trembling finger to him.

And onto her finger he slid the symbol of love and eternity—a white gold ring with the biggest diamond he could possibly afford encircled by tiny sparkling ones. He caught her hand in his own and pulled her off the couch into his arms, and then he pressed his lips to hers as the roomful of onlookers cheered.

"Woo-hoo!" Allie shouted.

"And I was hoping Mike would officiate." James looked at the pastor.

"I would be honored."

"When?" Layla asked, hugging Fatima and Allie on either side of her.

"I was thinking right after school lets out, before the baby comes." James rubbed a hand over Rain's belly. "I want her to be born into an official family."

"Babies belong in families and families should be forever." Fatima's grin almost matched Rain's.

"So what do you think?" James asked the precious woman in his arms. "You haven't said anything except, 'Oh, James.'"

"Yes, yes, a thousand times yes." Rain kissed him again.

And James said yes once and for all to a future with his wife, with his child, and with a God he could no longer deny.

Looking out over the frothing waves to the gentle blue horizon beyond, Layla clung to Fatima on one side of her and Allie on the other as their new tight-knit group of girlfriends all huddled together along the shoreline of Virginia Beach for what would most certainly be the first and last time. Sam in Atlanta had answered her call right away, and matters had fallen quickly into place, just like Doug had predicted. Layla nuzzled her cheek against Fatima's silky tresses and took in a deep draught of fresh sea-scented air.

"This was a good idea," Sarah said.

"It would have been a crime for her to leave without getting to see the ocean." Rain patted Fatima's hand from her other side.

"Mmm..." said Allie with a sigh. "I forget sometimes how much I love this place."

"Have you ever been to the beach before, Fatima?" Shondra leaned forward for a better peek at the look of awe on Fatima's delicate features.

Fatima smiled. "Once. My brothers were allowed to swim, but I had to sit under the shade covered up alongside my mother. I am not sure if looking at it is going to be quite enough," she said with a twinkle in her eye.

"Don't let the warm air fool you," Sarah said. "That water is still like ice."

"We're not sending you off to the far ends of the earth with the sniffles, young lady," Shondra chided, although Layla suspected she might not want to risk getting her high-maintenance hair wet and chuckled at the thought.

"But what if I end up somewhere in the middle of the desert?"

Rain shot a questioning glance over Fatima's head to Layla and said, "This might be her only chance."

That's when the certainty hit Layla—sometimes you just had to do something daring and bold, no matter how foolish it might seem from the outside—something to make you feel utterly alive.

"Let's do it!" Layla cried.

She, Fatima, and Rain rushed for the water, pulling the reluctant remainder of their posse in tow. As the frigid water washed up to envelop their jean-clad legs, drenching them and biting at their skin with bitter cold, Fatima began to laugh with the pure joy of a child, splashing and spinning and—at long last—free.

Then they all frolicked like children in the endless ocean. The closing of one chapter, but the opening of something new.

THIRTY-SEVEN

A clatter against her window woke Sarah. She bolted up in bed as fear shot through her. Then it came again, and again in a rhythmic fashion that suggested friend not foe. She hurried to the window before the noise woke Fatima. The girl had had an overwhelming day and didn't need a scare on top of it. Everyone had said their goodbyes already, and tomorrow Fatima would be heading for Atlanta bright and early.

Pulling aside the curtain, Sarah realized she had been partly right in her guess. Jesse stood in the shadows, scooping another handful of gravel from the drive. Not exactly foe but not friend either. She'd been ignoring his calls and texts all week. The stubborn guy should get the hint.

As he stood, she pressed her face close to the window and made a shushing motion. He gestured for her to come out. Not wanting to create a stir for Fatima's sake, she had no choice but to comply. She slipped on a pair of shoes with her pajamas then hustled outside, clicking the doors softly in her wake. Thank goodness the night was warm.

"What are you doing here?" She crossed her arms over her chest like a shield.

He closed the distance between them and took her by the elbows, tugging her near. "Don't be like that. I had to wait until my aunt got home from work to borrow her car. I've been worried about you.

Why won't you answer my calls?" His mouth descended toward hers. Despite the warmth and tingles flowing through her at his seductive tone, she managed to rip herself away from his grasp.

"The timing isn't great, but I'm glad you're here. We need to talk."

"I've always got time for you, sweet cheeks."

That nickname made her feel so cheap.

He reached around her and swatted her rear.

Sarah would have sworn he left a trail of sludge in his wake, sullying her all over again. She backed up a few steps. "Look, we need to end this. Now. I don't know what I was thinking. I can't marry a guy like you. We don't have anything in common." At least she hoped not. Today's meeting had shown her more than ever that she didn't have the connection with God she needed, but his presence had been so real in that room. She had never sensed anything quite like that before. It made her long for a real connection with God more than ever.

Jesse cocked an eyebrow. "So you want to marry me?"

"I...no...that's not what I said. It's just that I don't want to be doing all the...stuff...we've been doing with someone I don't plan to marry. You know that. You know I didn't intend for any of it to happen until my wedding night."

"But I love you, babe. Come on." He held out his arms again. "I'll help you get rid of all that tension. I'll take you to heaven and back."

That was more accurate than Jesse realized. Sarah couldn't deny the ecstasy she'd felt in his arms—nor the cold, hard crash to reality that always followed it. She wanted off this roller coaster. "No. It's over."

"Unless I marry you? Come on, Sarah, we're too young for that. That doesn't mean we shouldn't enjoy each other."

Sarah felt her resolve wavering all over again. Did that mean he'd marry her someday, just not now? He said he loved her. Could that be enough? Was it just her own moral code making her miserable?

Was it that she was judging herself according to her parents' beliefs rather than her own?

Her arms fell to her sides. "I don't know, Jesse. Are you saying that you would marry me? Eventually?"

Sensing her weakness, Jesse caught her in his arms and swung her around against the side of his aunt's car. Before she could stop him, he pressed his lips to hers, turning her resolve to a mound of jelly all over again.

"You didn't answer," she whispered. "Would you marry me eventually?"

He chuckled, low and sexy, as he trailed kisses down her neck. His hand traveled up her thigh.

"Jesse!" She smacked his hand away and pressed against his chest. "Please, answer."

He pulled back just enough to run his fingers through his hair. "I'm not sure I'm the marrying type, but what's it matter when we're so good together?"

His mouth caught hers again, but somehow his words sank through the haze and splashed against her heart like a bucket full of cold water.

She shoved him off of her, completely this time, and stomped away. Holding out her arms to block his advances, she hollered. "That's it, Jesse. We're through. I mean it. I'll get Mr. Fletcher to send you packing if I have to."

Jesse rubbed his mouth, wiping her kiss away. "You'll be back. In a few days, you'll come running to me." He got in the car, slammed the door, and sped away.

But she wouldn't. Would she? Even now her heart was collapsing in her chest, caving at the sight of him driving away. She caught back a sob with her hand. Although she hadn't thought he was right for her, she had believed that he loved her, assumed he would marry her if that's what she wanted. His rejection cut like a knife, and she couldn't deal with the pain. She had given everything to Jesse, and she could never get it back. How could she have been such a fool?

Sarah headed into the house and grabbed a bottle of wine off the rack. Surely the Fletchers wouldn't miss just one. Somehow, she needed to escape the awful ache in her heart, and this was the only way she knew. It wasn't as if God should comfort her now. She'd brought this on herself. No doubt he had far more punishment still in store.

Noah did not like the way this guy Sam stared at Fatima with the same moon-eyed expression that Rob did, and that Noah probably did too for that matter, but the guy knew his stuff, and he seemed like a pro. If he had a little crush on Fatima, well, then he'd work all that much harder to protect her.

"Don't worry, I've got this," Sam said.

"She's in good hands." Sam's sister, Nisreen, put a protective arm around Fatima. "We've done this many times." Although Nisreen was a few inches taller than Fatima, not quite as beautiful, and the gold in her hair was likely from the salon, the two girls did bear a remarkable resemblance.

"I am still amazed at how God worked everything out." Noah shook his head.

"Amazed...annoyed," Rob grumbled. "But even though we're losing you, I'm really glad you'll be safe."

"Me too." Fatima grinned and cuddled into Nisreen's side. "It is all too good to be true."

"Allah is more gracious than most Muslims give him credit for," Sam said. "I have seen this again and again in my work. In fact, I've come to have great respect for the teachings of Isa Masi as well, but we'll have plenty of time to talk about that on our trip."

Noah didn't know if that was a good idea, and Rob looked ready to argue, but Pastor Mike cut them off by grasping Sam's shoulder. "You're a good man. What do you say, Fatima?"

"I would like that." Fatima took a deep breath and stood a bit taller.

Noah could barely believe this was the bruised and broken girl from the balcony. Fatima looked ready to tackle the world and her new life.

"Well." Noah blinked back tears. "I guess this is good-bye. It hardly seems fair when I just found you."

Fatima moved away from Nisreen and offered him a hug. "Good-bye, my praying man. You don't know this, but you saved my life. I clung to the picture of you the whole way to Virginia. I know this hasn't turned out the way you wished, but you mean the world to me, and it's for the best."

Her sweet words brought some small comfort to his aching heart. God had used him, just not the way he wished.

"I know I didn't save your life or anything, but can I have a hug too?" Rob asked hopefully, extending his arms.

Fatima maneuvered her way to a quick side hug instead. "Thank you, Rob. You have been a good friend. I will miss you as well." She offered her hand to Mike. "And you too, Pastor Mike. I can never repay any of you."

"Just be safe and happy." Mike shook her hand. "That's all the payment we need."

"All right." Nisreen claimed Fatima again. "Let's go in and you can freshen up. We have a lot to plan before your trip."

The women disappeared through the doorway of the suburban Atlanta home. Noah's gut twisted, and the grimace on Rob's face suggested he suffered from the same malady.

"So where will she go?" Mike asked Sam.

"I'm not sure yet." Sam patted his heart. "But I will guard her like my own sister, and I'll try to get word to Layla once she's settled."

"I guess we have to trust her into God's care then," Pastor Mike said.

"True," Noah agreed, fully aware that it would be easier said than done.

A part of him wanted to run off to Lebanon after her, but a little tug in his heart reminded him that he'd have to let her go eventually. He suspected that he'd veered off God's path significantly by falling in love with her.

Rob patted him on the back. "Come on, buddy. I know it's hard, but we have to go."

The unexpected camaraderie gave Noah the strength to turn and walk to the car, leaving Fatima, perhaps forever.

THIRTY-EIGHT

Layla sat with Sarah and Rain by the lake behind the Fletchers' house watching white flowers on the pear trees fluttering in the warm spring breeze. Fatima was gone for good—safe, but far from their reach. They'd just received the call a few minutes earlier, and they'd arranged this little party to say good-bye to her over the phone, but no one seemed to be in a festive mood.

"So what now?" Layla asked.

"Now we get back to regular life, I guess." Rain plucked at the grass. "We have not one but two weddings to plan. Layla, I want you and Allie to be my bridesmaids."

"Of course, as long as the dress isn't tacky."

Rain gave her a little shove. "Just for that I'm going to make you wear bright yellow ruffles and lace. With polka dots! Oh, Sarah, I hope you don't feel left out."

Sarah pushed strands of blond hair from her face. "Don't be silly. Besides, I'm Allie's maid of honor, and we get to pick our own dresses."

Neither Rain nor Layla were scheduled to be in Allie's wedding since Rain would have a newborn and Layla was planning to be in Lebanon most of the summer and still hadn't pinned down her travel plans. Plus, Allie had a bunch of cousins who'd come crawling out of the woodwork at the wedding announcement, clamoring to be a part. Hopefully Layla and Rain would both make the momentous day, though.

"Picking your own dresses is a good idea," Rain said. "What do you think, Layla?"

"Whatever you want. Seriously, I'm just so glad you and James worked everything out," Layla assured her.

"I'm not gonna lie. He had me worried for a while, but now I couldn't be happier. Except that Fatima won't be there. Man, am I going to miss that girl."

"We all will," Sarah said wistfully. "I'll certainly never forget her."

"But she's safe, and that's what matters most." Although Layla would miss Fatima more than anyone, she understood the danger more than anyone too. Neither of these girls had stared down the blade of a knife and faced their own mortality. She had thought she might become a martyr, a statistic, and she was glad Fatima would never have to experience that horror. Just thinking back on the day caused her palms to sweat.

Now with Fatima gone, Layla realized that all along she'd secretly feared Fatima's brothers would come after her too, and that this time she would not have the courage, the strength, to stand up to them— that she'd crumble, that she wouldn't have enough faith.

She'd let that same sort of fear cloud her relationship with Mo. He'd been so great at the meeting about Fatima. She needed to overcome her fear and take that final step to embrace a relationship with him. All marriages had issues, ups and downs, but if she could just find the courage, she knew they could work it out.

Sarah stood and brushed off the bottom of her shorts. "I'm going into the house for a drink. Would you guys like something? I think there's lemonade."

"Sure, I'd love some." Rain continued to pluck at the grass.

"Sounds great." Layla leaned back. Once Sarah was a few yards away, she whispered, "She seems different. Don't you think?"

"She certainly dresses differently. I like the change. There's a new humility about her."

"I don't know." Layla grimaced. "She seems so vulnerable, stripped of all her certainty, and a little sad."

"Allie mentioned she had a hard semester."

They chatted about wedding details for a few more moments while staring out over the tranquil lake. Then a scream broke the peaceful scene.

Layla jumped up and turned toward the house. Although at a distance, she made out the figures of two men in black leather.

The moment had finally come.

Layla did not crumble. She did not waver. Strength and courage filled her from on high, just like it had when her uncle threatened her. "Come on!" she shouted and raced directly toward them.

※

Sarah froze in place as the two men in black leather jackets descended upon her, and she knew the moment had come. God would finally punish her. She would get what she deserved, and she was ready for it.

"Where is she? Where is Fatima?" snarled one of the men.

At any cost, she must protect her friend. "I...I don't know any Fatima."

"Liar! Tell us the truth, you whore." The other guy rushed at her and slapped her hard across the side of her face. Blinding heat enveloped her. Bright light flashed then faded to black. The tray with glasses full of lemonade crashed to the concrete, shattering and splashing everywhere.

Sarah stumbled backward. *Liar. Whore.* The words echoed through her head, so utterly true. No wonder God was about to rain down fiery judgment upon her, but she would not let them break her. She would be strong for Fatima. "I don't know what you mean."

"Shut up." The shorter guy grabbed her and twisted her arm

behind her back. Sarah waited for the inevitable snap. "Tell us. Tell us where she is. We know she was here."

"Stop. Let her go!" Layla rushed toward them, waving her hands in front of her. "I'm the one you want, not Sarah."

Rain ran up behind Layla. "I called the cops. They're on their way."

Sarah wanted to scream. She couldn't drag these good women, not to mention Rain's innocent child, into her destruction. "No. Go! Run while you can."

"Absolutely not!" Layla stood with her feet braced wide and fists at her side.

Rain grasped Layla's shoulder. "We're not leaving you."

Sarah heard a whir and a click, then both girls gasped. The next thing she knew, something hard and cold pressed against her temple, rendering her speechless. A gun. It wouldn't be long now. She'd burn in hell for eternity just like she deserved. *Oh God, if it's not too late, please forgive me! Please accept me back into your fold.*

I already have. She sensed the answer well up from her heart. *I've been searching for you, reaching for you, all along.* But there was no time to linger on those thoughts.

"Layla Al-Rai, it has been a long time. Where are you hiding my little sister? Tell me now, or I swear this girl dies."

"I have no idea where she is, Shadi. That's the utter truth. She did stop here for a while, but she's gone, and she's not coming back."

Shadi yanked Sarah's arm again. She couldn't hold back a yelp as pain shot through it.

"Where is she?" he shouted.

The other guy put his hand on his own gun. "We're going to be nice, for the old times' sake, Layla, and give you until the count of three. One, two..."

"Wait!" Layla shouted. "Just let Fatima go. She'll never bother you again, I promise. Say you killed her if it makes you feel better. She's been through enough."

"Never," Shadi hissed in Sarah's ear. "Now where were we? Oh yes, one, two..."

"In the name of Jesus, I command you to stop!" Rain shouted.

"Not likely," the second guy spat.

A shot rang out overhead. Shadi twisted toward it, allowing Sarah to catch sight of Doug holding a high-tech rifle in each hand with ammo crisscrossed over his chest. The man looked like Rambo, only scarier. He towered almost two heads over the shorter men, and with his bulging biceps, he could easily snap either of their necks.

While her captor was distracted, Sarah managed to pull free and stumbled to the ground several feet away, but as she looked up, she saw Shadi's gun still pointing directly at her.

"Don't tick me off!" Doug said. "Back off now or you both die before you get a chance to cock those silly little pistols of yours."

Shadi took a step back and lowered his aim.

"Smart move," Doug said. "Now drop your weapon."

A gun clattered to the ground.

"And you, take yours out nice and slow by the handle and toss it."

The second guy obeyed.

Doug stepped closer and kicked the guns far away. "I don't know where this Fatima person is, but I know a little about how things are done in the Middle East. So let me explain this in simple words that you'll understand. This is my territory. Not just this house, not just this city, but this whole Hampton Roads area. You're on my territory, and I want you off. You touch one of these girls again, you die. I see your ugly mugs within fifty miles of here, you die. I have friends and my friends have friends. So go back to whatever hole you crawled out of before things get messy. Got it?"

They just glared at him.

"I said, do you understand?" He growled in a low whisper and pointed a gun to each of their heads.

Shadi swiped his hand. "We're wasting our time. Let's get out of here."

The other guy sneered, but they both turned and disappeared around the house.

Everyone froze, still and quiet, until the sound of a car roaring to life and screeching away met their ears.

Doug laid down one of his weapons and held out his hand to lift Sarah from the ground. He brushed dirt from her cheek and gazed deep into her eyes. If it hadn't been for the crew cut and tattoos, Sarah would have sworn he was Jesus in the flesh.

Rain and Layla ran to them, crushing Sarah in an embrace.

"I was so scared."

"They could have killed you."

"That was awful." Their words swished about Sarah.

"We need to get you to a hospital." Rain wrapped Sarah's arm around her shoulder.

"I'll tell you what," Doug said. "Why don't you ladies go find Sarah's purse and call her parents and the police. Give her a minute to collect herself."

"The police are already on their way," Rain said.

"Great." Doug took charge of Sarah, and Layla and Rain hurried toward the house.

Sarah sank back to the ground. She could hardly believe what had just transpired. God hadn't punished her. He'd saved her. He sent angels in the forms of Doug and Layla and Rain. There must be hope for her yet. "You were amazing."

Doug stripped off the rest of his weapons and shrugged. "Classic scare tactics. But you, young lady, have had a rough couple of weeks."

Sarah gaped. Her head had begun to pound. Surely he didn't

mean what she thought he did. "I'll be okay. I really don't think a doctor is necessary."

"So tell me, is there some other guy I need to chase out of town before I put these guns away?" Doug stared at her knowingly, but she didn't feel judged. It was as if he saw to her core and loved her anyway.

Strength and courage filled Sarah, along with a new determination. "That's okay. I think I can handle it now, but if you wouldn't mind me hanging around your house a little longer, that might be helpful."

"You're welcome to stay with us as long as you like." He whisked her off the ground like a small child. "But no more wine. Deal?"

Sarah's face heated for a whole different reason. "You knew about that too, huh?"

"I know everything." He winked at her. "And I just want what's best for you—which is not that creepy guy I saw in my driveway."

Sarah relaxed into Doug's capable arms. Just like she planned to give up control and relax into the arms of her Father God for the rest of her life.

THIRTY-NINE

Sarah sat across from Allie and her mother at the kitchen table of their family home. The tan and beige surroundings brought to mind thousands of conversations in this very room, but tonight would be different. She clutched tightly to her coffee mug, allowing the warmth to soak into her hands.

Tonight would be hard, there was no getting around that. She'd spent the past week wrapped in God's mercy and forgiveness—a palpable, soothing sensation that even her rational, logical brain could not ignore. She'd also spent hours quizzing Allie and Andy about their inside-out version of Christianity. It was starting to make sense. Although they had assured her God's forgiveness was a complete and finished work, Sarah knew she would not feel free of the past until she told her mother the truth.

She'd leave it to Mom to share with Dad. The subject was so personal. Plus, she couldn't bear to see the disappointment on his face. Sarah pushed her mug away with resolution.

"So what's the big mystery?" Mom asked, taking another sip of her own coffee. "You two have been downright conspiratorial."

"Mom," Sarah began. Wow, this was rough. She could barely find the words. "I...I need to apologize to you, and to Dad, but...but for some reason I feel like this is mostly between us."

Mom reached out and clasped Sarah's hand with compassion

glowing from her face. "Whatever is it, sugar? I'm just so glad you're safe after that awful run-in last week."

Not willing to be sidetracked, Sarah continued. "I've been lying to you. For months. I've been seeing a guy."

Mom bristled but seemed to be sticking to her "if you have nothing nice to say" rule.

Allie gave Sarah's shoulder a rub and nodded for her to continue.

"Please don't be mad at me. I promise, I've been punished a million times over. I messed up so bad. It was all just awful."

"Who?" Mom managed to push the single word out.

"Jesse Kinsella."

Mom pressed her lips tight together. "I trusted that boy. What did he do to you? Did he kiss you?"

Words escaped Sarah completely. She stared down at their enfolded hands.

Mom pulled her hands away and covered her mouth. "Oh dear Lord, no! Say it isn't so. Tell me you didn't give your precious gift to that...that...delinquent."

Sarah forced herself to look at Mom's ashen face. The woman looked like she might lose her lunch. Sarah's lack of an answer must have said it all.

Mom stood and paced the kitchen. She clutched her stomach. "I just knew it. I knew it! It's all my fault. I tried so hard to do everything right, to raise you girls with godly principles, but you can't get good fruit from a rotten tree. Oh Jesus, oh sweet, sweet, Jesus, forgive me. You're ruined and it's all my fault!"

Ruined, just like Sarah feared. She knew Mom would see it that way, but still it cut to hear the word.

"Mother." Allie stood and stomped her foot. "Sarah is not ruined. She is a priceless, worthy, redeemed child of God who made a mistake. This situation has changed her for the better. She has a real relationship with God now, much closer than it's ever been."

"That's true," Sarah mumbled.

Allie slapped the table now. "She has a whole beautiful, wonderful life ahead of her, and I won't sit here and let you tell her otherwise."

Mom collapsed back into her chair and buried her head in her arms atop the table. "I'm so sorry. You're right, Allie. I'm the problem. I've failed you. I've ruined you, just like I always feared I would!"

"Mom?" Sarah touched her shoulder. "You're not making any sense. What do you mean?"

"I knew it would come out. Why did I ever bother to hide it? I was a wanton, a heathen, as a young woman. I did everything I could not to pass that on, but I knew I was destined to fail."

"What are you talking about?" Allie asked. "I thought you were the perfect church girl."

"Oh, I pretended. I put on a good show, but I was a backslider, pure and simple. I'd sneak off with boys just like a harlot. And then... and then...dear Lord, I can't even say."

Allie and Sarah both dragged their chairs close to Mom, hugging her from either side.

"It's okay," Sarah said. "Whatever it is, God loves you and he forgave you thousands of years ago." It finally made sense to her. "You can't do anything to earn his grace. It's a gift."

"But you don't understand. I was so filthy. So evil," Mom sobbed.

"Mom, Andy told me a while back that there must be something from your past that makes you cling so tightly to rules. It's time to let it go. Just tell us what it is, and set yourself free. Secrets are a trick from Satan to trap people."

"And trust us," Sarah said. "We'll love you no matter what."

For a moment Mom said nothing. Then without preamble she shrieked, "I killed my baby!" and began to wail.

Sarah turned to Allie, but she looked equally confused.

Allie bit her lip and glanced around the room. "Mom, did you... have an abortion?"

"I was so...scared...so ashamed. But I killed it! I'm a murderer and a whore."

Both girls hugged their mother tighter and began to cry along with her.

"Dear God," Allie whispered. "I can't believe you held on to that guilt and shame all these years. Let it out, Mom. Let it all out."

They allowed their mother to cry for a good long time, embracing and soothing her the whole while, pouring out their love and acceptance on her in this most delicate moment.

When her sobbing subsided to sniffles, Sarah finally asked. "Does Dad know?"

"He thinks I'm perfect. Pure. Dear God, I have to tell him."

"Only if you want to." Allie kissed their mother's brow. "Like you've always taught us, the past is in the past."

"Unless you're keeping it buried where it can eat away at you." Sarah kissed her as well. "I'm so sorry that you've carried this burden your whole life. I think you should tell him. It will be good for you."

"I need to do it now before I lose my courage." Mom walked to the sink and wiped her face dry with a dishcloth. In the kitchen window, she checked her reflection, straightening her hair and blouse.

Then she gripped the edge of the counter. "What if he hates me for it?"

"I'm sure he'll be upset at first, but he'll forgive you," Sarah said. "Just like I know you'll both forgive me. That's what families do."

Mom nodded to her daughters. "I can do this."

"We'll be praying for you," Allie said.

Sarah and Allie clutched hands and prayed quietly as Mom slipped out of the kitchen.

A few minutes later, Rob came banging through the back door. He stopped and looked from girl to girl. Noah Dixon entered after him. Evidently the guys had bonded over their shared heartbreaks. "Man," Rob said, "what did we interrupt?"

Allie stood to refill her coffee. "We'll talk about it later. It's been a long afternoon. Want some?" She held out her mug.

"Sure," Rob said.

"Um, maybe I should go." Noah turned back toward the door.

"No, no," Sarah said. "Please stay. Allie, maybe you can fill Rob in on everything, and Noah and I will prepare the coffee."

"Good idea."

Allie and Rob headed toward the living room, leaving Sarah alone with Noah.

"So, rough afternoon?" Noah grinned.

Sarah liked his boyish freckles and sparkling blue eyes. He had an innocence about him. This was just the sort of guy she had dreamed of once upon a time. "Rough, but good."

"Good." Noah shuffled his feet as Sarah set to work filling mugs and adding cream and sugar.

"What do you take?"

"One of each is fine."

Noah glanced up at her several times as she prepared the coffee and carried it to the table. Finally she sat and motioned for him to join her.

"Um..." Noah picked up his mug but didn't seem to be able to think of anything else to say. He smiled and took a sip.

Sarah smiled into her own cup. She had no idea what to say to this guy either, but she was glad he'd stayed.

"Oh!" Noah's eyes lit. "Rob told me you speak Arabic. *Hal hayda sahih?*"

"*Aywa Sahih!* Yeah, I've been studying with an international program."

"Wow! That's so awesome. I sure wish my high school had that."

"But evidently you learned somewhere on your own."

"I studied for years through an online program, and I talked to every Arabic speaker I could find."

"And now you're some sort of missionary?" Sarah remained unclear on the details, other than the fact he'd been praying for Fatima in Detroit.

He grew more animated, gesturing with his hands now as he spoke. "Well, my dream is to go to the Middle East, but it's hard to find organizations to support that. They want you to have a degree in something practical, like engineering or teaching English as a second language, but I spent the last four years studying Arabic and Islam and attending Bible college. I'm so ready to just jump in there and get started, you know?"

Sarah giggled, amused by his obvious passion. "I absolutely know, but now you have this opportunity with Pastor Mike. That's pretty cool."

"I can hardly wrap my head around it. I mean, it's not overseas, but it's still amazing. You want to be a missionary too, right? Rob mentioned something about that."

Sarah nodded slowly. She paused to sip more coffee. "All my life that was the plan, but I had a really rough semester. I...well honestly, I fell away from the Lord. It was awful, but now I feel like I'm in a better place than ever. I just haven't gotten around to figuring out how all of this will affect my future. I thought I'd ruined everything for a while there, but maybe not."

Noah laid his large, strong hand over Sarah's petite one. "It's never too late to follow your dreams." He stared deep into her eyes, and she felt like she could see into his soul. There she spied the same strength and compassion she'd found in Doug Fletcher's eyes when he had seemed so much like Jesus to her.

She saw something else too. A spark of interest, perhaps...and hope.

"It's weird, I know, but when Fatima left," Noah said, "I felt like all the light walked out of my life. Already I'm realizing how ridiculously wrong I was." He gave her hand a little squeeze. "God works in crazy ways sometimes, but I'm glad I'm here."

Sarah turned over her hand to grasp his. "I'm glad too."

And in that moment, new possibilities, far better than she had ever hoped or imagined, opened before Sarah.

FORTY

Rain blinked away tears as she surveyed the Fletchers' backyard and the tranquil lake beyond. She wouldn't want to ruin her makeup. Friends and even a few family members milled about white folding chairs. Nearby, Sarah and Noah stared dreamily at each other as they chatted under a shady tree. Love was in the air.

She spotted Pastor Mike, dressed in a suit for once, preparing his notes and Bible on a small podium beneath an archway covered with a profusion of colorful flowers supplied by Mrs. Carmichael's and Mrs. Fletcher's gardens. Rain clutched tightly to a similar array of blossoms over her now enormous belly. The Fletchers' home had been the perfect choice for their wedding location—the place where James proposed, the place he had first seen an undeniable God in action.

"You look so beautiful, I can hardly stand it." Allie gave her a kiss on the cheek.

"You both look gorgeous too!" Rain reached out to swipe a strand of wind-blown hair from Layla's face.

Her bridesmaids had chosen simple pastel sundresses to complement Rain's gauzy white one with its empire waist. The coronets of flowers around their heads had been Rain's crazy idea, but they lent them the appearance of springtime fairies, and there was no denying how pretty they looked.

"I can't believe this day is actually here. I never even admitted to myself how much I wanted it," Rain said.

"It's going to be perfect." Layla smiled.

"And you were hardly a bridezilla at all," Allie teased.

"Hey!" Rain gave her a little shove. "There was no hardly about it."

"Except for the programs," Allie reminded her.

Rain stuffed down a tiny spark of anger. She wouldn't let anything ruin this perfect day, and the printer had promised the programs would arrive in the next ten minutes before the ceremony, but time was running out. She took a deep breath. "Whatever happens, it will be fine."

"Pretty impressive." Layla nudged Allie. "I don't see any smoke coming out of her ears at all."

They all shared a laugh that broke the tension of the missing programs.

"I can hardly wait for my turn," Allie said wistfully.

"Neither can Andy from what I can tell," Raid said, "but it will be here before you know it."

"Looks like your parents have ironed things out." Layla nodded in their direction.

"Yeah." Allie sighed. "I didn't want to say too much, but my mom shared something pretty tricky from her past. Dad was a real champ about it, but it took him a while to process everything."

Evidently the processing had gone just fine, since they now cuddled side by side as they sat awaiting the ceremony.

Just then, James came running out the back door.

"Hey, you aren't supposed to see me," Rain said, but she had to admit she was enjoying her glimpse of him in his loose white shirt over tan pants. He'd even pulled his dreadlocks back into a classy man-bun for the formal occasion.

"Please, woman, we've been living together for eight years. Besides, you'll want what's behind my back."

"The programs?" Dear God, let it be true. She'd spent the better part of a day designing them.

"Yep. Give me a kiss first."

Rain stood on her tip toes to comply. "Now turn them over before I rip off your arms to get them."

"Ah, there's my bridezilla." Allie giggled.

James handed over the beautiful programs with their faded background of wildflowers before Rain could carry out her threat. She glanced over the top one. Perfect...perfect... "Wait. It says my dad is walking me down the aisle. What the...?"

The backdoor swung open again. A middle-aged couple—woman white, man black—popped out onto the deck. "Surprise!" They were both dressed in brightly patterned African garb.

Rain's mind could hardly process the information her eyes were receiving. "Mom? George?"

James started laughing. "I told you it would be worth surprising her. Ah, man, I should have snapped a picture of that look on your face."

"How wonderful!" Layla squealed as Rain's parents crushed their daughter in an embrace.

"But...but...I didn't think you got my letter."

"We didn't," her mom said, running a hand lovingly down Rain's cheek, "but James kept trying, and we got one of his just in time."

"But...Africa!" They were supposed to be an ocean away.

"Africa will be just fine without us," her dad, a.k.a. George, said, giving her another squeeze. "Our daughter is getting married and our grandchild's about to be born."

"So..." Rain was almost afraid to ask, "you don't mind...that I'm getting married?"

"We only ever wanted you to follow your own path, sweetie. Besides, your father really learned to chill out in Africa."

"Well, now that you mention it, I'm a little surprised you're buckling to the establishment." Her dad looked at his Birkenstock sandals for a minute. At least some things hadn't changed. He lifted his head back up and chuckled. "I'm just kidding. We always knew you and James were forever. A piece of paper won't change that."

"I still can't believe it," Rain whispered. It truly was too perfect.

"Let me take those." Allie snatched up the programs. "I'll hand them out and let Pastor Mike and the guitarist know we're almost ready."

"Okay, I'll go get my groomsmen." James dropped a kiss on Rain's forehead and then bent over to plant another atop the mound of baby. He whispered in her ear. "I can't wait to make you mine forever. I love you...both of you."

Rain couldn't hold back the tears another minute. Her makeup would just have to deal with it. She had believed for, prayed for, fought for this magical day throughout the last year, and nothing could take it away from her.

The next few minutes were a whirlwind as Layla and Allie repaired her makeup, everyone was seated, and the acoustic guitarist began playing soft, mellow music that perfectly matched the warm May day. They'd all survived this first year of school, Fatima was safe, and in just a few minutes, she would become Mrs. James Allen.

Allie and Layla walked gracefully down the white runner strewn with flower petals.

Rain's father held out his arm. "Are you ready?"

She wrapped hers through it. "Absolutely."

He led her down the aisle and into her forever life with James.

"In Jesus's name we pray, amen," Mo said.

Layla gave Mo's hands a squeeze, then opened her eyes. They had decided to bathe this visit with her parents in prayer. She could hardly believe she had been back in Virginia at Rain's wedding just two days ago. Much like the rest of the year, this spring was already flying by.

"So..." Mo said hopefully.

Layla took a deep breath and braced her hands against the seat of Mo's SUV. This time they would enter the house together. She would not risk letting her parents get into her head, and she would never let Mo suffer on the porch alone again. "So..." she said, "let's do this thing."

"Okay." Mo slid out of the car and walked around to open Layla's door.

She clutched tighter to his hand than she intended to as he pulled her to standing. "We can do this, right?"

"Of course we can," he assured her, wrapping his arm around her shoulder and leading her toward the house.

Layla pasted on a smile as he knocked. Might as well try to get this meeting off on a good foot. Her father had grudgingly agreed to talk to Mo, but her mother had made no such promises.

Dad opened the door, a similar polite smile pasted on his face. "Layla! You're home, and this must be Mo."

"Nice to meet you, Mr. Al-Rai." Mo released Layla and reached his hand to her dad.

To his credit, Dad reached out and shook it. Then he turned to Layla and offered her a hug. He peered around them. "Can I help you with your bags?"

Layla didn't want to mention that whether or not she'd be staying depended on how this meeting went. "Oh, don't worry about those right now. Why don't we sit down and get to know each other a little bit first?"

"Of course." Dad stuffed his hands into the pockets of his dress pants. "Come right in." He led them to the small formal sitting room at the front of the house.

Mo twisted his head as he walked through the elaborate entry way. "This is a lovely home."

"Thanks," her dad said.

Behind his back, Mo widened his eyes to Layla and let out a silent whistle. Evidently even Mo hadn't realized how wealthy they really were. In fact, it had been extra kind of Dad to meet them at the door rather than letting the housekeeper get it.

As they settled themselves on a velvet sofa, Layla caught a flash of color at the archway. "Mom, is that you?"

No answer, but Layla heard some shuffling. "Mom, would you like to meet Mo?"

She heard a familiar huff, then Mom emerged wearing a nice dress and her best red headscarf that flattered her features and made her look five years younger. "So this is the boy," Mom said without ever really looking at him. She crossed her arms over her chest. "The boy you would betray your family for."

Not ready to be deterred by such amateur theatrics, Layla persisted. "Do you remember Mo? We went to kindergarten together. Mohammed Hamoudi?"

"Hmph," Mom said. "Such a name for a man who is now a... Christian." She practically spat the last word. Then she shot a cold look straight at Mo.

Layla felt him bristle beside her, but he maintained his composure and stood to his feet. "Nice to meet you again, Mrs. Al-Rai. My mother sends her kind regards."

That's when Mom let down her guard and really stopped to look at him. "Mohammed. Mohammed Hamoudi." Her demeanor shifted to curiosity. "Son of Yasmeen Hamoudi? My dear, sweet friend Yasmeen? I remember you now." She lifted her hands into the air. "Well, why didn't someone say so?"

Mom marched straight at Mo as the rest of them held their breath.

"Look at you." She reached out and pinched his cheeks affectionately. "I remember this adorable little face." The fact that he towered over her by at least eight inches did not seem to deter her in the least. "Mo!" She shouted it this time, and then began to laugh.

"Of course! I should have known. We always said you two would be perfect for each other."

Then she turned to Layla. "*Ya habibti!* Why on earth didn't you tell me he was Yasmeen's boy? Foolish, foolish girl!"

Still reeling at this unexpected twist, Layla just laughed. "I tried to—"

Mom cut her off. "Why you're just as cute as you were as a five-year-old. But too skinny! Who has been feeding you?" She tugged him by the arm. "Come, come and I'll feed you. I have some hummus and baba ganoush and olives and bread right now. The rest of the family will be here in an hour for dinner. We'll fatten you right up."

As they rounded the corner and disappeared, Layla and Dad glanced at each other and stood to follow.

"Well, this is an interesting turn of events," Dad said.

"You're telling me."

As they caught up with the others passing through the giant living room, Mom called over her shoulder. "Layla, I've been looking at some of those American bridal magazines. You know, winter is a beautiful time for a wedding. Around December, I think. You look so lovely in deep winter colors."

Mo craned his neck to shoot Layla a look of wonder.

She just shrugged her shoulders. God most certainly did work in mysterious ways, and she was excited to be along for the ride. There would be plenty of time to set boundaries with her parents and to sort through her future plans with Mo. What mattered most in this moment was seeing her mother accepting Mo into her home and into her heart.

Dad reached over and gave her hand a squeeze. "I know things haven't gone as we expected, but I want you to know that I'm really proud of you. You've grown into an amazing woman."

She couldn't help but duck her head in her shy mouse fashion at the unexpected compliment. "You always taught me to seek the truth, Dad."

"I'm starting to understand."

As they entered the kitchen, Mom was already plying Mo with Lebanese food.

"Layla, I hope you like your men fat," he said, "because if your mother has anything to do with it…"

"Oh hush, you." Mom swatted Mo.

Layla smiled as she crossed to Mo and laid a hand on his arm. "I love you, now and forever. A few extra pounds won't change that."

"I love you too."

They resisted the urge to kiss in front of her parents, although the moment seemed to call for it.

"Oh, they are too sweet. Too perfect!" Layla's mother clasped her hands together.

And in that moment, Layla saw a new future. One with her family, her Mo, and her newfound faith, all weaving together in unexpected but wonderful ways.

AUTHOR'S NOTES

I have spent over two decades married to a Middle Eastern man with a heart to reach Muslims. He grew up in Lebanon with as many Muslim friends as Christian and is still close with some of them today. Because of that, I have always wanted to write the story of a Muslim woman. The last time I was in Lebanon, a beautiful, stylish young Muslim woman caught my eye, and she became my inspiration for Layla.

I meant no disrespect by having my Muslim character accept Christ. I hope that if you haven't read the first book, you will consider going back and following Layla's story from the beginning. It was always my intention to write her tale with compassion, respect, and love. I took pieces from a number of different stories of former Muslims I have met, wove them together, and added a good dose of fiction. My belief is that this is a story that deserves to be told, and more than that, a story that needs to be told.

In this second book, I dive into the darker side of Islam—a radical, violent side that many try to discredit as not being Islamic at all. But as the book illustrates, this dark side does have roots in the foundations of Islam. While I don't want this to drive anyone to fear or hatred, especially not in our current political climate, it is important to know the truth so that, as the Bible instructs us, we can be "wise as serpents and innocent as doves." We cannot simply turn a blind eye to the truth, especially when the basic human rights of so many women around the world are being violated.

You might wonder why I didn't more directly address the current refugee situation. The simple reason is that I initially wrote this book in early 2014, and I decided to stay faithful to the original story rather than try to tack on a new issue. However, I believe there are overriding truths in this book that can be applied to our current crisis. The majority of Muslims are wonderful people, and we should love and reach out to them. But there are also some very scary radicals out there, and we need to use wisdom and discretion.

I hope that your fictional relationships with Layla, Mo, and Fatima will help you to look at Muslims with new eyes and see them as fully rounded people with their own hopes, dreams, and desires. I hope they will help you to grow in understanding of a vast culture full of all sorts of individuals, as rich and varied as our own.

Meanwhile, I also hope that you learned something about yourself and about the importance of taking risks. My greatest prayer is that this book in some way moved you even one step closer in your relationship with God, and that it better equipped you to help reach a hurting world with the love of Jesus.

ACKNOWLEDGEMENTS

My thanks to my husband, his family, and all of his many friends who have been instrumental in teaching me about Islam and the Middle East. Thank you to Brother Rasheed and Sister Amani, who allowed me to reference their very powerful and effective television shows in this series.

Thank you to my beta readers, Marsha Staples, Angela Andrews, and Suzie Johnson. And of course, thank you to all of my friends and family who have supported me along my writing journey in so many ways. Finally, thank you to WhiteFire Publishing, who believed in me and is willing to take a risk with books off the beaten path.

DISCUSSION QUESTIONS

1. What is the difference between religion and spirituality?
2. Have you ever met and/or befriended any Muslim individuals? Which character or characters in the book did they most remind you of?
3. Each character in the book had to take a risk for what they believed in. What are some of the biggest risks you've had to take for your beliefs?
4. Do you think Sarah's story rang true? Why do you think she cracked and lost her faith for a time?
5. Do you have a personal relationship with God? If so, what drew you to him? If not, what might be the missing ingredient that would draw you to him?
6. Which character in the book did you most relate to and why?
7. Have you ever stopped to think how aspects of your culture affect your religion? Do you think that people sometimes confuse culture and religion?
8. Layla was tempted to compromise truth for peace. Which do you think is the most important and why?
9. Characters in the book experienced several arguably supernatural experiences. How did these affect the outcome of the story? Do you believe that God still moves in supernatural ways today?
10. What do you think Fatima's future might look like? If you could write her story, what would happen next?

DON'T MISS...

Dance from Deep Within
Deep Within Seires, Book 1

Three unlikely friends learn to dance to the song of the Spirit.

YOU MAY ALSO ENJOY

Hold the Light
by April McGowan

To an artist, the light is everything.
So what's Amber supposed to do when faced with blindness?

Love, Lace and Minor Alterations
by V. Joy Palmer

This bridal consultant has about had enough of everyone *else's* happily ever after.